Other Star Wars Books By Timothy Zahn

VOLUME 2

DARK FORCE RISING

TIMOTHY ZAHN

1 3 5 7 9 10 8 6 4 2

Del Rey
20 Vauxhall Bridge Road
London SW1V 2SA

Del Rey is part of the Penguin Random House group
of companies whose addresses can be found at global.
penguinrandomhouse.com.

First published in Great Britain by Bantam Books in 1992
This edition published by Del Rey in 2020

www.penguin.co.uk

A CIP catalogue record for this book is available from
the British Library.

ISBN 9781787466333

Typeset in 11/14.5pt Sabon LT Pro by Jouve (UK), Milton Keynes
Printed and bound in Great Britain by Clays Ltd, Elcograf S.p.A.

Penguin Random House is committed to a sustainable future
for our business, our readers and our planet. This book is made
from Forest Stewardship Council® certified paper.

A long time ago in a galaxy far, far away. . . .

CHAPTER ONE

⟨⟩

Directly ahead, the star was a marble-sized yellow-orange ball, its intensity moderated by its distance and by the viewports' automatic sunscreens. Surrounding it and the ship itself were the stars, a spattering of blazing white pinpricks in the deep blackness of space. Directly beneath the ship, in the western part of the Great Northern Forest of the planet Myrkr, dawn was approaching.

The last dawn that some in that forest would ever see.

Standing at one of the side bridge viewports of the Imperial Star Destroyer *Chimaera*, Captain Pellaeon watched as the fuzzy terminator line crept toward the target zone on the planet below. Ten minutes ago, the ground forces surrounding the target had reported themselves ready; the *Chimaera* itself had been holding blockade position for nearly an hour. All that was missing now was the order to attack.

Slowly, feeling almost furtive about it, Pellaeon turned his head a couple of centimeters to the side. Behind him and to his right, Grand Admiral Thrawn was seated at his command station, his blue-skinned face expressionless, his glowing red eyes focused on the bank of status readouts wrapped around his chair. He hadn't spoken or moved from that position since the last of the ground forces had reported in, and Pellaeon could tell the bridge crew was beginning to get restless.

For his own part, Pellaeon had long since stopped trying to second-guess Thrawn's actions. The fact that the late Emperor had seen fit to make Thrawn one of the twelve Grand Admirals was evidence of his own confidence in the man – all the more so given Thrawn's not-entirely-human heritage and the Emperor's well-known prejudices in such matters. Moreover, in the year since Thrawn had taken command of the *Chimaera* and had begun the task of rebuilding the Imperial Fleet, Pellaeon had seen the Grand Admiral's military genius demonstrated time and again. Whatever his reason for holding off the attack, Pellaeon knew it was a good one.

As slowly as he'd turned away, he turned back to the viewport. But his movements had apparently not gone unnoticed. 'A question, Captain?' Thrawn's smoothly modulated voice cut through the low hum of bridge conversation.

'No, sir,' Pellaeon assured him, turning again to face his superior.

For a moment those glowing eyes studied him, and Pellaeon unconsciously braced himself for a reprimand, or worse. But Thrawn, as Pellaeon still had a tendency to forget, did not have the legendary and lethal temper that had been the hallmark of the Lord Darth Vader. 'You're perhaps wondering why we haven't yet attacked?' the Grand Admiral suggested in that same courteous tone.

'Yes, sir, I was,' Pellaeon admitted. 'All our forces appear to be in position.'

'Our military forces are, yes,' Thrawn agreed. 'But not the observers I sent into Hyllyard City.'

Pellaeon blinked. 'Hyllyard City?'

'Yes. I find it unlikely that a man of Talon Karrde's cunning would set up a base in the middle of a forest without also setting up security contacts with others outside the immediate area. Hyllyard City is too far from Karrde's base for anyone there to directly witness our attack; hence, any sudden flurries of activity in the city will imply the existence of a more subtle line of communication. From that we'll be able to identify Karrde's contacts and put them under long-term surveillance. Eventually, they'll lead us to him.'

'Yes, sir,' Pellaeon said, feeling a frown crease his forehead. 'Then you're not expecting to take any of Karrde's own people alive.'

The Grand Admiral's smile turned brittle. 'On the contrary. I fully expect our forces to find an empty and abandoned base.'

Pellaeon threw a glance out the viewport at the partly lit planet below. 'In that case, sir . . . why are we attacking it?'

'Three reasons, Captain. First, even men like Talon Karrde occasionally make mistakes. It could well be that in the rush to evacuate his base he left some crucial bit of information behind. Second, as I've already mentioned, an attack on the base may lead us to his contacts in Hyllyard City. And third, it provides our ground forces with some badly needed field experience.'

The glowing eyes bored into Pellaeon's face. 'Never forget, Captain, that our goal is no longer merely the pitiful rear-guard harassment of the past five years. With Mount

Tantiss and our late Emperor's collection of Spaarti cylinders in our hands, the initiative is once again ours. Very soon now we'll begin the process of taking planets back from the Rebellion; and for that we'll need an army every bit as well trained as the officers and crew of the Fleet.'

'Understood, Admiral,' Pellaeon said.

'Good.' Thrawn lowered his gaze to his displays. 'It's time. Signal General Covell that he may begin.'

'Yes, sir,' Pellaeon said, leaving the viewport and returning to his station. He gave the readouts a quick check and tapped his comm switch, peripherally aware as he did so that Thrawn had likewise activated his own comm. Some private message to his spies in Hyllyard City? 'This is the *Chimaera*,' Pellaeon said. 'Launch the attack.'

'Acknowledged, *Chimaera*,' General Covell said into his helmet comlink, careful to keep the quiet scorn in his gut from getting through to his voice. It was typical – typical and disgustingly predictable. You scrambled around like mad hellions, got your troops and vehicles on the ground and set up . . . and then you stood around waiting for those strutting Fleet people in their spotless uniforms and nice clean ships to finish sipping their tea and finally get around to letting you loose.

Well, get yourselves comfortable, he thought sardonically in the direction of the Star Destroyer overhead. Because whether Grand Admiral Thrawn was interested in real results or just a good rousing show, he was going to get his money's worth. Reaching to the board in front of him, he keyed for local command frequency. 'General Covell to all units: we've got the light. Let's go.'

The acknowledgements came in; and with a shiver

from the steel deck beneath him, the huge AT-AT walker was off, lumbering its deceptively awkward-looking way through the forest toward the encampment a kilometer away. Ahead of the AT-AT, occasionally visible through the armored transparisteel viewport, a pair of AT-ST scout walkers ran in twin-point formation, tracking along the AT-AT's path and watching for enemy positions or booby traps.

Not that such futile gestures would do Karrde any good. Covell had directed literally hundreds of assault campaigns in his years of Imperial service, and he knew full well the awesome capabilities of the fighting machines under his command.

Beneath the viewport, the holographic tactical display was lit up like a decorative disk, the winking red, white, and green lights showing the positions of Covell's circle of AT-ATs, AT-STs, and hoverscout attack vehicles, all closing on Karrde's encampment in good order.

Good, but not perfect. The north-flank AT-AT and its support vehicles were lagging noticeably behind the rest of the armored noose. 'Unit Two, bring it up,' he said into his comlink.

'Trying, sir,' the voice came back, tinny and distant through the strange dampening effects of Myrkr's metal-rich flora. 'We're encountering some thick vine clusters that are slowing down our scout walkers.'

'Is it bothering your AT-AT any?'

'No, sir, but I wanted to keep the flank together—'

'Pattern coherence is a fine goal during academy maneuvers, Major,' Covell cut him off. 'But not at the expense of an overall battle plan. If the AT-STs can't keep up, leave them behind.'

'Yes, sir.'

Covell broke the connection with a snort. The Grand Admiral was right about one thing, at least: his troops were going to need a lot more battle seasoning before they would be up to real Imperial standards. Still, the raw material was there. Even as he watched, the north flank reformed itself, with the hoverscouts spreading forward to take up the AT-STs' former point positions while the lagging AT-STs themselves fell back into rear-guard deployment.

The energy sensor beeped a proximity warning: they were coming up on the encampment. 'Status?' he asked his crew.

'All weapons charged and ready,' the gunner reported, his eyes on the targeting displays.

'No indications of resistance, active or passive,' the driver added.

'Stay alert,' Covell ordered, keying for command frequency again. 'All units: move in.'

And with a final crash of mangled vegetation, the AT-AT broke through into the clearing.

It was an impressive sight. From all four sides of the open area, in nearly perfect parade-ground unison, the other three AT-ATs appeared from the forest cover in the predawn gloom, the AT-STs and hoverscouts clustered around their feet quickly fanning out on all sides to encircle the darkened buildings.

Covell gave the sensors a quick but thorough check. Two energy sources were still functioning, one in the central building, the other in one of the outer barracks-style structures. There was no evidence of operating sensors, or of weapons or energy fields. The life-form analyzer ran through its complicated algorithms and concluded that the outer buildings were devoid of life.

The large main building, on the other hand . . .

'I'm getting approximately twenty life-form readings from the main building, General,' the number four AT-AT commander reported. 'All in the central section.'

'They don't register as human, though,' Covell's driver murmured.

'Maybe they're being shielded,' Covell grunted, looking out the viewport. Still no movement from the encampment. 'Let's find out. Assault squads: go.'

The hoverscouts popped their aft hatchways, and from each came a squad of eight soldiers, laser rifles held tautly across battle-armored chests as they dropped to the ground. Half of each squad took up backstop position, their rifles trained on the encampment from the partial cover of their hoverscout, while the other half sprinted across the open ground to the outer line of buildings and sheds. There, they assumed covering positions, allowing their comrades in the rear to similarly advance. It was a centuries-old military tactic, executed with the kind of squeamish determination that Covell would have expected of green troops. Still, the raw material was definitely there.

The soldiers continued their leap-frog approach to the main building, with small groups breaking off the main encirclement to check out each of the other structures as they passed. The point men reached the central building – a brilliant flash lit up the forest as they blasted down the door – a slightly confused scramble as the rest of the troops piled through.

And then, silence.

For a handful of minutes the silence continued, punctuated only by occasional short commands from the troop commanders. Covell listened, watching the sensors . . . and finally the report came through. 'General Covell, this is Lieutenant Barse. We've secured the target zone, sir. There's no-one here.'

Covell nodded. 'Very good, Lieutenant. How does it look?'

'Like they pulled out in a hurry, sir,' the other said. 'They left a fair amount of stuff behind, but it all looks pretty much like junk.'

'That'll be for the scanning crew to decide,' Covell told him. 'Any indication of booby traps or other unpleasant surprises?'

'None at all, sir. Oh – and those life-forms we picked up are nothing but these long furry animals living on the tree growing up through the center of the roof.'

Covell nodded again. Ysalamiri, he believed they were called. Thrawn had been making a big deal about the stupid creatures for a couple of months now, though what use they could possibly be to the war effort he couldn't guess. Eventually, he supposed, the Fleet people would get around to letting him in on the big secret. 'Set up a defensive honeycomb,' he odered the lieutenant. 'Signal the scanning crew when you're ready. And get comfortable. The Grand Admiral wants this place taken apart, and that's exactly what we're going to do.'

'Very good, General,' the voice said, almost too faint to hear despite the heavy amplification and computer scrubbing. 'Proceed with the dismantling.'

Seated at the *Wild Karrde*'s helm, Mara Jade half

turned to face the man standing behind her. 'I suppose that's it, then,' she said.

For a moment Talon Karrde didn't seem to hear her. He just stood there, gazing through the viewport at the distant planet, a tiny bluish-white crescent shape visible around the jagged edge of the sun-skimmer asteroid the *Wild Karrde* was snuggled up against. Mara was just about to repeat the comment when he stirred. 'Yes,' he said, that calm voice showing no hint of the emotion he was obviously feeling. 'I suppose it is.'

Mara exchanged glances with Aves, at the copilot station, then looked back up at Karrde. 'Shouldn't we be going, then?' she prompted.

Karrde took a deep breath . . . and as she watched him, Mara caught in his expression a glimmer of what the Myrkr base had meant to him. More than just a base, it had been his home.

With an effort, she suppressed the thought. So Karrde had lost his home. Big deal. She'd lost far more than that in her lifetime and had survived just fine. He'd get over it. 'I asked if we should get going.'

'I heard you,' Karrde said, the flicker of emotion vanishing again into that slightly sardonic facade of his. 'I think perhaps we ought to wait a little longer. See if we left anything behind that might point in the direction of our Rishi base.'

Mara looked at Aves again. 'We were pretty thorough,' Aves said. 'I don't think there was any mention of Rishi anywhere except the main computer, and that left with the first group out.'

'I agree,' Karrde said. 'Are you willing to stake your life on that assessment?'

Aves's lip twitched. 'Not really.'

'Nor am I. So we wait.'

'What if they spot us?' Mara persisted. 'Skulking behind asteroids is the oldest trick on the list.'

'They won't spot us.' Karrde was quietly positive. 'Actually, I doubt the possibility will even occur to them. The average man running from the likes of Grand Admiral Thrawn is unlikely to stop running until he's a good deal farther away than this.'

Are you willing to stake your life on that assessment? Mara thought sourly. But she kept the retort to herself. He was probably right; and anyway, if the *Chimaera* or any of its TIE fighters started toward *Wild Karrde*, they would have no trouble punching the engines up to power and going to lightspeed well ahead of the attack.

The logic and tactics seemed clean. But still, Mara could feel something nagging at the back of her mind. Something that didn't feel good about all this.

Gritting her teeth, she adjusted the ship's sensors to their highest sensitivity and checked once more that the engine prestart sequence was keyed in and ready. And then settled in to wait.

The scanning crew was fast, efficient, and thorough; and it took them just over thirty minutes to come up completely dry.

'Well, so much for that.' Pellaeon grimaced as he watched the negative reports scroll up his display. A good practice session for the ground forces, perhaps, but otherwise the whole exercise seemed to have been pretty useless. 'Unless your observers have picked up any reactions in Hyllyard City,' he added, turning to face Thrawn.

The Grand Admiral's glowing red eyes were on his displays. 'There was a small twitch, as a matter of fact,' he said. 'Cut off almost before it began, but I think the implications are clear.'

Well, that was something, anyway. 'Yes, sir. Shall I have Surveillance begin equipping a long-term ground team?'

'Patience, Captain,' Thrawn said. 'It may not be necessary, after all. Key for a midrange scan, and tell me what you see.'

Pellaeon swiveled back to his command board and tapped for the appropriate readout. There was Myrkr itself, of course, and the standard TIE fighter defense cloud ranged around the *Chimaera*. The only other object anywhere within midrange distance – 'You mean that little asteroid out there?'

'That's the one,' Thrawn nodded. 'Nothing remarkable about it, is there? No, don't do a sensor focus,' he added, almost before the thought of doing one had even occurred to Pellaeon. 'We wouldn't want to prematurely flush our quarry, would we?'

'Our quarry?' Pellaeon repeated, frowning at the sensor data again. The routine sensor scans that had been done of the asteroid three hours earlier had come up negative, and nothing could have sneaked up on it since then without being detected. 'With all due respect, sir, I don't see any indication that anything's out there.'

'I don't either,' Thrawn agreed. 'But it's the only sizable cover available for nearly ten million kilometers around Myrkr. There's really no other place for Karrde to watch our operation from.'

Pellaeon pursed his lips. 'Your permission, Admiral,

but I doubt Karrde is foolish enough to just sit around waiting for us to arrive.'

The glowing red eyes narrowed, just a bit. 'You forget, Captain,' he said softly, 'that I've met the man. More importantly, I've seen the sort of artwork he collects.' He turned back to his displays. 'No; he's out there. I'm sure of it. Talon Karrde is not merely a smuggler, you see. Perhaps not even primarily a smuggler. His real love is not goods or money but information. More than anything else in the galaxy, he craves knowledge . . . and the knowledge of what we have or have not found here is too valuable a gem for him to pass up.'

Pellaeon studied the Grand Admiral's profile. It was, in his opinion, a pretty tenuous leap of logic. But on the other hand, he'd seen too many similar leaps borne out not to take this one seriously. 'Shall I order a TIE fighter squadron to investigate, sir?'

'As I said, Captain, patience,' Thrawn said. 'Even in sensor stealth mode with all engines shut down, he'll have made sure he can power up and escape before any attack force could reach him.' He smiled at Pellaeon. 'Or rather, any attack force from the *Chimaera*.'

A stray memory clicked: Thrawn, reaching for his comm just as Pellaeon was giving the ground forces the order to attack. 'You sent a message to the rest of the fleet,' he said. 'Timing it against my attack order to mask the transmission.'

Thrawn's blue-black eyebrows lifted a fraction. 'Very good, Captain. Very good, indeed.'

Pellaeon felt a touch of warmth on his cheeks. The Grand Admiral's compliments were few and far between. 'Thank you, sir.'

Thrawn nodded. 'More precisely, my message was to a single ship, the *Constrainer*. It will arrive in approximately ten minutes. At which point' – his eyes glittered – 'we'll see just how accurate my reading of Karrde has been.'

Over the *Wild Karrde*'s bridge speakers, the reports from the scanning crew were beginning to taper off. 'Doesn't sound like they've found anything,' Aves commented.

'Like you said, we were thorough,' Mara reminded him, hardly hearing her own words. The nameless thing nagging at the back of her mind seemed to be getting stronger. 'Can we get out of here now?' she asked, turning to look at Karrde.

He frowned down at her. 'Try to relax, Mara. They can't possibly know we're here. There's been no sensor-focus probe of the asteroid, and without one there's no way for them to detect this ship.'

'Unless a Star Destroyer's sensors are better than you think,' Mara retorted.

'We know all about their sensors,' Aves soothed. 'Ease up, Mara, Karrde knows what he's doing. The *Wild Karrde* has probably the tightest sensor stealth mode this side of—'

He broke off as the bridge door opened behind them; and Mara turned just as Karrde's two pet vornskrs bounded into the room.

Dragging, very literally, their handler behind them.

'What are you doing here, Chin?' Karrde asked.

'Sorry, Capt',' Chin puffed, digging his heels into the deck and leaning back against the taut leashes. The effort was only partially successful; the predators were still pulling him slowly forward. 'I couldn't stop them. I thought maybe they wanted to see you, hee?'

'What's the matter with you two, anyway?' Karrde chided the animals, squatting down in front of them. 'Don't you know we're busy?'

The vornskrs didn't look at him. Didn't even seem to notice his presence, for that matter. They continued staring straight ahead as if he wasn't even there.

Staring directly at Mara.

'Hey,' Karrde said, reaching over to slap one of the animals lightly across the muzzle. 'I'm talking to you, Sturm. What's gotten into you, anyway?' He glanced along their unblinking line of sight—

Paused for a second and longer look. 'Are you doing something, Mara?'

Mara shook her head, a cold shiver tingling up her back. She'd seen that look before, on many of the wild vornskrs she'd run into during that long three-day trek through the Myrkr forest with Luke Skywalker.

Except that those vornskr stares hadn't been directed at her. They'd been reserved instead for Skywalker. Usually just before they attacked him.

'That's Mara, Sturm,' Karrde told the animal, speaking to it as he might a child. 'Mara. Come on, now – you saw her all the time back home.'

Slowly, almost reluctantly, Sturm stopped his forward pull and turned his attention to his master. 'Mara,' Karrde repeated, looking the vornskr firmly in the eye. 'A friend. You hear that, Drang?' he added, reaching over to grip the other vornskr's muzzle. 'She's a friend. Understand?'

Drang seemed to consider that. Then, as reluctantly as Sturm had, he lowered his head and stopped pulling. 'That's better,' Karrde said, scratching both vornskrs briefly behind their ears and standing up again. 'Better take them back down, Chin. Maybe walk them around the main hold – give them some exercise.'

'If I can find a clear track through all the stuff in there, hee?' Chin grunted, twitching back on the leashes. 'Come on, littles – we go now.'

With only a slight hesitation the two vornskrs allowed him to take them off the bridge. Karrde watched as the door shut behind them. 'I wonder what that was all about,' he said, giving Mara a thoughtful look.

'I don't know,' she told him, hearing the tightness in her voice. With the temporary distraction now gone, the strange dread she'd been feeling was back again in full force. She swiveled back to her board, half expecting to see a squadron of TIE fighters bearing down on them.

But there was nothing. Only the *Chimaera*, still sitting harmlessly out there in orbit around Myrkr. No threat any of the *Wild Karrde*'s instruments could detect. But the tingling was getting stronger and stronger . . .

And suddenly she could sit still no longer. Reaching out to the control board, she keyed for engine prestart.

'Mara!' Aves yelped, jumping in his seat as if he'd been stung. 'What in—?'

'They're coming,' Mara snarled back, hearing the strain of a half dozen tangled emotions in her voice. The die was irrevocably cast – her activation of the *Wild Karrde*'s engines would have set sensors screaming all over the *Chimaera*. Now there was nowhere to go but out.

She looked up at Karrde, suddenly afraid of what his expression might be saying. But he was just standing there looking down at her, a slightly quizzical frown on his face. 'They don't appear to be coming,' he pointed out mildly.

She shook her head, feeling the pleading in her eyes. 'You have to believe me,' she said, uncomfortably aware that she didn't really believe it herself. 'They're getting ready to attack.'

'I believe you,' he said soothingly. Or perhaps he, too, recognized that there weren't any other choices left. 'Aves: lightspeed calculation. Take the easiest course setting that's not anywhere toward Rishi; we'll stop and reset later.'

'Karrde—'

'Mara is second in command,' Karrde cut him off. 'As such, she has the right and the duty to make important decisions.'

'Yeah, but—' Aves stopped, the last word coming out pinched as he strangled it off. 'Yeah,' he said between clenched teeth. Throwing a glower at Mara, he turned to the nav computer and got to work.

'You might as well get us moving, Mara,' Karrde continued, stepping over to the vacant communications chair and sitting down. 'Keep the asteroid between us and the *Chimaera* as long as you can.'

'Yes, sir,' Mara said. Her tangle of emotions was starting to dissolve now, leaving a mixture of anger and profound embarrassment in its wake. She'd done it again. Listened to her inner feelings – tried to do things she knew full well she couldn't do – and in the process had once again wound up clutching the sharp end of the bayonet.

And it was probably the last she'd hear of being Karrde's second in command, too. Command unity in front of Aves was one thing, but once they were out of here and he could get her alone there was going to be hell to pay. She'd be lucky if he didn't bounce her out of his organization altogether. Jabbing viciously at her board, she swung the *Wild Karrde* around, turning its nose away from the asteroid and starting to drive toward deep space—

And with a flicker of pseudomotion, something big shot in from lightspeed, dropping neatly into normal space not twenty kilometers away.

An Imperial Interdictor Cruiser.

Aves yelped a startled-sounding curse. 'We got company,' he barked.

'I see it,' Karrde said. As cool as ever . . . but Mara could hear the tinge of surprise in his voice, too. 'What's our time to lightspeed?'

'It'll be another minute,' Aves said tautly. 'There's a lot of junk in the outer system for the computer to work through.'

'We have a race, then,' Karrde said. 'Mara?'

'Up to point seven three,' she said, nursing as much power as she could out of the still-sluggish engines. He was right; it was indeed going to be a race. With their four huge gravity-wave generators capable of simulating planet-sized masses, Interdictor Cruisers were the Empire's weapon of choice for trapping an enemy ship in normal space while TIE fighters pounded it to rubble. But coming in fresh out of lightspeed itself, the Interdictor would need another minute before it could power up those generators. If she could get the *Wild Karrde* out of range by then . . .

'More visitors,' Aves announced. 'A couple of squadrons of TIE fighters coming from the *Chimaera*.'

'We're up to point eight six power,' Mara reported. 'We'll be ready for lightspeed as soon as the nav computer gives me a course.'

'Interdictor status?'

'Grav generators are powering up,' Aves said. On Mara's tactical display a ghostly cone appeared, showing the area where the lightspeed-dampening field would soon exist. She changed course slightly, aiming for the nearest edge, and risked a glance at the nav computer display. Almost ready. The hazy grav cone was rapidly becoming more substantial . . .

The computer scope pinged. Mara wrapped her hand around the three hyperspace control levers at the front of the control board and gently pulled them toward her. The *Wild Karrde* shuddered slightly, and for a second it seemed that the Interdictor had won their deadly race. Then, abruptly, the stars outside burst into starlines.

They'd made it.

Aves heaved a sigh of relief as the starlines faded into the mottled sky of hyperspace. 'Talk about slicing the mynock close to the hull. How do you suppose they tumbled that we were out there, anyway?'

'No idea,' Karrde said, his voice cool. 'Mara?'

'I don't know, either.' Mara kept her eyes on her displays, not daring to look at either of them. 'Thrawn may have just been playing a hunch. He does that sometimes.'

'Lucky for us he's not the only one who gets hunches,' Aves offered, his voice sounding a little strange. 'Nice going, Mara. Sorry I jumped on you.'

'Yes,' Karrde seconded. 'A very good job indeed.'

'Thanks,' Mara muttered, keeping her eyes on her control board and blinking back the tears that had suddenly come to her eyes. So it was back. She'd hoped fervently that her locating of Skywalker's X-wing out in deep space had been an isolated event. A fluke, more his doing than hers.

But no. It was all coming back, as it had so many times

before in the past five years. The hunches and sensory flickers, the urges and the compulsions.

Which meant that, very soon now, the dreams would probably be starting again, too.

Angrily, she swiped at her eyes, and with an effort unclenched her jaw. It was a familiar enough pattern . . . but this time things were going to be different. Always before there'd been nothing she could do about the voices and urges except to suffer through the cycle. To suffer, and to be ready to break out of whatever niche she'd managed to carve for herself when she finally betrayed herself to those around her.

But she wasn't a serving girl in a Phorliss cantina this time, or a come-up flector for a swoop gang on Capsioril, or even a hyperdrive mechanic stuck in the backwater of the Ison Corridor. She was second in command to the most powerful smuggler in the galaxy, with the kind of resources and mobility she hadn't had since the death of the Emperor.

The kind of resources that would let her find Luke Skywalker again. And kill him.

Maybe then the voices would stop.

For a long minute Thrawn stood at the bridge viewport, looking out at the distant asteroid and the now superfluous Interdictor Cruiser near it. It was, Pellaeon thought uneasily, almost the identical posture the Grand Admiral had assumed when Luke Skywalker had so recently escaped a similar trap. Holding his breath, Pellaeon stared at Thrawn's back, wondering if another of the *Chimaera*'s crewers was about to be executed for this failure.

Thrawn turned around. 'Interesting,' he said, his voice conversational. 'Did you note the sequence of events, Captain?'

'Yes, sir,' Pellaeon said cautiously. 'The target was already powering up before the *Constrainer* arrived.'

'Yes,' Thrawn nodded. 'And it implies one of three things. Either Karrde was about to leave anyway, or else he panicked for some reason—' The red eyes glittered. 'Or else he was somehow warned off.'

Pellaeon felt his back stiffen. 'I hope you're not suggesting, sir, that one of our people tipped him.'

'No, of course not.' Thrawn's lip twitched slightly. 'Loyalties of your crewers aside, no-one on the *Chimaera* knew the *Constrainer* was on its way; and no-one on the *Constrainer* could have sent any messages here without our detecting them.' He stepped over to his command station and sat down, a thoughtful look on his face. 'An interesting puzzle, Captain. One I'll have to give some thought to. In the meantime, we have more pressing matters. The task of acquiring new warships, for one. Have there been any recent responses to our invitation?'

'Nothing particularly interesting, Admiral,' Pellaeon said, pulling up the comm log and giving it a quick scan to refresh his memory. 'Eight of the fifteen groups I contacted have expressed interest, though none were willing to commit themselves to anything specific. We're still waiting on the others.'

Thrawn nodded. 'We'll give them a few weeks. If there've been no results after that time, we'll make the invitation a bit more compulsory.'

'Yes, sir.' Pellaeon hesitated. 'There's also been another communication from Jomark.'

Thrawn turned his glowing eyes on Pellaeon. 'I would very much appreciate it, Captain,' he said, biting off each word, 'if you would try to make it clear to our exalted Jedi Master C'baoth that if he persists in these communications he's going to subvert the whole purpose of putting him on Jomark in the first place. If the Rebels get even a hint of any connection between us, he can forget about Skywalker ever showing up there.'

'I *have* explained it to him, sir,' Pellaeon grimaced. 'Numerous times. His reply is always that Skywalker *is* going to show up. And then he demands to know when you're going to get around to delivering Skywalker's sister to him.'

For a long moment Thrawn said nothing. 'I suppose there'll be no shutting him up until he gets what he wants,' he said at last. 'Nor of getting any uncomplaining work out of him, either.'

'Yes, he was grumbling about the attack coordination you've been having him do,' Pellaeon nodded. 'He's warned me several times that he can't predict exactly when Skywalker will arrive on Jomark.'

'And implied that a horrible retribution would fall upon us if he's not there when that happens,' Thrawn growled. 'Yes, I know the routine well. And I'm getting rather tired of it.' He took a deep breath, let it out slowly. 'Very well, Captain. The next time C'baoth calls, you may inform him that the Taanab operation will be his last for the immediate future. Skywalker isn't likely to make it to Jomark for at least two more weeks – the little pot of political confusion we've stirred up in the Rebellion high command should occupy him at least that long. As to Organa Solo and her unborn Jedi . . . you may also inform him that from now on I'll be taking a personal hand in that matter.'

Pellaeon threw a quick glance over his shoulder, to where the Grand Admiral's bodyguard, Rukh, stood silently near the aft bridge door. 'Does that mean you'll be taking the Noghri off the job, sir?' he asked quietly.

'Do you have a problem with that, Captain?'

'No, sir. May I respectfully remind the Grand Admiral, though, that the Noghri have never liked leaving a mission uncompleted.'

'The Noghri are servants of the Empire,' Thrawn countered coldly. 'More to the point, they're loyal to me personally. They will do as they're told.' He paused. 'However, I'll take your concerns under advisement. At any rate, our task here at Myrkr is completed. Order General Covell to bring his force back up.'

'Yes, sir,' Pellaeon said, signaling the communications officer to relay the message.

'I'll want the general's report on file in three hours,' Thrawn continued. 'Twelve hours after that I want his recommendations as to the three best infantry troopers and two best mechanized operators in the assault. Those five men will be transferred to the Mount Tantiss operation and given immediate transport to Wayland.'

'Understood,' Pellaeon nodded, dutifully logging the orders in Covell's file. Such recommendations had been part of standard Imperial procedure for several weeks now, ever since the Mount Tantiss operation had begun in earnest. But Thrawn nevertheless still periodically went out of his way to mention it to his officers. Perhaps as a not-so-subtle reminder of how vitally important those recommendations were to the Grand Admiral's sweeping plan to crush the Rebellion.

Thrawn looked out the viewport again at the planet beneath them. 'And while we await the general's return, you'll contact Surveillance regarding that long-term team for Hyllyard City.' He smiled. 'It's a very large galaxy, Captain, but even a man like Talon Karrde can run for only so long. Eventually, he'll have to come to rest.'

It wasn't really deserving of its name, the High Castle of Jomark. Not in Joruus C'baoth's estimation, anyway. Short and dirty, its stonework ill-fitting in places and as alien as the long-gone race that had built it, it squatted uneasily between two of the larger crags on what was left of an ancient volcanic cone. Still, with the rest of the rim circling around in the distance, and the brilliant blue waters of Ring Lake four hundred meters almost straight down beneath him, C'baoth could allow that the natives had at least found some good scenery to build their castle on. Their castle, or temple, or whatever. It had been a good place for a Jedi Master to move into, if only because the colonists seemed to hold the place in awe. Then too, the dark island that filled the center of the crater and gave the lake its ring shape provided a suitably hidden landing site for Thrawn's annoyingly endless stream of shuttles.

But it was neither the scenery, nor the power, nor even the Empire that held C'baoth's thoughts as he stood on the castle terrace and gazed down into Ring Lake. It was, instead, the strange flicker he'd just felt in the Force.

He'd felt it before, this flicker. Or at least he thought he had. Threads to the past were always so hard to follow, so easily lost in the mists and the hurryings of the present. Even of his own past he had only glimpses of memory, scenes as if from a history record. He rather thought he remembered someone trying to explain the reasons to him once, but the explanation was long gone in the darkness of the past.

It didn't matter anyway. Memory wasn't important; concentration wasn't important; his own past wasn't important. He could call upon the Force when he wanted to, and *that* was what was important. As long as he could do that, no-one could ever hurt him or take away what he had.

Except that Grand Admiral Thrawn had already taken it away. Hadn't he?

C'baoth looked around the terrace. Yes. Yes; this wasn't the home and city and world he'd chosen to mold and command as his own. This wasn't Wayland, which he'd wrested from the Dark Jedi whom the Emperor had set to guard his Mount Tantiss storehouse. This was Jomark, where he was waiting for . . . someone.

He stroked his fingers through his long white beard, forcing himself to concentrate. He was waiting for Luke Skywalker – that was it. Luke Skywalker was going to come to him, and Luke Skywalker's sister and her as-yet-unborn twins, and he would turn all of them into his followers. Grand Admiral Thrawn had promised them to him, in return for his help to the Empire.

He winced at the thought. It was hard, this help that Grand Admiral Thrawn wanted. He had to concentrate hard to do what they wanted; to hold his thoughts and feelings closely in line, and for long periods at a time. On Wayland he hadn't had to do anything like that, not since he'd fought against the Emperor's Guardian.

He smiled. It had been a grand battle, that fight against the Guardian. But even as he tried to remember it, the details skittered away like straws in the wind. It had been too long ago.

Long ago . . . like these flickers in the Force had been.

C'baoth's fingers slipped away from his beard, to the medallion nestled against the skin of his chest. Squeezing the warm metal against his palm, he fought against the mists of the past, trying to see beyond them. Yes. Yes, he was not mistaken. These same flickers had come three times before in the past few seasons. Had come, had stayed for a time, and then once again had gone dormant. Like someone who had learned how to utilize the Force for a time, but then somehow forgotten.

He didn't understand it. But it was of no threat to him, and so wasn't important.

Above him, he could sense now the Imperial Star Destroyer entering high orbit, far above the clouds where none of the others on Jomark would see it. When night fell, the shuttle would come, and they would take him off somewhere – Taanab, he thought – to help coordinate yet another of these multiple Imperial attacks.

He wasn't looking forward to the effort and pain. But it would all be worth it when he had his Jedi. He would remake them in his own image, and they would be his servants and his followers all the days of their lives.

And then even Grand Admiral Thrawn would have to admit that he, Joruus C'baoth, had found the true meaning of power.

CHAPTER TWO

'I'm sorry, Luke,' Wedge Antilles' voice said over the comm, the words punctuated by occasional spittings of static. 'I've tried every handle I can think of, including pulling all the rank I've got and some I haven't. It's still no go. Some data pusher up the riser somewhere has issued orders that the Sluissi's own defense ships have absolute top priority for repair work. Until we can find this guy and talk him into a special dispensation, we're not going to get anyone to touch your X-wing.'

Luke Skywalker grimaced, feeling four hours' worth of frustration welling up in his throat. Four precious hours wasted, with the end still not in sight, while on Coruscant the future of the entire New Republic was even now teetering on the edge. 'Did you get this data pusher's name?' he asked.

'I couldn't even get that,' Wedge said. 'Every line I've tried has disappeared about three layers up from the mechanics themselves. I'm still trying, but this whole place has gone kind of baffy.'

'A major Imperial attack will do that to you,' Luke conceded with a sigh. He could understand why the Sluissi had set their priorities the way they had; but it wasn't like he was just going off on a joyride, either. It was a good six-day flight from here to Coruscant as it was, and every hour that he was delayed was one more hour the political forces trying to oust Admiral Ackbar would have to consolidate their position. 'Keep trying, OK? I've got to get out of here.'

'Sure,' Wedge said. 'Look, I know you're worried about what's happening on Coruscant. But any one person can only do so much. Even a Jedi.'

'I know,' Luke agreed reluctantly. And Han was on his way back, and Leia was already there . . . 'I just hate sitting around being out of it.'

'Me, too.' Wedge lowered his voice a bit. 'You've still got one other option. Don't forget that.'

'I won't,' Luke promised. It was certainly an option he'd been tempted to take his friend up on. But Luke wasn't officially a member of the New Republic military any more; and with the New Republic forces here at the shipyards still at full alert, Wedge could face an immediate court martial for handing his X-wing over to a civilian. Councilor Borsk Fey'lya and his anti-Ackbar faction might not want to bother making an example out of someone as relatively low in rank as a starfighter wing commander. But then again, they might.

Wedge, of course, knew all that better than Luke did. Which made the offer that much more generous. 'I appreciate it,' Luke told him. 'But unless things get really desperate, it'll probably be better all around if I just wait for mine to get fixed.'

'OK. How's General Calrissian doing?'

'He's in roughly the same boat as my X-wing,' Luke said dryly. 'Every doctor and medical droid in the place is tied up treating battle injuries. Digging minor bits of metal and glass out of someone who's not currently bleed-ing is kind of low on their priority list at the moment.'

'I'll bet he's really pleased with that.'

'I've seen him a lot happier,' Luke admitted. 'I'd better go give the medics another push. Why don't you get back to prodding the Sluissi bureaucracy from your end – if we both push hard enough, maybe we can meet in the middle.'

Wedge chuckled. 'Right. Talk to you later.'

With one final crackle of static, the comm cut off. 'And good luck,' Luke added softly as he got up from the public-use comm desk and headed off across the Sluis Van Central reception area toward the medical corridor. If the rest of the Sluissi equipment had been damaged as much as their in-system communications, it could be a long time indeed before anyone had enough spare time to put a couple of new hyperdrive motivators into a civil-ian's X-wing.

Still, things weren't quite as dark as they could have been, he decided as he maneuvered his way carefully through the hurrying crowds that seemed to be going in all directions at once. There were several New Republic ships here, whose work crews might be more willing than the Sluissi themselves to bend the rules for a former offi-cer like Luke. And if worse came to worst, he could try calling Coruscant to see if Mon Mothma could expedite matters any.

The drawback to that approach was that calling for help would probably give the appearance of weakness . . . and to show weakness in front of Councilor Fey'lya was not the right signal to be sending now.

Or so it seemed to him. On the other hand, showing

that he could get the head of the New Republic to give him personal attention could as easily be seen instead as a sign of strength and solidarity.

Luke shook his head in mild frustration. It was, he supposed, a generally useful trait for a Jedi to be able to see both sides of an argument. It did, however, make the machinations of politics seem even murkier than they already were. Another good reason why he'd always tried to leave politics to Leia.

He could only hope that she'd be equal to this particular challenge.

The medical wing was as crowded as the rest of the huge Sluis Van Central space station, but here at least a large percentage of the inhabitants were sitting or lying quietly off to the side instead of running around. Threading his way between the chairs and parked float gurneys, Luke reached the large ward room that had been turned into a waiting area for low-priority patients. Lando Calrissian, his expression and sense hovering somewhere between impatience and boredom, was sitting off in the far corner, holding a medpack desensitizer against his chest with one hand while balancing a borrowed data pad with the other. He was scowling at the latter as Luke came up. 'Bad news?' Luke asked.

'No worse than everything else that's happened to me lately,' Lando said, dropping the data pad onto the empty chair beside him. 'The price of hfredium has dropped again on the general market. If it doesn't come up a little in the next month or two, I'm going to be out a few hundred thousand.'

'Ouch,' Luke agreed. 'That's the main product of your Nomad City complex, isn't it?'

'One of several main products, yes,' Lando said with a grimace. 'We're diversified enough that normally it wouldn't hurt us much. The problem is that lately I've been stockpiling the stuff, expecting the price to go up. Now it's done just the opposite.'

Luke suppressed a smile. That was Lando, all right. Respectable and legitimate though he might have become, he was still not above dabbling in a little manipulative gambling on the side. 'Well, if it helps any, I've got some good news for you. Since all the ships that the Imperials tried to steal belonged directly to the New Republic, we won't have to go through the local Sluissi bureaucracy to get your mole miners back. It'll just be a matter of submitting a proper claim to the Republic military commander and hauling them out of here.'

The lines in Lando's face eased a little. 'That's great, Luke,' he said. 'I really appreciate it – you have no idea what I had to go through to get hold of those mole miners in the first place. Finding replacements would be a major headache.'

Luke waved the thanks away. 'Under the circumstances, it was the least we could do. Let me go over to the routing station, see if I can hurry things up a little for you. Are you finished with the data pad?'

'Sure, take it back. Anything new on your X-wing?'

'Not really,' Luke said, reaching past him to pick up the data pad. 'They're still saying it'll take another few hours at least to—'

He caught the abrupt change in Lando's sense a second before the other's hand suddenly snaked up to grip his arm. 'What is it?' Luke asked.

Lando was staring at nothing, his forehead furrowed

with concentration as he sniffed the air. 'Where were you just now?' he demanded.

'I went through the reception area to one of the public comm desks,' Luke said. Lando wasn't just sniffing the air, he realized suddenly: he was sniffing at Luke's sleeve. 'Why?'

Lando let Luke's arm drop. 'It's carababba tabac,' he said slowly. 'With some armudu spice mixed in. I haven't smelled that since . . .' He looked up at Luke, his sense abruptly tightening even further. 'It's Niles Ferrier. Has to be.'

'Who's Niles Ferrier?' Luke asked, feeling his heart-beat start to pick up speed. Lando's uneasiness was contagious.

'Human – big and built sort of thick,' Lando said. 'Dark hair, probably a beard, though that comes and goes. Probably smoking a long thin cigarra. No, of course he was smoking – you got some of the smoke on you. Do you remember seeing him?'

'Hang on.' Luke closed his eyes, reaching inward with the Force. Short-term memory enhancement was one of the Jedi skills he'd learned from Yoda. The pictures flowed swiftly backward in time: his walk to the medical wing, his conversation with Wedge, his hunt for a public comm desk—

And there he was. Exactly as Lando had described him, passing no more than three meters away. 'Got him,' he told Lando, freezing the picture in his memory.

'Where's he going?'

'Uh . . .' Luke replayed the memory forward again. The man wandered in and out of his field of vision for a minute, eventually disappearing entirely as Luke found the comm desks he'd been hunting for. 'Looks like he and a couple of others were heading for Corridor Six.'

Lando had punched up a station schematic on the data pad. 'Corridor Six . . . blast.' He stood up, dropping both the data pad and the desensitizer onto his chair. 'Come on, we'd better go check this out.'

'Check what out?' Luke asked, taking a long step to catch up as Lando hurried off through the maze of waiting patients to the door. 'Who is this Niles Ferrier, anyway?'

'He's one of the best spaceship thieves in the galaxy,' Lando threw over his shoulder. 'And Corridor Six leads to one of the staging areas for the repair teams. We'd better get out there before he palms a Corellian gunship or something and flies off with it.'

They made their way through the reception area and under the archway labeled 'Corridor Six' in both delicate Sluissi carioglyphs and the blockier Basic letters. Here, to Luke's surprise, the crowds of people that seemed to be everywhere else had dropped off to barely a trickle. By the time they'd gone a hundred meters along the corridor, he and Lando were alone.

'You *did* say this was one of the repair staging areas, didn't you?' he asked, reaching out with Jedi senses as they walked. The lights and equipment in the offices and workrooms around them seemed to be functioning properly, and he could sense a handful of droids moving busily about their business. But apart from that the place seemed to be deserted.

'Yes, I did,' Lando said grimly. 'The schematic said Corridors Five and Three are also being used but there ought to be enough traffic to keep this one busy, too. I don't suppose you have a spare blaster on you?'

Luke shook his head. 'I don't carry a blaster any more. Do you think we should call station security?'

'Not if we want to find out what Ferrier's up to. He'll be all through the station computer and comm system by now – call security and he'll just pull out and disappear back under a rock somewhere.' He peered into one of the open office doorways as they passed it. 'This is vintage Ferrier, all right. One of his favorite tricks is to fiddle work orders to route everyone out of the area he wants to—'

'Hold it,' Luke cut him off. At the edge of his mind . . . 'I think I've got them. Six humans and two aliens, the nearest about two hundred meters straight ahead.'

'What kind of aliens?'

'I don't know. I've never run into either species before.'

'Well, watch them. Aliens in Ferrier's gang are usually hired for their muscle. Let's go.'

'Maybe you should stay here,' Luke suggested, unhooking his lightsaber from his belt. 'I'm not sure how well I'll be able to protect you if they decide to make a fight of it.'

'I'll take my chances,' Lando told him. 'Ferrier knows me; maybe I can keep it from coming down to a fight. Besides, I've got an idea I want to try.'

They were just under twenty meters from the first human when Luke caught the change in sense from the group ahead. 'They've spotted us,' he murmured to Lando, shifting his grip slightly on his lightsaber. 'You want to try talking to them?'

'I don't know,' Lando murmured back, craning his neck to look down the seemingly deserted corridor ahead. 'We might need to get a little closer—'

It came as a flicker of movement from one of the

doorways, and an abrupt ripple in the Force. 'Duck!'
Luke barked, igniting his lightsaber. With a *snap-hiss* the
brilliant green-white blade appeared—

And moved almost of its own accord to neatly block
the blaster bolt that shot toward them.

'Get behind me!' Luke ordered Lando as a second bolt
sizzled the air toward them. Guided by the Force, his
hands again shifted the lightsaber blade into the path of
the attack. A third bolt spattered from the blade, followed by a fourth. From a doorway farther down the
corridor a second blaster opened up, adding its voice to
the first.

Luke held his ground, feeling the Force flowing into
him and out through his arms, evoking an odd sort of
tunnel vision effect that turned mental spotlights on the
attack itself and relative darkness on everything else.
Lando, half crouched directly behind him, was only a
hazy sense in the back of his mind; the rest of Ferrier's
people were even dimmer. Setting his teeth firmly
together, letting the Force control his defense, he kept
his eyes moving around the corridor, alert for new
threats.

He was looking directly at the odd shadow when it
detached itself from the wall and started forward.

For a long minute he didn't believe what he was seeing.
There was no texture or detail to the shadow; nothing
but a slightly fluid shape and nearly absolute blackness.
But it was real . . . and it was moving toward them. 'Lando!'
he shouted over the scream of blaster shots. 'Five meters
away – forty degrees left. Any ideas?'

He heard the hissing intake of air from behind him.
'Never seen anything like it. Retreat?'

With an effort, Luke pulled as much of his concentration as he dared away from their defense and turned it toward the approaching shadow. There was indeed something there – one of the alien intelligences, in fact, that he'd sensed earlier. Which implied it was one of Ferrier's people . . .

'Stay with me,' he told Lando. This was going to be risky, but turning tail and running wouldn't accomplish anything. Moving slowly, keeping his stance balanced and yet fluid, he headed directly toward the shadow.

The alien halted, its sense clearly surprised that a potential prey would be advancing instead of backing away from it. Luke took advantage of the momentary hesitation to move farther toward the corridor wall to his left. The first blaster, its shots starting to come close to the mobile shadow as it tracked Luke's movement, abruptly ceased fire. The shadow's form shifted slightly, giving Luke the impression of something looking over its shoulder. He continued moving to his left, drawing the second blaster's fire toward the shadow as he did so; and a second later it, too, fell reluctantly silent.

'Good job,' Lando murmured approvingly in his ear. 'Allow me.'

He took a step back from Luke. 'Ferrier?' he called. 'This is Lando Calrissian. Listen, if you want to keep your pal here in one piece, you'd better call him off. This is Luke Skywalker, Jedi Knight. The guy who took down Darth Vader.'

Which wasn't strictly true, of course. But it was close enough. Luke *had*, after all, defeated Vader in their last lightsaber duel, even if he hadn't actually gone on to kill him.

Regardless, the implications weren't lost on the unseen men down the corridor. He could sense the doubt and consternation among them; and even as he lifted his lightsaber a little higher, the shadow stopped its approach. 'What was your name?' someone called.

'Lando Calrissian,' Lando repeated. 'Think back to that botched Phraetiss operation about ten years ago.'

'Oh, I remember,' the voice said grimly. 'What do you want?'

'I want to offer you a deal,' Lando said. 'Come on out and we'll talk.'

There was a moment of hesitation. Then, the big man from Luke's memory track stepped out from behind a group of crates that had been stacked against the corridor wall, the simmering cigarra still clenched between his teeth. 'All of you,' Lando insisted. 'Come on, Ferrier, bring them out. Unless you seriously think you can hide them from a Jedi.'

Ferrier's eyes flicked to Luke. 'The mystic Jedi powers have always been exaggerated,' he sneered. But his lips moved inaudibly; and, even as he approached them, five humans and a tall, thin, green-scaled insectoid alien emerged one by one from concealment.

'That's better,' Lando said approvingly, stepping out from behind Luke. 'A Verpine, huh?' he added, waving toward the insectoid alien. 'Got to hand it to you, Ferrier – you're fast. Maybe thirty hours since the Imperials pulled out, and already you're on board. And with a tame Verpine, yet. You ever heard of Verpine, Luke?'

Luke nodded. The alien's appearance wasn't familiar, but the name was. 'They're supposed to be geniuses at fixing and reassembling high-tech devices.'

'And it's a well-deserved reputation,' Lando said. 'Rumor has it they're the ones who helped Admiral Ackbar design the B-wing starfighter. You shifted specialties to palming damaged ships, Ferrier? Or did your Verpine come aboard just for the occasion?'

'You mentioned a deal,' Ferrier said coldly. 'So deal.'

'I want to know first if you were in on the Sluis Van attack from the beginning,' Lando said, matching Ferrier's tone. 'If you're working for the Empire, we can't deal.'

One of the gang, blaster in hand, took a quiet preparatory breath. Luke shifted his lightsaber toward him slightly in warning, and the brief thought of heroics faded quickly away. Ferrier looked at the man, back at Lando. 'The Empire's sent out a call for ships,' he said grudgingly. 'Warships in particular. They're paying a bounty of twenty percent above market value for anything over a hundred thousand tons that can fight.'

Luke and Lando exchanged a quick glance. 'Odd request,' Lando said. 'They lose one of their shipyard facilities or something?'

'They didn't say, and I didn't ask,' Ferrier said acidly. 'I'm a businessman; I give the customer what he wants. You here to deal, or just talk?'

'I'm here to deal,' Lando assured him. 'You know, Ferrier, it seems to me that you're in sort of a jam here. We've nailed you red-handed in the process of trying to steal New Republic warships. We've also pretty well proved that Luke can take all of you without any trouble. All I have to do is whistle up Security and the whole bunch of you will be off to a penal colony for the next few years.'

The shadow, which had been standing still, took a step forward. 'The Jedi might survive,' Ferrier said darkly. 'But you wouldn't.'

'Maybe; maybe not,' Lando said easily. 'Regardless, it's not the sort of situation a businessman like yourself wants to be in. So here's the deal: you leave now, and we'll let you get out of the Sluis Van system before we drop the hammer with the authorities.'

'How very generous of you,' Ferrier said, heavily sarcastic. 'So what do you *really* want? A cut of the operation? Or just a wad of money?'

Lando shook his head. 'I don't want your money. I just want you out of here.'

'I don't take well to threats.'

'Then take it as a friendly warning for past associations' sake,' Lando said, his voice hard. 'But take it seriously.'

For a long minute the only sound in the corridor was the quiet background hum of distant machinery. Luke held himself in combat stance, trying to read the shifting emotions in Ferrier's sense. 'Your "deal" would cost us a lot of money,' Ferrier said, shifting the cigarra to the other side of his mouth.

'I realize that,' Lando conceded. 'And believe it or not, I *am* sorry. But the New Republic can't afford to lose any ships at the moment. However, you might try over at the Amorris system. Last I heard, the Cavrilhu pirate gang was using that as a base, and they're always in need of expert maintenance people.' He looked appraisingly at the shadow. 'And extra muscle, too.'

Ferrier followed his gaze. 'Ah, you like my wraith, do you?'

'Wraith?' Luke frowned.

'They call themselves Defel,' Ferrier said. 'But I think "wraith" suits them so much better. Their bodies absorb all visible light – some sort of evolved survival mechanism.' He eyed Luke. 'And what do *you* think of this deal, Jedi? Enforcer of law and justice that you are?'

Luke had expected the question. 'Have you stolen anything here?' he countered. 'Or done anything illegal other than breaking into the station's assignment computer?'

Ferrier's lip twisted. 'We also shot at a couple of bizits who were poking their noses in where they shouldn't have,' he said sarcastically. 'That count?'

'Not when you didn't hit them,' Luke countered evenly. 'As far as I'm concerned, you can leave.'

'You're too kind,' Ferrier growled. 'So is that it?'

'That's it,' Lando nodded. 'Oh, and I want your slicer access code, too.'

Ferrier glared at him, but gestured to the Verpine standing behind him. Silently, the tall green alien lurched forward and handed Lando a pair of data cards. 'Thank you,' Lando said. 'All right. I'll give you one hour to get your ship up and out of the system before we drop the hammer. Have a good trip.'

'Yeah, we'll do that,' Ferrier bit out. 'So good to see you, Calrissian. Maybe next time I can do *you* a favor.'

'Give Amorris a try,' Lando urged him. 'I'd bet they've got at least a couple of old Sienar patrol ships you could relieve them of.'

Ferrier didn't reply. In silence, the group passed Lando and Luke and headed back down the empty corridor toward the reception area. 'You sure telling him about Amorris was a good idea?' Luke murmured as he watched them go. 'The Empire's likely to get a patrol ship or two out of the deal.'

'Would you rather they have gotten hold of a Calamarian Star Cruiser?' Lando countered. 'Ferrier's probably good enough to have palmed one. Certainly with things as confused out there as they are.' He shook his head thoughtfully. 'I wonder what's going on over in the Empire. It doesn't make sense to pay premium prices for used ships when you've got the facilities to make your own.'

'Maybe they're having some trouble,' Luke suggested, closing down the lightsaber and returning it to his belt. 'Or maybe they've lost one of their Star Destroyers but managed to save the crew and need ships to put them on.'

'I suppose that's possible,' Lando conceded doubtfully. 'Hard to imagine an accident that would destroy any ship beyond repair but leave the crew alive. Well, we can get the word back to Coruscant. Let the Intelligence hotshots figure out what it means.'

'If they're not all too busy playing politics,' Luke said. Because if Councilor Fey'lya's group was also trying to take over Military Intelligence . . . He shook the thought away. Worrying about the situation wasn't productive. 'So what now? We give Ferrier his hour and then hand those slicer codes over to the Sluissi?'

'Oh, we'll give Ferrier his hour, all right,' Lando said, frowning thoughtfully at the departing group. 'But the slicer codes are another matter. It occurred to me on the way in that if Ferrier was using them to divert workers from this end of the station, there's no particular reason why we can't also use them to bump your X-wing to the top of the priority stack.'

'Ah,' Luke said. It was, he knew, not exactly the sort of marginally legal activity a Jedi should participate in. But under the circumstances – and given the urgency of the situation back on Coruscant – bending some rules in this case was probably justified. 'When do we get started?'

'Right now,' Lando said, and Luke couldn't help wincing at the quiet relief in the other's voice and sense. Clearly, he'd been half afraid that Luke would raise those same awkward ethical questions about the suggestion. 'With any luck, you'll be up and ready to fly before I have to give these things to the Sluissi. Come on, let's go find a terminal.'

CHAPTER THREE

✦

'Landing request acknowledged and confirmed, *Millennium Falcon*,' the voice of the Imperial Palace air control director came over the comm. 'You're cleared for pad eight. Councilor Organa Solo will meet you.'

'Thanks, Control,' Han Solo said, easing the ship down toward the Imperial City and eyeing with distaste the dark cloud cover that hung over the whole region like some brooding menace. He'd never put much stock in omens, but those clouds sure didn't help his mood any.

And speaking of bad moods ... Reaching over, he tapped the ship's intercom switch. 'Get ready for landing,' he called. 'We're coming into our approach.'

'Thank you, Captain Solo,' C-3PO's stiffly precise voice came back. A little stiffer than usual, actually; the droid must still be nursing a wounded ego. Or whatever it was that passed for ego in droids.

Han shut off the intercom, lip twisting with some annoyance of his own as he did so. He'd never really liked droids much. He'd used them occasionally, but never more than he'd absolutely had to. Threepio wasn't as bad as some of those he'd known ... but then, he'd never spent six days alone in hyperspace with any of the others, either.

He'd tried. He really had, if for no other reason than that Leia rather liked Threepio and would have wanted them to get along. The first day out from Sluis Van he'd let Threepio sit up front in the cockpit with him, enduring the droid's prissy voice and trying valiantly to hold something resembling a real conversation with him. The second day, he'd let Threepio do most of the talking, and had spent a lot of his time working in maintenance crawlways where there wasn't room for two. Threepio had accepted the limitation with typical mechanical cheerfulness, and had chattered at him from outside the crawlway access hatches.

By the afternoon of the third day, he'd banned the droid from his presence entirely.

Leia wouldn't like it when she found out. But she'd have liked it even less if he'd given in to his original temptation and converted the droid into a set of backup alluvial dampers.

The *Falcon* was through the cloud layer now and in sight of the monstrosity that was the Emperor's old palace. Banking slightly, Han confirmed that pad eight was clear and brought them down.

Leia must have been waiting just inside the canopy that shrouded the pad's accessway, because she was already beside the ship as Han lowered the *Falcon*'s ramp. 'Han,' she said, her voice laced with tension. 'Thank the Force you're back.'

'Hi, sweetheart,' he said, being careful not to press too hard against the increasingly prominent bulge of her belly as he hugged her. The muscles in her shoulders and back felt tight beneath his arms. 'I'm glad to see you, too.'

She clutched him to her for a moment, then gently disengaged. 'Come on – we've got to go.'

Chewbacca was waiting for them just inside the access-way, his bowcaster slung over his shoulder in ready position. 'Hey, Chewie,' Han nodded, getting a growled Wookiee greeting in return. 'Thanks for taking care of Leia.'

The other rumbled something strangely noncommittal in reply. Han eyed him, decided this wasn't the time to press for details of their stay on Kashyyyk. 'What've I missed?' he asked Leia instead.

'Not much,' she said as she led the way down the ramp corridor and into the Palace proper. 'After that first big flurry of accusations, Fey'lya's apparently decided to cool things down. He's talked the Council into letting him take over some of Ackbar's internal security duties, but he's been behaving more like a caretaker than a new administrator. He's also hinted broadly that he'd be available to take charge of the Supreme Command, but he hasn't done any real pushing in that direction.'

'Doesn't want anyone to panic,' Han suggested. 'Accusing someone like Ackbar of treason is a big enough bite for people to chew on as it is. Anything more and they might start choking on it.'

'That's my feeling, too,' Leia agreed. 'Which should give us at least a little breathing space to try and figure out this bank thing.'

'Yeah, what's the lowdown on that, anyway?' Han asked. 'All you told me was that some routine bank check had found a big chunk of money in one of Ackbar's accounts.'

'It turns out it wasn't just a routine check,' Leia said. 'There was a sophisticated electronic break-in at that central clearing bank on Coruscant the morning of the Sluis

Van attack, with several big accounts being hit. The investigators ran a check on all the accounts the bank served and discovered that there'd been a large transfer into Ackbar's account that same morning from the central bank on Palanhi. You familiar with Palanhi?'

'Everybody knows Palanhi,' Han said sourly. 'Little crossroads planet with an overblown idea of their own importance.'

'And the firm belief that if they can stay neutral enough they can play both sides of the war to their own profit,' Leia said. 'Anyway, the central bank there claims that the money didn't come from Palanhi itself and must have been transferred through them. So far our people haven't been able to backtrack it any further.'

Han nodded. 'I'll bet Fey'lya's got some ideas where it came from.'

'The ideas aren't unique to him,' Leia sighed. 'He was just the first one to voice them, that's all.'

'And to make himself a few points at Ackbar's expense,' Han growled. 'Where've they put Ackbar, anyway? The old prison section?'

Leia shook her head. 'He's under a sort of loose house arrest in his quarters while the investigation is under way. More evidence that Fey'lya's trying not to ruffle any more feathers than he has to.'

'Or else that he knows full well there isn't enough here to hang a stunted Jawa from,' Han countered. 'Has he got anything on Ackbar besides the bank thing?'

Leia smiled wanly. 'Just the near-fiasco at Sluis Van. And the fact that it was Ackbar who sent all those warships out there in the first place.'

'Point,' Han conceded, trying to recall the old Rebel

Alliance regulations on military prisoners. If he remembered correctly, an officer under house arrest could receive visitors without those visitors first having to go through more than minor amounts of bureaucratic datawork.

Though he could easily be wrong about that. They'd made him learn all that stuff back when he'd first let them slap an officer's rank on him after the Battle of Yavin. But regulations were never something he'd taken seriously. 'How much of the Council does Fey'lya have on his side?' he asked Leia.

'If you mean *solidly* on his side, only a couple,' she said. 'If you mean leaning in his direction . . . well, you'll be able to judge for yourself in a minute.'

Han blinked. Lost in his own mulling of the mess, he hadn't really paid attention to where Leia was taking him. Now, with a start, he suddenly realized they were walking down the Grand Corridor that linked the Council chamber with the much larger Assemblage auditorium. 'Wait a minute,' he protested. '*Now?*'

'I'm sorry, Han,' she sighed. 'Mon Mothma insisted. You're the first person back who was actually at the Sluis Van attack, and there are a million questions they want to ask you about it.'

Han looked around the corridor: at the high, convoluted vaulting of the ceiling; the ornate carvings and cut-glass windows alternating on the walls; the rows of short, greenish-purple saplings lining each side. The Emperor had supposedly designed the Grand Corridor personally, which probably explained why Han had always disliked the place. 'I knew I should have sent Threepio out first,' he growled.

Leia took his arm. 'Come on, soldier. Take a deep breath and let's get it over with. Chewie, you'd better wait out here.'

The usual Council chamber arrangement was a scaled-up version of the smaller Inner Council room: an oval table in the center for the Councilors themselves, with rows of seats along the walls for their aides and assistants. Today, to Han's surprise, the room had been reconfigured more along the lines of the huge Assemblage Commons. The seats were in neat, slightly tiered rows, with each Councilor surrounded by his or her assistants. In the front of the room, on the lowest level, Mon Mothma sat alone at a simple lectern, looking like a lecturer in a classroom. 'Whose idea was this?' Han murmured as he and Leia started down the side aisle toward what was obviously a witness chair next to Mon Mothma's desk.

'Mon Mothma set it up,' she murmured. 'I'd be willing to bet it was Fey'lya's idea, though.'

Han frowned. He'd have thought that underlining Mon Mothma's preeminent role in the Council like this would be the last thing Fey'lya would want. 'I don't get it.'

She nodded toward the lectern. 'Giving Mon Mothma the whole spotlight helps calm any fears that he plans to make a bid for her position. At the same time, putting the Councilors and their aides together in little groups tends to isolate the Councilors from each other.'

'I get it,' Han nodded back. 'Slippery little fuzzball, isn't he?'

'Yes, he is,' Leia said. 'And he's going to milk this Sluis Van thing for all it's worth. Watch yourself.'

They reached the front and separated, Leia going to the first row and sitting down next to her aide, Winter, Han continuing on to Mon Mothma and the witness chair waiting for him. 'You want me sworn in or anything?' he asked without preamble.

Mon Mothma shook her head. 'That won't be necessary, Captain Solo,' she said, her voice formal and a little strained. 'Please sit down. There are some questions the Council would like to ask you about the recent events at the Sluis Van shipyards.'

Han took his seat. Fey'lya and his fellow Bothans, he saw, were in the group of front-row seats next to Leia's group. There were no empty seats anywhere that might have signified Admiral Ackbar's absence, at least not in the front where they should have been. The Councilors, seated according to rank, had apparently shuffled positions so as to each be closer to the front. Another reason for Fey'lya to have pushed this configuration, Han decided: at the usual oval table, Ackbar's seat might have been left vacant.

'First of all, Captain Solo,' Mon Mothma began, 'we would like you to describe your role in the Sluis Van attack. When you arrived, what happened subsequently – that sort of thing.'

'We got there pretty much as the battle was starting,' Han said. 'Came in just ahead of the Star Destroyers. We picked up a call from Wedge – that's Wing Commander Wedge Antilles of Rogue Squadron – saying that there were TIE fighters loose in the shipyards—'

'Excuse me?' Fey'lya interrupted smoothly. 'Just who is the "we" here?'

Han focused on the Bothan. On those violet eyes, that

soft, cream-colored fur, that totally blank expression. 'My crew consisted of Luke Skywalker and Lando Calrissian.' As Fey'lya no doubt knew perfectly well already. Just a cheap trick to throw Han off stride. 'Oh, and two droids. You want their serial numbers?'

A slight rustle of not-quite humor ran through the room, and Han had the minor satisfaction of seeing that creamcolored fur flatten a little. 'Thank you, no,' Fey'lya said.

'Rogue Squadron was engaged with a group of approximately forty TIE fighters and fifty stolen mole miners that had somehow been smuggled into the shipyards,' Han continued. 'We gave them some assistance with the fighters, figured out that the Imperials were using the mole miners to try and steal some of the capital ships that had been pressed into cargo duty, and were able to stop them. That's about it.'

'You're too modest, Captain Solo,' Fey'lya spoke up again. 'According to the reports we've received here, it was you and Calrissian who managed single-handedly to thwart the Empire's scheme.'

Han braced himself. Here it came. He and Lando had stopped the Imperials, all right . . . only they'd had to fry the nerve centers of over forty capital ships to do it. 'I'm sorry about wrecking the ships,' he said, looking Fey'lya straight in the eye. 'Would you rather the Imperials have taken them intact?'

A ripple ran through the Bothan's fur. 'Really, Captain Solo,' he said soothingly. 'I have no particular quarrel with your method of stopping the Empire's attempt at grand larceny, costly though it might have been. You had only what you could work with. Within your constraints, you and the others succeeded brilliantly.'

Han frowned, feeling suddenly a little off balance. He had expected Fey'lya to try to make him the man under the hammer on this one. For once, the Bothan seemed to have missed a bet. 'Thank you, Councilor,' he said, for lack of anything better to say.

'Which is not to say that the Empire's attempt and near-victory are not important,' Fey'lya said, his fur rippling in the opposite direction this time as he looked around the room. 'On the contrary. At the best, they speak of serious misjudgements on the part of our military commanders. At the worst ... they may speak of treason.'

Han felt his lip twist. So that was it. Fey'lya hadn't changed his stripes; he'd simply decided not to waste a golden opportunity like this on a nobody like Han. 'With all due respect, Councilor,' he spoke up quickly, 'what happened at Sluis Van wasn't Admiral Ackbar's fault. The whole operation—'

'Excuse me, Captain Solo,' Fey'lya cut him off. 'And with all due respect to *you*, let me point out that the reason those capital ships were sitting at Sluis Van in the first place, undermanned and vulnerable, was that Admiral Ackbar had ordered them there.'

'There isn't anything like treason involved,' Han insisted doggedly. 'We already know that the Empire's got a tap into our communications—'

'And who's responsible for such failures of security?' Fey'lya shot back. 'Once again, the blame falls squarely around Admiral Ackbar's shoulders.'

'Well, then, *you* find the leak,' Han snapped. Peripherally, he could see Leia shaking her head urgently at him, but he was too mad now to care whether he was being properly respectful or not. 'And while you're at it, I'd like to see how well *you* would do up against an Imperial Grand Admiral.'

The low-level buzz of conversation that had begun in the room cut off abruptly. 'What was that last?' Mon Mothma asked.

Silently, Han swore at himself. He hadn't meant to spring this on anyone until he'd had a chance to check it out himself at the Palace archives. But it was too late now. 'The Empire's being led by a Grand Admiral,' he muttered. 'I saw him myself.'

The silence hung thick in the air. Mon Mothma recovered first. 'That's impossible,' she said, sounding more like she wanted to believe it than that she really did. 'We've accounted for all the Grand Admirals.'

'I saw him myself,' Han repeated.

'Describe him,' Fey'lya said. 'What did he look like?'

'He wasn't human,' Han said. 'At least, not completely. He had a roughly human build, but he had light blue skin, a kind of bluish black hair, and eyes that glowed red. I don't know what species he was.'

'Yet we know that the Emperor didn't like nonhumans,' Mon Mothma reminded him.

Han looked at Leia. The skin of her face was tight, her eyes staring at and through him with a kind of numb horror. She understood what this meant, all right. 'He was wearing a white uniform,' he told Mon Mothma. 'No other Imperial officers wore anything like that. And the contact I was with specifically called him a Grand Admiral.'

'Obviously a self-granted promotion,' Fey'lya said briskly. 'Some regular admiral or perhaps a leftover Moff trying to rally the remains of the Empire around him. Anyway, that's beside the immediate point.'

'Beside the *point*?' Han demanded. 'Look, Councilor, if there's a Grand Admiral running around loose—'

'If there is,' Mon Mothma interrupted firmly, 'we'll soon know for certain. Until then, there seems little value in holding a debate in a vacuum. Council Research is hereby directed to look into the possibility that a Grand Admiral might still be alive. Until such an investigation has been completed, we will continue with our current inquiry into the circumstances of the Sluis Van attack.' She looked at Han, then turned and nodded at Leia. 'Councilor Organa Solo, you may begin the questioning.'

Admiral Ackbar's high-domed, salmon-colored head bent slightly to the side, his huge round eyes swiveling in their sockets in a Calamarian gesture Leia couldn't recall ever having seen before. Surprise? Or was it perhaps dread?

'A Grand Admiral,' Ackbar said at last, his voice sounding even more gravelly than usual. 'An Imperial Grand Admiral. Yes. That would indeed explain a great many things.'

'We don't actually *know* that it's a real Grand Admiral yet,' Leia cautioned him, throwing a glance at the stony look on her husband's face. Han, clearly, had no doubts of his own. Neither did she, for that matter. 'Mon Mothma's having Research look into it.'

'They won't find anything,' Ackbar said, shaking his head. A more human gesture, that, of the sort he usually tried to use when dealing with humans. Good; that meant he was getting back on balance. 'I had a thorough search made of the Imperial records when we first took Coruscant back from the Empire. There's nothing in there but a list of the Grand Admirals' names and a little about their assignments.'

'Erased before they pulled out,' Han growled.

'Or perhaps never there to begin with,' Leia suggested. 'Remember that these weren't just the best and brightest military leaders the Emperor could find. They were also part of his plan to bring the Imperial military more personally under his control.'

'As was the Death Star project itself,' Ackbar said. 'I agree, Councilor. Until the Grand Admirals were fully integrated both militarily *and* politically, there was no reason to publish details of their identities. And every reason to conceal them.'

'So,' Han said. 'Dead end.'

'It appears that way,' Ackbar agreed. 'Any information we're going to get will have to come from current sources.'

Leia looked at Han. 'You mentioned you were with a contact when you saw this Grand Admiral, but you didn't give us the contact's name.'

'That's right,' Han nodded. 'I didn't. And I'm not going to. Not now, anyway.'

Leia frowned at that unreadable sabacc face, stretching out with all her rudimentary Jedi skills to try to sense his purpose and feelings. It didn't get her very far. *If only I had more time to practice*, she thought ruefully. But if the Council had needed all her time before, it was going to need even more than that now. 'Mon Mothma's going to want to know, eventually,' she warned him.

'And I'm going to tell her, eventually,' he came back. 'Until then, it's going to be our little secret.'

'As in "leverage"?'

'You never can tell.' A shadow of something crossed Han's face. 'The name's not going to do the Council any good right now, anyway. The whole group's probably buried themselves away somewhere. If the Empire hasn't caught up with them.'

'You don't know how to find them?' Leia asked.

Han shrugged. 'There's a ship I promised to get out of impoundment for them. I can try that.'

'Do what you can,' Ackbar said. 'You said Councilor Organa Solo's brother was with you at Sluis Van?'

'Yes, sir,' Han said. 'His hyperdrive needed some repairs, but he should've only been a couple of hours behind me.' He looked at Leia. 'Oh, and we're going to have to get Lando's ship back to him at Sluis Van.'

Ackbar made a noise that sounded something like a choked whistle: the Calamarian equivalent of a grunt. 'We'll need to hear testimony from both of them,' he said. 'And from Wing Commander Antilles, as well. It's vital that we learn how the Empire was able to smuggle such a large force past so many sensors.'

Leia threw Han a look. 'According to Wedge's preliminary report, they apparently were inside a freighter whose hold registered empty.'

Ackbar's eyes swiveled in their sockets. 'Empty? Not merely unreadable, as if from a sensor misfire or static-damping?'

'Wedge said it was empty,' Han told him. 'He ought to know the difference between that and static-damping.'

'Empty.' Ackbar seemed to slump a little in his seat. 'Which can only mean the Empire has finally developed a workable cloaking shield.'

'It's starting to look that way,' Leia agreed soberly. 'I suppose the only good news is that they must still have some bugs left in the system. Otherwise, they could have simply cloaked the whole Sluis Van task force and torn the place to ribbons.'

'No,' Ackbar said, shaking his massive head. 'That's something we won't have to worry about, at least. By its very nature a cloaking shield would be more danger to the user than it was worth. A cloaked warship's own sensor beams would be as useless as those of its enemies, leaving it to flail about totally blind. Worse, it if were under power, the enemy could locate it by simply tracking its drive emissions.'

'Ah,' Leia said. 'I hadn't thought of that.'

'There have been rumors for years that the Emperor was developing a cloaking shield,' Ackbar said. 'I've put a good deal of thought into the contingency.' He harrumphed. 'But the weaknesses are of small comfort. A cloaking shield in the hands of a Grand Admiral would still be a dangerous weapon indeed. He would find ways to use it against us.'

'He already has,' Han muttered.

'Apparently so.' Ackbar's swiveling eyes locked onto Leia's face. 'You must get me cleared of this ridiculous charge, Councilor. As soon as possible. For all his ambition and self-confidence, Councilor Fey'lya hasn't the tactical skills we need against a threat of this magnitude.'

'We'll get you released, Admiral,' Leia promised, wishing she felt that confident. 'We're working on it right now.'

There was a diffident knock, and behind Leia the door opened. 'Excuse me,' the squat G-2RD droid said in a mechanically resonant voice. 'Your time has expired.'

'Thank you,' Leia said, suppressing her frustration as she stood up. She wanted desperately to have more time with Ackbar, to explore with him both this new Imperial threat and also discuss the legal strategies they might use in his defense. But arguing with the droid would gain her nothing, and might get her visiting privileges revoked entirely. Guard droids were allowed that kind of discretion, and the 2RD series in particular was reputed to be a touchy lot. 'I'll be back soon, Admiral,' she told Ackbar. 'Either this afternoon or tomorrow.'

'Goodbye, Councilor.' There was just a brief hesitation – 'And to you, Captain Solo. Thank you for coming.'

'Goodbye, Admiral,' Han said.

They stepped from the room and started down the wide corridor, the G-2RD taking up position at the door behind them. 'That must have hurt,' Han commented.

'What must have?' Leia asked.

'Thanking me for coming.'

She frowned up at him, but there was nothing but seriousness in his face. 'Oh, come on, Han. Just because you resigned your commission—'

'He considers me one step up from a complete traitor,' Han finished for her.

An obvious retort about persecution complexes flashed through Leia's mind. 'Ackbar's never been what you'd call an outgoing person,' she said instead.

Han shook his head. 'I'm not imagining it, Leia. Ask Lando sometime – he gets the same kind of treatment. You leave the military and you might as well be tauntaun spit as far as Ackbar is concerned.'

Leia sighed. 'You have to understand the Mon Calamari ethos, Han. They were never a warlike species at all until the Empire started enslaving them and ravaging their world. Those wonderful Star Cruisers of theirs were originally passenger liners, you know, that we helped them convert into warships. Maybe it's not so much anger at you for quitting as it is some sort of residual guilt at himself and his people for taking up warfare in the first place.'

'Even if they were forced into it?'

Leia shrugged uncomfortably. 'I don't think anyone ever goes into a war without the nagging feeling that there might have been some other way. Even when every other way has already been tried and hasn't worked. I know *I* felt it when I first joined the Rebellion – and believe me, people like Mon Mothma and Bail Organa had tried everything. For an inherently peaceful race like the Mon Calamari, the feeling must be even worse.'

'Well ... maybe,' Han conceded grudgingly. 'I just wish they'd work it through for themselves and leave the rest of us out of it.'

'They are,' Leia assured him. 'We've just got to give them time.'

He looked down at her. 'You haven't told me yet why you and Chewie left Kashyyyk and came back here.'

Leia squeezed thumb and forefinger together. Eventually, she knew, she would have to tell Han about the deal she'd made with the Noghri commando Khabarakh. But walking down a public corridor of the Imperial Palace wasn't the place for that kind of discussion. 'There didn't seem any point in staying,' she told him. 'There was another attack—'

'There *what*?'

'Relax, we fought it off,' she soothed him. 'And I've

made arrangements that should keep me safe, at least for the next couple of weeks. I'll tell you about it later, when we're someplace more secure.'

She could feel his eyes boring into her; could sense the suspicion in his mind that there was something she wasn't telling him. But he recognized as well as she did the danger of speaking secrets out in the open. 'All right,' he muttered. 'I just hope you know what you're doing.'

Leia shivered, focusing on the sense of the twins she carried within her. So potentially strong in the Force . . . and yet so utterly helpless. 'So do I,' she whispered.

CHAPTER FOUR

JORUUS C'BAOTH. HUMAN. BORN IN REITHCAS, ON
BORTRAS, ON 4\3\112, PRE-EMPIRE DATE.

Luke made a face as he watched the words scroll
up the Old Senate Library computer screen. What was
it about new regimes, he wondered, that one of their
first official acts always seemed to be the creation of a
new dating system, which they then went and applied
to all existing historical records? The Galactic Empire
had done that, as had the Old Republic before it. He
could only hope that the New Republic wouldn't follow suit. History was hard enough to keep track of as
it was.

ATTENDED MIRNIC UNIVERSITY 6\4\95 TO 4\32\90 PE.
ATTENDED JEDI TRAINING CENTER ON KAMPARAS 2\15\90
TO 8\33\88 PE. PRIVATE JEDI TRAINING BEGUN 9\88 PE;
INSTRUCTOR UNKNOWN. GRANTED TITLE OF JEDI KNIGHT
3\6\86 PE. OFFICIALLY ASSUMED TITLE OF JEDI MASTER
4\3\74 PE. SUMMARY ENDS. FURTHER DETAILS OF
SCHOOLING AND TRAINING?

'No,' Luke said, frowning. C'baoth had *assumed* the title of Jedi Master? He'd always been under the impression that that title, like the rank of Jedi Knight itself, was something that was granted by the rest of the Jedi community and not simply self-proclaimed. 'Give me the highlights of his record as a Jedi.'

MEMBER OF ANDO DEMILITARIZATION OBSERVATION
GROUP 8\82 TO 7\81 PE. MEMBER OF SENATE
INTERSPECIES ADVISORY COMMITTEE 9\81 TO 6\79 PE.
PERSONAL JEDI ADVISER TO SENATOR PALPATINE 6\79 TO 5\77—

'Stop,' Luke ordered, a sudden shiver running up his back. Jedi adviser to Senator *Palpatine*? 'Detail C'baoth's service to Senator Palpatine.'

The computer seemed to consider the request. UNAVAILABLE, the answer came at last.

'Unavailable, or just classified?' Luke countered.

UNAVAILABLE, the computer repeated.

Luke grimaced. But there was little he could do about it for the moment. 'Continue.'

MEMBER OF JEDI FORCE ASSEMBLED TO OPPOSE THE
DARK JEDI INSURRECTION ON BPFASSH 7\77 TO 1\74 PE.
ASSISTED IN RESOLVING ALDERAAN ASCENDANCY
CONTENTION 11\70 PE. ASSISTED JEDI MASTER TRA'S
M'INS IN MEDIATION OF DUINUOGWUIN-GOTAL CONFLICT
1\68 TO 4\66 PE. NAMED AMBASSADOR AT LARGE TO
XAPPYH SECTOR 8\21\62 PE BY SENATE. HIGHLY
INSTRUMENTAL IN CONVINCING SENATE TO AUTHORIZE
AND FUND OUTBOUND FLIGHT PROJECT. ONE OF SIX JEDI
MASTERS ATTACHED TO PROJECT 7\7\65 PE. NO RECORD

EXISTS AFTER PROJECT DEPARTURE FROM YAGA MINOR,
4\1\64. HIGHLIGHTS SUMMARY ENDS. FURTHER
INFORMATION?

Luke leaned back in his chair, gazing at the display and
chewing at the inside of his cheek. So not only had C'baoth
once been an adviser to the man who would someday
declare himself Emperor, but he'd also been part of the
attack against those Dark Jedi from the Sluis sector that
Leia had told him about. One of whom had survived long
enough to face Master Yoda on Dagobah . . .

There was a soft footstep behind him. 'Commander?'

'Hello, Winter,' Luke said without turning. 'Looking
for me?'

'Yes,' Winter said, coming up to stand beside him. 'Princess Leia would like to see you whenever you're finished
here.' She nodded at the display, running a hand through
her silky white hair as she did so. 'More Jedi research?'

'Sort of,' Luke told her, sliding a data card into the
terminal's slot. 'Computer: copy complete record of Jedi
Master Joruus C'baoth.'

'Joruus C'baoth,' Winter repeated thoughtfully. 'Wasn't
he involved in the big ascendancy flap on Alderaan?'

'That's what the record says,' Luke nodded. 'You know
anything about that?'

'No more than any other Alderaanian,' Winter said.
Even with her rigid control some of the pain leaked
through to her voice, and Luke found himself wincing in
sympathy with it. For Leia, he knew, the destruction of
Alderaan and the loss of her family was a heartrending
but slowly fading ache in the back corners of her mind.
For Winter, with her perfect and indelible memory, the

pain would probably go on for ever. 'The question was whether the line of ascent to Viceroy should go to Bail Organa's father or one of the other family lines,' Winter continued. 'After the third voting deadlock they appealed to the Senate to mediate the issue. C'baoth was one of the delegation they sent, which took less than a month to decide that the Organas had the proper claim.'

'Did you ever see any pictures of C'baoth?' Luke asked.

Winter considered. 'There was a group holo in the archives that showed the entire mediation team,' she said after a moment. 'C'baoth was – oh, about average height and build, I suppose. Fairly muscular, too, which I remembered thinking seemed rather odd for a Jedi.' She looked at Luke, coloring slightly. 'I'm sorry; I didn't mean that to sound derogatory.'

'No problem,' Luke assured her. It was a common misconception, he'd discovered: with mastery over the Force, people just assumed there was no reason for a Jedi to cultivate physical strength. It had taken Luke himself several years to truly appreciate the subtle ways in which control of the body was linked to control of the mind. 'What else?'

'He had graying hair and a short, neatly trimmed beard,' Winter said. 'He was wearing the same brown robe and white undertunic that a lot of Jedi seemed to favor. Other than that, there wasn't anything particularly notable about him.'

Luke rubbed his chin. 'How old did he look?'

'Oh . . . I'd say somewhere around forty,' Winter said. 'Plus or minus five years, perhaps. Age is always hard to ascertain from a picture.'

'That would fit with the record here,' Luke agreed, retrieving the data card from the slot. But if the record was right . . . 'You said Leia wanted to see me?' he asked, standing up.

'If it's convenient,' Winter nodded. 'She's in her office.'

'OK. Let's go.'

They left the library and started down the cross corridor linking the research areas with the Council and Assemblage chambers. 'You know anything about the planet Bortras?' he asked Winter as they walked. 'Specifically, anything about how long its people live?'

She thought a moment. 'I've never read anything that mentioned it one way or another. Why?'

Luke hesitated; but however the Imperials were getting information out of the New Republic's inner sanctum, Winter was certainly far above suspicion. 'The problem is that if this alleged Jedi out on Jomark really is Joruus C'baoth, he has to be over a hundred by now. I know there are some species that live longer than that, but he's supposed to be human.'

Winter shrugged. 'There are always exceptions to a race's normal life span,' she pointed out. 'And a Jedi, in particular, might have techniques that would help extend that span.'

Luke thought about that. It was possible, he knew. Yoda had certainly had a long life – a good nine hundred years – and as a general rule, smaller species usually had shorter life spans than larger ones. But *usually* didn't mean *always*; and after many hours of record searches, Luke still hadn't figured out just what species Yoda had belonged to. Perhaps a better approach might be to try to find out how long the Emperor had lived.

'So you think Joruus C'baoth is alive?' Winter asked into his thoughts.

Luke glanced around. They'd reached the Grand Corridor now, which because of its location was usually fairly brimming with humans and others standing around in little conversation groups of their own, all of them too far away to eavesdrop. 'I had a brief mental contact with another Jedi while I was on Nkllon,' he said, lowering his voice. 'Afterward, Leia told me that there were rumors C'baoth had been seen on Jomark. I don't know what other conclusion to come to.'

Winter was silent. 'Any comments?' Luke prompted her.

She shrugged. 'Anything having to do with Jedi and the Force are out of my personal experience, Commander,' she said. 'I really can't comment one way or another on that. But . . . I'd have to say that the impression I got of C'baoth from Alderaanian history makes me skeptical.'

'Why?'

'It's just an impression, you understand,' Winter emphasized. 'Nothing I would ever have mentioned if you hadn't asked. C'baoth struck me as the sort of person who loved being in the middle of things. The sort who, if he couldn't lead, control, or help in a particular situation, would still be there just so he'd be visible.'

They were passing by one of the purple-and-green ch'hala trees lining the Grand Corridor now, close enough for Luke to see the subtle moirélike turmoil of color taking place beneath the thin transparent outer bark. 'I suppose that fits with what I read,' he conceded, reaching out to slide a fingertip across the slender tree trunk as they walked. The subtle turmoil exploded at his touch into a flash of angry red across the quiet purple, the color shooting out around the trunk like ripples in a cylindrical pond, circling it again and again as it flowed up and down the trunk before finally fading to burgundy and then back to purple again. 'I don't know if you knew it, but he apparently promoted himself from Jedi Knight to Jedi Master. Seems like kind of a conceited thing to do.'

'Yes, it does,' Winter agreed. 'Though at least by the time he came to Alderaan there didn't seem to be any dispute about it. My point is that someone who likes the spotlight that much wouldn't have stayed so completely out of the war against the Empire.'

'And a good point it is, too,' Luke admitted, half turning to watch the last bit of red fade away on the ch'hala tree he'd touched. The Nkllon contact with the mysterious Jedi had been like that: there for a short time, and then gone without a trace. Was C'baoth perhaps no longer fully in control of his powers? 'New subject, then. What do you know about this Outbound Flight project the Old Republic put together?'

'Not much,' she said, frowning with concentration. 'It was supposedly an attempt to search for life outside the galaxy proper, but the whole thing was so buried in secrecy they never released any details. I'm not even sure whether or not it was ever launched.'

'The records say it was,' Luke said, touching the next ch'hala tree in line as they passed by, eliciting another flash of red. 'They also say that C'baoth was attached to the project. Does that mean he would have been aboard?'

'I don't know,' Winter said. 'There were rumors that several Jedi Masters would be going along, but again there was no official confirmation of that.' She looked sideways at him. 'Are you thinking that might be why he wasn't around during the Rebellion?'

'It's possible,' Luke said. 'Of course, that would just raise another whole set of questions. Like what happened to them and how he got back.'

Winter shrugged. 'I suppose there's one way to find out.'

'Yeah.' Luke touched the last tree in line. 'Go to Jomark and ask him. I guess I'll have to.'

Leia's office was grouped with the other Inner Council suites just off the cross hallway that linked the Grand Corridor with the more intimate Inner Council meeting room. Luke and Winter entered the outer reception area, to find a familiar figure waiting there. 'Hello, Threepio,' Luke said.

'Master Luke – how good to see you again,' the gold-skinned droid gushed. 'I trust you're well?'

'I'm fine,' Luke told him. 'Artoo said to say hello when I saw you, by the way. They've got him over at the space-port helping with some maintenance on my X-wing, but I'll be bringing him back later this evening. You can see him then.'

'Thank you, sir.' Threepio tilted his head slightly, as if suddenly remembering that he was supposed to be acting as a receptionist here. 'Princess Leia and the others are expecting you,' he said, touching the inner chamber release. 'Please go on in.'

'Thank you,' Luke said, nodding gravely. No matter how ridiculous Threepio might look in any given situation, there was always a certain inherent dignity about him, a dignity that Luke usually tried to respond to in kind. 'Let us know if anyone else comes.'

'Of course, sir,' Threepio said.

They went into the inner chamber to find Leia and Han holding a quiet conversation over a computer display on Leia's desk. Chewbacca, sitting alone near the door with his bowcaster across his knees, growled a greeting as they entered.

'Ah – Luke,' Leia said, looking up. 'Thanks for coming.' She shifted her attention to Winter. 'That'll be all for now, Winter.'

'Yes, Your Highness,' Winter nodded. With her usual grace, she glided from the room.

Luke looked at Han. 'I hear you dropped a double-sized thermal detonator on the Council yesterday.'

Han grimaced. 'I tried. Not that anyone really believed me.'

'One of those instances where politics drifts off into the realm of wishful thinking,' Leia said. 'The last thing anyone wants to believe is that in our sweep we somehow missed one of the Emperor's Grand Admirals.'

'Sounds more like willful denial than wishful thinking to me,' Luke said. 'Or do they have another theory as to how we got edged so neatly into that Sluis Van trap?'

Leia grimaced. 'Some of them say that's where Ackbar's collusion comes in.'

'Ah,' Luke murmured. So *that* was the thrust of Fey'lya's scheme. 'I hadn't heard any of the details yet.'

'So far, Fey'lya's been playing the sabacc cards close to the fur,' Han growled. '*He* claims he's trying to be fair; *I* think he's just trying not to rock all the stabilizers at once.'

Luke frowned at him. There was something else in his friend's face and sense . . . 'And maybe something more?' he prompted.

Han and Leia exchanged glances. 'Maybe,' Han said. 'You notice how quickly after the Sluis Van attack Fey'lya dropped the hammer on Ackbar. Either he's one of the great opportunists of all time—'

'Which we already know he is,' Leia put in.

'—or else,' Han continued grimly, 'he knew in advance what was going to happen.'

Luke looked at Leia. At the strain in her face and sense . . . 'You realize what you're saying,' he said quietly. 'You're accusing a member of the Council of being an Imperial agent.'

Leia's sense seemed to flinch. Han's didn't even flicker. 'Yeah, I know,' Han said. 'Isn't that what he's accusing Ackbar of?'

'The problem is timing, Han,' Leia said, her tone one of strained patience. 'As I've already tried to explain. If we accuse Fey'lya of anything now, it'll just look like we're trying to take the pressure off Ackbar by turning Fey'lya's charges back against him. Even if it were true – and I don't think it is – it would still come across as a cheap and rather mindless trick.'

'Maybe that's why he was so quick to finger Ackbar in the first place,' Han countered. 'So that we couldn't turn it back on him. That ever occur to you?'

'Yes, it has,' Leia said. 'Unfortunately, it doesn't change the situation. Until we've cleared Ackbar, we can't go making accusations against Fey'lya.'

Han snorted. 'Come on, Leia. Political waddlefooting is fine in its place, but we're talking about the survival of the New Republic here.'

'Which could fall completely apart over this without anyone ever firing a shot,' Leia retorted hotly. 'Face it, Han – this whole thing is still being held together with hope and crating tape. You get a few wild accusations flying around, and half the races in the old Rebel Alliance might decide to pull out and go their separate ways.'

Luke cleared his throat. 'If I can say something . . . ?'

They looked at him, the tension in the room fading a little. 'Sure, kid, what is it?' Han said.

'I think we all agree that, whatever his agenda or possible sponsors, Fey'lya is up to *something*,' Luke said. 'Maybe it would help to find out what that something is. Leia, what do we know about Fey'lya?'

She shrugged. 'He's a Bothan, obviously, though he grew up on the Bothan colony world of Kothlis instead of on Bothawui proper. He joined the Rebel Alliance right after the Battle of Yavin, bringing a good-sized group of his fellow Bothans in with him. His people served mainly in support and reconnaissance, though they saw some occasional action, too. He was involved in a number of wide-ranging interstellar business activities before joining the Alliance – shipping, merchandising, some mining, assorted other ventures. I'm pretty sure he's kept up with some of them since then, but I don't know which ones.'

'Are they on file?' Luke asked.

She shook her head. 'I've been through his file five times, and I've checked every other reference to him I could find. Nothing.'

'That's where we want to start our backtrack, then,' Han decided. 'Quiet business stuff is always good for digging up dirt.'

Leia threw him a patient look. 'It's a big galaxy, Han. We don't even know where to start looking.'

'I think we can figure it out,' Han assured her. 'You said the Bothans saw some action after Yavin. Where?'

'Any number of places,' Leia said, frowning. She swiveled the computer around to face her, tapped in a command. 'Let's see . . .'

'You can skip any battle they were ordered into,' Han told her. 'Also any time there were only a few of them there as part of a big multispecies force. I just want the places where a bunch of Fey'lya's people really threw themselves into it.'

It was clear from Leia's face that she didn't see where Han was going with this, a sentiment Luke could readily identify with. But she fed in the parameters without comment. 'Well . . . I suppose the only one that really qualifies would be a short but violent battle off New Cov in the Churba sector. Four Bothan ships took on a *Victory*-class Star Destroyer that was snooping around, keeping it busy until a Star Cruiser could come to their assistance.'

'New Cov, huh?' Han repeated thoughtfully. 'That system get mentioned anywhere in Fey'lya's business stuff?'

'Uh . . . no, it doesn't.'

'Fine,' Han nodded. 'Then that's where we start.'

Leia threw Luke a blank look. 'Did I miss something?'

'Oh, come on, Leia,' Han said. 'You said yourself that the Bothans pretty much sat out the real war everywhere they could. They didn't take on a *Victory* Star Destroyer at New Cov just for the fun of it. They were protecting something.'

Leia frowned. 'I think you're reaching.'

'Maybe,' Han agreed. 'Maybe not. Suppose it was Fey'lya and not the Imperials that sneaked that money into Ackbar's account? Transferring a block fund through Palanhi from the Churba sector would be easier than sending it in from any of the Imperial systems.'

'That takes us back to accusing Fey'lya of being an Imperial agent,' Luke warned.

'Maybe not,' Han argued. 'Could be the timing of the

transfer was coincidence. Or maybe one of the Bothans got a whiff of the Empire's intentions and Fey'lya figured he could use it to take down Ackbar.'

Leia shook her head. 'It's still nothing we can take to the Council,' she said.

'I'm not going to take it to the Council,' Han told her. 'I'm going to take Luke, and we're going to go to New Cov and check it out ourselves. Quiet like.'

Leia looked at Luke, an unspoken question forming in her mind. 'There's nothing I can do here to help,' he said. 'It's worth a look, anyway.'

'All right,' Leia sighed. 'But keep it quiet.'

Han gave her a tight grin. 'Trust me.' He raised an eyebrow at Luke. 'You ready?'

Luke blinked. 'You mean right now?'

'Sure, why not? Leia's got the political end covered here OK.'

There was a flicker of sense from Leia, and Luke looked over just in time to see her wince. Her eyes met Luke's, her sense pleading with him to keep quiet. *What is it?* he asked her silently.

Whether she would have answered him or not he never found out. From over at the door Chewbacca growled out the whole story.

Han turned to stare at his wife, his mouth falling open. 'You promised *what*?' he breathed.

She swallowed visibly. 'Han, I had no choice.'

'No choice? No *choice*? I'll give you a choice – no, you're not going.'

'Han—'

'Excuse me,' Luke interrupted, standing up. 'I have to go check out my X-wing. I'll see you both later.'

'Sure, kid,' Han growled, not looking at him.

Luke stepped to the door, catching Chewbacca's eye as he passed and nodding toward the outer office. Clearly, the Wookiee had already come to the same conclusion. Heaving his massive bulk to his feet, he followed Luke from the room.

The door slid shut behind them, and for a long moment they just stared at each other. Leia broke the silence first. 'I have to go, Han,' she said softly. 'I promised Khabarakh I'd meet him. Don't you understand?'

'No, I don't understand,' Han retorted, trying hard to hold on to his temper. The gut-wrenching fear he'd felt after that near-miss on Bpfassh was back, churning hard at his stomach. Fear for Leia's safety, and the safety of the twins she carried. His son and daughter ... 'These whatever-they-ares—'

'Noghri,' she supplied the word.

'—these Noghri have been taking potshots at you every chance they've had for a couple of months now. You remember Bpfassh and that mock-up of the *Falcon* they tried to sucker us into getting aboard? And the attack on Bimmisaari before that – they came within a hair of snatching us right out of the middle of a market-place. If it hadn't been for Luke and Chewie they'd have done it, too. These guys are *serious*, Leia. And now you tell me you want to fly out alone and visit their planet? You might as well turn yourself over to the Empire and save some time.'

'I wouldn't be going if I thought that,' she insisted. 'Khabarakh knows I'm Darth Vader's daughter, and for whatever reason, that seems to be very important to them.

Maybe I can use that leverage to turn them away from the Empire and onto our side. Anyway, I have to try.'

Han snorted. 'What is this, some kind of crazy Jedi thing? Luke was always getting all noble and charging off into trouble, too.'

Leia reached over to lay her hand on his arm. 'Han . . . I know it's a risk,' she said quietly. 'But it may be the only chance we ever have of resolving this. The Noghri need help – Khabarakh admitted that. If I can give them that help – if I can convince them to come over to our side – that'll mean one less enemy for us to have to deal with.' She hesitated. 'And I can't keep running for ever.'

'What about the twins?'

He had the guilty satisfaction of seeing her wince. 'I know,' she said, a shiver running through her as she reached her other hand up to hold her belly. 'But what's the alternative? To lock them away in a tower of the Palace somewhere with a ring of Wookiee guards around them? They'll never have any chance of a normal life as long as the Noghri are trying to take them from us.'

Han gritted his teeth. So she knew. He hadn't been sure before, but he was now. Leia knew that what the Empire had been after this whole time was her unborn children.

And knowing that, she still wanted to meet with the Empire's agents.

For a long minute he gazed at her, his eyes searching the features of that face he'd grown to love so deeply over the years, his memory bringing up images of the past as he did so. The young determination in her face as, in the middle of a blazing firefight, she'd grabbed Luke's blaster rifle away from him and shot them an escape route into the Death Star's detention-level garbage chute. The sound of her voice in the middle of deadly danger at Jabba's, helping him through the blindness and tremor and disorientation of hibernation sickness. The wiser, more mature determination visible through the pain in her eyes as, lying wounded outside the Endor bunker, she had nevertheless summoned the skill and control to coolly shoot two stormtroopers off Han's back.

And he remembered, too, the wrenching realization he'd had at that same time: that no matter how much he tried, he would never be able to totally protect her from the dangers and risks of the universe. Because no matter how much he might love her – no matter how much he might give of himself to her – she could never be content with that alone. Her vision extended beyond him, just as it extended beyond herself, to all the beings of the galaxy.

And to take that away from her, whether by force or even by persuasion, would be to diminish her soul. And to take away part of what he'd fallen in love with in the first place.

'Can I at least go with you?' he asked quietly.

She reached up to caress his cheek, smiling her thanks through the sudden moisture in her eyes. 'I promised I'd go alone,' she whispered, her voice tight with emotion. 'Don't worry, I'll be all right.'

'Sure.' Abruptly, Han got to his feet. 'Well, if you're going, you're going. Come on – I'll help you get the *Falcon* prepped.'

'The *Falcon*?' she repeated. 'But I thought you were going to New Cov.'

'I'll take Lando's ship,' he called over his shoulder as he strode to the door. 'I've got to get it back to him, anyway.'

'But—'

'No argument,' he cut her off. 'If this Noghri of yours has something besides talking in mind, you'll stand a better chance in the *Falcon* than you will in the *Lady Luck*.' He opened the door and stepped into the reception area.

And stopped short. Standing directly between him and the door, looking for all the world like a giant hairy thundercloud, Chewbacca was glowering at him. 'What?' Han demanded.

The Wookiee's comment was short, sharp, and very much to the point. 'Well, *I* don't much like it, either,' Han told him bluntly. 'What do you want me to do, lock her up somewhere?'

He felt Leia come up behind him. 'I'll be all right, Chewie,' she assured him. 'Really I will.'

Chewbacca growled again, making it abundantly clear what he thought of her assessment. 'You got any suggestions, let's hear 'em,' Han said.

Not surprisingly, he did. 'Chewie, I'm sorry,' Leia said. 'I promised Khabarakh I'd come alone.'

Chewbacca shook his head violently, showing his teeth as he growled his opinion of that idea. 'He doesn't like it,' Han translated diplomatically.

'I got the gist, thank you,' Leia retorted. 'Listen, you two; for the last time—'

Chewbacca cut her off with a bellow that made her jump half a meter backward. 'You know, sweetheart,' Han said, 'I really think you ought to let him go with you. At least as far as the rendezvous point,' he added quickly as she threw him a glare. 'Come on – you know how seriously Wookiees take this life debt thing. You need a pilot, anyway.'

For just a second he could see the obvious counter-argument in her eyes: that she was perfectly capable of flying the *Falcon* herself. But only for a second. 'All right,' she sighed. 'I guess Khabarakh won't object to that. But once we reach the rendezvous, Chewie, you do as I tell you, whether you like it or not. Agreed?'

The Wookiee thought about it, rumbled agreement. 'OK,' Leia said, sounding relieved. 'Let's get going, then. Threepio?'

'Yes, Your Highness?' the droid said hesitantly. For once, he'd had the brains to sit quietly at the reception desk and keep his loose change out of the discussion. It was a marked improvement over his usual behavior, Han decided. Maybe he ought to let Chewbacca get angry more often.

'I want you to come with me, too,' Leia told the droid. 'Khabarakh spoke Basic well enough, but the other Noghri may not, and I don't want to have to depend on their translators to make myself understood.'

'Of course, Your Highness,' Threepio said, tilting his head slightly to the side.

'Good.' Leia turned to look up at Han, licked her lips. 'I guess we'd better get going.'

There were a million things he could have said to her. A million things he wanted to say. 'I guess,' he said instead, 'you'd better.'

CHAPTER FIVE

'You'll forgive me,' Mara said conversationally as she finished the last bit of wiring on her comm board, 'if I say that as a hideout, this place stinks.'

Karrde shrugged as he hefted a sensor pack out of its box and set it down on the side table with an assortment of other equipment. 'I agree it's not Myrkr,' he said. 'On the other hand, it has its compensations. Who'd ever think of looking for a smuggler's nest in the middle of a swamp?'

'I'm not referring to the ship drop,' Mara told him, reaching beneath her loose-flowing tunic sleeve to readjust the tiny blaster sheathed to her left forearm. 'I mean *this* place.'

'Ah. *This* place.' Karrde glanced out the window. 'I don't know. A little public, perhaps, but that, too, has its compensations.'

'A little public?' Mara echoed, looking out the window herself at the neat row of cream-white buildings barely five meters away and the crowds of brightly clad humans and aliens hurrying along just outside. 'You call this a *little* public?'

'Calm down, Mara,' Karrde said. 'When the only viable

places to live on a planet are a handful of deep valleys, of course things are going to get a bit crowded. The people here are used to it, and they've learned how to give each other a reasonable degree of privacy. Anyway, even if they wanted to snoop, it wouldn't do them much good.'

'Mirror glass won't stop a good sensor probe,' Mara countered. 'And crowds mean cover for Imperial spies.'

'The Imperials have no idea where we are.' He paused and threw her an odd look. 'Unless you know differently.'

Mara turned away. So that was how it was going to be this time. Previous employers had reacted to her strange hunches with fear, or anger, or simple bald-faced hatred. Karrde, apparently, was going to go for polite exploitation. 'I can't turn it on and off like a sensor pack,' she growled over her shoulder. 'Not any more.'

'Ah,' Karrde said. The word implied he understood; the tone indicated otherwise. 'Interesting. Is this a remnant of some previous Jedi training?'

She turned to look at him. 'Tell me about the ships.'

He frowned. 'Excuse me?'

'The ships,' she repeated. 'The capital warships that you were very careful not to tell Grand Admiral Thrawn about, back when he visited us on Myrkr. You promised to give me the details later. This is later.'

He studied her, a slight smile creasing his lips. 'All right,' he said. 'Have you ever heard of the *Katana* fleet?'

She had to search her memory. 'That was the group also called the Dark Force, wasn't it? Something like two hundred Dreadnaught-class Heavy Cruisers that were lost about ten years before the Clone Wars broke out. All the ships were fitted with some kind of new-style full-rig slave circuitry, and when the system malfunctioned, the whole fleet jumped to lightspeed together and disappeared.'

'Nearly right,' Karrde said. 'The Dreadnaughts of that era in particular were ridiculously crew-intensive ships, requiring upwards of sixteen thousand men each. The full-rig slave circuitry on the *Katana* ships cut that complement down to around two thousand.'

Mara thought about the handful of Dreadnaught cruisers she'd known. 'Must have been an expensive conversion.'

'It was,' Karrde nodded. 'Particularly since they played it as much for public relations as they did for pure military purposes. They redesigned the entire Dreadnaught interior for the occasion, from the equipment and interior decor right down to the dark gray hull surfacing. That last was the origin of the nickname "Dark Force", incidentally, though there was some suggestion that it referred to the smaller number of interior lights a two-thousand-crewer ship would need. At any rate, it was the Old Republic's grand demonstration of how effective a slave-rigged fleet could be.'

Mara snorted. 'Some demonstration.'

'Agreed,' Karrde said dryly. 'But the problem wasn't in the slave circuitry itself. The records are a little vague – suppressed by those in charge at the time, no doubt – but it appears that one or more of the fleet's crewers picked up a hive virus at one of the ports of call on their maiden voyage. It was spread throughout all two hundred ships while in dormant state, which meant that when it suddenly flared up it took down nearly everybody at once.'

Mara shivered. She'd heard of hive viruses leveling whole planetary populations in pre-Clone Wars days, before the medical science of the Old Republic and later the Empire had finally figured out how to deal with the things. 'So it killed the crews before they could get to help.'

'Apparently in a matter of hours, though that's just an educated guess,' Karrde said. 'What turned the whole thing from a disaster into a debacle was the fact that this particular hive virus had the charming trait of driving its victims insane just before it killed them. The dying crewers lasted just long enough to slave their ships together ... which meant that when the *Katana* command crew also went crazy and took off, the entire fleet went with them.'

'I remember now,' Mara nodded slowly. 'That was supposedly what started the big movement toward decentralization in automated ship functions. Away from big, all-powerful computers into hundreds of droids.'

'The movement was already on its way, but the *Katana* fiasco pretty well sealed the outcome,' Karrde said. 'Anyway, the fleet disappeared somewhere into the depths of interstellar space and was never heard from again. It was a big news item for a while, with some of the less reverent members of the media making snide wordplays on the "Dark Force" name, and for a few years it was considered a hot prospect by salvage teams who had more enthusiasm than good sense. Once it finally dawned on them just how much empty space was available in the galaxy to lose a couple hundred ships in, the flurry of interest ended. At any rate, the Old Republic soon had bigger problems on its hands. Aside from the occasional con artist who'll try to sell you a map of its location, you never hear about the fleet any more.'

'Right.' It was, of course, obvious now where Karrde was going with this. 'So how did you happen to find it?'

'Purely by accident, I assure you. In fact, it wasn't until several days afterward that I realized what exactly I'd found. I suspect none of the rest of the crew ever knew at all.'

Karrde's gaze defocused, his eyes flattening with the memory. 'It was just over fifteen years ago,' he said, his voice distant, the thumbs of his intertwined hands rubbing slowly against each other. 'I was working as navigator/sensor specialist for a small, independent smuggling group. We'd rather botched a pickup and had had to shoot our way past a pair of Carrack cruisers on our way out. We made it all right, but since I hadn't had the time to do a complete lightspeed calculation, we dropped back to realspace a half light-year out to recalculate.' His lip twitched. 'Imagine our surprise when we discovered a pair of Dreadnaughts waiting directly in our path.'

'Lying dead in space.'

Karrde shook his head. 'Actually, they weren't, which was what threw me for those first few days. From all appearances, the ships seemed to be fully functional, with both interior and running lights showing and even a standby sensor scan in operation. Naturally, we assumed it was part of the group we'd just tangled with, and the captain made an emergency jump to lightspeed to get us out of there.'

'Not a good idea,' Mara murmured.

'It seemed the lesser of the two evils at the time,' Karrde said grimly. 'As it turned out, we came close to being fatally wrong on that account. The ship hit the mass shadow of a large comet on the way out, blowing the main hyperdrive and nearly wrecking the rest of the ship on the spot. Five of our crew were killed in the collision, and another three died of injuries before we could limp back to civilization on the backup hyperdrive.'

There was a moment of silence. 'How many of you were left?' Mara asked at last.

Karrde focused on her, his usual sardonic smile back on his face. 'Or in other words, who else might know about the fleet?'

'If you want to put it that way.'

'There were six of us left. As I said, though, I don't think any of the others realized what it was we'd found. It was only when I went back to the sensor records and discovered that there were considerably more than just the two Dreadnaughts in the area that I began to have my own suspicions.'

'And the records themselves?'

'I erased them. After memorizing the coordinates, of course.'

Mara nodded. 'You said this was fifteen years ago?'

'That's right,' Karrde nodded back. 'I've thought about going back and doing something with the ships, but I never had the time to do it properly. Unloading two hundred Dreadnaughts on the open market isn't something you rush into without a good deal of prior preparation. Even if you have markets for all of them, which has always been problematic.'

'Until now.'

He cocked an eyebrow. 'Are you suggesting I sell them to the Empire?'

'They're in the market for capital ships,' she reminded him. 'And they're offering value plus twenty percent.'

He cocked an eyebrow at her. 'I thought you didn't much care for the Empire.'

'I don't,' she retorted. 'What's the other option – give them to the New Republic?'

He held her gaze. 'That might be more profitable in the long run.'

Mara's left hand curled into a tight fist, her stomach churning with mixed feelings. To let the Dreadnaughts fall into the hands of the New Republic, successor to the Rebel Alliance that had destroyed her life, was a hateful thought. But on the other hand, the Empire without the Emperor was only a pale shadow of its former self, hardly even worthy of the name any more. It would be pearls before swine to give the Dark Force to them.

Or would it? With a Grand Admiral in charge of the Imperial Fleet again, perhaps there was now a chance for the Empire to regain some of its old glory. And if there was ... 'What are you going to do?' she asked Karrde.

'At the moment, nothing,' Karrde said. 'It's the same problem we faced with Skywalker, after all: the Empire will be swifter to exact vengeance if we go against them, but the New Republic looks more likely to win in the end. Giving Thrawn the *Katana* fleet would only delay the inevitable. The most prudent course right now is to stay neutral.'

'Except that giving Thrawn the Dreadnaughts might get him off our exhaust trail,' Mara pointed out. 'That would be worth the trade right there.'

Karrde smiled faintly. 'Oh, come now, Mara. The Grand Admiral may be a tactical genius, but he's hardly omniscient. He can't possibly have any idea where we are. And he certainly has more important things to do than spend his resources chasing us down.'

'I'm sure he does,' Mara agreed reluctantly. But she couldn't help remembering how, even at the height of his power and with a thousand other concerns, the Emperor had still frequently taken the time to exact vengeance on someone who'd crossed him.

Beside her the comm board buzzed, and Mara reached over to key the channel. 'Yes?'

'Lachton,' a familiar voice came from the speaker. 'Is Karrde around?'

'Right here,' Karrde called, stepping to Mara's side. 'How's the camouflage work going?'

'We're about done,' Lachton said. 'We ran short of flash-netting, though. Do we have any more?'

'There's some at one of the dumps,' Karrde told him. 'I'll send Mara to get it; can you have someone come in to pick it up?'

'Sure, no problem. I'll send Dankin – he hasn't got much to do at the moment anyway.'

'All right. The netting will be ready by the time he gets here.'

Karrde gestured, and Mara keyed off the channel. 'You know where the Number Three dump is?' he asked her.

She nodded. 'Four twelve Wozwashi Street. Three blocks west and two north.'

'Right.' He peered out the window. 'Unfortunately, it's still too early for repulsorlift vehicles to be on the streets. You'll have to walk.'

'That's all right,' Mara assured him. She felt like a little exercise, anyway. 'Two boxes be enough?'

'If you can handle that many,' he told her, looking her

up and down as if making sure her outfit conformed to local Rishi standards of propriety. He needn't have bothered; one of the first rules the Emperor had drummed into her so long ago was to blend in as best she could with her surroundings. 'If not, Lachton can probably make do with one.'

'All right. I'll see you later.'

Their townhouse was part of a row of similar structures abutting one of the hundreds of little market areas that dotted the whole congested valley. For a moment Mara stood in the entry alcove of their building, out of the busy flow of pedestrian traffic, and looked around her. Through the gaps between the nearest buildings she could see the more distant parts of the city-vale, most of it composed of the same cream-white stone so favored by the locals. In places, she could see all the way to the edge, a few small buildings perched precariously partway up the craggy mountains that rose sharply into the sky on all sides. Far up those mountains, she knew, lived loose avian tribes of native Rishii, who no doubt looked down in bemused disbelief at the strange creatures who had chosen the most uncomfortably hot and humid spots of their planet in which to live.

Dropping her gaze from the mountains, Mara gave the immediate area a quick scan. Across the street were more townhouses; between her and them was the usual flow of brightly clad pedestrians hurrying to and from the market area to the east. Reflexively, her eyes flicked across the townhouses, though with each window composed of mirror glass there wasn't a lot there for her to see. Also reflexively, she glanced across each of the narrow pedestrian alleyways between the buildings.

Between two of them, back at the building's rear where he was hardly visible, was the motionless figure of a man wearing a blue scarf and patterned green tunic.

Staring in her direction.

Mara let her gaze drift on as if she hadn't seen him, her heart thudding suddenly in her throat. Stepping out of the alcove, she turned east toward the market and joined the flow of traffic.

She didn't stay with it long, though. As soon as she was out of the mysterious loiterer's line of sight, she began cutting her way across the flow, heading across the street toward the townhouse row. She reached it three buildings down from the loiterer, ducked into the alleyway, and hurried toward the rear. If he was indeed monitoring Karrde's place, there was a good chance she could take him from behind.

She reached the rear of the buildings and circled around . . . only to find that her quarry had vanished.

For a moment she stood there, looking around her for any sign of the man's whereabouts, wondering what to do now. There was none of the insistent tingling that had gotten them away from Myrkr at the last second; but as she'd told Karrde, it wasn't a talent she could turn on and off.

She looked down at the ground where the man had been standing. There were a few faint footprints in the thin coating of dust that had collected at the corner of the townhouse, giving the impression that the man had been there long enough to shuffle his feet a few times. A half dozen steps away, right in the center of another layer of dust, was a clear footprint pointing toward the west behind the row of townhouses.

Mara looked in that direction, feeling her lip twist. A deliberate lead-on, obviously – footprints in dust never came out that clear and unsmudged unless carefully planted. And she was right. A hundred meters directly ahead, strolling casually along the rear of the buildings toward a north–south street, was the man in the blue scarf and patterned tunic. A not-very-subtle invitation to follow him.

OK, friend, she thought as she started off after him. *You want to play? Let's play.*

She had closed the gap between them to perhaps ninety meters when he reached the cross flow of traffic and turned north into it. Another clear invitation, this time to close the gap further lest she lose him.

But Mara had no intention of taking him up on this one. She'd memorized the geography of the city-vale their first day here, and it was pretty obvious that his intention was to lead her up to the more sparsely populated industrial areas to the north, where presumably he could deal with her without the awkward presence of witnesses. If she could get there first, she might be able to turn things around on him. Double-checking the blaster beneath her left sleeve, she cut through an alley between the buildings to her right and headed north.

The valley stretched for nearly a hundred fifty kilometers in a roughly east-west direction, but at this point its north–south dimension was only a few kilometers. Mara kept up her pace, continually revising her course to avoid crowds and other impediments. Gradually, the houses and shops began to give way to light industry; and, finally, she judged she'd come far enough. If her quarry had kept with the leisurely pace of a man who didn't want to lose a tracker, she should now have enough time to prepare a little reception for him.

There was, of course, always the possibility that he'd shifted to one of the other north–south streets somewhere along the way, changed direction east or west, or even doubled back completely and returned to Karrde's townhouse. But as she looked carefully around the corner of a building into the street he'd first turned onto, she discovered that his imagination was as limited as his surveillance technique. Halfway down the block, he was crouched motionless behind a row of storage barrels with his back to her, his blue scarf thrown back out of the way across his patterned green tunic, something that was probably a weapon clutched ready in his hand. Waiting, no doubt, for her to stroll into his trap. *Amateur*, she thought, lip twisting in contempt. Watching him closely, not even bothering with her blaster, she eased around the corner and started silently toward him.

'That's far enough,' a mocking voice said from behind her.

Mara froze. The figure crouched by the barrels ahead of her didn't even twitch . . . and it was only then that she belatedly realized that it was far too still to be simply waiting in ambush. Far too still, for that matter, to even be alive.

Slowly, keeping her arms stretched straight out to her sides, she turned around. The man facing her was of medium height, with a somewhat bulky build and dark, brooding eyes. His undertunic hung open to reveal a light-armor vest beneath it. In his hand, of course, was a blaster. 'Well, well, well,' he sneered. 'What we got here?

'Bout time you showed up – I was startin' to think you'd gotten lost or somethin'.'

'Who are you?' Mara asked.

'Oh, no, Red, I'm the one what's askin' the questions here. Not that I need to, 'course. That fancy stuff on top pret' well tells me aw I need t'know.' He gestured with his blaster at her red-gold hair. 'Shoulda gotten rid o' that – hide it or dyed it, y'know. Dead give'way. Pardon the 'spression.'

Mara took a careful breath, forcing her muscles to unknot. 'What do you want with me?' she asked, keeping her voice calm.

'Same thin' ev'ry man reall' wants,' he grinned slyly. 'A pile o' hard cold cash.'

She shook her head. 'In that case, I'm afraid you've picked the wrong person. I've only got about fifty on me.'

He grinned even wider. 'Cute, Red, but you're wastin' your time. I know who y'are, aw right. You 'n' your pals are gonna make me real rich. C'mon – let's go.'

Mara didn't move. 'Perhaps we can work a deal,' she suggested, feeling a drop of sweat trickle down between her shoulder blades. She knew better than to be fooled by the other's careless speech and manner – whoever and whatever he was, he knew exactly what he was doing.

On the plus side, she still had the blaster hidden beneath her sleeve; and she would give long odds that her assailant wouldn't expect that a weapon that potent might be small enough to conceal there. The fact that he hadn't already searched her seemed to confirm that assessment.

But whatever she was going to do, she had to do it

now, while she was still facing him. Unfortunately, with her hands spread apart there was no way for her to get at her weapon without telegraphing the movement. Somehow, she needed to distract him.

'A deal, huh?' he asked lazily. 'What kind o' deal you got in mind?'

'What kind of deal do you want?' she countered. If there'd been a box anywhere near her feet, she might have been able to scoop it up with her foot and throw it at him. But though there was a fair amount of junk littering the streets in this part of town, nothing suitable was within reach. Her half-boots were firmly fastened around her ankles, impossible to get loose without him noticing. Rapidly, she ran through an inventory of items she was carrying or wearing – nothing.

But the Emperor's intensive training had included direct manipulation of the Force as well as the long-range communication abilities that had been her primary value to his regime. Those skills had vanished at the moment of his death, reappearing only briefly and erratically in the years since then.

But if the sensory tingles and hunches had started again, perhaps the power was back, too . . .

'I'm sure we can double whatever you've been offered,' she said. 'Maybe even throw in something extra to sweeten the pot.'

His grin turned evil. 'That's a real gen'rous offer, Red. Real gen'rous. Lotta men'd jump on that right away, sure 'nough. Me' – he lifted the blaster a little higher – 'I like stayin' with a sure thing.'

'Even if it means settling for half the money?' Two meters behind him, piled carelessly up against a retaining wall, was a small stack of scrap metal parts waiting to be picked up. A short length of shield tubing, in particular, seemed to be rather precariously positioned on one edge of a battered power cell case.

Setting her teeth, clearing her thoughts as best she could, Mara reached her mind out toward the tubing.

'On my pad, half a sure thing's better than twice o' nothin',' the man said. 'Anyway, I don't 'spect you can outbid the Empire.'

Mara swallowed. She'd suspected it from the first; but the confirmation still sent a shiver up her back. 'You might be surprised at our resources,' she said. The length of tubing twitched, rolled a couple of millimeters—

'Naw, don't think so,' the other said easily. 'C'mon, let's go.'

Mara tilted a finger back toward the dead man crouched at the box behind her. 'You mind telling me first what happened here?'

Her assailant shrugged. 'What's t' tell? I needed a decoy; he was wanderin' around the wrong place at the wrong time. End o' story.' His grin suddenly vanished. 'Enough stallin'. Turn around and start walkin' . . . unless you're lookin' t' spite me by makin' me settle for the death fee instead.'

'No,' Mara murmured. She took a deep breath, straining with every bit of strength she possessed, knowing that this was her last best chance—

And behind her captor, the tubing fell with a muffled clank onto the ground.

He was good, all right. The tubing had hardly even finished its fall before he'd dropped to one knee, spinning around and spraying the area behind him with a splattering of quick cover fire as he searched for whoever was sneaking up on him. It took less than a second for him to recognize his mistake, and with another spray of blaster fire he spun back again.

But one second was all Mara needed. His desperate blaster spray was still tracking toward her when she shot him neatly in the head.

For a long moment she just stood there, breathing hard, muscles trembling with reaction. Then, glancing around to make sure no-one was running to see what all the commotion was about, she holstered her weapon and knelt down beside him.

There was, as she'd expected, precious little to find. An ID – probably forged – giving his name as Dengar Roth, a couple of spare power clips for his blaster, a backup vibroblade knife, a data card and data pad, and some working capital in both local and Imperial currency. Stuffing the ID and data card into her tunic, she left the money and weapons where they were and got back to her feet. 'There's your twice of nothing,' she muttered, looking down at the body. 'Enjoy it.'

Her eyes shifted to the piece of shield tubing that had saved her life. She'd been right. The twitches of power, as well as the hunches, were back. Which meant the dreams wouldn't be far behind.

She swore under her breath. If they came, they came, and there was nothing much she could do except endure them. For the moment she had other, more pressing matters to deal with. Taking one final look around, she headed for home.

Karrde and Dankin were waiting when she arrived back at the townhouse, the latter all but pacing the floor in his nervousness. '*There* you are,' he snapped as she slipped in through the back door. 'Where the blazes—?'

'We've got trouble,' Mara cut him off, handing the Dengar Roth ID to Karrde and brushing past them to the still largely disassembled communications room. Pushing aside a box of cables, she found a data pad and plugged in the card.

'What kind of trouble?' Karrde asked, coming up behind her.

'The bounty hunter kind,' Mara said, handing him the data pad. Neatly framed in the center of the display, under a large *20,000*, was Karrde's face. 'We're probably all in there,' she told him. 'Or at least as many as Grand Admiral Thrawn knew about.'

'So I'm worth twenty thousand now,' Karrde murmured, paging quickly through the card. 'I'm flattered.'

'Is that all you're going to say?' Mara demanded.

He looked at her. 'What would you like me to say?' he asked mildly. 'That you were right and I was wrong about the Empire's interest in us?'

'I'm not interested in laying blame,' she told him stiffly. 'What I want to know is what we're going to do about it.'

Karrde looked at the data pad again, a muscle tightening briefly in his jaw. 'We're going to do the only prudent thing,' he said. 'Namely, retreat. Dankin, get on the secure comm and tell Lachton to start pulling the drop apart again. Then call Chin and his team and have them go over and repack the stuff in the equipment dumps. You can stay and help Mara and me here. I want to get off Rishi by midnight if at all possible.'

'Got it,' Dankin said, already keying the encrypt codes into the comm board.

Karrde handed the data pad back to Mara. 'We'd better get busy.'

She stopped him with a hand on his arm. 'And what happens when we run out of backup bases?'

He locked eyes with her. 'We don't give up the Dreadnaughts under duress,' he said, lowering his voice to just above a whisper. 'Not to Thrawn; not to anyone else.'

'We may have to,' she pointed out.

His eyes hardened. 'We may choose to,' he corrected her. 'We will never *have* to. Is that clear?'

Mara grimaced to herself. 'Yes.'

'Good.' Karrde flicked a glance over her shoulder to where Dankin was speaking urgently into the comm. 'We have a lot of work to do. Let's get to it.'

Mara would have bet that they couldn't reassemble their equipment in less than twenty-four hours. To her mild surprise, the crews had everything packed and ready to go barely an hour after local midnight. With suitably generous applications of funds to spaceport officials, they were off Rishi and to lightspeed an hour after that.

And later that night, as the *Wild Karrde* drove through the mottled sky of hyperspace, the dreams started again.

CHAPTER SIX

From a distance it had looked like a standard-issue Bulk Cruiser: old, slow, minimally armed, with very little going for it in a fight except its size. But as with so very much of warfare, appearances in this case turned out to be deceiving; and if Grand Admiral Thrawn hadn't been on the *Chimaera*'s bridge, Pellaeon had to admit that he might have been caught a bit by surprise.

But Thrawn had been on the bridge, and had recognized immediately the unlikelihood that the Rebellion's strategists would have put such an important convoy under the protection of such a weak ship. And so, when the Bulk Cruiser's bays suddenly erupted with three full squadrons of A-wing starfighters, the *Chimaera*'s TIE interceptors were already in space and swarming to the attack.

'Interesting tactic,' Thrawn commented as the gap between the *Chimaera* and the Rebel convoy began to sparkle with laser flashes. 'If not especially innovative. The idea of converting Bulk Cruisers to starfighter carriers was first proposed over twenty years ago.'

'I don't recall it ever being implemented,' Pellaeon said, feeling a twinge of uneasiness as he eyed the tactical displays. A-wings were faster even than those cursed X-wings, and he wasn't at all sure how well his TIE interceptors would handle them.

'Excellent fighters, A-wings,' Thrawn said, as if reading Pellaeon's thoughts. 'Not without their limitations, though. Particularly here – high-speed craft like that are far more suited to hit-and-fade operations than to escort duty. Forcing them to remain near a convoy largely neutralizes their speed advantage.' He cocked a blue-black eyebrow at Pellaeon. 'Perhaps we're seeing the result of Admiral Ackbar's removal as Supreme Commander.'

'Perhaps.' The TIE interceptors did indeed seem to be holding their own against the A-wings; and the *Chimaera* itself was certainly having no trouble with the Bulk Cruiser. Beyond the battlefront, the rest of the convoy was trying to huddle together, as if that would do them any good. 'Ackbar's people are still in charge, though. Obviously.'

'We've been over this territory already, Captain,' Thrawn said, his voice cooling slightly. 'Planting a vacuum-tight collection of evidence against Ackbar would have ruined him far too quickly. The more subtle attack will still neutralize him, but it will also send ripples of uncertainty and confusion through the Rebellion's entire political system. At the very least, it will distract and weaken them just at the moment when we'll be launching the Mount Tantiss campaign. At its best, it could split the entire Alliance apart.' He smiled. 'Ackbar himself is replaceable, Captain. The delicate political balance the Rebellion has created for itself is not.'

'I understand all that, Admiral,' Pellaeon growled. 'My concern is with your assumption that that Bothan on the

Council can be relied upon to push things so close to your theoretical breakup point.'

'Oh, he'll push, all right,' Thrawn said, his smile turning sardonic as he gazed out at the battle blazing on around the enemy convoy. 'I've spent many hours studying Bothan art, Captain, and I understand the species quite well. There's no doubt at all that Councilor Fey'lya will play his part beautifully. As beautifully as if we were pulling his strings directly.'

He tapped a key on his board. 'Starboard batteries: one of the Frigates in the convoy is easing into attack position. Assume it's an armed backup and treat it accordingly. Squadrons A-2 and A-3, move to protect that flank until the Frigate has been neutralized.'

The batteries and TIE wing commander acknowledged, and some of the turbolaser fire began to track on the Frigate. 'And what happens if Fey'lya wins?' Pellaeon persisted. 'Quickly, I mean, before all this political confusion has a chance to set in. By your own analysis of the species, any Bothan who's risen as high as Fey'lya has would have to be highly intelligent.'

'Intelligent, yes, but not necessarily in any way that's dangerous to us,' Thrawn said. 'He'd have to be a survivor, certainly, but that kind of verbal skill doesn't necessarily translate into military competence.' He shrugged. 'Actually, a victory by Fey'lya would merely prolong the whole awkward situation for the enemy. Given the kind of support Fey'lya's been cultivating among the Rebellion military, the politicians would have to go through another polarizing struggle when they realized their mistake and tried to replace him.'

'Yes, sir,' Pellaeon said, suppressing a sigh. It was the

kind of tangled subtlety that he'd never really felt comfortable with. He just hoped the Grand Admiral was right about the potential gains; it would be a shame for Intelligence to have engineered such a brilliantly successful bank job and then not get anything of real value out of it.

'Trust me, Captain,' Thrawn said into his unspoken worries. 'I dare say the wasting of political effort has already begun, in fact. Ackbar's staunchest allies would hardly have left Coruscant at this critical point unless they were desperately searching for evidence to clear him.'

Pellaeon frowned at him. 'Are you saying that Solo and Organa Solo are heading for the Palanhi system?'

'Solo only, I think,' Thrawn corrected thoughtfully. 'Organa Solo and the Wookiee are most likely still trying to find a place to hide from our Noghri. But Solo will be going to Palanhi, firmly convinced by Intelligence's electronic sleight-of-hand that the trail leads through that system. Which is why the *Death's Head* is on its way there right now.'

'I see,' Pellaeon murmured. He'd noticed that order on the daily log and had wondered why Thrawn was pulling one of their best Imperial Star Destroyers off battle duty. 'I hope it will be equal to the task. Solo and Skywalker have both proved hard to trap in the past.'

'I don't believe Skywalker is going to Palanhi,' Thrawn told him, his face settling into a somewhat sour expression. 'Our esteemed Jedi Master apparently called it correctly. Skywalker has decided to pay a visit to Jomark.'

Pellaeon stared at him. 'Are you sure, Admiral? I haven't seen anything from Intelligence to that effect.'

'The information wasn't from Intelligence,' Thrawn said. 'It came from Delta Source.'

'Ah,' Pellaeon said, feeling his own expression go a little sour. The *Chimaera*'s Intelligence section had been nagging him for months now to find out what exactly this Delta Source was that seemed to feed such clear and precise information to the Grand Admiral from the very heart of the Imperial Palace. So far all Thrawn would say was that Delta Source was firmly established and that the information gained through it should be treated as absolutely reliable.

Intelligence hadn't even been able to figure out whether Delta Source was a person, a droid, or some exotic recording system that was somehow able to elude the Rebellion's hourly counterintelligence sweeps of the Palace. It irritated them no end; and Pellaeon had to admit he didn't much like being kept in the dark about it, either. But Thrawn had personally activated Delta Source, and long years of unwritten protocol in such matters gave him the right to keep the contact confidential if he chose. 'I'm sure C'baoth will be pleased to hear it,' he said. 'I presume you'll want to give him the news yourself.'

He thought he'd hidden his irritation with C'baoth reasonably well. Apparently, he'd thought wrong. 'You're still upset about Taanab,' Thrawn said, turning to gaze out at the battle. It wasn't a question.

'Yes, sir, I am,' Pellaeon said stiffly. 'I've been over the records again, and there's only one possible conclusion. C'baoth deliberately went beyond the battle plan Captain Aban had laid out – went beyond it to the point of disobeying a direct order. I don't care who C'baoth is or whether he felt justified or not. What he did constitutes mutiny.'

'It did indeed,' Thrawn agreed calmly. 'Shall I throw him out of the Imperial service altogether, or simply demote him in rank?'

Pellaeon glared at the other. 'I'm serious, Admiral.'

'So am I, Captain,' Thrawn countered, his voice abruptly cold. 'You know full well what's at stake here. We need to utilize every weapon at our disposal if we're to defeat the Rebellion. C'baoth's ability to enhance coordination and battle efficiency between our forces is one of those weapons; and if he can't handle proper military discipline and protocol, then we bend the rules for him.'

'And what happens when we've bent the rules so far that they come around and stab us in the back?' Pellaeon demanded. 'He ignored a direct order at Taanab – maybe next time it'll be two orders. Then three, then four, until finally he's doing what he damn well pleases and to blazes with the Empire. What's to stop him?'

'Initially, the ysalamiri,' Thrawn said, gesturing at the odd-looking tubular frameworks scattered around the bridge, each with an elongated furry creature wrapped around it. Each of them creating a bubble in the Force where none of C'baoth's Jedi tricks would work. 'That's what they're here for, after all.'

'That's all well and good,' Pellaeon said. 'But in the long run—'

'In the long run, I will stop him,' Thrawn cut him off, touching his board. 'Squadron C-3, watch your port-zenith flank. There's a blister on that Frigate that could be a cluster trap.'

The commander acknowledged, the TIE interceptors

veering away in response. A second later, half a heartbeat too late, the blister abruptly exploded, sending a withering hail of concussion grenades outward in all directions. The rearmost of the TIE interceptors was caught by the edge of the fiery flower, shattering in a brilliant secondary explosion. The rest, out of range, escaped the booby trap unharmed.

Thrawn turned his glowing eyes on Pellaeon. 'I understand your concerns, Captain,' he said quietly. 'What you fail to grasp – what you've always failed to grasp – is that a man with C'baoth's mental and emotional instabilities can never be a threat to us. Yes, he has a great deal of power, and at any given moment he could certainly do considerable damage to our people and equipment. But by his very nature he's unable to use that power for any length of time. Concentration, focus, long-term thinking – those are the qualities that separate a warrior from a mere flailing fighter. And they're qualities C'baoth will never possess.'

Pellaeon nodded heavily. He still wasn't convinced, but there was clearly no use in arguing the point further. Not now, anyway. 'Yes, sir.' He hesitated. 'C'baoth will also want to know about Organa Solo.'

Thrawn's eyes glittered; but the annoyance, Pellaeon knew, wasn't directed at him. 'You will tell Master C'baoth that I've decided to allow the Noghri one last chance to find and capture her. When we've finished here, I'll be taking that message to them. Personally.'

Pellaeon glanced back at the entrance to the bridge, where the Noghri bodyguard Rukh stood his usual silent vigil. 'You're calling a convocate of the Noghri commandos?' he asked, suppressing a shiver. He'd been to one such mass meeting once, and facing a whole roomful of those quiet gray-skinned killers was not an experience he was anxious to repeat.

'I think matters have gone beyond simply calling a convocate,' Thrawn said coldly. 'You'll instruct Navigation to prepare a course from the rendezvous point to the Honoghr system. The entire Noghri populace, I think, needs to be reminded of who it is they serve.'

He shifted his glare out the viewport at the battle and tapped his board. 'TIE command: recall all fighters to the ship,' he ordered. 'Navigation: begin calculations for a return to the rendezvous point.'

Pellaeon frowned out the viewport. The modified Bulk Cruiser and backup Frigate were pretty much dead where they lay, but the convoy itself was largely undamaged. 'We're letting them go?'

'There's no need to destroy them,' Thrawn said. 'Stripping them of their defense is an adequate object lesson for the moment.'

He tapped a key, and a tactical holo of this section of the galaxy appeared between their two stations. Blue lines marked the Rebellion's main trade routes; those sheathed in red marked ones the Imperial forces had hit in the past month. 'There's more to these attacks than simple harassment, Captain. Once this group has told their story, all future convoys from Sarka will demand upgraded protection. Enough such attacks, and the Rebellion will face the choice of either tying up large numbers of its ships with escort duty or effectively abandoning cargo shipment through these border sectors. Either way, it will put them at a serious disadvantage when we launch the Mount Tantiss campaign.' He smiled grimly. 'Economics and psychology, Captain. For now, the more civilian survivors there are to spread the tale of Imperial power, the better. There'll be time enough for destruction later.' He glanced at his board, looked back out the viewport. 'Speaking of Imperial power, any news on our ship hunt?'

'We've had five more capital ships turned in to various Imperial bases in the past ten hours,' Pellaeon told him. 'Nothing larger than an old Star Galleon, but it's a start.'

'We're going to need more than just a start, Captain,' Thrawn said, craning his neck slightly to watch the returning TIE interceptors. 'Any word on Talon Karrde?'

'Nothing since that tip from Rishi,' Pellaeon told him, tapping the proper log for an update. 'The bounty hunter who sent it was killed shortly afterward.'

'Keep up the pressure,' Thrawn ordered. 'Karrde knows a great deal about what happens in this galaxy. If there are any capital ships lying unused out there, he'll know where they are.'

Personally, Pellaeon thought it pretty unlikely that a mere smuggler, even one with Karrde's connections, would have better information sources than the vast Imperial Intelligence network. But he'd also dismissed the possibility that Karrde might be hiding Luke Skywalker out at that base on Myrkr. Karrde was turning out to be full of surprises. 'There are a lot of people out there hunting for him,' he told the Grand Admiral. 'Sooner or later, one of them will find him.'

'Good.' Thrawn glanced around the bridge. 'In the meantime, all units will continue their assigned harassment of the Rebellion.' His glowing red eyes bored into Pellaeon's face. 'And they will continue, too, to maintain a watch for the *Millennium Falcon* and the *Lady Luck*. After the Noghri have been properly primed for their task, I want their prey to be ready for them.'

C'baoth awakened suddenly, his black-edged dreams giving way to the sudden realization that someone was approaching.

For a moment he lay there in the darkness, his long white beard scratching gently against his chest as he breathed, his mind reaching out through the Force to track along the road from the High Castle to the cluster of villages at the base of the rim mountains. It was hard to concentrate – so very hard – but with a perverse grimness he ignored the fatigue-driven pain and kept at it. There ... no ... *there*. A lone man riding a Cracian Thumper, laboring over one of the steeper sections of the roadway. Most likely a messenger, come to bring him some news from the villagers below. Something trifling, no doubt, but something that they felt their new Master should know.

Master. The word echoed through C'baoth's mind, sparking a windblown tangle of thoughts and feelings. The Imperials who pleaded for him to help them fight their battles – they called him Master, too. So had the people of Wayland, whose lives he had been content to rule before Grand Admiral Thrawn and his promise of Jedi followers had lured him away.

The people of Wayland had meant it. The people on Jomark weren't quite sure yet whether they did or not. The Imperials didn't mean it at all.

C'baoth felt his lip twist in disgust. No, they most certainly did not. They made him fight their battles for them – drove him by their disbelief to do things he hadn't attempted for years and years. And then, when he'd succeeded in doing the impossible, they still held tightly to their private contempt for him, hiding it behind those ysalamiri creatures and the strange empty spaces they somehow created in the Force.

But he knew. He'd seen the sideways looks among the officers, and the brief but muttered discussions between them. He'd felt the edginess of the crew, submitting by Imperial order to his influences on their combat skills but clearly disliking the very thought of it. And he'd watched Captain Aban sit there in his command chair on the *Bellicose*, shouting and blaspheming at him even while calling him Master, spitting anger and impotent rage as C'baoth calmly inflicted his punishment on the Rebel ship that had dared to strike at his ship.

The messenger below was approaching the High Castle gate now. Reaching out with the Force to call his robe to him, C'baoth got out of bed, feeling a brief rush of vertigo as he stood erect. Yes, it had been difficult, that business of taking command of the *Bellicose*'s turbolaser crews for the few seconds it had required to annihilate that Rebel ship. It had gone beyond any previous stretch of concentration and control, and the mental aches he was feeling now were the payment for that stretch.

He tightened the robe sash around him, thinking back. Yes, it had been hard. And yet, at the same time, it had also been strangely exhilarating. On Wayland, he had personally commanded a whole city-state, one with a larger population than that which nestled beneath the High Castle. But there, he'd long since gone beyond the need to impose his will by force. The humans and Psadans had submitted to his authority early on; even the Myneyr-shi, with their lingering resentment of his rule, had learned to obey his orders without question.

The Imperials, as well as the people of Jomark, were going to have to learn that same lesson.

Back when Grand Admiral Thrawn had first goaded C'baoth into this alliance, he'd implied that C'baoth had been too long without a real challenge. Perhaps the Grand Admiral had also secretly thought that this challenge of running the Empire's war would prove too much for a single Jedi Master to handle.

C'baoth smiled tightly in the darkness. If that was what the glowing-eyed Grand Admiral thought, he was going to be in for a surprise. Because when Luke Sky-walker finally got here, C'baoth would face perhaps the most subtle challenge of his life: to bend and twist another Jedi to his will without the other even being aware of what was happening to him.

And when he'd succeeded, there would be two of them . . . and who could tell what might be possible then?

The messenger had dismounted from his Thumper and was standing beside the gate now, his sense that of a man prepared to await the convenience of his Master, no matter how long that wait might be. That was good: exactly the proper attitude. Giving his robe sash one final tug, C'baoth headed through the maze of darkened rooms toward the door to hear what his new subjects wished to tell him.

CHAPTER SEVEN

With a delicacy that always seemed so incongruous in a being his size, Chewbacca maneuvered the *Falcon* into his precisely selected orbital slot above the lush green moon of Endor. Rumbling under his breath, he switched over the power linkages and cut the engines back to standby.

Seated in the copilot seat, Leia took a deep breath, wincing as one of the twins kicked her from inside. 'Doesn't look like Khabarakh's here yet,' she commented, realizing even as she said it how superfluous the comment was. She'd been watching the sensors from the moment they dropped out of lightspeed; and given there were no other ships anywhere in the system, there wasn't much chance that they could have missed him. But with the familiar engine roar now cut back down to a whisper, the silence felt strange and even a little eerie to her.

Chewbacca growled a question. 'We wait, I guess,' Leia shrugged. 'Actually, we're almost a day early – we got here faster than I'd expected.'

Chewbacca turned back to his board, growling his own interpretation of the Noghri's absence. 'Oh, come on,' Leia chided him. 'If he'd decided to make this meeting into a trap, don't you think they'd have had a couple of Star Destroyers and an Interdictor Cruiser waiting to meet us?'

'Your Highness?' Threepio's voice called from down the tunnel. 'I'm sorry to disturb you, but I believe I've located the fault in the Carbanti countermeasures package. Could you ask Chewbacca to step back for a moment?'

Leia raised her eyebrows in mild surprise as she looked at Chewbacca. As was depressingly normal with the *Falcon*, several bits of equipment had gone out early in the flight from Coruscant. Up to his elbows with more important repairs, Chewbacca had assigned the relatively low-priority work on the Carbanti to Threepio. Leia had had no objections, though given the results the last time Threepio had tried to work on the *Falcon*, she hadn't expected very much to come of it. 'We'll make a repair droid out of him yet,' she said to Chewbacca. 'Your influence, no doubt.'

The Wookiee snorted his opinion of that as he got out of the pilot's seat and headed back to see what Threepio had found. The cockpit door slid open, closed again behind him.

Leaving the cockpit that much quieter.

'You see that planet down there, my dears?' Leia murmured, rubbing her belly gently. 'That's Endor. Where the Rebel Alliance finally triumphed over the Empire, and the New Republic began.'

Or at least, she amended silently to herself, that was what the histories someday would say. That the death of the Empire occurred at Endor, with all the rest of it merely a mopping-up action.

A mopping-up action which had lasted five years, so

far. And could wind up lasting another twenty, the way things were going.

She let her eyes drift across the brilliant mottled green world turning slowly beneath them, wondering yet again why she'd chosen this place for her rendezvous with Khabarakh. True, it was a system that practically every being in both the Republic and Imperial sections of the galaxy had heard of and knew how to find. And with the major planes of contention long gone from this sector, it was a quiet enough place for two ships to meet.

But there were memories here, too, some of which Leia would just as soon not bring to mind. Before they'd triumphed, they'd very nearly lost everything.

From down the tunnel, Chewbacca roared a question. 'Hang on, I'll check,' Leia called back. Leaning over the board, she keyed a switch. 'It reads "standby/modulo",' she reported. 'Wait a minute – now it reads "system ready". Do you want me to—?'

And abruptly, without any warning, a black curtain seemed to drop across her vision . . .

Slowly, she became aware that there was a metallic voice calling to her. 'Your Highness,' it said over and over again. 'Your Highness. Can you hear me? Please, Your Highness, can you hear me?'

She opened her eyes, vaguely surprised to discover they were closed, to find Chewbacca leaning over her with an open medpack gripped in one huge hand, an agitated Threepio hovering like a nervous mother bird behind him. 'I'm all right,' she managed. 'What happened?'

'You shouted for help,' Threepio put in before Chewbacca could answer. 'At least, we thought it was for help,' he amended helpfully. 'You were brief and rather incoherent.'

'I don't doubt it,' Leia told him. It was starting to come back now, like moonlight through the edge of a cloud. The menace, the rage; the hatred, the despair. 'You didn't feel it, did you?' she asked Chewbacca.

He growled a negative, watching her closely. 'I felt nothing either,' Threepio put in.

Leia shook her head. 'I don't know what it could have been. One minute I was sitting there, and then the next—'

She broke off, a sudden horrible thought striking her. 'Chewie – where does this orbit take us? Does it ever pass through the position where the Death Star blew up?'

Chewbacca stared at her a moment, rumbling something deep in his throat. Then, shifting the medpack to his other hand, he reached past her to key the computer. The answer came almost immediately.

'Five minutes ago,' Leia murmured, feeling cold. 'That would be just about right, wouldn't it?'

Chewbacca growled an affirmative, then a question. 'I really don't know,' she had to admit. 'It sounds a little like something Luke went through on – during his Jedi training,' she amended, remembering just in time that Luke still wanted Dagobah's significance to be kept a secret. 'But he saw a vision. All I felt was . . . I don't know. It was anger and bitterness; but at the same time, there was something almost sad about it. No – sad isn't the right word.' She shook her head, sudden tears welling inexplicably up in her eyes. 'I don't know. Look, I'm all right. You two can go on back to what you were doing.'

Chewbacca rumbled under his breath again, clearly not convinced. But he said nothing else as he closed the medpack and pushed past Threepio. The cockpit door slid open for him; with the proverbial Wookiee disdain for subtlety, he locked it in that position before disappearing down the tunnel into the main body of the ship.

Leia focused on Threepio. 'You, too,' she told him. 'Go on – you still have work to do back there. I'm all right. Really.'

'Well . . . very well, Your Highness,' the droid said, clearly no happier than Chewbacca was. 'If you're certain.'

'I am. Go on, scat.'

Threepio dithered another moment, then obediently shuffled out of the cockpit.

And the silence resumed. A silence that was thicker, somehow, than it had been before. And much darker.

Leia set her teeth firmly together. 'I will not be intimidated,' she said aloud to the silence. 'Not here; not anywhere.'

The silence didn't reply. After a minute Leia reached over to the board and keyed in a course alteration that would keep them from again passing through the spot where the Emperor had died. Refusing to be intimidated, after all, didn't mean deliberately asking for trouble.

And after that, there was nothing left to do but wait. And wonder if Khabarakh would indeed come.

The topmost bit of the walled city Ilic poked through the clutching trees of the jungle pressing tightly around it, looking to Han for all the world like some sort of dome-topped, silver-skinned droid drowning in a sea of green quicksand. 'Any idea how we land on that thing?' he asked.

'Probably through those vents near the top,' Lando

said, pointing at the *Lady Luck*'s main display. 'They read large enough for anything up to about W-class space barge to get into.'

Han nodded, fingers plucking restlessly at the soft armrest of his copilot seat. There weren't a lot of things in the galaxy that could make him nervous, but having to sit there while someone else made a tricky landing was one of them. 'This is even a crazier place to live than that Nomad City thing of yours,' he growled.

'No argument from me,' Lando agreed, adjusting their altitude a bit. Several seconds later than Han would have done it. 'At least on Nkllon we don't have to worry about getting eaten by some exotic plant. But that's economics for you. At last count there were eight cities in this part of New Cov, and two more being built.'

Han grimaced. And all because of those same exotic plants. Or to be specific, the exotic biomolecules that could be harvested from them. The Covies seemed to think the profit was worth having to live in armored cities all the time. No-one knew what the plants thought about it. 'They're still crazy,' he said. 'Watch out – they may have magnetic airlocks on those entrance ducts.'

Lando gave him a patient look. 'Will you relax? I *have* flown ships before, you know.'

'Yeah,' Han muttered. Setting his teeth together, he settled in to suffer through the landing.

It wasn't as bad as he'd expected. Lando got his clearance from Control and guided the *Lady Luck* with reasonable skill into the flaring maw of one of the entrance ducts, following the curved pipe down and inward to a brightly lit landing area just beneath the transparisteel dome that topped the city walls. Inbound customs were a mere formality, though given the planet's dependence on exports, the outbound scrutiny would probably be a lot tighter. They were officially welcomed to Ilic by a professional greeter with a professional smile, given a data card with maps of the city and surrounding territory, and then turned loose.

'That wasn't so hard,' Lando commented as they rode a sliding spiral ramp down through the spacious open center. At each level walkways led outward from the ramp to the market, administrative, and living areas of the city. 'Where are we supposed to be meeting Luke?'

'Three more levels down, in one of the entertainment districts,' Han told him. 'The Imperial library didn't have much detail on this place, but it did mention a little tap-cafe called the Mishra attached to some half-size version they've got of the old Grandis Mon theater on Coruscant. I got the impression it was kind of a watering hole for local big shots.'

'Sounds like a good place to meet,' Lando agreed. He threw Han a sideways look. 'So. You ready to show me the hook yet?'

Han frowned. 'Hook?'

'Come on, you old pirate,' Lando snorted. 'You pick me up at Sluis Van, ask for a lift out to New Cov, send Luke on ahead for this cloak-and-blade rendezvous – and you expect me to believe you're just going to wave good-bye now and let me go back to Nkllon?'

Han gave his friend his best wounded look. 'Come on, Lando—'

'The hook, Han. Let me see the hook.'

Han sighed theatrically. 'There isn't any hook, Lando,' he said. 'You can leave for Nkllon any time you want to.

'Course,' he added casually, 'if you hung around a little and gave us a hand, you might be able to work a deal here to unload any spare metals you had lying around. Like, oh, a stockpile of hfredium or something.'

Carefully keeping his eyes forward, he could still feel the heat of Lando's glare. 'Luke told you about that, didn't he?' Lando demanded.

Han shrugged. 'He might have mentioned it,' he conceded.

Lando hissed between clenched teeth. 'I'm going to strangle him,' he announced. 'Jedi or not, I'm going to strangle him.'

'Oh, come on, Lando,' Han soothed. 'You hang around a couple of days, you listen to people's jabberings, you maybe dig us out a lead or two about what Fey'lya's got going here, and that's it. You go home and back to your mining operation, and we never bother you again.'

'I've heard *that* before,' Lando countered. But Han could hear the resignation in his voice. 'What makes you think Fey'lya's got contacts on New Cov?'

'Because during the war, this was the only place his Bothans ever seemed to care about defending—'

He broke off, grabbing Lando's arm and turning both of them hard to the right toward the central column of the spiral walkway. 'What—' Lando managed.

'Quiet!' Han hissed, trying to simultaneously hide his face and still watch the figure he'd spotted leaving the ramp one level down. 'That Bothan down there to the left – see him?'

Lando turned slightly, peering in the indicated direction out of the corner of his eye. 'What about him?'

'It's Tav Breil'lya. One of Fey'lya's top aides.'

'You're kidding,' Lando said, frowning down at the alien. 'How can you tell?'

'That neckpiece he wears – some kind of family crest or something. I've seen it dozens of times at Council meetings.' Han chewed at his lip, trying to think. If that really was Breil'lya over there, finding out what he was up to could save them a lot of time. But Luke was probably sitting in the tapcafe downstairs right now waiting for them . . . 'I'm going to follow him,' he told Lando, shoving his data pad and the city map into the other's hands. 'You head down to the Mishra, grab Luke, and catch up with me.'

'But—'

'If you're not with me in an hour I'll try calling on the comlink,' Han cut him off, stepping toward the outside of the ramp. They were nearly to the Bothan's level now. 'Don't call me – I might be someplace I wouldn't want a callbeep going off.' He stepped off the ramp onto the walkway.

'Good luck,' Lando called softly after him.

There was a good scattering of aliens among the humans wandering around Ilic, but Breil'lya's cream-colored fur stood out of the crowd enough to make him easy to follow. Which was just as well. If Han could recognize the Bothan, the Bothan could probably recognize him right back, and it would be risky to have to get too close.

Luckily, the alien didn't seem to even consider the possibility that anyone might be following him. He kept up a steady pace, never turning around, as he headed past cross streets and ships and atria toward the outer city wall. Han stayed with him, wishing he hadn't been so quick to give the city map to Lando. It might have been nice to have some idea where he was going.

They passed through one final atrium and reached a section of warehouse-type structures abutting a vast mural that seemed to have been painted directly on the inner city wall. Breil'lya went straight to one of the buildings near the mural and disappeared through the front door.

Han ducked into a convenient doorway about thirty meters down the street from the warehouse. The door Breil'lya had gone through, he could see, carried the faded sign Amethyst Shipping and Storage above it. 'I just hope it's on the map,' he muttered under his breath, pulling his comlink from his belt.

'It is,' a woman's voice came softly from behind him.

Han froze. 'Hello?' he asked tentatively.

'Hello,' she said back. 'Turn around, please. Slowly, of course.'

Han did as ordered, the comlink still in hand. 'If this is a robbery—'

'Don't be silly.' The woman was short and slender, perhaps ten years older than him, with close-cut graying hair and a thin face which under other circumstances would look friendly enough. The blaster pointed in his direction was some unfamiliar knockoff of a BlasTech DL-18 – not nearly as powerful as his own DL-44, but under the circumstances the difference didn't matter a whole lot. 'Put the comlink on the ground,' she continued. 'Your blaster, too, as long as you're down there.'

Silently, Han crouched down, drawing his weapon out with exaggerated caution. Under cover of the motion, with most of her attention hopefully on the blaster, he flicked on the comlink. Laying both on the ground, he straightened and took a step back, just to prove that he knew the proper procedure for prisoners. 'Now what?'

'You seem interested in the little get-together yonder,' she said, stooping to retrieve the blaster and comlink. 'Perhaps you'd like a guided tour.'

'That would be great,' Han told her, raising his hands and hoping that she wouldn't think to look at the comlink before putting it away in one of the pockets in her jumpsuit.

She didn't look at it. She did, however, shut it off. 'I think I'm insulted,' she said mildly. 'That has to be the oldest trick on the list.'

Han shrugged, determined to maintain at least a little dignity here. 'I didn't have time to come up with any new ones.'

'Apology accepted. Come on, let's go. And lower your hands – we don't want any passersby wondering, now, do we?'

'Of course not,' Han said, dropping his hands to his sides.

They were halfway to the Amethyst when, off in the distance, a siren began wailing.

It was, Luke thought as he looked around the Mishra, almost like an inverted replaying of his first visit to the Mos Eisley cantina on Tatooine all those years ago.

True, the Mishra was light-years more sophisticated than that dilapidated place had been, with a correspondingly more upscale clientele. But the bar and tables were crowded with the same wide assortment of humans and aliens, the smells and sounds were equally variegated, and the band off in the corner was playing similar

music – a style, obviously, that had been carefully tai-
lored to appeal to a multitude of different races.

There was one other difference, too. Crowded though
the place might be, the patrons were leaving Luke a
respectful amount of room at the bar.

He took a sip of his drink – a local variant of the hot
chocolate Lando had introduced him to, this one with a
touch of mint – and glanced over at the entrance. Han
and Lando should have been only a couple of hours
behind him, which meant they could be walking in at any
minute. He hoped so, anyway. He'd understood Han's
reasons for wanting the two ships to come into Ilic separ-
ately, but with all the threats that seemed to be hanging
over the New Republic, they couldn't really afford to
waste time. He took another sip—

And from behind him came an inhuman bellow.

He spun around, hand automatically yanking his lightsaber from his belt, as the sound of a chair crashing over
backwards added an exclamation point to the bellow.
Five meters away from him, in the middle of a circle of
frozen patrons, a Barabel and a Rodian stood facing each
other over a table, both with blasters drawn.

'No blasters! No blasters!' an SE4 servant droid called,
waving his arms for emphasis as he scuttled toward the
confrontation. In the flick of an eye, the Barabel shifted
aim and blew the droid apart, bringing his blaster back
to bear on the Rodian before the other could react.

'Hey!' the bartender said indignantly. 'That's going to
cost you—'

'Shut up,' the Barabel cut him off with a snarl. 'Rodian
will pay you. After he pay me.'

The Rodian drew himself up to his full height – which

still left him a good half meter shorter than his opponent – and spat something in a language Luke didn't understand. 'You lie,' the Barabel spat back. 'You cheat. I know.'

The Rodian said something else. 'You no like?' the Barabel countered, his voice haughty. 'You do anyway. I call on Jedi for judgement.'

Every eye in the tapcafe had been riveted to the confrontation. Now, in almost perfect unison, the gazes turned to Luke. 'What?' he asked cautiously.

'He wants you to settle the dispute,' the bartender said, relief evident in his voice.

A relief that Luke himself was far from feeling. 'Me?'

The bartender gave him a strange look. 'You're the Jedi Knight Luke Skywalker, aren't you?' he asked, gesturing at the lightsaber in Luke's hand.

'Yes,' Luke admitted.

'Well, then,' the bartender concluded, waving a hand toward the disputants.

Except that, Jedi or no Jedi, Luke didn't have a drop of legal authority here. He opened his mouth to tell the bartender that—

And then took another look into the other's eyes.

Slowly, he turned back around, the excuses sticking unsaid in his throat. It wasn't just the bartender, he saw. Everyone in the tapcafe, it seemed, was looking at him with pretty much the same expression. An expression of expectation and trust.

Trust in the judgement of a Jedi.

Taking a quiet breath, sternly ordering his pounding heart to calm down, he started through the crowd toward the confrontation. Ben Kenobi had introduced him to the Force; Yoda had taught him how to use the Force for self-control and self-defense. Neither had ever taught him anything about mediating arguments.

'All right,' he said as he reached the table. 'The first thing you're going to do – both of you – is put away your weapons.'

'Who first?' the Barabel demanded. 'Rodians collect bounty – he shoot if I disarm.'

This was certainly getting off to a great start. Suppressing a sigh, Luke ignited his lightsaber, holding it out so that the brilliant green blade was directly between the opposing blasters. 'No-one is going to shoot anyone,' he said flatly. 'Put them away.'

Silently, the Barabel complied. The Rodian hesitated a second longer, then followed suit. 'Now tell me the problem,' Luke said, shutting down the lightsaber but keeping it ready in his hand.

'He hire me for tracking job,' the Barabel said, jabbing a keratin-plated finger at the Rodian. 'I do what he say. But he no pay me.'

The Rodian said something indignant sounding. 'Just a minute – we'll get to you,' Luke told him, wondering how he was going to handle that part of the cross-examination. 'What sort of job was it?'

'He ask me hunt animal nest for him,' the Barabel said. 'Animals bothering little ships – eating at sides. I do what he says. He burn animal nest, get money. But then he pay me in no-good money.' He gestured down at a now scattered pile of gold-colored metal chips.

Luke picked one up. It was small and triangular, with an intricate pattern of lines in the center, and inscribed with a small '100' in each corner. 'Anyone ever seen this currency before?' he called, holding it up.

'It's new Imperial scrip,' someone dressed in an expensive business coat said with thinly veiled contempt. 'You can only spend it on Imperial-held worlds and stations.'

Luke grimaced. Another reminder, if he'd needed one, that the war for control of the galaxy was far from over. 'Did you tell him beforehand that you'd be paying in this?' he asked the Rodian.

The other said something in his own language. Luke glanced around the circle, wondering if asking for a translator would diminish his perceived status here. 'He says that that was how he was paid,' a familiar voice said; and Luke turned to see Lando ease his way to the front of the crowd. 'Says he argued about it, but that he didn't have any choice in the matter.'

'That *is* how the Empire's been doing business lately,' someone in the crowd offered. 'At least around here.'

The Barabel spun toward the other. 'I no want your judgement,' he snarled. 'Only Jedi give judgement.'

'All right, calm down,' Luke told him, fingering the chit and wondering what he was going to do. If this really was the way the Rodian had been paid . . . 'Is there any way to convert these into something else?' he asked the Rodian.

The other answered. 'He says no,' Lando translated. 'You can use them for goods and services on Imperial worlds, but since no-one in the New Republic will take them, there's no official rate of exchange.'

'Right,' Luke said dryly. He might not have Lando's experience in under-the-plate operations, but he hadn't been born yesterday, either. 'So what's the *un*official exchange rate?'

'No idea, actually,' Lando said, looking around the crowd. 'Must be someone here who works both sides of the street, though.' He raised his voice. 'Anyone here do business with the Empire?'

If they did, they were keeping quiet about it. 'Shy, aren't you?' Luke murmured.

'About admitting Imperial dealings to a Jedi?' Lando countered. 'I'd be shy, too.'

Luke nodded, feeling a sinking sense in the pit of his stomach as he studied the Rodian's tapirlike snout and passive, multifaceted eyes. He'd hoped that he could simply smooth out the problem and thereby avoid the need to pass any kind of real judgement. Now, he had no choice but to rule on whether the Rodian was in fact deliberately trying to cheat his partner.

Closing his eyes down to slits, he composed his mind and stretched out his senses. It was a long shot, he knew; but most species showed subtle physiological changes when under stress. If the Rodian was lying about the payment – and if he thought that Luke's Jedi skills could catch him at it – he might react enough to incriminate himself.

But even as Luke ran through the sensory enhancement techniques, something else caught his attention. It was an odor: a faint whiff of carababba tabac and armudu. The same combination Lando had called his attention to on the Sluis Van space station . . .

Luke opened his eyes and looked around the crowd. 'Niles Ferrier,' he called. 'Will you step forward, please.'

There was a long pause, punctuated only by Lando's sudden hissing intake of air at Ferrier's name. Then, with a rustle of movement from one side of the circle, a famil- iar bulky figure pushed his way to the front. 'What do you want?' he demanded, his hand resting on the butt of his holstered blaster.

'I need to know the unofficial exchange rate between Imperial and New Republic currencies,' Luke said. 'I thought perhaps you could tell me what it is.'

Ferrier studied him with ill-concealed scorn. 'This is your problem, Jedi. Leave me out of it.'

There was a low rumble of displeasure from the crowd. Luke didn't reply, but held Ferrier in a level gaze; and after a moment, the other's lip twisted. 'The last time I did business on the other side, we settled on a five to four Empire/Republic conversion,' he growled.

'Thank you,' Luke said. 'That seems straightforward enough, then,' he continued, turning to the Rodian. 'Pay your associate with New Republic currency at a five/four exchange rate and take the Empire scrip back for the next time you work in their territory.'

The Rodian spat something. 'That is lie!' the Barabel snarled back.

'He says he doesn't have enough in New Republic currency,' Lando translated. 'Knowing Rodians, I'd tend to agree with the Barabel.'

'Perhaps.' Luke stared hard into the Rodian's faceted eyes. 'Perhaps not. But there might be another way.' He looked back at Ferrier, raised his eyebrows questioningly.

The other was sharp, all right. 'Don't even think of it, Jedi,' he warned.

'Why not?' Luke asked. 'You work both sides of the border. You're more likely to be able to spend Imperial scrip than the Barabel could.'

'Suppose I don't want to?' Ferrier countered. 'Suppose I don't plan to go back any time soon. Or maybe I don't want to get caught with that much Imperial scrip on me. Fix it yourself, Jedi – I don't owe you any favors.'

The Barabel whirled on him. 'You talk respect,' he snarled. 'He is Jedi. You talk respect.'

A low rumble of agreement rippled through the crowd. 'Better listen to him,' Lando advised. 'I don't think you'd want to get in a fight here, especially not with a Barabel. They've always had a soft spot for Jedi.'

'Yeah – right behind their snouts,' Ferrier retorted. But his eyes were flicking around the crowd now, and Luke caught the subtle shift in his sense as he began to realize just how much in the minority his opinion of Luke was.

Or perhaps he was realizing that winding up in the middle of an official flap might buy him more attention than he really wanted to have. Luke waited, watching the other's sense flicker with uncertainty, waiting for him to change his mind.

When it happened, it happened quickly. 'All right, but it'll have to be a five/three exchange,' Ferrier insisted. 'The five/four was a fluke – no telling if I'll ever get that again.'

'It is cheat,' the Barabel declared. 'I deserve more from Rodian.'

'Yes, you do,' Luke agreed. 'But under the circumstances, this is probably the best you're going to get.' He looked at the Rodian. 'If it helps any,' he added to the Barabel, 'remember that you can pass a warning to the rest of your people about dealing with this particular Rodian. Not being able to hire expert Barabel hunters will hurt him far more in the long run than he might cost you now.'

The Barabel made a grating noise that was probably the equivalent of a laugh. 'Jedi speak truth,' he said. 'Punishment is good.'

Luke braced himself. This part the Barabel wasn't going to be nearly so happy about. 'You will, however, have to pay for the repair of the droid you shot. Whatever the Rodian said or did, he is not responsible for that.'

The Barabel stared at Luke, his needle teeth making small, tight biting motions. Luke returned the cold gaze, senses alert to the Force for any intimation of attack. 'Jedi again speak truth,' the alien said at last. Reluctantly, but firmly. 'I accept judgement.'

Luke let out a quiet sigh of relief. 'Then the matter is closed,' he said. He looked at Ferrier, then raised his lightsaber to his forehead in salute to the two aliens and turned away.

'Nicely done,' Lando murmured in his ear as the crowd began to break up.

'Thanks,' Luke murmured, his mouth dry. It had worked, all right . . . but it had been more luck than skill, and he knew it. If Ferrier hadn't been there – or if the ship thief hadn't decided to back down – Luke had no idea how he would have solved the dispute. Leia and her diplomatic training would have done better than he had; even Han and his long experience at hard bargaining would have done as well.

It was an aspect of Jedi responsibility that he'd never considered before. But it was one he'd better start thinking about, and fast.

'Han's following one of Fey'lya's Bothan pals up on Level Four,' Lando was saying as they moved through the crowd toward the exit. 'Spotted him from the west-central ramp and sent me to—'

He stopped short. From outside the Mishra the sound of wailing sirens had started. 'I wonder what that is,' he said, a touch of uneasiness in his voice.

'It's an alarm,' one of the tapcafe patrons said, his

forehead wrinkled in concentration as he listened. The pitch of the siren changed; changed again . . . 'It's a raid.'

'A raid?' Luke frowned. He hadn't heard of any pirate activity in this sector. 'Who's raiding you?'

'Who else?' the man retorted. 'The Empire.'

Luke looked at Lando. 'Uh-oh,' he said quietly.

'Yeah,' Lando agreed. 'Come on.'

They left the Mishra and headed out into the wide avenue. Oddly enough, there were no signs of the panic Luke would have expected to find. On the contrary, the citizens of Ilic seemed to be continuing about their daily business as if nothing untoward was happening. 'Maybe they don't realize what's going on,' he suggested doubtfully as they headed for one of the spiral ramps.

'Or else they've got a quiet agreement with the Empire,' Lando countered sourly. 'Maybe the leadership finds it politically handy to align themselves with the New Republic, but they also want to keep in the Empire's good graces. Since they can't pay anything as overt as tribute, they instead let the Imperials come in every so often and raid their stocks of refined biomolecules. I've seen that sort of thing done before.'

Luke looked around at the unconcerned crowds. 'Only this time it might backfire on them.'

'Like if the Imperials spot the *Lady Luck* and your X-wing on the landing records.'

'Right. Where did you say Han was?'

'Last I saw, he was on Level Four heading west,' Lando said, digging out his comlink. 'He told me not to call him, but I think this qualifies as an unforeseen circumstance.'

'Wait a minute,' Luke stopped him. 'If he's anywhere

near this aide of Fey'lya's – and if Fey'lya is working some kind of deal with the Empire . . . ?'

'You're right.' Lando swore under his breath as he put the comlink away. 'So what do we do?'

They'd reached the ramp now and stepped onto the section spiraling upward. 'I'll go find Han,' Luke said. 'You get up to the landing area and see what's happening. If the Imperials haven't actually landed yet, you might be able to get into the air control computer and erase us from the list. Artoo can help if you can get him out of my X-wing and over to a terminal without being caught.'

'I'll give it a try.'

'OK.' A stray memory flicked through Luke's mind – 'I don't suppose the *Lady Luck*'s equipped with one of those full-rig slave circuits you talked about back on Nkllon, is it?'

Lando shook his head. 'It's rigged, but only with a simple homing setup. Nothing much more than straight-line motion and a little maneuvering. It'd never be able to get to me through the middle of an enclosed city like this.'

And even if it could, Luke had to admit, it wouldn't do them much good. Short of blasting a huge hole through the outer wall, the only way out of Ilic for anything the size of a spaceship was through the exit ducts above the landing area. 'It was just a thought,' he said.

'Here's where Han got off,' Lando said, pointing. 'He headed that way.'

'Right.' Luke stepped off the ramp. 'See you soon. Be careful.'

'You, too.'

CHAPTER EIGHT

✦

The graying woman took Han to a small office-type room in the Amethyst building, turned him over to a couple of other guard types there, and disappeared with his blaster, comlink, and ID in hand. Han tried once or twice to strike up a conversation with the guards, got no response from either of them, and had just about resigned himself to sitting quietly, listening to the sirens outside, when the woman returned, accompanied by another, taller woman with the unmistakable air of authority about her.

'Good day to you,' the tall woman said, nodding at Han. 'Captain Han Solo, I believe?'

With his ID in her hand, there didn't seem much point in denying it. 'That's right,' he said.

'We're honored by your visit,' she said, her tone putting a slightly sardonic edge to the polite words. 'Though a bit surprised by it.'

'I don't know why – the visit was your idea,' Han countered. 'You always pick people up off the street like this?'

'Just special ones.' The tall woman's eyebrows lifted slightly. 'You want to tell me who you are and who sent you?'

Han frowned. 'What do you mean, who am I? You've got my ID right there.'

'Yes, I do,' the woman nodded, turning the card over in her hand. 'But there's some difference of opinion as to whether or not it's genuine.' She looked out the door and beckoned—

And Tav Breil'lya stepped past her into the room. 'I was right,' the Bothan said, his cream-colored fur rippling in an unfamiliar pattern. 'As I told you when I first saw his ID. He is an impostor. Almost certainly an Imperial spy.'

'What?' Han stared at him, the whole situation tilting slightly off vertical. He looked at the alien's neckpiece – it was Tav Breil'lya, all right. 'What did you call me?'

'You're an Imperial spy,' Breil'lya repeated, his fur rippling again. 'Come to destroy our friendship, or even to kill us all. But you'll never live to report back to your masters.' He turned to the tall woman. 'You must destroy him at once, Sena,' he urged. 'Before he has the chance to summon your enemies here.'

'Let's not do anything rash, Council-Aide Breil'lya,' Sena soothed. 'Irenez has a good picket screen in position.' She looked at Han. 'Would you care to respond to the Council-Aide's accusations?'

'We have no interest in the ravings of an Imperial spy,' Breil'lya insisted before Han could speak.

'On the contrary, Council-Aide,' Sena countered. 'Around here, we have an interest in a great many things.' She turned back to Han, lifted his ID. 'Do you have any proof other than this that you're who you claim to be?'

'It doesn't matter who he is,' Breil'lya jumped in again, his voice starting to sound a little strained. 'He's seen you, and he must certainly know that we have some kind of arrangement. Whether he's from the Empire or the

New Republic is irrelevant – both are your enemies, and both would use such information against you.'

Sena's eyebrows lifted again. 'So now his identity doesn't matter,' she said coolly. 'Does that mean you're no longer certain he's an impostor?'

Breil'lya's fur rippled again. Clearly, he wasn't as quick on his verbal feet as his boss. 'He's a very close likeness,' the other muttered. 'Though a proper dissection would quickly establish for certain who he is.'

Sena smiled slightly. But it was a smile of understanding, not of humor . . . and suddenly Han realized that the confrontation had been as much a test of Breil'lya as it had been of him. And if Sena's expression was anything to go by, the Bothan had just flunked it. 'I'll keep that recommendation in mind,' she told him dryly.

There was a soft beep, and the gray-haired woman pulled out a comlink and spoke quietly into it. She listened, spoke again, and looked up at Sena. 'Picket line reports another man approaching,' she said. 'Medium build, dark blond hair, dressed in black' – she threw a glance at Breil'lya – 'and carrying what appears to be a lightsaber.'

Sena looked at Breil'lya, too. 'I believe that ends the discussion,' she said. 'Have one of the pickets meet him, Irenez, and ask him if he'll join us. Make it clear that's a *request*, not an order. Then return Captain Solo's weapon and equipment to him.' She turned to Han, nodded gravely to him as she returned his ID. 'My apologies, Captain. You understand we have to be cautious. Particularly given the coincidence of this.' She gestured toward the outside wall.

Han frowned, wondering what she meant. Then he got

it: she was indicating the sirens still wailing outside. 'No problem,' he assured her. 'What are the sirens for, anyway?'

'It's an Imperial raid,' Irenez said, handing him his blaster and comlink.

Han froze. 'A raid?'

'It's no big deal,' Sena assured him. 'They come by every few months and take a percentage of the refined biomolecules that have been packaged for export. It's a covert form of taxation the city governments have worked out with them. Don't worry, they never come any farther in than the landing level.'

'Yeah, well, they may change the routine a little this time,' Han growled, flicking on his comlink. He half expected someone to try to stop him, but no-one even twitched. 'Luke?'

'I'm here, Han,' the younger man's voice came back. 'My escort tells me I'm being brought to where you are. You all right?'

'Just a little misunderstanding. Better get in here fast – we got company.'

'Right.'

Han shut off the comlink. Sena and Irenez, he saw, had meanwhile been having a quiet conversation of their own. 'If you're as touchy about Imperials as Breil'lya implied, you might want to find a hole to disappear into,' he advised.

'Our escape route's ready,' Sena assured him as Irenez left the room. 'The question is what to do with you and your friend.'

'You can't just turn them loose,' Breil'lya insisted, trying one last time. 'You know full well that if the New Republic learns about you—'

'The Commander is being notified,' Sena cut him off. 'He'll decide.'

'But—'

'That's all, Council-Aide,' she cut him off again, her voice suddenly hard. 'Join the others at the lift shaft. You'll accompany me on my ship.'

Breil'lya threw one last unreadable look at Han, then silently left the room.

'Who's this Commander of yours?' Han asked.

'I can't tell you that.' Sena studied him a moment. 'Don't worry, though. Despite what Breil'lya said, we're not enemies of the New Republic. At least, not at the moment.'

'Oh,' Han said. 'Great.'

There was the sound of footsteps from the hallway outside. A few seconds later, accompanied by two young men with holstered blasters, Luke stepped into the room.

'Han,' Luke greeted his friend, giving Sena a quick once-over. 'You all right?'

'I'm fine,' Han assured him. 'Like I said, a little misunderstanding. The lady here – Sena—' He paused expectantly.

'Let's just leave it at Sena for now,' she said.

'Ah,' Han said. He'd hoped to get her last name, but clearly she wasn't in the habit of giving it out. 'Anyway, Sena thought I was an Imperial spy. And speaking of Imperials—'

'I know,' Luke nodded. 'Lando's gone up to see if he can clear our ships from the landing record.'

'He won't be able to,' Han shook his head. 'Not in time. And they're bound to pull the landing list.'

Luke nodded agreement. 'Then we'd better get up there.'

'Unless you'd all rather come with us,' Sena offered.

'There's plenty of room on our ship, and it's hidden away where they won't find it.'

'Thanks, but no,' Han said. He wasn't about to go off with these people until he knew a lot more about them. Whose side they were on, for starters. 'Lando won't want to leave his ship.'

'And I need to get my droid back,' Luke added.

Irenez slipped back into the room. 'Everyone's on their way down, and the ship's being prepared,' she told Sena. 'And I got through to the Commander.' She handed the tall woman a data pad.

Sena glanced at it, nodded, and turned back to Han. 'There's a service shaft near here that opens up into the west edge of the landing area,' she told him. 'I doubt the Imperials know about it; it's not on any of the standard city maps. Irenez will guide you up there and give you what help she can.'

'That's really not necessary,' Han told her.

Sena held up the data pad. 'The Commander has instructed me to give you whatever aid you require,' she said firmly. 'I'd appreciate it if you'd allow me to carry out my orders.'

Han looked at Luke, raised his eyebrows. Luke shrugged slightly in return: if there was treachery in the offer, his Jedi senses weren't picking it up. 'Fine, she can tag along,' he said. 'Let's go.'

'Good luck,' Sena said, and disappeared out the door.

Irenez gestured to the door after her. 'This way, gentlemen.'

The service shaft was a combination stairway and lift-car tube set into the outer city wall, its entrance almost invisible against the swirling pattern of that section of the mural. The liftcar itself was nowhere to be seen – probably, Han decided, still ferrying Sena's group to wherever it was they'd stashed their ship. With Irenez in the lead, they started up the stairs.

It was only three levels up to the landing area. But three levels in a city with Ilic's high-ceilinged layout translated into a lot of stairs. The first level ran to fifty-three steps; after that, Han stopped counting. By the time they slipped through another disguised door into the landing area and took cover behind a massive diagnostic analyzer, his legs were beginning to tremble with fatigue. Irenez, in contrast, wasn't even breathing hard.

'Now what?' Luke asked, looking cautiously around the analyzer. He wasn't breathing hard, either.

'Let's find Lando,' Han said, pulling out his comlink and thumbing his call. 'Lando?'

'Right here,' the other's whispered voice came back instantly. 'Where are you?'

'West end of the landing area, about twenty meters from Luke's X-wing. How about you?'

'About ninety degrees away from you toward the south,' Lando answered. 'I'm behind a stack of shipping boxes. There's a stormtrooper standing guard about five meters away, so I'm sort of stuck here.'

'What sort of trouble are we looking at?'

'It looks like a full-fledged task force,' Lando said grimly. 'I saw three drop ships come in, and I think there were one or two on the ground when I got here. If they were fully loaded, that translates to a hundred sixty to two hundred men. Most of them are regular army troops, but there are a few stormtroopers in the crowd, too. There aren't too many of either still up here – most of them headed on down the ramps a few minutes ago.'

'Probably gone to search the city for us,' Luke murmured.

'Yeah.' Han eased up to look over the analyzer. The top of Luke's X-wing was just visible over the nose of a W-23 space barge. 'Looks like Artoo's still in Luke's ship.'

'Yeah, but I saw them doing something over that way,' Lando warned. 'They may have put a restraining bolt on him.'

'We can handle that.' Han scanned as much of the area around them as he could see. 'I think we can make it to the X-wing without being spotted. You told me on the trip here that you had a beckon call for the *Lady Luck*, right?'

'Right, but it's not going to do me any good,' Lando said. 'With all these boxes around, there's no place I can set it down without opening myself to fire.'

'That's OK,' Han told him, feeling a tight smile twist at his lip. Luke might have the Force, and Irenez might be able to climb stairs without getting winded; but he would bet heavily that he could outdo both of them in sheer chicanery. 'You just get it moving toward you when I give the word.'

He switched off the comlink. 'We're going over to the X-wing,' he told Luke and Irenez, adjusting his grip on his blaster. 'You ready?'

He got two acknowledgements, and with a last look around the area headed as quickly as silence permitted across the floor. He reached the space barge lying across their path without incident, paused there to let the others catch up—

'Shh!' Luke hissed.

Han froze, pressing himself against the barge's corroded hull. Not four meters away a stormtrooper standing guard was starting to turn in their direction.

Clenching his teeth, Han raised his blaster. But even as he did so, his peripheral vision caught Luke's hand making some sort of gesture; and suddenly the Imperial spun around in the opposite direction, pointing his blaster rifle toward a patch of empty floor. 'He thinks he heard a noise,' Luke whispered. 'Let's go.'

Han nodded, and sidled around to the other side of the barge. A few seconds later they were crouched beside the X-wing's landing skids. 'Artoo?' Han stage-whispered upward. 'Come on, short stuff, wake up.'

There was a soft and rather indignant beep from the top of the X-wing. Which meant the Imperials' restraining bolt hadn't shut the droid down entirely, just blocked out his control of the X-wing's systems. Good. 'OK,' he called to the droid. 'Get your comm sensor warmed up and get ready to record.'

Another beep. 'Now what?' Irenez asked.

'Now we get cute,' Han told her, pulling out his comlink. 'Lando? You ready?'

'As ready as I'm going to be,' the other came back.

'OK. When I give the signal, turn on your beckon call and get the *Lady Luck* moving. When I tell you again, shut it off. Got that?'

'Got it. I hope you know what you're doing.'

'Trust me.' Han looked at Luke. 'You got your part figured out?'

Luke nodded, holding up his lightsaber. 'I'm ready.'

'OK, Lando. Go.'

For a long moment nothing happened. Then, through

the background noise of the landing area, came the distinctive whine of repulsorlifts being activated. Half standing up, Han was just in time to see the *Lady Luck* rise smoothly up from among the other docked ships.

From somewhere in the same general vicinity came a shout, followed by the multiple flash of blaster fire. Another three weapons opened up almost immediately, all four tracking the *Lady Luck* as it made a somewhat ponderous turn and began floating south toward Lando's hiding place.

'You know it'll never get there,' Irenez muttered in Han's ear. 'As soon as they figure out where it's going, they'll be all over him.'

'That's why it's not going to get to him,' Han countered, watching the *Lady Luck* closely. Another couple of seconds and every stormtrooper and Imperial soldier in the place ought to have his attention solidly fixed on the rogue ship . . . 'Ready, Luke . . . *now.*'

And suddenly Luke was gone, a single leap taking him to the top of the X-wing. Over the commotion Han heard the *snap-hiss* as Luke ignited his lightsaber, could see the green glow reflected from the nearest ships and equipment. The glow and sound shifted subtly as Luke made a short slice—

'Restraining bolt's off,' Luke called down. 'Now?'

'Not yet,' Han told him. The *Lady Luck* was about a quarter of the way to the far wall, blaster bolts still scattering off its armored underside. 'I'll tell him when. You get ready to fly interference.'

'Right.' The X-wing rocked slightly as Luke moved forward and dropped into the cockpit, its own repulsorlifts beginning to whine as Artoo activated them.

A whine that no-one else out in all that confusion had a hope of hearing. The *Lady Luck* was halfway to the wall now ... 'OK, Lando, shut down,' Han ordered. 'Artoo, your turn. Call it back this way.'

With full access again to the X-wing's transmitters, it was a simple task for the droid to duplicate the signal from Lando's beckon call. The *Lady Luck* shuddered to a halt, reoriented itself to the new call, and started across the landing area again toward the X-wing.

It wasn't something the Imperials had expected. For a second the blaster fire faltered as the soldiers chasing the yacht skidded to a halt; and by the time the fire resumed in earnest, the *Lady Luck* was nearly to the X-wing.

'Now?' Luke called.

'Now,' Han called back. 'Put 'er down and clear us a path.'

Artoo twittered, and the *Lady Luck* again halted in midair, this time dropping smoothly to the ground. There was a shout that sounded like triumph from the Imperials ... but if so, it was the shortest triumph on record. The *Lady Luck* touched down—

And without warning, the X-wing leaped into the air. Pulling a tight curve around the *Lady Luck*, Luke swooped back down, wingtip lasers spitting a corridor of destruction across the startled soldiers' line of approach.

Given time, the Imperials would regroup. Han had no intention of giving them that time. 'Come on,' he snapped to Irenez, leaping to his feet and making a mad dash for the *Lady Luck*. He was probably on the ramp before the soldiers even noticed him, and was up and through the hatch before anyone was able to get off a shot. 'Stay here and guard the hatch,' he shouted back as Irenez charged in behind him. 'I'm going to go pick up Lando.'

Luke was still roaring around creating havoc as Han

scrambled into the cockpit and dived into the pilot's seat, throwing a quick look at the instruments as he did so. All the systems seemed to be ready; and anything that wasn't was going to have to do so on the way up. 'Grab onto something!' he shouted back to Irenez and lifted.

The stormtrooper Lando had mentioned as being near his position was nowhere in sight as Han brought the *Lady Luck* swinging over to the pile of shipping boxes. Luke was right with him, the X-wing's lasers making a mess of the landing area floor as he kept the Imperials pinned down. Han dropped the ship to within a half meter of the floor, entrance ramp swiveled toward the boxes. There was a flicker of motion, visible for just a second through the cockpit's side viewport—

'We've got him,' Irenez shouted from the hatch. 'Go!'

Han swiveled the ship around, throwing full power to the repulsorlifts and heading upward into one of the huge exit ducts overhead. There was a slight jolt as he cleared the magnetic seal on the end, and then they were out in clear air, screaming hard for space.

Four TIE fighters were skulking around just above the city, waiting for trouble. But they apparently weren't waiting for it to come this quickly. Luke got three of them on the fly, and Han took out the fourth.

'Nothing like cutting it close to the wire,' Lando panted as he slid into the copilot's seat and got busy with his board. 'What have we got?'

'Looks like a couple more drop ships coming in,' Han told him, frowning. 'What are you doing?'

'Running a multisensor airflow analysis,' Lando said. 'It'll show up any large irregularities on the hull. Like if someone's attached a homing beacon to us.'

Han thought back to that escape from the first Death Star, and their near-disastrous flight to Yavin with just such a gadget snugged aboard. 'I wish I had a system like that for the *Falcon*.'

'It'd never work,' Lando commented dryly. 'Your hull's so irregular already the system would go nuts just trying to map it.' He keyed off the display. 'OK; we're clear.'

'Great.' Han threw a glance out to the left. 'We're clear of those drop ships, too. They don't have a hope of catching us now.'

'Yes, but that might,' Irenez said, pointing at the mid-range scope.

Which showed an Imperial Star Destroyer behind them, already leaving orbit and moving into pursuit. 'Great,' Han growled, kicking in the main drive. Using it this close to the ground wasn't going to do New Cov's plant life any good, but that was the least of his worries at the moment. 'Luke?'

'I see it,' Luke's voice came back through the comm speaker. 'Any ideas besides running for it?'

'I think running for it sounds like a great idea,' Han said. 'Lando?'

'Calculating the jump now,' the other said, busy with the nav computer. 'It ought to be ready by the time we're far enough out.'

'There's another ship coming up from below,' Luke said. 'Right out of the jungle.'

'That's ours,' Irenez said, peering over Han's shoulder. 'You can parallel them by changing course to one twenty-six mark thirty.'

The Star Destroyer was picking up speed, the scope now showing a wedge of TIE fighters sweeping along ahead of it. 'We'd do better to split up,' Han said.

'No – stay with our ship,' Irenez said. 'Sena said we've got help coming.'

Han took another look at the ship climbing for deep space. A small transport, with a fair amount of speed but not much else going for it. Another look at the approaching TIE fighters—

'They're going to be in range before we can make the jump,' Lando murmured, echoing Han's thought.

'Yeah. Luke, you still there?'

'Yes. I think Lando's right.'

'I know. Any way you can pull that Nkllon stunt again? You know – scramble the pilots' minds a little?'

There was noticeable hesitation from the comm. 'I don't think so,' Luke said at last. 'I – don't think it's good for me to do that sort of thing. You understand?'

Han didn't, really, but it probably didn't matter. For a moment he'd forgotten that he wasn't in the *Falcon*, with a pair of quad lasers and shields and heavy armor. The *Lady Luck*, for all Lando's modifications, wasn't anything to take on even confused TIE fighter pilots with. 'All right, skip it,' he told Luke. 'Sena just better be right about this help of hers.'

The words were hardly out of his mouth when a flash of brilliant green light shot past the *Lady Luck*'s cockpit canopy. 'TIE fighters coming in from portside,' Lando snapped.

'They're trying to cut us off,' Luke said. 'I'll get rid of them.'

Without waiting for comment, he dropped his X-wing below the *Lady Luck*'s vector and with a roar of main drive swung off to the left toward the incoming TIE fighters. 'Watch yourself,' Han muttered after him, giving the rear scope another look. The pursuing batch of fighters was still closing fast. 'Your ship got any weapons?' he asked Irenez.

'No, but it's got good armor and plenty of deflector power,' she told him. 'Maybe you should get ahead of them, let them take the brunt of the attack.'

'Yeah, I'll think about it,' Han said, wincing at the woman's ignorance of this kind of fight. TIE pilots didn't much care which ship was first in line when they attacked; and sitting close enough to another ship to hide in its deflector shield was to give up your maneuverability.

Off to portside, the incoming group of TIE fighters scattered out of the way as Luke drove through their formation, wingtip lasers blazing away madly. A second wave of Imperials behind the first closed to intercept as Luke pulled a hard one-eighty and swung back on the tails of the first wave. Han held his breath; but even as he watched, the X-wing managed somehow to thread its way unscathed through the melee and take off at full throttle at an angle from the *Lady Luck*'s vector, the whole squadron hot on his tail.

'Well, so much for that group,' Irenez commented.

'Any maybe for Luke, too,' Lando countered harshly as he jabbed at the comm. 'Luke, you all right?'

'I got a little singed, but everything's still running,' Luke's voice came back. 'I don't think I can get back to you.'

'Don't try,' Han told him. 'As soon as you're clear, jump to lightspeed and get out of here.'

'What about you?'

Luke's last word was partially drowned out by a sudden twitter from the comm. 'That's the signal,' Irenez said. 'Here they come.'

Han frowned, searching the sky outside the front view-port. As far as he could see, there was nothing out there but stars—

And then, in perfect unison, three large ships suddenly dropped out of hyperspace into triangular formation directly ahead of them.

Lando inhaled sharply. 'Those are old Dreadnaught cruisers.'

'That's our help,' Irenez said. 'Straight down the middle of the triangle – they'll cover for us.'

'Right,' Han gritted, shifting the *Lady Luck*'s vector a few degrees, and trying to coax a little more speed out of its engines. The New Republic had a fair number of Dreadnaughts, and at six hundred meters long each they were impressive enough warships. But even three of them working together would be hard pressed to take out an Imperial Star Destroyer.

Apparently, the Dreadnaught's commander agreed. Even as the Star Destroyer behind the *Lady Luck* opened up with its huge turbolaser batteries, the Dreadnaughts began pelting the larger ship with a furious barrage of ion cannon blasts, trying to temporarily knock out enough of its systems for them to get away.

'That answer your question?' Han asked Luke.

'I think so,' Luke said dryly. 'OK, I'm gone. Where do I meet you?'

'You don't,' Han told him. He didn't like that answer much, and he suspected Luke would like it even less. But it couldn't be helped. With a dozen TIE fighters currently between the *Lady Luck* and the X-wing, suggesting a rendezvous point on even what was supposed to be a secure comm channel would be an open invitation for the

Empire to send their own reception committee on ahead. 'Lando and I can handle the mission on our own,' he added. 'If we run into any problems, we'll contact you through Coruscant.'

'All right,' Luke said. Sure enough, he didn't sound happy about it. But he had enough sense to recognize there was no other safe way. 'Take care, you two.'

'See you,' Han said, and cut the transmission.

'So now it's *my* mission, too, huh?' Lando growled from the copilot's seat, his tone a mixture of annoyance and resignation. 'I knew it. I just *knew* it.'

Sena's transport was into the triangular pocket between the Dreadnaughts now, still driving for all it was worth. Han kept the *Lady Luck* with them, staying as close above the transport's tail as he could without getting into its exhaust. 'You got some particular place you'd like us to drop you?' he asked, looking back at Irenez.

She was gazing out the viewport at the underside of the Dreadnaught they were passing beneath. 'Actually, our Commander was rather hoping you'd accompany us back to our base,' she said.

Han threw a look at Lando. There had been something in her tone that implied the request was more than merely a suggestion. 'And just how hard was your Commander hoping this?' Lando asked.

'Very much.' She dropped her gaze from the Dreadnaught. 'Don't misunderstand – it's not an order. But when I spoke to him, the Commander seemed extremely interested in meeting again with Captain Solo.'

Han frowned. '*Again?*'

'Those were his words.'

Han looked at Lando, found the other looking back at

him. 'Some old friend you've never mentioned?' Lando asked.

'I don't recall having any friends who own Dreadnaughts,' Han countered. 'What do you think?'

'I think I'm being nicely maneuvered into a corner here,' Lando said, a little sourly. 'Aside from that, whoever this Commander is, he seems to be in contact with your Bothan pals. If you're trying to find out what Fey'lya's up to, he'd be the one to ask.'

Han thought it over. Lando was right, of course. On the other hand, the whole thing could just as easily be a trap, with this talk about old friends being designed to lure him in.

Still, with Irenez sitting behind him with a blaster riding her hip, there wasn't really a graceful way to get out of it if she and Sena chose to press the point. They might as well be polite about it. 'OK,' he told Irenez. 'What course do we set?'

'You don't,' she said, nodding upward.

Han followed her gaze. One of the three Dreadnaughts they'd passed had now swung around to fly parallel with them. Ahead, Sena's ship was heading up toward one of a pair of brightly lit docking ports. 'Let me guess,' he said to Irenez.

'Just relax and let us do the flying,' she said, with the first hint of humor that he'd yet seen from her.

'Right,' Han sighed.

And with the flashes of the rear guard battle still going on behind them, he eased the *Lady Luck* up toward the docking port. Luke, he reminded himself, had apparently not sensed any treachery from Sena or her people back in the city.

But then, he hadn't sensed any deceit from the Bimms on Bimmisaari, either, just before that first Noghri attack.

This time the kid better be right.

The first Dreadnaught gave a flicker of pseudomotion and vanished into hyperspace, taking the transport and the *Lady Luck* with it. A few seconds later, the other two Dreadnaughts ceased their ion bombardment of the Star Destroyer and, through a hail of turbolaser blasts from still-operating Imperial batteries, made their own escape.

And Luke was alone. Except, of course, for the squadron of TIE fighters still chasing him.

From behind him came an impatient and rather worried-sounding trill. 'OK, Artoo, we're going,' he assured the little droid. Reaching over, he pulled the hyperdrive lever; and the stars became starlines, and turned to mottled sky, and he and Artoo were safe.

Luke took a deep breath, let it out in a sigh. So that was it. Han and Lando were gone, to wherever Sena and her mysterious Commander had taken them, and there really wasn't any way for him to track them down. Until they surfaced again and got in touch with him, he was out of the mission.

But perhaps that was for the best.

There was another warble from behind, a questioning one this time. 'No, we're not going back to Coruscant, Artoo,' he told the droid, an echo of *déjà vu* tugging at him. 'We're going to a little place called Jomark. To see a Jedi Master.'

CHAPTER NINE

The little fast-attack patrol ship had dropped out of hyperspace and closed to within a hundred kilometers of the *Falcon* before the ship's sensors even noticed its presence. By the time Leia got to the cockpit, the pilot had already made contact.

'Is that you, Khabarakh?' she called, slipping into the copilot's seat beside Chewbacca.

'Yes, Lady Vader,' the Noghri's gravelly, catlike voice mewed. 'I have come alone, as I promised. Are you also alone?'

'My companion Chewbacca is with me as pilot,' she said. 'As is a protocol droid. I would like to bring the droid along to help with translation, if I may. Chewbacca, as we agreed, will stay here.'

The Wookiee turned to her with a growl. 'No,' she said firmly, remembering just in time to mute the transmitter. 'I'm sorry, but that was the promise I made to Khabarakh. You'll stay here on the *Falcon*, and that's an order.'

Chewbacca growled again, more insistently this time . . . and with a sudden prickly sensation on the back of her neck, Leia became acutely aware of something she hadn't really thought about for years. Namely, that the

Wookiee was quite capable of ignoring pretty much any order he chose to.

'I have to go alone, Chewie,' she said in a low voice. Force of will wasn't going to work here; she was going to have to go for logic and reason. 'Don't you understand? That was the arrangement.'

Chewbacca rumbled. 'No,' Leia shook her head. 'My safety isn't a matter of strength any more. My only chance is to convince the Noghri that I can be trusted. That when I make promises I keep them.'

'The droid will pose no problem,' Khabarakh decided. 'I will bring my ship alongside for docking.'

Leia switched the transmitter back on. 'Fine,' she said. 'I also have one case of clothing and personal items to bring along, if I may. Plus a sensor/analyzer package, to test the air and soil for anything that might be dangerous to me.'

'The air and soil where we shall be is safe.'

'I believe you,' Leia said. 'But I am not responsible only for my own safety. I carry within me two new lives, and I must protect them.'

The comm speaker hissed. 'Heirs of the Lord Vader?'

Leia hesitated; but genetically, if not philosophically, it was true enough. 'Yes.'

Another hiss. 'You may bring what you wish,' he said. 'I must be allowed to scan them, though. Do you bring weapons?'

'I have my lightsaber,' Leia said. 'Are there any animals on your world dangerous enough for me to need a blaster?'

'Not any more,' Khabarakh said, his voice grim. 'Your lightsaber, too, will be acceptable.'

Chewbacca snarled something quietly vicious, his wickedly curved climbing claws sliding involuntarily in and out of their fingertip sheaths. He was, Leia realized abruptly, on the edge of losing control . . . and perhaps of taking matters into those huge hands of his—

'What is the problem?' Khabarakh demanded.

Leia's stomach tightened. *Honesty*, she reminded herself. 'My pilot doesn't like the idea of me going off alone with you,' she conceded. 'He has a – well, you wouldn't understand.'

'He is under a life debt to you?'

Leia blinked at the speaker. She hadn't expected Khabarakh to have ever heard of the Wookiee life debt, much less know anything about it. 'Yes,' she said. 'The original life debt was to my husband, Han Solo. During the war Chewie extended it to include my brother and me.'

'And now to the children you bear within you?'

Leia looked at Chewbacca. 'Yes.'

For a long minute the comm was silent. The patrol ship continued toward them, and Leia found herself gripping the seat arms tightly as she wondered what the Noghri was thinking. If he decided that Chewbacca's objections constituted betrayal of their arrangement . . .

'The Wookiee code of honor is similar to our own,' Khabarakh said at last. 'He may come with you.'

Chewbacca gave a throaty rumble of surprise, a surprise that slid quickly into suspicion. 'Would you rather he have said you had to stay here?' Leia countered, her own surprise at the Noghri's concession quickly covered up by relief that the whole thing had been resolved so easily. 'Come on, make up your mind.'

The Wookiee rumbled again, but it was clear that he'd rather walk into a trap with her than let her walk into one alone. 'Thank you, Khabarakh, we accept,' Leia told the Noghri. 'We'll be ready whenever you get here. How long will the trip to your world take, by the way?'

'Approximately four days,' Khabarakh said. 'I await the honor of your presence aboard my ship.'

The comm went silent. *Four days*, Leia thought, a shiver running up her back. Four days in which to learn all that she could about both Khabarakh and the Noghri people.

And to prepare for the most important diplomatic mission of her life.

As it turned out, she didn't learn much about the Noghri culture during the trip. Khabarakh kept largely to himself, splitting his time between the sealed cockpit and his cabin. Occasionally he would come by to talk to Leia, but the conversations were short and invariably left her with the uncomfortable feeling that he was still very ambivalent about his decision to bring her to his home. When they'd set up this meeting back on the Wookiee world of Kashyyyk, she had suggested that he discuss the question with friends or confidants; but as they neared the end of the voyage and his dark nervousness grew, she began to pick up little hints that he had not, in fact, done so. The decision had been made entirely on his own.

It was not, to her way of thinking, a very auspicious beginning. It implied either a lack of trust in his friends or else a desire to absolve them from responsibility should the whole thing go sour. Either way, not exactly the sort of situation that filled her with confidence.

With their host generally keeping to himself, she and Chewbacca were forced to come up with their own entertainment. For Chewbacca, with his innate mechanical interests, such entertainment consisted mainly of wandering through the ship and poking his nose into every room, access hatch, and crawlway he could find – studying the ship, as he ominously put it, in case they needed at some point to fly it themselves. Leia, for her part, spent most of the trip in her cabin with Threepio, trying to deduce a possible derivation of *Mal'ary'ush*, the only Noghri word she knew, with the hope of at least getting some idea of where in the galaxy they might be going. Unfortunately, with six million languages to draw on, Threepio could come up with any number of possible etymologies for the word, ranging from reasonable to tenuous to absurd and right back again. It was an interesting exercise in applied linguistics, but ultimately more frustating than useful.

In the middle of the fourth day, they reached the Noghri world . . . and it was even worse than she'd expected.

'It's incredible,' she breathed, a hard knot forming in her throat as she pressed close to Chewbacca to stare through the ship's only passenger viewport at the world they were rapidly approaching. Beneath the mottling of white clouds the planetary surface seemed to be a uniform brown, relieved only by the occasional deep blue of lakes and small oceans. No greens or yellows, no light purples or blues – none of the colors, in fact, that usually signified plant life. For all she could tell, the entire planet might have been dead.

Chewbacca growled a reminder. 'Yes, I know Khabarakh said it had been devastated in the war,' she agreed soberly.

'But I didn't realize he really meant the *whole* planet had been hit.' She shook her head, feeling sick at heart. Wondering which side had been most responsible for this disaster.

Most responsible. She swallowed hard at the reflexively defensive words. There was no *most responsible* here, and she knew it. Khabarakh's world had been destroyed during a battle in space . . . and there had been only two sides to the war. Whatever had happened to turn this world into a desert, the Rebel Alliance could not avoid its share of the guilt. 'No wonder the Emperor and Vader were able to turn them against us,' she murmured. 'We have to find some way to help them.'

Chewbacca growled again, gestured out the viewport. The terminator line was coming up over the horizon now, a fuzzy strip of twilight between day and night; and there, fading through to the darkness beyond, was what looked like an irregular patch of pale green. 'I see it,' Leia nodded. 'You suppose that's all that's left?'

The Wookiee shrugged, offered the obvious suggestion. 'Yes, I suppose that would be the simplest way to find out,' Leia agreed. 'I really don't know if I want to ask him, though. Let's wait until we're closer and can see more of—'

She felt Chewbacca go stiff beside her a split second before his bellow split the air and left her ears ringing. 'What—?'

And then she saw it, and her stomach knotted abruptly with shock. There, just coming over the curve of the planet, was an Imperial Star Destroyer.

They'd been betrayed.

'No,' she breathed, staring out at the huge arrowhead shape. No mistake – it was a Star Destroyer, all right. 'No. I can't believe Khabarakh would do this.'

The last words were spoken to empty air; and with a second shock, she realized that Chewbacca was no longer beside her. Spinning around, she saw a flash of brown as he vanished down the corridor leading to the cockpit.

'No!' she shouted, pushing away from the bulkhead and taking off after him as fast as she could run. 'Chewie, no!'

The order was a waste of air, and she knew it. The Wookiee had murder in his heart, and he would get to Khabarakh even if he had to tear down the cockpit door with his bare hands.

The first *clang* sounded as she was halfway down the corridor; the second came as she rounded the slight curve and came within sight of the door. Chewbacca was raising his massive fists for a third blow—

When, to Leia's amazement, the door slid open.

Chewbacca seemed surprised, too, but he didn't dwell on it long. He was through the door before it was completely open, charging into the cockpit with a ululating Wookiee battle yell. 'Chewie!' Leia shouted again, diving through herself.

Just in time to see Khabarakh, seated at the pilot's station, throw up his right arm and somehow send Chewbacca spinning past him to crash with a roar into the underside of the control board.

Leia skidded to a halt, not quite believing what she'd just seen. 'Khabarakh—'

'I did not call them,' the Noghri said, half turning to face her. 'I did not betray my word of honor.'

Chewbacca thundered his disbelief as he fought to scramble to his feet in the cramped space. 'You must stop him,' Khabarakh shouted over the Wookiee's roar. 'Must keep him quiet. I must give the recognition signal or all will be lost.'

Leia looked past him at the distant Star Destroyer, her teeth clenched hard together. *Betrayal* ... but if Khabarakh had planned a betrayal, why had he let Chewbacca come along? Whatever that fighting technique was he'd used to deflect Chewbacca's first mad rush, it wasn't likely to work a second time.

She focused again on Khabarakh's face; on those dark eyes, protruding jaw, and needle-sharp teeth. He was watching her, ignoring the threat of the enraged Wookiee behind him, his hand poised ready over the comm switch. A beep sounded from the board, and his hand twitched toward the switch before stopping again. The board beeped again – 'I have not betrayed you, Lady Vader,' Khabarakh repeated, a note of urgency in his voice. 'You must believe me.'

Leia braced herself. 'Chewie, be quiet,' she said. 'Chewie? Chewie, be *quiet*.'

The Wookiee ignored the order. Finally back on his feet, he roared his war cry again and lunged for Khabarakh's throat. The Noghri took the charge head-on this time, grabbing Chewbacca's huge wrists in his wiry hands and holding on for all he was worth.

It wasn't enough. Slowly but steadily, Khabarakh's arms were bent steadily backwards as Chewbacca forced his way forward. 'Chewie, I said stop,' Leia tried again. 'Use your head – if he was planning a trap, don't you think he'd have timed it for when we were asleep or something?'

Chewbacca spit out a growl, his hands continuing their unwavering advance. 'But if he doesn't check in, they'll *know* something's wrong,' she countered. 'That's a sure way to bring them down on us.'

'The Lady Vader speaks truth,' Khabarakh said, his voice taut with the strain of holding back Chewbacca's hands. 'I have not betrayed you, but if I give no recognition signal you *will* be betrayed.'

'He's right,' Leia said. 'If they come to investigate, we lose by default. Come on, Chewie, it's our only hope.'

The Wookiee snarled again, shaking his head firmly. 'Then you leave me no choice,' Khabarakh said.

And without warning, the cockpit flashed with blue light, dropping Chewbacca to the floor like a huge sack of grain. 'What—?' Leia gasped, dropping to her knees beside the motionless Wookiee. 'Khabarakh!'

'A stun weapon only,' the Noghri said, breathing rapidly as he swiveled back to his board. 'A built-in defense.'

Leia twisted her head to glare at him, furious at what he'd done ... a fury that faded reluctantly behind the logic of the situation. Chewbacca had been fully prepared to throttle the life out of Khabarakh; and from personal experience, she knew how hard it was to calm down an angry Wookiee, even when you were his friend to begin with.

And Khabarakh *had* tried talking first. 'Now what?' she asked the Noghri, digging a hand through Chewbacca's thick torso hair to check his heartbeat. It was steady, which meant the stun weapon hadn't played any of its rare but potentially lethal tricks on the Wookiee's nervous system.

'Now be silent,' Khabarakh said, tapping his comm switch and saying something in his own language. Another mewing Noghri voice replied, and for a few minutes they conversed together. Leia remained kneeling at Chewbacca's side, wishing she'd had time to bring Threepio up before the discussion started. It would have been nice to know what the conversation was all about.

But finally it ended, and Khabarakh signed off. 'We are safe now,' he said, slumping a little in his seat. 'They are persuaded it was an equipment malfunction.'

'Let's hope so,' Leia said.

Khabarakh looked at her, a strange expression on his nightmare face. 'I have not betrayed you, Lady Vader,' he said quietly, his voice hard and yet oddly pleading. 'You must believe me. I have promised to defend you, and I will. To my own death, if need be.'

Leia stared at him . . . and whether through some sensitivity of the Force or merely her own long diplomatic experience, she finally understood the position Khabarakh was now in. Whatever waverings or second thoughts he might have been feeling during the voyage, the Star Destroyer's unexpected appearance had burned those uncertainties away. Khabarakh's word of honor had been brought into question, and he was now in the position of having to conclusively prove that he had not broken that word.

And he would have to go to whatever lengths such proof demanded. Even if it killed him.

Earlier, Leia had wondered how Khabarakh could possibly understand the concept of the Wookiee life debt. Perhaps the Noghri and Wookiee cultures were more alike than she'd realized.

'I believe you,' she told him, climbing to her feet and sitting down in the copilot seat. Chewbacca she would have to leave where he was until he was awake enough to help her move him. 'What now?'

Khabarakh turned back to his board. 'Now we must make a decision,' he said. 'My intention had been to bring you to ground in the city of Nystao, waiting until full dark to present you to my clan dynast. But that is now impossible. Our Imperial lord has come, and is holding a convocate of the dynasts.'

The back of Leia's neck tingled. 'Your Imperial lord is the Grand Admiral?' she asked carefully.

'Yes,' Khabarakh said. 'That is his flagship, the *Chimaera*. I remember the day that the Lord Darth Vader first brought him to us,' he added, his mewing voice becoming reflective. 'The Lord Vader told us that his duties against the Emperor's enemies would now be taking his full attention. That the Grand Admiral would henceforth be our lord and commander.' He made a strange, almost purring sound deep in his chest. 'There were many who were sad that day. The Lord Vader had been the only one save the Emperor who cared for Noghri wellbeing. He had given us hope and purpose.'

Leia grimaced. That purpose being to go off and die as death commandos at the Emperor's whim. But she couldn't say things like that to Khabarakh. Not yet, anyway. 'Yes,' she murmured.

At her feet, Chewbacca twitched. 'He will be fully awake soon,' Khabarakh said. 'I would not like to stun him again. Can you control him?'

'I think so,' Leia said. They were coming in low toward the upper atmosphere now, on a course that would take them directly beneath the orbiting Star Destroyer. 'I hope they don't decide to do a sensor focus on us,' she murmured. 'If they pick up three lifeforms here, you're going to have a lot of explaining to do.'

'The ship's static-damping should prevent that,' Khabarakh assured her. 'It is at full power.'

Leia frowned. 'Aren't they likely to wonder about that?'

'No. I explained it was part of the same malfunction that caused the transmitter problem.'

There was a low rumble from Chewbacca, and Leia looked down to see the Wookiee's eyes glaring impotently up at her. Fully alert again, but without enough motor control yet to do anything. 'We've cleared outer control,' she told him. 'We're heading down to – where *are* we going, Khabarakh?'

The Noghri took a deep breath, let it out in an odd sort of whistle. 'We will go to my home, a small village near the edge of the Clean Land. I will hide you there until our lord the Grand Admiral leaves.'

Leia thought about that. A small village situated off the mainstream of Noghri life ought to be safely out of the way of wandering Imperials. On the other hand, if it was anything like the small villages she'd known, her presence there would be common knowledge an hour after they put down. 'Can you trust the other villagers to keep quiet?'

'Do not worry,' Khabarakh said. 'I will keep you safe.'

But he hesitated before he said it . . . and as they headed into the atmosphere, Leia noted uneasily that he hadn't really answered the question.

The dynast bowed one last time and stepped back to the line of those awaiting their turn to pay homage to their leader. Thrawn, seated in the gleaming High Seat of the Common Room of Honoghr, nodded gravely to the departing clan leader and motioned to the next. The other stepped forward, moving in the formalized dance that seemed to indicate respect, and bowed his forehead to the ground before the Grand Admiral.

Standing two meters to Thrawn's right and a little behind him, Pellaeon shifted his weight imperceptibly between feet, stifled a yawn, and wondered when this ritual would be over. He'd been under the impression they'd come to Honoghr to try to inspire the commando teams, but so far the only Noghri they'd seen had been ceremonial guards and this small but excessively boring collection of clan leaders. Thrawn presumably had his reasons for wading through the ritual, but Pellaeon wished it would hurry up and be over. With a galaxy still to win back for the Empire, sitting here listening to a group of gray-skinned aliens drone on about their loyalty seemed a ridiculous waste of time.

There was a touch of air on the back of his neck. 'Captain?' someone said quietly in his ear – Lieutenant Tschel, he tentatively identified the voice. 'Excuse me, sir, but Grand Admiral Thrawn asked to be informed immediately if anything out of the ordinary happened.'

Pellaeon nodded slightly, glad of any interruption. 'What is it?'

'It doesn't seem dangerous, sir, or even very important,' Tschel said. 'A Noghri commando ship on its way in almost didn't give the recognition response in time.'

'Equipment trouble, probably,' Pellaeon said.

'That's what the pilot said,' Tschel told him. 'The odd thing is that he begged off putting down at the Nystao landing area. You'd think that someone with equipment problems would want his ship looked at immediately.'

'A bad transmitter isn't exactly a crisis-level problem,' Pellaeon grunted. But Tschel had a point; and Nystao was the only place on Honoghr with qualified spaceship repair facilities. 'We have an ID on the pilot?'

'Yes, sir. His name's Khabarakh, clan Kihm'bar. I pulled up what we have on him,' he added, offering Pellaeon a data pad.

Surreptitiously, Pellaeon took it, wondering what he should do now. Thrawn had indeed left instructions that he was to be notified of any unusual activity anywhere in the system. But to interrupt the ceremony for something so trivial didn't seem like a good idea.

As usual, Thrawn was one step ahead of him. Lifting a hand, he stopped the Noghri clan dynast's presentation and turned his glowing red eyes on Pellaeon. 'You have something to report, Captain?'

'A small anomaly only, sir,' Pellaeon told him, steeling himself and stepping to the Grand Admiral's side. 'An incoming commando ship was slow to transmit its recognition signal, and then declined to put down at the Nystao landing area. Probably just an equipment problem.'

'Probably,' Thrawn agreed. 'Was the ship scanned for evidence of malfunction?'

'Ah . . .' Pellaeon checked the data pad. 'The scan was inconclusive,' he told the other. 'The ship's static-damping was strong enough to block—'

'The incoming ship was static-damped?' Thrawn interrupted, looking sharply up at Pellaeon.

'Yes, sir.'

Wordlessly, Thrawn held up a hand. Pellaeon gave him

the data pad, and for a moment the Grand Admiral frowned down at it, skimming the report. 'Khabarakh, clan Kihm'bar,' he murmured to himself. 'Interesting.' He looked up at Pellaeon again. 'Where did the ship go?'

Pellaeon looked in turn at Tschel. 'According to the last report, it was headed south,' the lieutenant said. 'It might still be in range of our tractor beams, sir.'

Pellaeon turned back to Thrawn. 'Shall we try to stop it, Admiral?'

Thrawn looked down at the data pad, his face tight with concentration. 'No,' he said at last. 'Let it land, but track it. And order a tech team from the *Chimaera* to meet us at the ship's final destination.' His eyes searched the line of Noghri dynasts, came to rest on one of them. 'Dynast Ir'khaim, clan Kihm'bar, step forward.'

The Noghri did so. 'What is your wish, my lord?' he mewed.

'One of your people has come home,' Thrawn said. 'We go to his village to welcome him.'

Ir'khaim bowed. 'At my lord's request.'

Thrawn stood up. 'Order the shuttle to be prepared, Captain,' he told Pellaeon. 'We leave at once.'

'Yes, sir,' Pellaeon said, nodding the order on to Lieutenant Tschel. 'Wouldn't it be easier, sir, to have the ship and pilot brought here to us?'

'Easier, perhaps,' Thrawn acknowledged, 'but possibly not as illuminating. You obviously didn't recognize the pilot's name; but Khabarakh, clan Kihm'bar, was once part of commando team twenty-two. Does *that* jog any memories?'

Pellaeon felt his stomach tighten. 'That was the team that went after Leia Organa Solo on Kashyyyk.'

'And of which team only Khabarakh still survives,' Thrawn nodded. 'I think it might be instructive to hear from him the details of that failed mission. And to find out why it's taken him this long to return home.'

Thrawn's eyes glittered. 'And to find out,' he added quietly, 'just why he's trying so hard to avoid us.'

CHAPTER TEN

I t was full dark by the time Khabarakh brought the ship to ground in his village, a tight-grouped cluster of huts with brightly lit windows. 'Do ships land here often?' Leia asked as Khabarakh pointed the ship toward a shadowy structure standing apart near the center of the village. In the glare of the landing lights the shadow became a large cylindrical building with a flat cone-shaped roof, the circular wall composed of massive vertical wooden pillars alternating with a lighter, shimmery wood. Just beneath the eaves she caught a glint of a metal band encircling the entire building.

'It is not common,' Khabarakh said, cutting the repulsorlifts and running the ship's systems down to standby. 'Neither is it unheard of.'

In other words, it was probably going to attract a fair amount of attention. Chewbacca, who had recovered enough for Leia to help into one of the cockpit passenger seats, was obviously thinking along the same lines. 'The villagers are all close family of the clan Kihm'bar,' Khabarakh said in answer to the Wookiee's slightly slurred question. 'They will accept my promise of protection as their own. Come.'

Leia unstrapped and stood up, suppressing a grimace as she did so. But they were here now, and she could only hope that Khabarakh's confidence was more than just the unfounded idealism of youth.

She helped Chewbacca unstrap and together they followed the Noghri back toward the main hatchway, collecting Threepio from her cabin on the way. 'I must go first,' Khabarakh said as they reached the exit. 'By custom, I must approach alone to the *dukha* of the clan Kihm'bar upon arrival. By law, I am required to announce out-clan visitors to the head of my family.'

'I understand,' Leia said, fighting back a fresh surge of uneasiness. She didn't like this business of Khabarakh having conversations with his fellow Noghri that she wasn't in on. Once again, there wasn't a lot she could do about it. 'We'll wait here until you come and get us.'

'I will be quick,' Khabarakh promised. He palmed the door release twice, slipping outside as the panel slid open and then shut again.

Chewbacca growled something unintelligible under his breath. 'He'll be back soon,' Leia soothed him, making a guess as to what was bothering the Wookiee.

'I'm certain he is telling the truth,' Threepio added helpfully. 'Customs and rituals of this sort are very common among the more socially primitive prespaceflight cultures.'

'Except that this culture isn't prespaceflight,' Leia pointed out, her hand playing restlessly with the grip of her lightsaber as she stared at the closed hatchway in front of her. Khabarakh could at least have left the door open so that they would be able to see when he was coming back.

Unless, of course, he didn't *want* them to see when he was coming back.

'That is evident, Your Highness,' Threepio agreed, his voice taking on a professional tone. 'I feel certain, however, that their status in that regard has been changed only recent—Well!' he broke off as Chewbacca abruptly pushed past him and lumbered back toward the center of the ship.

'Where are you going?' Leia called after the Wookiee. His only reply was some comment about the Imperials that she wasn't quite able to catch. 'Chewie, get back here,' she snapped. 'Khabarakh will be back any minute.'

This time the Wookiee didn't bother to answer. 'Great,' Leia muttered, trying to decide what to do. If Khabarakh came back and found Chewbacca gone – but if he came and found *both* of them gone – 'As I was saying,' Threepio went on, apparently deciding that the actions of rude Wookiees were better left ignored, 'all the evidence I have gathered so far about this culture indicates that they were until recently a nonspacefaring people. Khabarakh's reference to the *dukha* – obviously a clan center of some sort – the familial and clan structures themselves, plus this whole preoccupation with your perceived royal status—'

'The high court of Alderaan had a royal hierarchy, too,' Leia reminded him tartly, still looking back along the empty corridor. No, she decided, she and Threepio had better stay here and wait for Khabarakh. 'Most other people in the galaxy didn't consider us to be socially primitive.'

'No, of course not,' Threepio said, sounding a little embarrassed. 'I didn't mean to imply any such thing.'

'I know,' Leia assured him, a little embarrassed herself at jumping on Threepio like that. She'd known what he meant. 'Where *is* he, anyway?'

The question had been rhetorical; but even as she voiced it the hatchway abruptly slid open again. 'Come,' Khabarakh said. His dark eyes flickered over Leia and Threepio – 'Where is the Wookiee?'

'He went back into the ship,' Leia told him. 'I don't know why. Do you want me to go and find him?'

Khabarakh made a sound halfway between a hiss and a purr. 'There is no time,' he said. 'The maitrakh is waiting. Come.'

Turning, he started back down the ramp. 'Any idea how long it will take you to pick up the language?' Leia asked Threepio as they followed.

'I really cannot say, Your Highness,' the droid answered as Khabarakh led them across a dirt courtyard past the large wooden building they'd seen on landing – the clan *dukha*, Leia decided. One of the smaller structures beyond it seemed to be their goal. 'Learning an entirely new language would be difficult indeed,' Threepio continued. 'However, if it is similar to any of the six million forms of communication with which I am familiar—'

'I understand,' Leia cut him off. They were almost to the lighted building now; and as they approached, a pair of short Noghri standing in the shadows pulled open the double doors for them. Taking a deep breath, Leia followed Khabarakh inside.

From the amount of light coming through the windows she would have expected the building's interior to be uncomfortably bright. To her surprise, the room they entered was actually darker than it had been immediately outside. A glance to the side showed why: the brightly lit 'windows' were in fact standard self-powered lighting panels, with the operational sides facing outward. Except for a small amount of spillage from the panels, the interior of the building was lit only by a pair of floating-wick lamps. Threepio's assessment of the society echoed through her mind; apparently, he'd known what he was talking about.

In the center of the room, standing silently in a row facing her, were five Noghri.

Leia swallowed hard, sensing somehow that the first words should be theirs. Khabarakh stepped to the Noghri in the center and dropped to his knees, ducking his head to the floor and splaying out his hands to his sides. The same gesture of respect, she remembered, that he'd extended to her back in the Kashyyyk holding cell. '*Llyr'ush mir lakh svoril'lae*,' he said. '*Mir'lae karah siv Mal'ary'ush vir'ae Vader'ush.*'

'Can you understand it?' Leia murmured to Threepio.

'To a degree,' the droid replied. 'It appears to be a dialect of the ancient trade language—'

'*Sha'vah*!' the Noghri in the center of the line spat.

Threepio recoiled. 'She said, "Quiet",' he translated unnecessarily.

'I understood the gist,' Leia said, drawing herself up and bringing the full weight of her Royal Alderaanian Court upbringing to bear on the aliens facing her. Deference to local custom and authority was all well and good; but she was the daughter of their Lord Darth Vader, and there were certain discourtesies that such a person should not put up with. 'Is this how you speak to the *Mal'ary'ush*?' she demanded.

Six Noghri heads snapped over to look at her. Reaching out with the Force, Leia tried to read the sense behind those gazes; but as always, this particular alien mind seemed totally closed to her. She was going to have to play it by ear. 'I asked a question,' she said into the silence.

The Noghri in the center took a step forward, and with the motion Leia noticed for the first time the two small hard bumps on the alien's upper chest beneath the loose tunic. A female? 'Maitrakh?' she murmured to Threepio, remembering the word Khabarakh had used earlier.

'A female who is leader of a local family or subclan structure,' the droid translated, his voice nervous and almost too low to hear. Threepio hated being yelled at.

'Thank you,' Leia said, eyeing the Noghri. 'You are the maitrakh of this family?'

'I am she,' the Noghri said in heavily accented but understandable Basic. 'What proof do you offer to your claim of *Mal'ary'ush*?'

Silently, Leia held out her hand. The maitrakh hesitated, then stepped up to her and gingerly sniffed it. 'Is it not as I said?' Khabarakh asked.

'Be silent, thirdson,' the maitrakh said, raising her head to stare into Leia's eyes. 'I greet you, Lady Vader. But I do not welcome you.'

Leia held her gaze steadily. She could still not sense anything from any of the aliens, but with her thoughts extended she could tell that Chewbacca had left the ship and was approaching the house. Approaching rather rapidly, and with a definite agitation about him. She hoped he wouldn't charge brashly in and ruin what little civility remained here. 'May I ask why not?' she asked the maitrakh.

'Did you serve the Emperor?' the other countered. 'Do you now serve our lord, the Grand Admiral?'

'No, to both questions,' Leia told her.

'Then you bring discord and poison among us,' the maitrakh concluded darkly. 'Discord between what was and what now is.'

She shook her head. 'We do not need more discord on Honoghr, Lady Vader.'

The words were barely out of her mouth when the doors behind Leia swung open again and Chewbacca strode into the room.

The maitrakh started at the sight of the Wookiee, and one of the other Noghri uttered something startled-sounding. But any further reactions were cut off by Chewbacca's snarled warning. 'Are you sure they're Imperials?' Leia asked, a cold fist clutching her heart. *No, she pleaded silently. Not now. Not yet.*

The Wookiee growled the obvious: that a pair of *Lambda*-class shuttles coming from orbit and from the direction of the city of Nystao could hardly be anything else.

Khabarakh moved up beside the maitrakh, said something urgently in his own language. 'He says he has sworn protection to us,' Threepio translated. 'He asks that the pledge be honored.'

For a long moment Leia thought the maitrakh was going to refuse. Then, with a sigh, she bowed her head slightly. 'Come with me,' Khabarakh said to Leia, brushing past her and Chewbacca to the door. 'The maitrakh has agreed to hide you from our lord the Grand Admiral, at least for now.'

'Where are we going?' Leia asked as they followed him out into the night.

'Your droid and your analysis equipment I will hide among the decon droids that are stored for the night in an outer shed,' the Noghri explained, pointing to a windowless building fifty meters away. 'You and the Wookiee will be more of a problem. If the Imperials have sensor equipment with them, your life-sign profiles will register as different from Noghri.'

'I know,' Leia said, searching the sky for the shuttles' running lights and trying to remember everything she could about life-form identification algorithms. Heart rate was one of the parameters, she knew, as were ambient atmosphere, respiratory byproducts, and molecule-chain EM polarization effects. But the chief long-range parameter was—'We need a heat source,' she told Khabarakh. 'As big a one as possible.'

'The bake house,' the Noghri said, pointing to a windowless building three down from where they stood. At its back was a squat chimney from which wisps of smoke could be seen curling upward in the backwash of light from the surrounding structures.

'Sounds like our best chance,' Leia agreed. 'Khabarakh, you hide Threepio; Chewie, come with me.'

The Noghri were waiting for them as they stepped from the shuttle: three females standing side by side, with two children acting as honor wardens by the doors of the clan *dukha* building. Thrawn glanced at the group, threw an evaluating sweep around the area, and then turned to Pellaeon. 'Wait here until the tech team arrives, Captain,' he ordered Pellaeon quietly. 'Get them started on a check of the communications and countermeasures equipment in the ship over there. Then join me inside.'

'Yes, sir.'

Thrawn turned to Ir'khaim. 'Dynast,' he invited, gesturing at the waiting Noghri. The dynast bowed and strode toward them. Thrawn threw a glance at Rukh, who'd taken Ir'khaim's former position at the Grand Admiral's side, and together they followed. There was the usual welcoming ritual, and then the females led the way into the *dukha*.

The shuttle from the *Chimaera* was only a couple of minutes behind them. Pellaeon briefed the tech team and got them busy, then crossed to the *dukha* and went in.

He'd expected that the maitrakh would have managed to round up perhaps a handful of her people for this impromptu late-evening visit by their glorious lord and master. To his surprise, he found that the old girl had in fact turned out half the village. There was a double row of them, children as well as adults, lining the *dukha* walls from the huge genealogy wall chart back to the double doors and around again to the meditation booth opposite the chart. Thrawn was seated in the clan High Seat two-thirds of the way to the back of the room with Ir'khaim standing again at his side. The three females who'd met the shuttle stood facing them with a second tier of elders another pace back. Standing with the females, his steel-gray skin a marked contrast to their older, darker gray, was a young Noghri male.

Pellaeon had, apparently, missed nothing more important than a smattering of the nonsense ritual the Noghri never seemed to get enough of. As he moved past the silent lines of aliens to stand at Thrawn's other side, the young male stepped forward and knelt before the High Seat. 'I greet you, my lord,' he mewed gravely, spreading his arms out to his sides. 'You honor my family and the clan Kihm'bar with your presence here.'

'You may rise,' Thrawn told him. 'You are Khabarakh, clan Kihm'bar?'

'I am, my lord.'

'You were once a member of the Imperial Noghri commando team twenty-two,' Thrawn said. 'A team that ceased to exist on the planet Kashyyyk. Tell me what happened.'

Khabarakh might have twitched. Pellaeon couldn't tell for sure. 'I filed a report, my lord, immediately upon leaving that world.'

'Yes, I read the report,' Thrawn told him coolly. 'Read it very carefully, and noted the questions it left unanswered. Such as how and why you survived when all others in your team were killed. And how it was you were able to escape when the entire planet had been alerted to your presence. And why you did not return immediately to either Honoghr or one of our other bases after your failure.'

This time there was definitely a twitch. Possibly a reaction to the word *failure*. 'I was left unconscious by the Wookiees during the first attack,' Khabarakh said. 'I awakened alone and made my way back to the ship. Once there, I deduced what had happened to the rest of the team from official information sources. I suspect they simply were unprepared for the speed and stealth of my ship when I made my escape. As to my whereabouts afterward, my lord—' He hesitated. 'I transmitted my report, and then left for a time to be alone.'

'Why?'

'To think, my lord, and to meditate.'

'Wouldn't Honoghr have been a more suitable place for such meditation?' Thrawn asked, waving a hand around the *dukha*.

'I had much to think about. My lord.'

For a moment Thrawn eyed him thoughtfully. 'You were slow to respond when the request for a recognition signal came from the surface,' he said. 'You then refused to land at the Nystao port facilities.'

'I did not refuse, my lord. I was never ordered to land there.'

'The distinction is noted,' Thrawn said dryly. 'Tell me why you chose to come here instead.'

'I wished to speak with my maitrakh. To discuss my meditations with her, and to ask forgiveness for my ... failure.'

'And have you done so?' Thrawn asked, turning to face the maitrakh.

'We have begun,' she said in atrociously mangled Basic. 'We have not finished.'

At the back of the room, the *dukha* doors swung open and one of the tech team stepped inside. 'You have a report, Ensign?' Thrawn called to him.

'Yes, Admiral,' the other said, crossing the room and stepping somewhat gingerly around the assembled group of Noghri elders. 'We've finished our preliminary set of comm and countermeasures tests, sir, as per orders.'

Thrawn shifted his gaze to Khabarakh. 'And?'

'We think we've located the malfunction, sir. The main transmitter coil seems to have overloaded and back-fed into a dump capacitor, damaging several nearby circuits. The compensator computer rebuilt the pathway, but the bypass was close enough to one of the static-damping command lines for the resulting inductance surge to trigger it.'

'An interesting set of coincidences,' Thrawn said, his glowing eyes still on Khabarakh. 'A natural malfunction, do you think, or an artificial one?'

The maitrakh stirred, as if about to say something. Thrawn looked at her, and she subsided. 'Impossible to say, sir,' the tech said, choosing his words carefully. Obviously, he hadn't missed the fact that this was skating him close to the edge of insult in the middle of a group of Noghri who might decide to take offense at it. 'Someone who knew what he was doing could probably have pulled it off. I have to say, though, sir, that compensator computers in general have a pretty low reputation among mechanics. They're OK on the really serious stuff that can get unskilled pilots into big trouble, but on noncritical reroutes like this they've always had a tendency to foul up something else along the way.'

'Thank you.' If Thrawn was annoyed that he hadn't caught Khabarakh red-handed in a lie, it didn't show in his face. 'Your team will take the ship back to Nystao for repairs.'

'Yes, sir.' The tech saluted and left.

Thrawn looked back at Khabarakh. 'With your team destroyed, you will of course have to be reassigned,' he said. 'When your ship has been repaired you will fly it to the Valrar base in Glythe sector and report there for duty.'

'Yes, my lord,' Khabarakh said.

Thrawn stood up. 'You have much to be proud of here,' he said, inclining his head slightly to the maitrakh. 'Your family's service to the clan Kihm'bar and to the Empire will be long remembered by all of Honoghr.'

'As will your leadership and protection of the Noghri people,' the maitrakh responded.

Flanked by Rukh and Ir'khaim, Thrawn stepped down from the chair and headed back toward the double doors. Pellaeon took up the rear, and a minute later they were once again out in the chilly night air. The shuttle was standing ready, and without further comment or ritual Thrawn led the way inside. As they lifted, Pellaeon caught just a glimpse out the viewport of the Noghri filing out of the *dukha* to watch their departing leaders. 'Well, *that* was pleasant,' he muttered under his breath.

Thrawn looked at him. 'A waste of time, you think, Captain?' he asked mildly.

Pellaeon glanced at Ir'khaim, seated farther toward the front of the shuttle. The dynast didn't seem to be listening to them, but it would probably still pay to be tactful. 'Diplomatically, sir, I'm sure it was worthwhile to demonstrate that you care about all of Honoghr, including the outer villages,' he told Thrawn. 'Given that the commando ship really *had* malfunctioned, I don't think anything else was gained.'

Thrawn turned to stare out the side viewport. 'I'm not so sure of that, Captain,' he said. 'There's something not quite right back there. Rukh, what's your reading of our young commando Khabarakh?'

'He was unsettled,' the bodyguard told him quietly. 'That much I saw in his hands and his face.'

Ir'khaim swiveled around in his chair. 'It is a naturally unsettling experience to face the lord of the Noghri,' he said.

'Particularly when one's hands are wet with failure?' Rukh countered.

Ir'khaim half rose from his seat, and for a pair of heartbeats the air between the two Noghri was thick with tension. Pellaeon felt himself pressing back in his seat cushions, the long and bloody history of Noghri clan rivalry flooding fresh into his consciousness ... 'This mission has generated several failures,' Thrawn said calmly into the taut silence. 'In that, the clan Kihm'bar hardly stands alone.'

Slowly, Ir'khaim resumed his seat. 'Khabarakh is still young,' he said.

'He is indeed,' Thrawn agreed. 'One reason, I presume, why he's such a bad liar. Rukh, perhaps the Dynast Ir'khaim would enjoy the view from the forward section. Please escort him there.'

'Yes, my lord.' Rukh stood up. 'Dynast Ir'khaim?' he said, gesturing toward the forward blast door.

For a moment the other Noghri didn't move. Then, with obvious reluctance, he stood up. 'My lord,' he said stiffly, and headed down the aisle.

Thrawn waited until the door had closed on both aliens before turning back to Pellaeon. 'Khabarakh is hiding something, Captain,' he said, a cold fire in his eyes. 'I'm certain of it.'

'Yes, sir,' Pellaeon said, wondering how the Grand Admiral had come to that conclusion. Certainly the routine sensor scan they'd just run hadn't picked up anything. 'Shall I order a sensor focus on the village?'

'That's not what I meant,' Thrawn shook his head. 'He wouldn't have brought anything incriminating back to Honoghr with him – you can't hide anything for long in one of these close-knit villages. No, it's something he's not telling us about that missing month. The one where he claims he was off meditating by himself.'

'We might be able to learn something from his ship,' Pellaeon suggested.

'Agreed,' Thrawn nodded. 'Have a scanning crew go over it before the techs get to work. Every cubic millimeter of it, interior and exterior both. And have Surveillance put someone on Khabarakh.'

'Ah – yes, sir,' Pellaeon said. 'One of our people, or another Noghri?'

Thrawn cocked an eyebrow at him. 'The ridiculously obvious or the heavily political, in other words?' he asked dryly. 'Yes, you're right, of course. Let's try a third option: does the *Chimaera* carry any espionage droids?'

'I don't believe so, sir,' Pellaeon said, punching up the question on the shuttle's computer link. 'No. We have some Arakyd Viper probe droids, but nothing of the more compact espionage class.'

'Then we'll have to improvise,' Thrawn said. 'Have Engineering put a Viper motivator into a decon droid and rig it with full-range optical and auditory sensors and a recorder. We'll have it put in with the group working out of Khabarakh's village.'

'Yes, sir,' Pellaeon said, keying in the order. 'Do you want a transmitter installed, too?'

Thrawn shook his head. 'No, a recorder should be sufficient. The antenna would be difficult to conceal from view. The last thing we want is for some curious Noghri to see it and wonder why this one was different.'

Pellaeon nodded his understanding. Especially since that might lead the aliens to start pulling decon droids apart for a look inside. 'Yes, sir. I'll have the order placed right away.'

Thrawn's glowing eyes shifted to look out the viewport. 'There's no particular rush here,' he said thoughtfully. 'Not now. This is the calm before the storm, Captain; and until the storm is ready to unleash, we might as well spend our time and energy making sure our illustrious Jedi Master will be willing to assist us when we want him.'

'Which means bringing Leia Organa Solo to him.'

'Exactly.' Thrawn looked at the forward blast door. 'And if my presence is what the Noghri need to inspire them, then my presence is what they'll have.'

'For how long?' Pellaeon asked.

Thrawn smiled tightly. 'For as long as it takes.'

CHAPTER ELEVEN

'Han?' Lando's voice came from the cabin intercom beside the bunk. 'Wake up.'

'Yeah, I'm awake,' Han grunted, swiping at his eyes with one hand and swiveling the repeater displays toward him with the other. If there was one thing his years on the wrong side of the law had hammered into him, it was the knack of going from deep sleep to full alertness in the space between heartbeats. 'What's up?'

'We're here,' Lando announced. 'Wherever *here* is.'

'I'll be right up.'

They were in sight of their target planet by the time he'd dressed and made his way to the *Lady Luck*'s cockpit. 'Where's Irenez?' he asked peering out at the mottled blue-green crescent shape they were rapidly approaching. It looked pretty much like any of a thousand other planets he'd seen.

'She's gone back to the aft control station,' Lando told him. 'I got the impression she wanted to be able to send down some recognition codes without us looking over her shoulder.'

'Any idea where we are?'

'Not really,' Lando said. 'Transit time was forty-seven hours, but that doesn't tell us a whole lot.'

Han nodded, searching his memory. 'A Dreadnaught can pull, what, about Point Four?'

'About that,' Lando agreed. 'When it's really in a hurry, anyway.'

'Means we aren't any more than a hundred fifty light-years from New Cov, then.'

'I'd guess we're closer than that, myself,' Lando said. 'It wouldn't make much sense to use New Cov as a contact point if they were that far away.'

'Unless New Cov was Breil'lya's idea and not theirs,' Han pointed out.

'Possible,' Lando said. 'I still think we're closer than a hundred fifty light-years, though. They could have taken their time getting here just to mislead us.'

Han looked up at the Dreadnaught that had been hauling them through hyperspace for the past two days. 'Or to have time to organize a reception committee.'

'There's that,' Lando nodded. 'I don't know if I mentioned it, but after they apologized for getting the magnetic coupling off-center over our hatch I went back and took a look.'

'You didn't mention it, but I did the same thing,' Han said sourly. 'Looked kind of deliberate, didn't it?'

'That's what I thought, too,' Lando said. 'Like maybe they wanted an excuse to keep us cooped up down here and not wandering around their ship.'

'Could be lots of good and innocent reasons for that,' Han reminded him.

'And lots of not-so-innocent ones,' Lando countered.

'You sure you don't have any idea who this Commander of theirs might be?'

'Not even a guess. Probably be finding out real soon, though.'

The comm crackled on. '*Lady Luck*, this is Sena,' a familiar voice said. 'We've arrived.'

'Yes, we noticed,' Lando told her. 'I expect you'll want us to follow you down.'

'Right,' she said. 'The *Peregrine* will drop the magnetic coupling whenever you're ready to fly.'

Han stared at the speaker, barely hearing Lando's response. A ship called the *Peregrine* . . . ?

'You still with me?'

Han focused on Lando, noticing with mild surprise that the other's conversation with Sena had ended. 'Yeah,' he said. 'Sure. It's just – that name, *Peregrine*, rang an old bell.'

'You've heard of it?'

'Not the ship, no,' Han shook his head. 'The Peregrine was an old Corellian scare legend they used to tell when I was a kid. He was some old ghostly guy who'd been cursed to wander around the world for ever and never find his home again. Used to make me feel real creepy.'

From above came a clang; and with a jolt they were free of the Dreadnaught. Lando eased them away from the huge warship, looking up as it passed by overhead. 'Well, try to remember it was just a legend,' he reminded Han.

Han looked at the Dreadnaught. 'Sure,' he said, a little too quickly. 'I know that.'

———

They followed Sena's freighter down and were soon skimming over what appeared to be a large grassy plain dotted with patches of stubby coniferous trees. A wall of craggy cliffs loomed directly ahead – an ideal spot, Han's old smuggler instincts told him, to hide a spaceship support and servicing base. A few minutes later his hunch was borne out as, sweeping over a low ridge, they came to the encampment.

An encampment that was far too large to be merely a servicing base. Rows upon rows of camouflaged structures filled the plain just beneath the cliffs: everything from small living quarters to larger admin and supply sheds to still larger maintenance and tool buildings, up to a huge camo-roofed refurbishing hangar. The perimeter was dotted with the squat, turret-topped cylinders of Golan Arms anti-infantry batteries and a few of the longer Speizoc anti-vehicle weapons, along with some KAAC Freerunner assault vehicles parked in defensive posture.

Lando whistled softly under his breath. 'Would you look at that?' he said. 'What *is* this, someone's private army?'

'Looks that way,' Han agreed, feeling the skin on the back of his neck starting to crawl. He'd run into private armies before, and they'd never been anything but trouble.

'I think I'm starting not to like this,' Lando decided, easing the *Lady Luck* gingerly over the outer sentry line. Ahead, Sena's freighter was approaching a landing pad barely visible against the rest of the ground. 'You sure you want to go through with this?'

'What, with three Dreadnaughts standing on our

heads out there?' Han snorted. 'I don't think we've got a whole lot of choice. Not in this crate, anyway.'

'Probably right,' Lando conceded, apparently too pre-occupied to notice the insult to his ship. 'So what do we do?'

Sena's freighter had dropped its landing skids and was settling onto the pad. 'I guess we go down and behave like invited guests,' Han said.

Lando nodded at Han's blaster. 'You don't think they'll object to their invited guests coming in armed?'

'Let 'em object first,' Han said grimly. 'Then we'll dis-cuss it.'

Lando put the *Lady Luck* down beside the freighter, and together he and Han made their way to the aft hatch-way. Irenez, her transmission chores finished, was waiting there for them, her own blaster strapped prominently to her hip. A transport skiff was parked outside, and as the three of them headed down the ramp, Sena and a handful of her entourage came around the *Lady Luck*'s bow. Most of the others were dressed in a casual tan uniform of an unfamiliar but vaguely Corellian cut; Sena, by con-trast, was still in the nondescript civilian garb she'd been wearing on New Cov.

'Welcome to our base of operations,' Sena said, waving a hand to encompass the encampment around them. 'If you'll come with us, the Commander is waiting to meet you.'

'Busy looking place you've got here,' Han commented as they all boarded the skiff. 'You getting ready to start a war or something?'

'We're not in the business of starting wars,' Sena said coolly.

'Ah,' Han nodded, looking around as the driver swung the skiff around and headed off through the camp. There was something about the layout that seemed vaguely familiar.

Lando got it first. 'You know, this place looks a lot like one of the old Alliance bases we used to work out of,' he commented to Sena. 'Only built on the surface instead of dug in underground.'

'It does look that way, doesn't it?' Sena agreed, her voice not giving anything away.

'You've had dealings with the Alliance, then?' Lando probed gently.

Sena didn't answer. Lando looked at Han, eyebrows raised. Han shrugged slightly in return. Whatever was going on here, it was clear the hired hands weren't in the habit of talking about it.

The skiff came to a halt beside an admin-type building indistinguishable from the others nearby except for the two uniformed guards flanking the doorway. They saluted as Sena approached, one of them reaching over to pull the door open. 'The Commander asked to see you for a moment alone, Captain Solo,' Sena said, stopping by the open door. 'We'll wait out here with General Calrissian.'

'Right,' Han said. Taking a deep breath, he stepped inside.

From its outside appearance he'd expected it to be a standard administrative center, with an outer reception area and a honeycomb of comfy executive offices stacked behind it. To his mild surprise, he found himself instead in a fully equipped war room. Lining the walls were comm and tracking consoles, including at least one crystal gravfield trap receptor and what looked like the ranging control for a KDY v-150 Planet Defender ion cannon like the one the Alliance had had to abandon on Hoth. In the center of the room a large holo display showed a sector's worth of stars, with a hundred multi-colored markers and vector lines scattered among the glittering white dots.

And standing beside the holo was a man.

His face was distorted somewhat by the strangely colored lights playing on it from the display; and it was, at any rate, a face Han had never seen except in pictures. But even so, recognition came with the sudden jolt of an overhead thunderclap. 'Senator Bel Iblis,' he breathed.

'Welcome to Peregrine's Nest, Captain Solo,' the other said gravely, coming away from the holo toward him. 'I'm flattered you still remember me.'

'It'd be hard for any Corellian to forget you, sir,' Han said, his numbed brain noting vaguely in passing that there were very few people in the galaxy who rated an automatic *sir* from him. 'But you . . .'

'Were dead?' Bel Iblis suggested, a half smile creasing his lined face.

'Well – yes,' Han floundered. 'I mean, everyone thought you died on Anchoron.'

'In a very real sense, I did,' the other said quietly, the smile fading from his face. Closer now, Han was struck with just how lined with age and stress the Senator's face was. 'The Emperor wasn't quite able to kill me at Anchoron, but he might just as well have done so. He took everything I had except my life: my family, my profession, even all future contacts with mainstream Corellian society. He forced me outside the law I'd worked so hard to create and maintain.' The smile returned, like a hint of sunshine around the edge of a dark cloud. 'Forced me to become a rebel. I imagine you understand the feeling.'

'Pretty well, yeah,' Han said, grinning lopsidedly in return. He'd read in school about the legendary presence of the equally legendary Senator Garm Bel Iblis; now, he was getting to see that charm up close. It made him feel like a schoolkid again. 'I still can't believe this. I wish we'd known sooner – we could really have used this army of yours during the war.'

For just a second a shadow seemed to cross Bel Iblis's face. 'We probably couldn't have done much to help,' he said. 'It's taken us a good deal of time to build up to what you see here.' His smile returned. 'But there'll be time to talk about that later. Right now, I see you standing there trying to figure out exactly when it was we met.'

Actually, Han had forgotten about Sena's references to a previous meeting. 'Tell you the truth, I haven't got a clue,' he confessed. 'Unless it was after Anchoron and you were in disguise or something.'

Bel Iblis shook his head. 'No disguise; but it wasn't something I'd really expect you to remember. I'll give you a hint: you were all of eleven at the time.'

Han blinked. 'Eleven?' he echoed. 'You mean in school?'

'Correct,' Bel Iblis nodded. 'Literally correct, in fact. It was at a convocation at your school, where you were being forced to listen to a group of us old fossils talk about politics.'

Han felt his face warming. The specific memory was still a blank, but that *was* how he'd felt about politicians at that time in his life. Though come to think of it, the opinion hadn't changed all that much over the years. 'I'm sorry, but I still don't remember.'

'As I said, I didn't expect you to,' Bel Iblis said. 'I, on the other hand, remember the incident quite well. During the question period after the talk you asked two irreverently phrased yet highly pointed questions: the first regarding the ethics of the anti-alien bias starting to creep into the legal structure of the Republic, the second about some very specific instances of corruption involving my colleagues in the Senate.'

It was starting to come back, at least in a vague sort of way. 'Yeah, I remember now,' Han said slowly. 'I think one of my friends dared me to throw those questions at you. He probably figured I'd get in trouble for not being polite. I was in trouble enough that it didn't bother me.'

'Setting your life pattern early, were you?' Bel Iblis suggested dryly. 'At any rate, they weren't the sort of questions I would have expected from an eleven-year-old, and they intrigued me enough to ask about you. I've been keeping a somewhat loose eye on you ever since.'

Han grimaced. 'You probably weren't very impressed by what you saw.'

'There were times,' Bel Iblis agreed. 'I'll admit to having been extremely disappointed when you were dismissed from the Imperial Academy – you'd shown considerable promise there, and I felt at the time that a strongly loyal officer corps was one of the few defenses the Republic still had left against the collapse toward Empire.' He shrugged. 'Under the circumstances, it's just as well that you got out when you did. With your obvious disdain for authority, you'd have been quietly eliminated in the Emperor's purge of those officers he hadn't been able to seduce to his side. And then things would have gone quite differently, wouldn't they?'

'Maybe a little,' Han conceded modestly. He glanced around the war room. 'So how long have you been here at – you called it Peregrine's Nest?'

'Oh, we never stay anywhere for very long,' Bel Iblis said, clapping a hand on Han's shoulder and gently but firmly turning him toward the door. 'Sit still too long and the Imperials will eventually find you. But we can talk business later. Right now, your friend outside is probably getting nervous. Come introduce me to him.'

Lando was indeed looking a little tense as Han and Bel Iblis stepped out into the sunlight again. 'It's all right,' Han assured him. 'We're with friends. Senator, this is Lando Calrissian, one-time general of the Rebel Alliance. Lando; Senator Garm Bel Iblis.'

He hadn't expected Lando to recognize the name of a long-past Corellian politician. He was right. 'Senator Bel Iblis,' Lando nodded, his voice neutral.

'Honored to meet you, General Calrissian,' Bel Iblis said. 'I've heard a great deal about you.'

Lando glanced at Han. 'Just Calrissian,' he said. 'The *General* is more a courtesy title now.'

'Then we're even,' Bel Iblis smiled. 'I'm not a Senator any more, either.' He waved a hand at Sena. 'You've met my chief adviser and unofficial ambassador-at-large, Sena Leikvold Midanyl. And—' He paused, looking around. 'I understood Irenez was with you.'

'She was needed back at the ship, sir,' Sena told him. 'Our other guest required some soothing.'

'Yes; Council-Aide Breil'lya,' Bel Iblis said, glancing in the direction of the landing pad. 'This could prove somewhat awkward.'

'Yes, sir,' Sena said. 'Perhaps I shouldn't have brought him here, but at the time I didn't see any other reasonable course of action.'

'Oh, I agree,' Bel Iblis assured her. 'Leaving him in the middle of an Imperial raid would have been more than simply awkward.'

Han felt a slight chill run through him. In the flush of excitement over meeting Bel Iblis, he'd completely forgotten what had taken them to New Cov in the first place. 'You seem to be on good terms with Breil'lya, Senator,' he said carefully.

Bel Iblis eyed him. 'And you'd like to know just what those good terms entail?'

Han steeled himself. 'As a matter of fact, sir . . . yes, I would.'

The other smiled slightly. 'You still have that underlying refusal to flinch before authority, don't you. Good. Come on over to the headquarters lounge and I'll tell you anything you want to know.' His smile hardened, just a little. 'And after that, I'll have some questions to ask you, as well.'

The door slid open, and Pellaeon stepped into the darkened antechamber of Thrawn's private command room. Darkened and apparently empty; but Pellaeon knew better than that. 'I have important information for the Grand Admiral,' he said loudly. 'I don't have time for these little games of yours.'

'They are not games,' Rukh's gravelly voice mewed

right in Pellaeon's ear, making him jump despite his best efforts not to. 'Stalking skills must be practiced or lost.'

'Practice on someone else,' Pellaeon growled. 'I have work to do.'

He stepped foward to the inner door, silently cursing Rukh and the whole Noghri race. Useful tools of the Empire they might well be; but he'd dealt with this kind of close-knit clan structure before, and he'd never found such primitives to be anything but trouble in the long run. The door to the command room slid open—

Revealing a darkness lit only by softly glowing candles.

Pellaeon stopped abruptly, his mind flashing back to that eerie crypt on Wayland, where a thousand candles marked the graves of offworlders who had come there over the past few years, only to be slaughtered by Joruus C'baoth. For Thrawn to have turned his command room into a duplicate of that . . .

'No, I haven't come under the influence of our unstable Jedi Master,' Thrawn's voice came dryly across the room. Over the candles, Pellaeon could just see the Grand Admiral's glowing red eyes. 'Look closer.'

Pellaeon did as instructed, to discover that the 'candles' were in fact holographic images of exquisitely delicate lighted sculptures. 'Beautiful, aren't they?' Thrawn said, his voice meditative. 'They're Corellian flame miniatures, one of that very short list of art forms which others have tried to copy but never truly been able to duplicate. Nothing more than shaped transoptical fibers, pseudoluminescent plant material, and a pair of Goorlish light sources, really; and yet, somehow, there's something about them that's never been captured by anyone else.'

The holographic flames faded away, and in the center of the room a frozen image of three Dreadnaught cruisers appeared. 'This was taken by the *Relentless* two days ago off the planet New Cov, Captain,' Thrawn continued in the same thoughtful tone. 'Watch closely.'

He started the recording. Pellaeon watched in silence as the Dreadnaughts, in triangular formation, opened fire with ion cannons toward the camera's point of view. Almost hidden in the fury of the assault, a freighter and what looked like a small pleasure yacht could be seen skittering to safety down the middle of the formation. Still firing, the Dreadnaughts began drawing back, and a minute later the whole group had jumped to lightspeed. The holo faded away, and the room lights came up to a gentle glow. 'Comments?' Thrawn invited.

'Looks like our old friends are back,' Pellaeon said. 'They seem to have recovered from that scare we gave them at Linuri. A nuisance, especially right now.'

'Unfortunately, indications are that they're about to become more than just a nuisance,' Thrawn told him. 'One of the two ships they were rescuing was identified by the *Relentless* as the *Lady Luck*. With Han Solo and Lando Calrissian aboard.' Pellaeon frowned. 'Solo and Calrissian? But—' He broke off sharply.

'But they were supposed to go to the Palanhi system,' Thrawn finished for him. 'Yes. An error on my part. Obviously, something more important came up than their concerns for Ackbar's reputation.'

Pellaeon looked back at where the holo had been. 'Such as adding new strength to the Rebellion military.'

'I don't believe they've merged quite yet,' Thrawn said, his forehead furrowed with thought. 'Nor do I believe

such an alliance is inevitable. That was a Corellian leading that task force, Captain – I'm sure of that now. And
there are only a few possibilities as to just who that Corellian might be.'

A stray memory clicked. 'Solo is Corellian, isn't he?'

'Yes,' Thrawn confirmed. 'One reason I think they're
still in the negotiation stage. If their leader is who I suspect, he might well prefer sounding out a fellow Corellian
before making any commitment to the Rebellion's
leaders.'

To Thrawn's left, the comm pinged. 'Admiral Thrawn?
We have the contact you requested with the *Relentless*.'

'Thank you,' Thrawn said, tapping a switch. In front
of the double circle of repeater displays a three-quarter-
sized hologram of an elderly Imperial officer appeared,
standing next to what appeared to be a detention block
control board. 'Grand Admiral,' the image said, nodding
gravely.

'Good day, Captain Dorja,' Thrawn nodded back.
'You have the prisoner I asked for?'

'Right here, sir,' Dorja said. He glanced to the side and
gestured; and from off-camera a rather bulky human
appeared, his hands shackled in front of him, his expression studiously neutral behind his neatly trimmed beard.
'His name's Niles Ferrier,' Dorja said. 'We picked him
and his crew up during the raid on New Cov.'

'The raid from which Skywalker, Solo and Calrissian
escaped,' Thrawn said.

Dorja winced. 'Yes, sir.'

Thrawn shifted his attention to Ferrier. 'Captain Ferrier,' he nodded. 'Our records indicate that you specialize
in spaceship theft. Yet you were picked up on New Cov

with a cargo of biomolecules aboard your ship. Would you care to explain?'

Ferrier shrugged fractionally. 'Palming ships isn't something you can do every day,' he said. 'It takes opportunities and planning. Taking the occasional shipping job helps make ends meet.'

'You're aware, of course, that the biomolecules were undeclared.'

'Yes, Captain Dorja told me that,' Ferrier said with just the right mixture of astonishment and indignation. 'Believe me, if I'd known I was being made a party to such cheating against the Empire—'

'I presume you're also aware,' Thrawn cut him off, 'that for such actions I can not only confiscate your cargo, but also your ship.'

Ferrier was aware of that, all right. Pellaeon could see it in the pinched look around his eyes. 'I've been very helpful to the Empire in the past, Admiral,' he said evenly. 'I've smuggled in loads of contraband from the New Republic, and only recently delivered three Sienar patrol ships to your people.'

'And were paid outrageous sums of money in all cases,' Thrawn reminded him. 'If you're trying to suggest we owe you for past kindnesses, don't bother. However . . . there may be a way for you to pay back this new debt. Did you happen to notice the ships attacking the *Relentless* as you were trying to sneak away from the planet?'

'Of course I did,' Ferrier said, a touch of wounded professional pride creeping into his voice. 'They were Rendili StarDrive Dreadnaughts. Old ones, by the look of them, but spry enough. Probably undergone a lot of refitting.'

'They have indeed.' Thrawn smiled slightly. 'I want them.'

It took Ferrier a handful of seconds for the offhanded sounding comment to register. When it did, his mouth dropped open. 'You mean . . . *me*?'

'Do you have a problem with that?' Thrawn asked coldly.

'Uh . . .' Ferrier swallowed. 'Admiral, with all due respect—'

'You have three standard months to get me either those ships or else their precise location,' Thrawn cut him off. 'Captain Dorja?'

Dorja stepped forward again. 'Sir.'

'You will release Captain Ferrier and his crew and supply them with an unmarked Intelligence freighter to use. Their own ship will remain aboard the *Relentless* until they've completed their mission.'

'Understood,' Dorja nodded.

Thrawn cocked an eyebrow. 'One other thing, Captain Ferrier. On the off chance that you might feel yourself tempted to abandon the assignment and make a run for it, the freighter you'll be given will be equipped with an impressive and totally unbreakable doomsday mechanism. With exactly three standard months set on its clock. I trust you understand.'

Above his beard, Ferrier's face had gone a rather sickly white. 'Yes,' he managed.

'Good.' Thrawn shifted his attention back to Dorja. 'I leave the details in your hands, Captain. Keep me informed of developments.'

He tapped a switch, and the hologram faded away. 'As I said, Captain,' Thrawn said, turning to Pellaeon, 'I don't think an alliance with the Rebellion is necessarily inevitable.'

'If Ferrier can pull it off,' Pellaeon said doubtfully.

'He has a reasonable chance,' Thrawn assured him. 'After all, we have a general idea ourselves of where they might be hidden. We just don't have the time and man-power at the moment to properly root them out. Even if we did, a large-scale attack would probably end up destroying the Dreadnaughts, and I'd rather capture them intact.'

'Yes, sir,' Pellaeon said grimly. The word *capture* had reminded him of why he'd come here in the first place. 'Admiral, the report on Khabarakh's ship has come in from the scanning team.' He held the data card over the double display circle.

For a moment Thrawn's glowing red eyes burned into Pellaeon's face, as if trying to read the reason for his sub-ordinate's obvious tension. Then, wordlessly, he took the data card from the captain's hand and slid it into his reader. Pellaeon waited, tightlipped, as the Grand Admiral skimmed the report.

Thrawn reached the end and leaned back in his seat, his face unreadable. 'Wookiee hairs,' he said.

'Yes, sir,' Pellaeon nodded. 'All over the ship.'

Thrawn was silent another few heartbeats. 'Your interpretation?'

Pellaeon braced himself. 'I can only see one, sir. Khabarakh didn't escape from the Wookiees on Kashy-yyk at all. They caught him . . . and then let him go.'

'After a month of imprisonment.' Thrawn looked up at Pellaeon. 'And interrogation.'

'Almost certainly,' Pellaeon agreed. 'The question is, what did he tell them?'

'There's one way to find out.' Thrawn tapped on the comm. 'Hangar bay, this is the Grand Admiral. Prepare my shuttle; I'm going to the surface. I'll want a troop shuttle and double squad of stormtroopers ready to accompany me, plus two flights of Scimitar assault bombers to provide air cover.'

He got an acknowledgement and keyed off. 'It may be, Captain, that the Noghri have forgotten where their loyalties lie,' he told Pellaeon, standing up and stepping out around the displays. 'I think it's time they were reminded that the Empire commands here. You'll return to the bridge and prepare a suitable demonstration.'

'Yes, sir.' Pellaeon hesitated. 'Do you want merely a reminder and not actual destruction?'

Thrawn's eyes blazed. 'For the moment, yes,' he said, his voice icy. 'Let them all pray that I don't change my mind.'

CHAPTER TWELVE

I t was the smell Leia noticed first as she drifted slowly awake: a smoky smell, reminiscent of the wood fires of the Ewoks of Endor but with a tangy sharpness all its own. A warm, homey sort of aroma, reminding her of the campouts she'd had as a child on Alderaan.

And then she woke up enough to remember where she was. Full consciousness flooded in, and she snapped open her eyes—

To find herself lying on a rough pallet in a corner of the Noghri communal bake house. Exactly where she'd been when she'd fallen asleep the night before.

She sat up, feeling relieved and a little ashamed. What with that unexpected visit last night by the Grand Admiral, she realized she'd half expected to wake up in a Star Destroyer detention cell. Clearly, she'd underestimated the Noghri's ability to stick by their promises.

Her stomach growled, reminding her it had been a long time since she'd eaten; a little lower down, one of the twins kicked a reminder of his own. 'OK,' she soothed. 'I get the hint. Breakfast time.'

She tore the top off a ration bar from one of her cases and took a bite, looking around the bake house as she chewed. Against the wall by the door, the double pallet that had been laid out for Chewbacca to sleep on was empty. For a moment the fear of betrayal again whispered to her; but a little concentration through the Force silenced any concerns. Chewbacca was somewhere nearby, with a sense that gave no indication of danger. *Relax*, she ordered herself sternly, pulling a fresh jumpsuit out of her case and starting to get dressed. Whatever these Noghri were, it was clear they weren't savages. They were honorable people, in their own way, and they wouldn't turn her over to the Empire. At least, not until they'd heard her out.

She downed the last bite of ration bar and finished dressing, making sure as always that her belt didn't hang too heavily across her increasingly swollen belly. Retrieving her lightsaber from its hiding place under the edge of the pallet, she fastened it prominently to her side. Khabarakh, she remembered, had seemed to find reassurance of her identity in the presence of the Jedi weapon; hopefully, the rest of the Noghri would also respond that way. Stepping to the bake house door, she ran through her Jedi calming exercises and went outside.

Three small Noghri children were playing with an inflatable ball in the grassy area outside the door, their grayish-white skin glistening with perspiration in the bright morning sunlight. A sunlight that wasn't going to last, Leia saw: a uniform layer of dark clouds extending all the way to the west was even now creeping its way east toward the rising sun. All for the best; a thick layer of clouds would block any direct telescopic observations the Star Destroyer up there might make of the village, as well as diffusing the non-Noghri infrared signatures she and Chewbacca were giving off.

She looked back down, to find that the three children had halted their game and formed a straight line in front of her. 'Hello,' she said, trying a smile on them.

The child in the middle stepped forward and dropped to his knees in an awkward but passable imitation of his elders' gesture of respect. '*Mal'ary'ush*,' he mewed. '*Miskh'ha'ra isf chrak'mi'sokh. Mir'es kha.*'

'I see,' Leia said, wishing fervently that she had Threepio with her. She was just wondering if she should risk calling him on the comlink when the child spoke again. 'Hai ghreet yhou, *Mal'ary'ush*,' he said, the Basic words coming out mangled but understandable. 'The maitrakh whaits for yhou hin the *dukha*.'

'Thank you,' Leia nodded gravely to him. Door wardens last night; official greeters this morning. Noghri children seemed to be introduced early into the rituals and responsibilities of their culture. 'Please escort me to her.'

The child made the respect gesture again and got back to his feet, heading off toward the large circular structure that Khabarakh had landed next to the night before. Leia followed, the other two children taking up positions to either side of her. She found herself throwing short glances at them as they walked, wondering at the light color of their skin. Khabarakh's skin was a steel gray; the maitrakh's had been much darker. Did the Noghri consist of several distinct racial types? Or was the darkening a natural part of their aging process? She made a mental note to ask Khabarakh about it when she had a chance.

The *dukha*, seen now in full daylight, was far more elaborate than she'd realized. The pillars spaced every few meters around the wall seemed to be composed of whole sections of tree trunk, stripped of bark and smoothed to a black marble finish. The shimmery wood that made up the rest of the wall was covered to perhaps half its height with intricate carvings. As they got closer, she could see that the reinforcing metal band that encircled the building just beneath the eaves was also decorated – clearly, the Noghri believed in combining function and art. The whole structure was perhaps twenty meters across and four meters high, with another three or four meters for the conical roof, and she found herself wondering how many more pillars they'd had to put inside to support the thing.

Tall double doors had been built into the wall between two of the pillars, flanked at the moment by two straight-backed Noghri children. They pulled open the doors as Leia approached; nodding her thanks, she stepped inside.

The interior of the *dukha* was no less impressive than its exterior. It was a single open room, with a thronelike chair two-thirds of the way to the back, a small booth with an angled roof and a dark-meshed window built against the wall between two of the pillars to the right, and a wall chart of some sort directly across from it on the left. There were no internal support pillars; instead, a series of heavy chains had been strung from the top of each of the wall pillars to the edge of a large concave dish hanging over the center of the room. From inside the dish – just inside its rim, Leia decided – hidden lights played upward against the ceiling, providing a softly diffuse illumination.

A few meters in front of the chart a group of perhaps twenty small children were sitting in a semicircle around Threepio, who was holding forth in their language with what was obviously some kind of story, complete with occasional sound effects. It brought to mind the condensed version of their struggle against the Empire that he'd given the Ewoks, and Leia hoped the droid would remember not to vilify Darth Vader here. Presumably he would; she'd drummed the point into him often enough during the voyage.

A small movement off to the left caught her eye: Chewbacca and Khabarakh were sitting facing each other on the other side of the door, engaged in some kind of quiet activity that seemed to involve hands and wrists. The Wookiee had paused and was looking questioningly in her direction. Leia nodded her assurance that she was all right, trying to read from his sense just what he and Khabarakh were doing. At least it didn't seem to involve ripping the Noghri's arms out of their sockets; that was something, anyway.

'Lady Vader,' a gravelly Noghri voice said. Leia turned back to see the maitrakh walking up to her. 'I greet you. You slept well?'

'Quite well,' Leia told her. 'Your hospitality has been most honorable.' She looked over at Threepio, wondering if she should call him back to his duties as translator.

The maitrakh misunderstood. 'It is the history time for the children,' she said. 'Your machine graciously volunteered to tell to them the last story of our lord Darth Vader.'

Vader's final, self-sacrificial defiance against the Emperor, with Luke's life hanging in the balance. 'Yes,' Leia murmured. 'It took until the end, but he was finally able to rid himself of the Emperor's web of deception.'

For a moment the maitrakh was silent. Then, she stirred. 'Walk with me, Lady Vader.'

She turned and began walking along the wall. Leia joined her, noticing for the first time that the *dukha*'s inner walls were decorated with carvings, too. A historical record of their family? 'My thirdson has gained a new respect for your Wookiee,' she said, gesturing toward Chewbacca and Khabarakh. 'Our lord the Grand Admiral came last eve seeking proof that my thirdson had deceived him about his flying craft being broken. Because of your Wookiee, he found no such proof.'

Leia nodded. 'Yes, Chewie told me last night about gimmicking the ship. I don't have his knowledge of spaceship mechanics, but I know it can't be easy to fake a pair of linked malfunctions the way he did. It's fortunate for all of us he had the foresight and skill to do so.'

'The Wookiee is not of your family or clan,' the maitrakh said. 'Yet you trust him, as if he were a friend?'

Leia took a deep breath. 'I never knew my true father, the Lord Vader, as I was growing up. I was instead taken to Alderaan and raised by the Viceroy as if I were his own child. On Alderaan, as seems to also be the case here, family relationships were the basis of our culture and society. I grew up memorizing lists of aunts and uncles and cousins, learning how to place them in order of closeness to my adoptive line.' She gestured to Chewbacca. 'Chewie was once merely a good friend. Now, he is part of my family. As much a part as my husband and brother are.'

They were perhaps a quarter of the way around the *dukha* before the maitrakh spoke again. 'Why have you come here?'

'Khabarakh told me his people needed help,' Leia said simply. 'I thought there might be something I could do.'

'Some will say you have come to sow discord among us.'

'You said that yourself last night,' Leia reminded her. 'I can only give you my word that discord is not my intention.'

The maitrakh made a long hissing sound that ended with a sharp double click of needle teeth. 'The goal and the end are not always the same, Lady Vader. Now we serve one overclan only. You would require service to another. This is the seed of discord and death.'

Leia pursed her lips. 'Does service to the Empire satisfy you, then?' she asked. 'Does it gain your people better life or higher honor?'

'We serve the Empire as one clan,' the maitrakh said. 'For you to demand our service would be to bring back the conflicts of old.' They had reached the wall chart now, and she gestured a thin hand up toward it. 'Do you see our history, Lady Vader?'

Leia craned her neck to look. Neatly carved lines of alien script covered the bottom two-thirds of the wall, with each word connected to a dozen others in a bewildering crisscross of vertical, horizontal, and angled lines, each cut seemingly of a different width and depth. Then she got it: the chart was a genealogical tree, either of the entire clan Kihm'bar or else just this particular family. 'I see it,' she said.

'Then you see the terrible destruction of life created by the conflicts of old,' the maitrakh said. She gestured to three or four places on the chart which were, to Leia, indistinguishable from the rest of the design. Reading Noghri genealogies was apparently an acquired skill. 'I do not wish to return to those days,' the maitrakh continued. 'Not even for the daughter of the Lord Darth Vader.'

'I understand,' Leia said quietly, shivering as the ghosts of Yavin, Hoth, Endor, and a hundred more rose up before her. 'I've seen more conflict and death in my lifetime than I ever thought possible. I have no wish to add to the list.'

'Then you must leave,' the maitrakh said firmly. 'You must leave and not come back while the Empire lives.'

They began to walk again. 'Is there no alternative?' Leia asked. 'What if I could persuade all of your people to leave their service to the Empire? There would be no conflict then among you.'

'The Emperor aided us when no-one else would,' the maitrakh reminded her.

'That was only because we didn't know about your need,' Leia said, feeling a twinge of conscience at the half truth. Yes, the Alliance had truly not known about the desperate situation here; and yes, Mon Mothma and the other leaders would certainly have wanted to help if they had. But whether they would have had the resources to actually do anything was another question entirely. 'We know now, and we offer you our help.'

'Do you offer us aid for our own sakes?' the maitrakh asked pointedly. 'Or merely to wrest our service from the Empire to your overclan? We will not be fought over like a bone among hungry *stava*.'

'The Emperor used you,' Leia said flatly. 'As the Grand Admiral uses you now. Has the aid they've given been worth the sons they've taken from you and sent off to die?'

They had gone another twenty steps or so before the maitrakh answered. 'Our sons have gone,' she said softly. 'But with their service they have bought us life. You came in a flying craft, Lady Vader. You saw what was done to our land.'

'Yes,' Leia said with a shiver. 'It – I hadn't realized how widespread the destruction had been.'

'Life on Honoghr has always been a struggle,' the maitrakh said. 'The land has required much labor to tame. You saw on the history the times when the struggle was lost. But after the battle in the sky . . .'

She shuddered, a peculiar kind of shaking that seemed to move from her hips upward to her shoulders. 'It was like a war between gods. We know now that it was only large flying craft high above the land. But then we knew nothing of such things. Their lightning flashed across the sky, through the night and into the next day, brightening the distant mountains with their fury. And yet, there was no thunder, as if those same gods were too angry even to shout at each other as they fought. I remember being more frightened of the silence than of any other part of it. Only once was there a distant crash like thunder. It was much later before we learned that one of our higher mountains had lost its uppermost peak. Then the lightning stopped, and we dared to hope that the gods had taken their war away from us.

'Until the groundshake came.'

She paused, another shudder running through her. 'The lightning had been the anger of the gods. The groundshake was their war hammer. Whole cities vanished as the ground opened up beneath them. Fire-mountains that had been long quiet sent out flame and smoke that darkened the sky over all the land. Forests and fields burned, as did cities and villages that had survived the groundshake itself. From those who had died came sickness, and still more died after them. It was as if the fury of the sky gods had come among the gods of the land, and they too were fighting among themselves.

'And then, when finally we dared to hope it was over, the strange-smelling rain began to fall.'

Leia nodded, the whole sequence of events painfully clear. One of the warring ships had crashed, setting off massive earthquakes and releasing toxic chemicals which had been carried by wind and rain to every part of the planet. There were any number of such chemicals in use aboard a modern warship, but it was only the older ships that carried anything as virulent as this chemical must have been.

Older ships . . . which had been virtually all the Rebel Alliance had had to fight with in the beginning.

A fresh surge of guilt twisted like a blade in her stomach. *We did this*, she thought miserably. *Our ship. Our fault.* 'Was it the rain that killed the plants?'

'The Empire's people had a name for what was in the rain,' the maitrakh said. 'I do not know what it was.'

'They came soon after the disaster, then. The Lord Vader and the others.'

'Yes.' The maitrakh waved her hands to encompass the area around them. 'We had gathered together here, all who were left alive and could make the journey. This place had always been a truce ground between clans. We had come here to try to find a way for survival. It was here that the Lord Vader found us.'

They walked in silence for another minute. 'Some believed then that he was a god,' the maitrakh said. 'All feared him and the mighty silver flying craft that had brought him and his attendants from the sky. But even amid the fear there was anger at what the gods had done to us, and nearly two tens of warriors chose to attack.'

'And were duly slaughtered,' Leia said grimly. The thought of effectively unarmed primitives taking on Imperial troops made her wince.

'They were not slaughtered,' the maitrakh retorted, and there was no mistaking the pride in her voice. 'Only three of the two tens died in the battle. In turn, they killed many of the Lord Vader's attendants, despite their lightning-weapons and rock-garments. It was only when the Lord Vader himself intervened that the warriors were defeated. But instead of destroying us, as some of the attendants counseled, he instead offered us peace. Peace, and the blessing and aid of the Emperor.'

Leia nodded, one more piece of the puzzle falling into place. She had wondered why the Emperor would have bothered with what to him would have been nothing more than a tiny group of primitive nonhumans. But primitive nonhumans with that kind of natural fighting skill were something else entirely. 'What sort of aid did he bring?'

'All that we needed,' the maitrakh said. 'Food and medicine and tools came at once. Later, when the strange rain began to kill our crops, he sent the metal droids to begin cleaning the poison from our land.'

Leia winced, freshly aware of her twins' vulnerability. But the analysis kit had found no trace of anything toxic in the air as they approached the village, and Chewbacca and Khabarakh had done similar tests on the soil. Whatever it was that had been in the rain, the decon droids had done a good job of getting rid of it. 'And still nothing will grow outside the cleaned land?'

'Only the *kholm*-grass,' the maitrakh said. 'It is a poor plant, of no use as food. But it alone can grow now, and even it no longer smells as it once did.'

Which explained the uniform brown color that she and Chewbacca had seen from space. Somehow, that particular plant had adapted to the toxic soil. 'Did any of the animals survive?' she asked.

'Some did. Those who could eat the *kholm-grass*, and those which in turn ate them. But they are few.'

The maitrakh lifted her head, as if looking in her mind's eye toward the distant hills. 'This place was never rich with life, Lady Vader. Perhaps that was why the clans had chosen it as a truce ground. But even in so desolate a place there were still animals and plants without count. They are gone now.'

She straightened up, visibly putting the memory behind her. 'The Lord Vader helped us in other ways, as well. He sent attendants to teach our sons and daughters the ways and customs of the Empire. He issued new orders to allow all clans to share the Clean Land, though for all clans to live beside one another this way had never happened since the beginning.' She gestured around her. 'And he sent mighty flying craft into the desolation, to find and bring to us our clan *dukhas*.'

She turned her dark eyes to gaze at Leia. 'We have an honorable peace, Lady Vader. Whatever the cost, we pay it gladly.'

Across the room, the children had apparently finished their lesson and were getting to their feet. One of them spoke to Threepio, making a sort of truncated version of their facedown bow. The droid replied, and the whole group turned and headed for the door, where two adults awaited them. 'Break time?' Leia asked.

'The clan lessons are over for today,' the maitrakh said. 'The children must now begin their share of the work of the village. Later, in the evening, they will have the lessons which will equip them to someday serve the Empire.'

Leia shook her head. 'It's not right,' she told the maitrakh as the children filed out of the *dukha*. 'No people should have to sell their children in return for life.'

The maitrakh gave a long hiss. 'It is the debt we owe,' she said. 'How else shall we pay it?'

Leia squeezed her thumb and forefinger together. How else, indeed? Clearly, the Empire was quite happy with the bargain it had made; and having seen the Noghri commandos in action, she could well understand its satisfaction. They wouldn't be interested in letting the Noghri buy out of their debt in any other way. And if the Noghri themselves considered their service to be a debt of honor to their saviors ... 'I don't know,' she had to concede.

A movement to the side caught her attention: Khabarakh, still sitting on the floor across the room, had fallen over onto his side, with Chewbacca's hand engulfing his wrist. It looked like fighting, except that Chewbacca's sense didn't indicate anger. 'What *are* they doing over there?' she asked.

'Your Wookiee has asked my thirdson to instruct him in our fighting methods,' the maitrakh answered, pride again touching her voice. 'Wookiees have great strength, but no knowledge of the subtlety of combat.'

It was probably not an assessment the Wookiees themselves would have agreed with. But Leia had to admit that Chewbacca, at least, had always seemed to rely mainly on brute force and bowcaster accuracy. 'I'm surprised he was willing to have Khabarakh teach him,' she said. 'He's never really trusted him.'

'Perhaps it is that same distrust that whets his interest,' the maitrakh said dryly.

Leia had to smile. 'Perhaps.'

For a minute they watched in silence as Khabarakh showed Chewbacca two more wrist and arm locks. They seemed to be variants of techniques Leia had learned in her youth on Alderaan, and she shivered once at the thought of those moves with Wookiee muscle behind them. 'You understand the cycle of our life now, Lady Vader,' the maitrakh said quietly. 'You must realize that we still hang by spider silk. Even now we do not have enough clean land to grow sufficient food. We must continue to buy from the Empire.'

'Payment for which requires that much more service from your sons.' Leia nodded, grimacing. Permanent debt – the oldest form of covert slavery in the galaxy.

'It also encourages the sending away of our sons,' the maitrakh added bitterly. 'Even if the Empire allowed it, we could not now bring all our sons home. We would not have food for them.'

Leia nodded again. It was as neat and tidy a box as she'd ever seen anyone trapped in. She should have expected no less from Vader and the Emperor. 'You'll never be entirely out of their debt,' she told the maitrakh bluntly. 'You know that, don't you? As long as you're useful to them, the Grand Admiral will make sure of that.'

'Yes,' the maitrakh said softly. 'It has taken a long time, but I now believe that. If all Noghri believed so, changes could perhaps be made.'

'But the rest of the Noghri still believe the Empire is their friend?'

'Not all believe so. But enough.' She stopped and gestured upward. 'Do you see the starlight, Lady Vader?'

Leia looked up at the concave dish that hung four meters off the ground at the intersection of the wall support chains. About a meter and a half across, it was composed of some kind of black or blackened metal and perforated with hundreds of tiny pinholes. With the light from the inside rim of the dish winking through like stars, the whole effect was remarkably like a stylized version of the night sky. 'I see it.'

'The Noghri have always loved the stars,' the maitrakh said, her voice distant and reflective. 'Once, long ago, we worshiped them. Even after we knew what they were they remained our friends. There were many among us who would have gladly gone with the Lord Vader, even without our debt, for the joy of traveling among them.'

'I understand,' Leia murmured. 'Many in the galaxy feel the same way. It's the common birthright of us all.'

'A birthright which we have now lost.'

'Not lost,' Leia said, dropping her gaze from the star dish. 'Only misplaced.' She looked over at Khabarakh and Chewbacca. 'Perhaps if I talked to all the Noghri leaders at once.'

'What would you say to them?' the maitrakh countered.

Leia bit at her lip. What *would* she say? That the

Empire was using them? But the Noghri perceived it as a debt of honor. That the Empire was pacing the cleanup job so as to keep them on the edge of self-sufficiency without ever reaching it? But at the rate the decontamination was going she would be hard-pressed to prove any such lagging, even to herself. That she and the New Republic could give the Noghri back their birthright? But why should they believe her?

'As you see, Lady Vader,' the maitrakh said into the silence. 'Perhaps matters will someday change. But until then, your presence here is a danger to us as much as to you. I will honor the pledge of protection made by my thirdson, and not reveal your presence to our lord the Grand Admiral. But you must leave.'

Leia took a deep breath. 'Yes,' she said, the word hurting her throat. She'd had such hopes for her diplomatic and Jedi skills here. Hopes that those skills, plus the accident of her lineage, would enable her to sweep the Noghri out from under the Empire's fist and bring them over to the New Republic.

And now the contest was over, almost before it had even begun. *What in space was I thinking about when I came here?* she wondered bleakly. 'I will leave,' she said aloud, 'because I don't wish to bring trouble to you or your family. But the day will come, maitrakh, when your people will see for themselves what the Empire is doing to them. When that happens, remember that I'll always be ready to assist you.'

The maitrakh bowed low. 'Perhaps that day will come soon, Lady Vader. I await it, as do others.'

Leia nodded, forcing a smile. Over before it had begun . . . 'Then we must make arrangements to—'

She broke off as, across the room, the double doors flew open and one of the child door wardens stumbled inside. '*Maitrakh!*' he all but squealed. '*Mira'kh saar khee hrach'mani vher ahk!*'

Khabarakh was on his feet in an instant; out of the corner of her eye, Leia saw Threepio stiffen. 'What is it?' she demanded.

'It is the flying craft of our lord the Grand Admiral,' the maitrakh said, her face and voice suddenly very tired and very alien.

'And it is coming here.'

CHAPTER THIRTEEN

For a single heartbeat Leia stared at the maitrakh, her muscles frozen with shock, her mind skidding against the idea as if walking on ice. No – it couldn't be. It *couldn't*. The Grand Admiral had been here just last night – surely he wouldn't be coming back again. Not so soon.

And then, in the distance, she heard the faint sound of approaching repulsorlifts, and the paralysis vanished. 'We've got to get out of here,' she said. 'Chewie—?'

'There is no time,' Khabarakh called, sprinting toward them with Chewbacca right on his heels. 'The shuttle must already be in sight beneath the clouds.'

Leia looked quickly around the room, silently cursing her moment of indecision. No windows; no other doors; no cover except the small booth that faced the wall genealogy chart from across the *dukha*.

No way out.

'Are you certain he's coming here?' Leia asked Khabarakh, realizing as she spoke that the question was a waste of breath. 'Here to the *dukha*, I mean?'

'Where else would he come?' Khabarakh countered darkly, his eyes on the maitrakh. 'Perhaps he was not fooled, as we thought.'

Leia looked around the *dukha* again. If the shuttle landed by the double doors, there would be a few seconds before the Imperials entered when the rear of the building would be out of their view. If she used those seconds to cut them an escape hole with her lightsaber . . .

Chewbacca's growled suggestion echoed her own train of thought. 'Yes, but cutting a hole isn't the problem,' she pointed out. 'It's how to seal it up afterward.'

The Wookiee growled again, jabbing a massive hand toward the booth. 'Well, it'll hide the hole from the inside, anyway,' Leia agreed doubtfully. 'I suppose that's better than nothing.' She looked at the maitrakh, suddenly aware that slicing away part of their ancient clan *dukha* might well qualify as sacrilege. 'Maitrakh—'

'If it must be done, then be it so,' the Noghri cut her off harshly. She was still in shock herself; but even as Leia watched she visibly drew herself together again. 'You must not be found here.'

Leia bit at the inside of her lip. She'd seen that same expression several times on Khabarakh's face during the trip from Endor. It was a look she'd come to interpret as regret for his decision to bring her to his home. 'We'll be as neat as possible,' she assured the maitrakh, pulling her lightsaber from her belt. 'And as soon as the Grand Admiral is gone, Khabarakh can get his ship back and take us away—'

She broke off as Chewbacca snarled for silence. Faintly, in the distance, they could hear the sound of the approaching shuttle; and then, suddenly, another all-too-familiar whine shot past the *dukha*.

'Scimitar assault bombers,' Leia breathed, hearing in the whine the crumbling of her impromptu plan. With

Imperial bombers flying cover overhead, it would be impossible for them to sneak out of the *dukha* without being spotted.

Which left them only one option. 'We'll have to hide in the booth,' she told Chewbacca, doing a quick estimation of its size as she hurried toward it. If the slanting roof that sloped upward from the front edge back to the *dukha* wall wasn't just for show, there should be barely enough room for both her and Chewbacca inside—

'Will you want me in there as well, Your Highness?'

Leia skidded to a halt, spinning around in shock and chagrin. Threepio – she'd forgotten all about him.

'There will not be room enough,' the maitrakh hissed. 'Your presence here has betrayed us, Lady Vader—'

'Quiet!' Leia snapped, throwing another desperate look around the *dukha*. But there was still no other place to hide.

Unless . . .

She looked at the star dish hanging over the middle of the room. 'We'll have to put him up there,' she told Chewbacca, pointing to it. 'Do you think you can—?'

There was no need to finish the question. Chewbacca had already grabbed Threepio and was heading at top speed toward the nearest of the tree-trunk pillars, throwing the frantically protesting droid over his shoulder as he ran. The Wookiee leaped upward at the pillar from two meters out, his hidden climbing claws anchoring him solidly to the wood. Three quick pulls got him to the top of the wall; and, with the half hysterical droid balanced precariously, he began to race hand over hand along the chain. 'Quiet, Threepio,' Leia called to him from the booth door, giving the interior a quick look. The ceiling did indeed follow the slanting roof, giving the back of the booth considerably more height than the front, and there was a low benchlike seat across the back wall. A tight fit, but they should make it. 'Better yet, shut down – they may have sensors going,' she added.

Though if they did, the whole game was over already. Listening to the approaching whine of repulsorlifts, she could only hope that after the negative sensor scan from the previous night, they wouldn't bother doing another one.

Chewbacca had reached the center now. Pulling himself partway up on the chain with one hand, he unceremoniously dumped Threepio into the star dish. The droid gave one last screech of protest, a screech that broke off halfway through as the Wookiee reached into the dish and shut him off. Dropping back to the floor with a thud, he hit the ground running as the repulsorlifts outside went silent.

'Hurry!' Leia hissed, holding the door open for him. Chewbacca made it across the *dukha* and dived through the narrow opening, jumping up on the bench and turning around to face forward, his head jammed up against the sloping ceiling and his legs spread to both sides of the bench. Leia slid in behind him, sitting down in the narrow gap between the Wookiee's legs.

There was just enough time to ease the door closed before the double doors a quarter of the way around the *dukha* slammed open.

Leia pressed against the back wall of the booth and Chewbacca's legs, forcing herself to breathe slowly and quietly and running through the Jedi sensory enhancement techniques Luke had taught her. From above her

Chewbacca's breathing rasped in her ears, the heat from his body flowing like an invisible waterfall onto her head and shoulders. She was suddenly and acutely aware of the weight and bulge of her belly and of the small movements of the twins within it; of the hardness of the bench she was sitting on; of the intermingling smells of Wookiee hair, the alien wood around her, and her own sweat. Behind her, through the wall of the *dukha*, she could hear the sound of purposeful footsteps and the occasional clink of laser rifles against stormtrooper armor, and said silent thanks that they'd scrubbed her earlier plan of trying to escape that way.

And from the inside of the *dukha*, she could hear voices.

'Good morning, maitrakh,' a calm, coolly modulated voice said. 'I see that your thirdson, Khabarakh, is here with you. How very convenient.'

Leia shivered, the rough rubbing of her tunic against her skin horribly loud in her ears. That voice had the unmistakable tone of an Imperial commander, but with a calmness and sheer weight of authority behind it. An authority that surpassed even the smug condescension she'd faced from Governor Tarkin aboard the Death Star.

It could only be the Grand Admiral.

'I greet you, my lord,' the maitrakh's voice mewed, her own tone rigidly controlled. 'We are honored by your visit.'

'Thank you,' the Grand Admiral said, his tone still polite but with a new edge of steel beneath it. 'And you, Khabarakh clan Kihm'bar. Are you also pleased at my presence here?'

Slowly, carefully, Leia eased her head to the right,

hoping to get a look at the newcomer through the dark mesh of the booth window. No good; they were all still over by the double doors, and she didn't dare get her face too close to the mesh. But even as she eased back to her previous position there was the sound of measured footsteps . . . and a moment later, in the center of the *dukha*, the Grand Admiral came into view.

Leia stared at him through the mesh, an icy chill running straight through her. She'd heard Han's description of the man he'd seen on Myrkr – the pale blue skin, the glowing red eyes, the white Imperial uniform. She'd heard, too, Fey'lya's casual dismissal of the man as an impostor, or at best a self-promoted Moff. And she'd wondered privately if Han might indeed have been mistaken.

She knew now that he hadn't been.

'Of course, my lord,' Khabarakh answered the Grand Admiral's question. 'Why should I not be?'

'Do you speak to your lord the Grand Admiral in such a tone?' an unfamiliar Noghri voice demanded.

'I apologize,' Khabarakh said. 'I did not mean disrespect.'

Leia winced. Undoubtedly not; but the damage was already done. Even with her relative inexperience of the subtleties of Noghri speech, the words had sounded too quick and too defensive. To the Grand Admiral, who knew this race far better than she did . . .

'What then *did* you mean?' the Grand Admiral asked, turning around to face Khabarakh and the maitrakh.

'I—' Khabarakh floundered. The Grand Admiral stood silently, waiting. 'I am sorry, my lord,' Khabarakh finally got out. 'I was overawed by your visit to our simple village.'

'An obvious excuse,' the Grand Admiral said. 'Possibly even a believable one ... except that you weren't over-awed by my visit last night.' He cocked an eyebrow. 'Or is it that you didn't expect to face me again so soon?'

'My lord—'

'What is the Noghri penalty for lying to the lord of your overclan?' the Grand Admiral interrupted, his cool voice suddenly harsh. 'Is it death, as it was in the old days? Or do the Noghri no longer prize such outdated concepts as honor?'

'My lord has no right to bring such accusations against a son of the clan Kihm'bar,' the maitrakh spoke up stiffly.

The Grand Admiral shifted his gaze slightly. 'You would be well advised to keep your counsel to yourself, maitrakh. This particular son of the clan Kihm'bar has lied to me, and I do not take such matters lightly.' The glowing gaze shifted back. 'Tell me, Khabarakh clan Kihm'bar, about your imprisonment on Kashyyyk.'

Leia squeezed her lightsaber hard, the cool metal ridges of the grip biting into the palm of her hand. It had been during Khabarakh's brief imprisonment on Kashyyyk that he'd been persuaded to bring her here to Honoghr. If Khabarakh blurted out the whole story—

'I do not understand,' Khabarakh said.

'Really?' the Grand Admiral countered. 'Then allow me to refresh your memory. You didn't escape from Kashyyyk as you stated in your report and repeated last night in my presence and in the presence of your family and your clan dynast. You were, in fact, captured by the Wookiees after the failure of your mission. And you spent that missing month not meditating, but undergoing interrogation in a Wookiee prison. Does that help your memory any?'

Leia took a careful breath, not daring to believe what she was hearing. However it was the Grand Admiral had learned about Khabarakh's capture, he'd taken that fact and run in exactly the wrong direction with it. They'd been given a second chance . . . if Khabarakh could hold on to his wits and poise a little longer.

Perhaps the maitrakh didn't trust his stamina, either. 'My thirdson would not lie about such matters, my lord,' she said before Khabarakh could reply. 'He has always understood the duties and requirement of honor.'

'Has he, now,' the Grand Admiral shot back. 'A Noghri commando, captured by the enemy for interrogation – and still alive? Is this the duty and requirement of honor?'

'I was not captured, my lord,' Khabarakh said stiffly. 'My escape from Kashyyyk was as I said it.'

For a half dozen heartbeats the Grand Admiral gazed in his direction in silence. 'And I say that you lie, Khabarakh clan Kihm'bar,' he said softly. 'But no matter. With or without your cooperation I will have the truth about your missing month . . . and whatever the price was you paid for your freedom. Rukh?'

'My lord,' the third Noghri voice said.

'Khabarakh clan Kihm'bar is hereby placed under arrest. You and Squad Two will escort him aboard the troop shuttle and take him back to the *Chimaera* for interrogation.'

There was a sharp hiss. 'My lord, this is a violation—'

'You will be silent, maitrakh,' the Grand Admiral cut her off. 'Or you will share in his imprisonment.'

'I will not be silent,' the maitrakh snarled. 'A Noghri

accused of treason to the overclan must be given over to
the clan dynasts for the ancient rules of discovery and
judgement. It is the law.'

'I am not bound by Noghri law,' the Grand Admiral
said coldly. 'Khabarakh has been a traitor to the Empire.
By Imperial rules will he be judged and condemned.'

'The clan dynasts will demand—'

'The clan dynasts are in no position to demand anything,' the Grand Admiral barked, touching the comlink
cylinder pocketed beside his tunic insignia. 'Do you
require a reminder of what it means to defy the Empire?'

Leia heard the faint sound of the maitrakh's sigh. 'No,
my lord,' she said, her voice conceding defeat.

The Grand Admiral studied her. 'You shall have one
anyway.'

He touched his comlink again—

And abruptly the interior of the *dukha* flashed with a
blinding burst of green light.

Leia jerked her head back into Chewbacca's legs,
squeezing her eyelids shut against the sudden searing
pain ripping through her eyes and face. For a single, horrifying second she thought that the *dukha* had taken a
direct hit, a turbolaser blast powerful enough to bring
the whole structure down in flaming ruin around them.
But the afterimage burned into her retina showed the
Grand Admiral still standing proud and unmoved; and
belatedly she understood.

She was trying desperately to reverse her sensory
enhancement when the thunderclap slammed like the
slap of an angry Wookiee into the side of her head.

She would later have a vague recollection of several
more turbolaser blasts, seen and heard only dimly

through the thick gray haze that clouded over her mind, as the orbiting Star Destroyer fired again and again into the hills surrounding the village. By the time her throbbing head finally dragged her back to full consciousness the Grand Admiral's reminder was over, the final thunderclap roiling away into the distance.

Cautiously, she opened her eyes, squinting a little against the pain. The Grand Admiral was still standing where he'd been, in the center of the *dukha* . . . and as the last thunderclap faded into silence he spoke. '*I* am the law on Honoghr now, maitrakh,' he said, his voice quiet and deadly. 'If I choose to follow the ancient laws, I will follow them. If I choose to ignore them, they will be ignored. Is that clear?'

The voice, when it came, was almost too alien to recognize. If the purpose of the Grand Admiral's demonstration had been to frighten the maitrakh half out of her mind, it had clearly succeeded. 'Yes, my lord.'

'Good.' The Grand Admiral let the brittle silence hang in the air for another moment. 'For loyal servants of the Empire, however, I am prepared to make compromises. Khabarakh will be interrogated aboard the *Chimaera*; but before that, I will allow the first stage of the ancient laws of discovery.' His head turned slightly. 'Rukh, you will remove Khabarakh clan Kihm'bar to the center of Nystao and present him to the clan dynasts. Perhaps three days of public shaming will serve to remind the Noghri people that we are still at war.'

'Yes, my lord.'

There was the sound of footsteps, and the opening and closing of the double doors. Hunched against the ceiling above her, his sense in unreadable turmoil, Chewbacca rumbled softly to himself. Leia clenched her teeth, hard enough to send flashes of pain through her still throbbing head. Public shaming . . . and something called the laws of discovery.

The Rebel Alliance had unwittingly destroyed Honoghr. Now, it seemed, she was going to do the same to Khabarakh.

The Grand Admiral was still standing in the middle of the *dukha*. 'You are very quiet, maitrakh,' he said.

'My lord ordered me to be silent,' she countered.

'Of course.' He studied her. 'Loyalty to one's clan and family is all well and good, maitrakh. But to extend that loyalty to a traitor would be foolish. As well as potentially disastrous to your family and clan.'

'I have not heard evidence that my thirdson is a traitor.'

The Grand Admiral's lip twitched. 'You will,' he promised softly.

He walked toward the double doors, passing out of Leia's sight, and there was the sound of the doors opening. The footsteps paused, clearly waiting; and a moment later the quieter paces of the maitrakh joined him. Both left, the doors closed again, and Leia and Chewbacca were alone.

Alone. In enemy territory. Without a ship. And with their only ally about to undergo an Imperial interrogation. 'I think, Chewie,' she said softly, 'we're in trouble.'

CHAPTER FOURTEEN

One of the first minor truths about interstellar flight that any observant traveler learned was that a planet seen from space almost never looked anything at all like the official maps of it. Scatterings of cloud cover, shadows from mountain ranges, contour-altering effects of large vegetation tracts, and lighting tricks in general, all combined to disguise and distort the nice clean computer-scrubbed lines drawn by the cartographers. It was an effect that had probably caused a lot of bad moments for neophyte navigators, as well as supplying the ammunition for innumerable practical jokes played on those same neophytes by their more experienced shipmates.

It was therefore something of a surprise to find that, on this particular day and coming in from this particular angle, the major continent of the planet Jomark did indeed look almost exactly like a precisely detailed map. Of course, in all fairness, it was a pretty small continent to begin with.

Somewhere on that picture-perfect continent was a Jedi Master.

Luke tapped his fingers gently on the edge of his control board, gazing out at the greenish-brown chunk of land now framed in his X-wing's canopy. He could sense the other Jedi's presence – had been able to sense it, in fact, since first dropping out of hyperspace – but so far he'd been unable to make a more direct contact. *Master C'baoth?* he called silently, trying one more time. *This is Luke Skywalker. Can you hear me?*

There was no response. Either Luke wasn't doing it right, or C'baoth was unable to reply . . . or else this was a deliberate test of Luke's abilities.

Well, he was game. 'Let's do a sensor focus on the main continent, Artoo,' he called, looking over his displays and trying to put himself into the frame of mind of a Jedi Master who'd been out of circulation for a while. The bulk of Jomark's land area was in that one small continent – not much more than an oversized island, really – but there were also thousands of much smaller islands scattered in clusters around the vast ocean. Taken all together, there were probably close to three hundred thousand square kilometers of dry land, which made for an awful lot of places to guess wrong. 'Scan for technology, and see if you can pick out the main population centers.'

Artoo whistled softly to himself as he ran the X-wing's sensor readings through his programmed life-form algorithms. He gave a series of beeps, and a pattern of dots appeared superimposed on the scope image. 'Thanks,' Luke said, studying it. Not surprisingly, most of the population seemed to be living along the coast. But there were a handful of other, small centers in the interior, as well. Including what seemed to be a cluster of villages near the southern shore of an almost perfectly ring-shaped lake.

He frowned at the image, keyed for a contour overlay. It wasn't just an ordinary lake, he saw now, but one that had formed inside what was left of a cone-shaped mountain, with a smaller cone making a large island in the center. Probably volcanic in origin, given the mountainous terrain around it.

A wilderness region thick with mountains, where a Jedi Master could have lived in privacy for a long time. And a cluster of villages nearby where he could have emerged from his isolation when he was finally ready to do so.

It was as good a place to start as any. 'OK, Artoo, here's the landing target,' he told the droid, marking it on his scope. 'I'll take us down; you watch the sensors and let me know if you spot anything interesting.'

Artoo beeped a somewhat nervous question. 'Yes, or anything suspicious,' Luke agreed. Artoo had never fully believed that the Imperial attack on them the last time they'd tried to come here had been purely coincidence.

They dropped in through the atmosphere, switching to repulsorlifts about halfway down and leveling off just below the tops of the highest mountains. Seen up close, the territory was rugged enough but not nearly as desolate as Luke had first thought. Vegetation was rich down in the valley areas between mountains, though it was sparse on the rocky sides of the mountains themselves. Most of the gaps they flew over seemed to have at least a couple of houses nestled into them, and occasionally even a village that had been too small for the X-wing's limited sensors to notice.

They were coming up on the lake from the southwest when Artoo spotted the mansion perched up on the rim.

'Never seen a design like that before,' Luke commented. 'You getting any life readings from it?'

Artoo warbled a moment: inconclusive. 'Well, let's give it a try,' Luke decided, keying in the landing cycle. 'If we're wrong, at least it'll be a downhill walk to everywhere else.'

The mansion was set into a small courtyard bordered by a fence that appeared more suited for decoration than defense. Killing the X-wing's forward velocity, he swung the ship parallel to the fence and set it down a few meters outside its single gate. He was in the process of shutting down the systems when Artoo's trilled warning made him look up again.

Standing just outside the gate, watching them, was the figure of a man.

Luke gazed at him, heart starting to beat a little harder. The man was old, obviously – the gray-white hair and long beard that the mountain winds were blowing half across his lined face were evidence enough of that. But his eyes were keenly alert, his posture straight and proud and unaffected by even the harder gusts of wind, and the half-open brown robe revealed a chest that was strongly muscled.

'Finish shutting down, Artoo,' Luke said, hearing the slight quaver in his voice as he slipped off his helmet and popped the X-wing's canopy. Standing up, he vaulted lightly over the cockpit side to the ground.

The old man hadn't moved. Taking a deep breath, Luke walked over to him. 'Master C'baoth,' he said, bowing his head slightly. 'I'm Luke Skywalker.'

The other smiled faintly. 'Yes,' he said. 'I know. Welcome to Jomark.'

'Thank you,' Luke said, letting his breath out in a quiet sigh. At last. It had been a long and circuitous journey, what with the unscheduled stopovers at Myrkr and Sluis Van. But at last he'd made it.

C'baoth might have been reading his mind. Perhaps he was. 'I expected you long before now,' he said reproachfully.

'Yes, sir,' Luke said. 'I'm sorry. Circumstances lately have been rather out of my control.'

'Why?' C'baoth countered.

The question took Luke by surprise. 'I don't understand.'

The other's eyes narrowed slightly. 'What do you mean, you don't understand?' he demanded. 'Are you or are you not a Jedi?'

'Well, yes—'

'Then you should be in control,' C'baoth said firmly. 'In control of yourself; in control of the people and events around you. Always.'

'Yes, Master,' Luke said cautiously, trying to hide his confusion. The only other Jedi Master he'd ever known had been Yoda . . . but Yoda had never talked like this.

For another moment C'baoth seemed to study him. Then, abruptly, the hardness in his face vanished. 'But you've come,' he said, the lines in his face shifting as he smiled. 'That's the important thing. They weren't able to stop you.'

'No,' Luke said. 'They tried, though. I must have gone through four Imperial attacks since I first started out this way.'

C'baoth looked at him sharply. 'Did you, now. Were they directed specifically at you?'

'One of them was,' Luke said. 'For the others I just happened to be in the wrong place at the wrong time. Or maybe the right place at the right time,' he corrected.

The sharp look faded from C'baoth's face, replaced by something distant. 'Yes,' he murmured, gazing into the distance toward the edge of the cliff and the ring-shaped lake far below. 'The wrong place at the wrong time. The epitaph of so many Jedi.' He looked back at Luke. 'The Empire destroyed them, you know.'

'Yes, I know,' Luke said. 'They were hunted down by the Emperor and Darth Vader.'

'And one or two other Dark Jedi with them,' C'baoth said grimly, his gaze turned inward. 'Dark Jedi like Vader. I fought the last of them on—' He broke off, shaking his head slowly. 'So long ago.'

Luke nodded uncomfortably, feeling as if he was standing in loose sand. All these strange topic and mood shifts were hard to follow. A result of C'baoth's isolation? Or was this another test, this time of Luke's patience? 'A long time ago,' he agreed. 'But the Jedi can live again. We have a chance to rebuild.'

C'baoth's attention returned to him. 'Your sister,' he said. 'Yes. She'll be giving birth to Jedi twins soon.'

'Potential Jedi, anyway,' Luke said, a little surprised that C'baoth had heard about Leia's pregnancy. The New Republic's publicists had given the news wide dissemination, but he'd have thought Jomark too far out of the mainstream to have picked up on it. 'The twins are the reason I came here, in fact.'

'No,' C'baoth said. 'The reason you came here was because I called you.'

'Well . . . yes. But—'

'There are no *buts*, Jedi Skywalker,' C'baoth cut him off sharply. 'To be a Jedi is to be a servant of the Force. I called you through the Force; and when the Force calls, you must obey.'

'I understand,' Luke nodded again, wishing that he really did. Was C'baoth just being figurative? Or was this yet another topic his training had skipped over? He was familiar enough with the general controlling aspects of the Force; they were what kept him alive every time he matched his lightsaber against blaster fire. But a literal 'call' was something else entirely. 'When you say the Force calls you, Master C'baoth, do you mean—?'

'There are two reasons why I called you,' C'baoth interrupted him again. 'First, to complete your training. And second . . . because I need your help.'

Luke blinked. 'My help?'

C'baoth smiled wanly, his eyes suddenly very tired. 'I am nearing the end of my life, Jedi Skywalker. Soon now I will be making that long journey from this life to what lies beyond.'

A lump caught in Luke's throat. 'I'm sorry,' was all he could think of to say.

'It's the way of all life,' C'baoth shrugged. 'For Jedi as well as for lesser beings.'

Luke's memory flicked back to Yoda, lying on his deathbed in his Dagobah home . . . and his own feeling of helplessness that he could do nothing but watch. It was not an experience he really wanted to go through again. 'How can I help?' he asked quietly.

'By learning from me,' C'baoth said. 'Open yourself to me; absorb from me my wisdom and experience and power. In this way will you carry on my life and work.'

'I see,' Luke nodded, wondering exactly what work the other was referring to. 'You understand, though, that I have work of my own to do—'

'And are you prepared to do it?' C'baoth said, arching his eyebrows. '*Fully* prepared? Or did you come here with nothing to ask of me?'

'Well, actually, yes,' Luke had to admit. 'I came on behalf of the New Republic, to ask your assistance in the fight against the Empire.'

'To what end?'

Luke frowned. He'd have thought the reasons self-evident. 'The elimination of the Empire's tyranny. The establishment of freedom and justice for all the beings of the galaxy.'

'Justice.' C'baoth's lip twisted. 'Do not look to lesser beings for justice, Jedi Skywalker.' He slapped himself twice on the chest, two quick movements of his finger-tips. '*We* are the true justice of this galaxy. We two, and the new legacy of Jedi that we will forge to follow us. Leave the petty battles to others, and prepare yourself for that future.'

'I . . .' Luke floundered, searching for a response to that.

'What is it your sister's unborn twins need?' C'baoth demanded.

'They need – well, they're someday going to need a teacher,' Luke told him, the words coming out with a strange reluctance. First impressions were always dicey, he knew; but right now he wasn't at all sure that this was the sort of man he wanted to be teaching his niece and nephew. C'baoth seemed to be too mercurial, almost on the edge of instability. 'It's sort of been assumed that I'd be teaching them when they're old enough, like I'm teaching Leia. The problem is that just being a Jedi doesn't necessarily mean you can be a good teacher.' He hesitated. 'Obi-wan Kenobi blamed himself for Vader's turn to the dark side. I don't want that to happen to Leia's children. I thought maybe you could teach me the proper methods of Jedi instruction—'

'A waste of time,' C'baoth said with an offhanded shrug. 'Bring them here. I'll teach them myself.'

'Yes, Master,' Luke said, picking his words carefully. 'I appreciate the offer. But as you said, you have your own work to do. All I really need are some pointers—'

'And what of you, Jedi Skywalker?' C'baoth interrupted him again. 'Have you yourself no need of further instruction? In matters of judgement, perhaps?'

Luke gritted his teeth. This whole conversation was leaving him feeling a lot more transparent than he really liked. 'Yes, I could use some more instruction in that area,' he conceded. 'I think sometimes that the Jedi Master who taught me expected me to pick that up on my own.'

'It's merely a matter of listening to the Force,' C'baoth said briskly. For a moment his eyes seemed to unfocus; then they came back again. 'But come. We will go down to the villages and I will show you.'

Luke felt his eyebrows go up. 'Right now?'

'Why not?' C'baoth shrugged. 'I have summoned a driver; he will meet us on the road.' His gaze shifted to something over Luke's shoulder. 'No – stay there,' he snapped.

Luke turned. Artoo had raised himself out of the X-wing's droid socket and was easing his way along the upper hull. 'That's just my droid,' he told C'baoth.

'He will stay where he is,' C'baoth bit out. 'Droids are an abomination – creations that reason, but yet are not genuinely part of the Force.'

Luke frowned. Droids were indeed unique in that way, but that was hardly a reason to label them as abominations. But this wasn't the time or the place to argue the point. 'I'll go help him back into his socket,' he soothed C'baoth, hurrying back to the ship. Drawing on the Force, he leaped up to the hull beside Artoo. 'Sorry, Artoo, but you're going to have to stay here,' he told the droid. 'Come on – let's get you back in.'

Artoo beeped indignantly. 'I know, and I'm sorry,' Luke said, herding the squat metal cylinder back to its socket. 'But Master C'baoth doesn't want you coming along. You might as well wait here as on the ground – at least this way you'll have the X-wing's computer to talk to.'

The droid warbled again, a plaintive and slightly nervous sound this time. 'No, I don't think there's any danger,' Luke assured him. 'If you're worried, you can keep an eye on me through the X-wing's sensors.' He lowered his voice to a murmur. 'And while you're at it, I want you to start doing a complete sensor scan of the area. See if you can find any vegetation that seems to be distorted, like that twisted tree growing over the dark side cave on Dagobah. OK?'

Artoo gave a somewhat bemused acknowledging beep. 'Good. See you later,' Luke said and dropped back to the ground. 'I'm ready,' he told C'baoth.

The other nodded. 'This way,' he said, and strode off along a path leading downward.

Luke hurried to catch up. It was, he knew, something

of a long shot: even if the spot he was looking for was within Artoo's sensor range, there was no guarantee that the droid would be able to distinguish healthy alien plants from unhealthy ones. But it was worth a try. Yoda, he had long suspected, had managed to stay hidden from the Emperor and Vader only because the dark side cave near his home had somehow shielded his own influence on the Force. For C'baoth to have remained unnoticed, it followed that Jomark must also have a similar focus of dark side power somewhere.

Unless of course, he *hadn't* gone unnoticed. Perhaps the Emperor had known all about him, but had deliberately left him alone.

Which would in turn imply . . . what?

Luke didn't know. But it was something he had better find out.

They had walked no more than two hundred meters when the driver and vehicle C'baoth had summoned arrived: a tall, lanky man on an old SoroSuub recreational speeder bike pulling an elaborate wheeled carriage behind it. 'Not much more than a converted farm cart, I'm afraid,' C'baoth said as he ushered Luke into the carriage and got in beside him. Most of the vehicle seemed to be made of wood, but the seats were comfortably padded. 'The people of Chynoo built it for me when I first came to them.'

The driver got the vehicles turned around – no mean trick on the narrow path – and started downward. 'How long were you alone before that?' Luke asked.

C'baoth shook his head. 'I don't know,' he said. 'Time was not something I was really concerned with. I lived, I thought, I meditated. That was all.'

'Do you remember when it was you first came here?' Luke persisted. 'After the Outbound Flight Mission, I mean.'

Slowly, C'baoth turned to face him, his eyes icy. 'Your thoughts betray you, Jedi Skywalker,' he said coldly. 'You seek reassurance that I was not a servant of the Emperor.'

Luke forced himself to meet the gaze. 'The Master who instructed me told me that I was the last of the Jedi,' he said. 'He wasn't counting Vader and the Emperor in that list.'

'And you fear that I'm a Dark Jedi, as they were?'

'Are you?'

C'baoth smiled; and to Luke's surprise, actually chuckled. It was a strange sound, coming out of that intense face. 'Come now, Jedi Skywalker,' he said. 'Do you really believe that Joruus C'baoth – *Joruus C'baoth* – would ever turn to the dark side?'

The smile faded. 'The Emperor didn't destroy me, Jedi Skywalker, for the simple reason that during most of his reign I was beyond his reach. And after I returned . . .'

He shook his head sharply. 'There is another, you know. Another besides your sister. Not a Jedi; not yet. But I've felt the ripples in the Force. Rising, and then falling.'

'Yes, I know who you're talking about,' Luke said. 'I've met her.'

C'baoth turned to him, his eyes glistening. 'You've *met* her?' he breathed.

'Well, I think I have,' Luke amended. 'I suppose it's possible there's someone else out there who—'

'What is her name?'

Luke frowned, searching C'baoth's face and trying unsuccessfully to read his sense. There was something there he didn't like at all. 'She called herself Mara Jade,' he said.

C'baoth leaned back into the seat cushions, eyes focused on nothing. 'Mara Jade,' he repeated the name softly.

'Tell me more about the Outbound Flight project,' Luke said, determined not to get dragged off the topic. 'You set off from Yaga Minor, remember, searching for other life outside the galaxy. What happened to the ship and the other Jedi Masters who were with you?'

C'baoth's eyes took on a faraway look. 'They died, of course,' he said, his voice distant. 'All of them died. I alone survived to return.' He looked suddenly at Luke. 'It changed me, you know.'

'I understand,' Luke said quietly. So that was why C'baoth seemed so strange. Something had happened to him on that flight . . . 'Tell me about it.'

For a long moment C'baoth was silent. Luke waited, jostled by the bumps as the carriage wheels ran over the uneven ground. 'No,' C'baoth said at last, shaking his head. 'Not now. Perhaps later.' He nodded toward the front of the carriage. 'We are here.'

Luke looked. Ahead he could see half a dozen small houses, with more becoming visible as the carriage cleared the cover of the trees. Probably fifty or so all told; small, neat little cottages that seemed to combine natural building elements with selected bits of more modern technology. About twenty people could be seen moving about at various tasks; most stopped what they were doing as the speeder bike and carriage appeared. The driver pulled to roughly the center of the village and stopped in front of a thronelike chair of polished wood protected by a small, dome-roofed pavilion.

'I had it brought down from the High Castle,' C'baoth explained, gesturing to the chair. 'I suspect it was a symbol of authority to the beings who carved it.'

'What's it used for now?' Luke asked. The elaborate throne seemed out of place, somehow, in such a casually rustic setting as this.

'It's from there that I usually give my justice to the people,' C'baoth said, standing up and stepping out of the carriage. 'But we will not be so formal today. Come.'

The people were still standing motionless, watching them. Luke reached out with the Force as he stepped out beside C'baoth, trying to read their overall sense. It seemed expectant, perhaps a little surprised, definitely awed. There didn't seem to be any fear; but there was nothing like affection, either. 'How long have you been coming here?' he asked C'baoth.

'Less than a year,' C'baoth said, setting off casually down the street. 'They were slow to accept my wisdom, but eventually I persuaded them to do so.'

The villagers were starting to return to their tasks now, but their eyes still followed the visitors. 'What do you mean, persuaded them?' Luke asked.

'I showed them that it was in their best interests to listen to me.' C'baoth gestured to the cottage just ahead. 'Reach out your senses, Jedi Skywalker. Tell me about that house and its inhabitants.'

It was instantly apparent what C'baoth was referring to. Even without focusing his attention on the place Luke could feel the anger and hostility boiling out of it. There was a flicker of something like murderous intent—'Uh-oh,' he said. 'Do you think we should—?'

'Of course we should,' C'baoth said. 'Come.' He stepped up to the cottage and pushed open the door. Keeping his hand on his lightsaber, Luke followed.

There were two men standing in the room, one holding a large knife toward the other, both frozen in place as they stared at the intruders. 'Put the knife down, Tarm,' C'baoth said sternly. 'Svan, you will likewise lay aside your weapon.'

Slowly, the man with the knife laid it on the floor. The other looked at C'baoth, back at his now unarmed opponent—'I said lay it aside!' C'baoth snapped.

The man cringed back, hastily pulled a small slug-thrower from his pocket and dropped it beside the knife. 'Better,' C'baoth said, his voice calm but with a hint of the fire still there. 'Now explain yourselves.'

The story came out in a rush from both men at once, a loud and confusing babble of charges and countercharges about some kind of business deal gone sour. C'baoth listened silently, apparently having no trouble following the windstorm of fact and assumption and accusation. Luke waited beside him, wondering how he was ever going to untangle the whole thing. As near as he could understand it, both men seemed to have equally valid arguments.

Finally, the men ran out of words. 'Very well,' C'baoth said. 'The judgement of C'baoth is that Svan will pay to Tarm the full wages agreed upon.' He nodded at each man in turn. 'The judgement will be carried out immediately.'

Luke looked at C'baoth in surprise. 'That's all?' he asked.

C'baoth turned a steely gaze on him. 'You have something to say?'

Luke glanced back at the two villagers, acutely aware that arguing the ruling in front of them might undermine whatever authority C'baoth had built up here. 'I just thought that more of a compromise might be in order.'

'There is no compromise to be made,' C'baoth said firmly. 'Svan is at fault, and he will pay.'

'Yes, but—'

Luke caught the flicker of sense a half second before Svan dived for the slugthrower. With a single smooth motion he had his lightsaber free of his belt and ignited. But C'baoth was faster. Even as Luke's green-white blade snapped into existence, C'baoth raised his hand; and from his fingertips flashed a sizzling volley of all-too-well-remembered blue lightning bolts.

Svan took the blast full in the head and chest, snapping over backwards with a scream of agony. He slammed into the ground, screaming again as C'baoth sent a second blast at him. The slugthrower flew from his hand, its metal surrounded for an instant by a blue-white coronal discharge.

C'baoth lowered his hand, and for a long moment the only sound in the room was a soft whimpering from the man on the floor. Luke stared at him in horror, the smell of ozone wrenching at his stomach. 'C'baoth—!'

'You will address me as *Master*,' the other cut him off quietly.

Luke took a deep breath, forcing calm into his mind and voice. Closing down his lightsaber, he returned it to his belt and went over to kneel beside the groaning man. He was obviously still hurting, but aside from some angry red burns on his chest and arms, he didn't seem to be seriously hurt. Laying his hand gently on the worst of the burns, Luke reached out with the Force, doing what he could to alleviate the other's pain.

'Jedi Skywalker,' C'baoth said from behind him. 'He is not permanently damaged. Come away.'

Luke didn't move. 'He's in pain.'

'That is as it should be,' C'baoth said. 'He required a lesson, and pain is the one teacher no-one will ignore. Now come away.'

For a moment Luke considered disobeying. Svan's face and sense were in agony . . .

'Or would you have preferred that Tarm lie dead now?' C'baoth added.

Luke looked at the slugthrower lying on the floor, then at Tarm standing stiffly with wide eyes and face the color of dirty snow. 'There were other ways to stop him,' Luke said, getting to his feet.

'But none that he will remember longer.' C'baoth locked eyes with Luke. 'Remember that, Jedi Skywalker; remember it well. For if you allow your justice to be forgotten, you will be forced to repeat the same lessons again and again.'

He held Luke's gaze a pair of heartbeats longer before turning back to the door. 'We're finished here. Come.'

The stars were blazing overhead as Luke eased open the low gate of the High Castle and stepped out of the courtyard. Artoo had clearly noticed his approach; as he closed the gate behind him the droid turned on the X-wing's landing lights, illuminating his path. 'Hi, Artoo,' Luke said, walking to the short ladder and wearily pulling himself up into the cockpit. 'I just came out to see how you and the ship were doing.'

Artoo beeped his assurance that everything was fine. 'Good,' Luke said, flicking on the scopes and keying for a status check anyway. 'Any luck with the sensor scan I asked for?'

The reply this time was less optimistic. 'That bad, huh?' Luke nodded heavily as the translation of Artoo's answer scrolled across the X-wing's computer scope. 'Well, that's what happens when you get up into mountains.'

Artoo grunted, a distinctly unenthusiastic sound, then warbled a question. 'I don't know,' Luke told him. 'A few more days at least. Maybe longer, if he needs me to stay.' He sighed. 'I don't know, Artoo. I mean, it's just never what I expect. I went to Dagobah expecting to find a great warrior, and I found Master Yoda. I came here expecting to find someone like Master Yoda . . . and instead I got Master C'baoth.'

Artoo gave a slightly disparaging gurgle, and Luke had to smile at the translation. 'Yes, well, don't forget that Master Yoda gave you a hard time that first evening, too,' he reminded the droid, wincing a little himself at the memory. Yoda had also given Luke a hard time at that encounter. It had been a test of Luke's patience and of his treatment of strangers.

And Luke had flunked it. Rather miserably.

Artoo warbled a point of distinction. 'No, you're right,' Luke had to concede. 'Even while he was still testing us Yoda never had the kind of hard edge that C'baoth does.'

He leaned back against his headrest, staring past the open canopy at the mountaintops and the distant stars beyond them. He was weary – wearier than he'd been, probably, since the height of that last climactic battle against the Emperor. It had been all he could do to come out here to check on Artoo. 'I don't know, Artoo. He hurt someone today. Hurt him a lot. And he pushed his way into an argument without being invited, and then forced an arbitrary judgement on the people involved, and—' He waved a hand helplessly. 'I just can't see Ben or Master Yoda acting that way. But he's a Jedi, just like they were. So which example am I supposed to follow?'

The droid seemed to digest that. Then, almost reluctantly, he trilled again. 'That's the obvious question,' Luke agreed. 'But why would a Dark Jedi of C'baoth's power bother playing games like this? Why not just kill me and be done with it?'

Artoo gave an electronic grunt, a list of possible reasons scrolling across the screen. A rather lengthy list – clearly, the droid had put a lot of time and thought into the question. 'I appreciate your concern, Artoo,' Luke soothed him. 'But I really don't think he's a Dark Jedi. He's erratic and moody, but he doesn't have the same sort of evil aura about him that I could sense in Vader and the Emperor.' He hesitated. This wasn't going to be easy to say. 'I think it's more likely that Master C'baoth is insane.'

It was possibly the first time Luke had ever seen Artoo actually startled speechless. For a minute the only sound was the whispering of the mountain winds playing through the spindly trees surrounding the High Castle. Luke stared at the stars and waited for Artoo to find his voice.

Eventually, the droid did. 'No, I don't know for sure

how something like that could happen,' Luke admitted as the question appeared on his screen. 'But I've got an idea.'

He reached up to lace his fingers behind his neck, the movement easing the pressure in his chest. The dull fatigue in his mind seemed to be matched by an equally dull ache in his muscles, the kind he sometimes got if he went through an overly strenuous workout. Dimly, he wondered if there was something in the air that the X-wing's biosensors hadn't picked up on. 'You never knew, but right after Ben was cut down – back on the first Death Star – I found out that I could sometimes hear his voice in the back of my mind. By the time the Alliance was driven off Hoth, I could see him, too.'

Artoo twittered. 'Yes, that's who I sometimes talked to on Dagobah,' Luke confirmed. 'And then right after the Battle of Endor, I was able to see not only Ben but Yoda and my father, too. Though the other two never spoke, and I never saw them again. My guess is that there's some way for a dying Jedi to – oh, I don't know; to somehow anchor himself to another Jedi who's close by.'

Artoo seemed to consider that, pointed out a possible flaw in the reasoning. 'I didn't say it was the tightest theory in the galaxy,' Luke growled at him, a glimmer of annoyance peeking through his fatigue. 'Maybe I'm way off the mark. But if I'm not, it's possible that the five other Jedi Masters from the Outbound Flight project wound up anchored to Master C'baoth.'

Artoo whistled thoughtfully. 'Right,' Luke agreed ruefully. 'It didn't bother me any to have Ben around – in fact, I wish he had talked to me more often. But Master C'baoth was a lot more powerful than I was. Maybe it was different with him.'

Artoo made a little moan, and another, rather worried suggestion appeared on the screen. 'I can't just leave him, Artoo,' Luke shook his head tiredly. 'Not with him like this. Not when there's a chance I can help him.'

He grimaced, hearing in the words a painful echo of the past. Darth Vader, too, had needed help, and Luke had similarly taken on the job of saving him from the dark side. And had nearly gotten himself killed in the process. *What am I doing?* he wondered silently. *I'm not a healer. Why do I keep trying to be one?*

Luke?

With an effort, Luke dragged his thoughts back to the present. 'I've got to go,' he said, levering himself out of the cockpit seat. 'Master C'baoth's calling me.'

He shut down the displays, but not before the translation of Artoo's worried jabbering scrolled across the computer display. 'Relax, Artoo,' Luke told him, leaning back over the open cockpit canopy to pat the droid reassuringly. 'I'll be all right. I'm a Jedi, remember? You just keep a good eye on things out here. OK?'

The droid trilled mournfully as Luke dropped down the ladder and onto the ground. He paused there, looking at the dark mansion, lit only by the backwash of the X-wing's landing lights. Wondering if maybe Artoo was right about them getting out of here.

Because the droid had a good point. Luke's talents didn't lean toward the healing aspects of the Force – that much he was pretty sure of. Helping C'baoth was going to be a long, time-consuming process, with no guarantee of success at the end of the road. With a Grand Admiral in command of the Empire, political infighting in the New Republic, and the whole galaxy hanging in the balance, was this really the most efficient use of his time?

He raised his eyes from the mansion to the dark shadows of the rim mountains surrounding the lake below. Snowcapped in places, barely visible in the faint light of Jomark's three tiny moons, they were reminiscent somehow of the Manarai Mountains south of the Imperial City on Coruscant. And with that memory came another one: Luke, standing on the Imperial Palace rooftop gazing at those other mountains, sagely explaining to Threepio that a Jedi couldn't get so caught up in galactic matters that he was no longer concerned about individual people.

The speech had sounded high and noble when he'd given it. This was his chance to prove that it hadn't been just words.

Taking a deep breath, he headed back toward the gate.

killed, fortunately, but it took us the better part of the night to cut them all free. With the storm still blazing on around us.'

'Things finally quieted down just before daylight,' Bel Iblis said. 'We were out of there by the next evening. Ah.'

The bartender had arrived with the next round of drinks. Twistlers, Bel Iblis had called them: a blend of Corellian brandy with some unidentified but very tart fruit extract. Not the sort of drink Han would have expected to find in a military camp, but not bad either. The Senator took two of the drinks off the tray and handed them across to Han and Sena; took the other two off—

'I'm still good, thanks,' Lando said before Bel Iblis could offer him one.

Han frowned across the table at his friend. Lando was sitting stiffly in his lounge chair, his face impassive, his glass still half full. His *first* glass, Han realized suddenly – Lando hadn't had a refill in the hour and a half since Bel Iblis had brought them here. He caught Lando's eye, raised his eyebrows fractionally. Lando looked back, his expression still stony, then dropped his gaze and took a small sip of his drink.

'It was about a month after Tangrene,' Bel Iblis went on, 'that we first met Borsk Fey'lya.'

Han turned back to him, feeling a twitch of guilt. He'd gotten so wrapped up in Bel Iblis's storytelling that he'd completely forgotten why he and Lando had set off on this mission in the first place. Probably that was what had Lando glaring crushed ice in his direction. 'Yeah – Fey'lya,' he said. 'What's your deal with him?'

'Considerably less of a deal than he'd like, I assure you,' Bel Iblis said. 'Fey'lya did us some favors during the height of the war years, and he seems to think we should be more grateful for them.'

'What sort of favors?' Lando asked.

'Small ones,' Bel Iblis told him. 'Early on he helped us set up a supply line through New Cov, and he whistled up some Star Cruisers once when the Imperials started nosing around the system at an awkward moment. He and some of the other Bothans also shifted various funds to us, which enabled us to buy equipment sooner than we otherwise would have. That sort of thing.'

'So how grateful are you?' Lando persisted.

Bel Iblis smiled slightly. 'Or in other words, what exactly does Fey'lya want from me?'

Lando didn't smile back. 'That'll do for starters,' he agreed.

'Lando,' Han said warningly.

'No, that's all right,' Bel Iblis said, his own smile fading. 'Before I answer, though, I'd like you to tell me a little about the New Republic hierarchy. Mon Mothma's position in the new government, Fey'lya's relationship to her – that sort of thing.'

Han shrugged. 'That's pretty much public record.'

'That's the official version,' Bel Iblis said. 'I'm asking what things are *really* like.'

Han glanced over at Lando. 'I don't understand,' he said.

Bel Iblis took a swallow of his Twistler. 'Well, then, let me be more direct,' he said, studying the liquid in his glass. 'What's Mon Mothma really up to?'

Han felt a trickle of anger in his throat. 'Is that what Breil'lya told you?' he demanded. 'That she's up to something?'

Bel Iblis raised his eyes over the rim of his glass. 'This has nothing to do with the Bothans,' he said quietly. 'It's about Mon Mothma. Period.'

Han looked back at him, forcing down his confusion as he tried to collect his thoughts. There were things he didn't like about Mon Mothma – a lot of things, when you came right down to it. Starting with the way she kept running Leia off her feet doing diplomacy stuff instead of letting her concentrate on her Jedi training. And there were other things, too, that drove him crazy. But when you came right down to it . . . 'As far as I know,' he told Bel Iblis evenly, 'the only thing she's trying to do is put together a new government.'

'With herself at its head?'

'Shouldn't she be?'

A shadow of something seemed to cross Bel Iblis's face, and he dropped his eyes to his glass again. 'I suppose it was inevitable,' he murmured. For a moment he was silent. Then he looked up again, seeming to shake himself out of the mood. 'So you'd say that you're becoming a republic in fact as well as in name?'

'I'd say that, yes,' Han nodded. 'What does this have to do with Fey'lya?'

Bel Iblis shrugged. 'It's Fey'lya's belief that Mon Mothma wields altogether too much power,' he said. 'I presume you'd disagree with that assessment?'

Han hesitated. 'I don't know,' he conceded. 'But she sure isn't running the whole show, like she did during the war.'

'The war's still going on,' Bel Iblis reminded him.

'Yeah. Well . . .'

'What does Fey'lya think ought to be done about it?' Lando spoke up.

Bel Iblis's lip twitched. 'Oh, Fey'lya has some rather personal and highly unsurprising ideas about the reapportionment of power. But that's Bothans for you. Give them a sniff of the soup pot and they climb all over each other to be in charge of the ladle.'

'Especially when they can claim to have been valued allies of the winning side,' Lando said. 'Unlike others I could mention.'

Sena stirred in her seat; but before she could say anything, Bel Iblis waved a hand at her. 'You're wondering why I didn't join the Alliance,' he said calmly. 'Why I chose instead to run my own private war against the Empire.'

'That's right,' Lando said, matching his tone. 'I am.'

Bel Iblis gave him a long, measuring look. 'I could give you several reasons why I felt it was better for us to remain independent,' he said at last. 'Security, for one. There was a great deal of communication going on between various units of the Alliance, with a correspondingly large potential for interception of that information by the Empire. For a while it seemed like every fifth Rebel base was being lost to the Imperials through sheer sloppiness in security.'

'We had some problems,' Han conceded. 'But they've been pretty well fixed.'

'Have they?' Bel Iblis countered. 'What about this information leak I understand you have right in the Imperial Palace?'

'Yeah, we know it's there,' Han said, feeling strangely like a kid who's been called on the carpet for not finishing his homework. 'We've got people looking into it.'

'They'd better do more than just look,' Bel Iblis warned. 'If our analysis of Imperial communiqués is correct, this leak has its own name – Delta Source – and is further-more reporting personally to the Grand Admiral.'

'OK,' Lando said. 'Security. Let's hear some of the other reasons.'

'Ease off, Lando,' Han said, glaring across the table at his friend. 'This isn't a trial, or—'

He broke off at a gesture from Bel Iblis. 'Thank you, Solo, but I'm quite capable of defending my own actions,' the Senator said. 'And I'll be more than happy to do so . . . when I feel the time is right for such a discussion.'

He looked at Lando, then at his watch. 'But right now, I have other duties to attend to. It's getting late, and I know you really haven't had time to relax since landing. Irenez has had your baggage taken to a vacant officers' efficiency back toward the landing pad. It's small, I'm afraid, but I trust you'll find it comfortable enough.' He stood up. 'Perhaps later over dinner we can continue this discussion.'

Han looked at Lando. *Such convenient timing*, the other's expression said; but he kept the thought to himself. 'Sounds fine,' Han told Bel Iblis for both of them.

'Good,' Bel Iblis smiled. 'I'll need Sena with me, but we'll point you in the direction of your quarters on our way out. Unless you'd rather I assign you a guide.'

'We can find it,' Han assured him.

'All right. Someone will come to get you for dinner. Until later, then.'

They walked in silence for probably half the distance to their quarters before Lando finally spoke. 'You want to go ahead and get it over with?'

'Get what over with?' Han growled.

'Chewing me out for not bowing and scraping in front of your pal the Senator,' Lando said. 'Do it and get it over with, because we have to talk.'

Han kept his eyes straight head. 'You weren't just not bowing and scraping, pal,' he bit out. 'I've seen Chewie in a bad mood be more polite than you were back there.'

'You're right,' Lando acknowledged. 'You want to be mad a little longer, or are you ready to hear my reasons?'

'Oh, this should be interesting,' Han said sarcastically. 'You've got a good reason to be rude to a former Imperial Senator, huh?'

'He's not telling us the truth, Han,' Lando said earnestly. 'Not the whole truth, anyway.'

'So?' Han said. 'Who says he has to tell strangers everything?'

'He brought us here,' Lando countered. 'Why do that and then lie to us about it?'

Han frowned sideways at his friend ... and through his annoyance he saw for the first time the tension lines in Lando's face. Whatever Lando was reaching for here, he was serious about it. 'OK,' he said, a little more calmly. 'What did he lie about?'

'This camp, for starters,' Lando said, gesturing toward the nearest building. 'The Senator said they move around a lot – fourteen sites in seven years, remember? But this place has been here a lot longer than half a year.'

Han looked at the building as they passed it. At the smoothness of the edges where the memory-plastic would fold up, at the signs of wear in the subfoundation ... 'There are other things, too,' Lando went on. 'That head-quarters lounge back there – did you notice all the decoration they had in that place? Probably a dozen sculptures scattered around on those corner ledges between the booths, plus a lot of light poles. And that doesn't even count all the stuff on the walls. There was a whole antique repeater display panel mounted over the main bar, a ship's chrono next to the exit—'

'I was there, too, remember?' Han cut him off. 'What's your point?'

'My point is that this place isn't ready to pack up and ship offplanet on three minutes' notice,' Lando said quietly. 'Not any more. And you don't get this soft and comfortable if you're still in the business of launching major attacks against Imperial bases.'

'Maybe they decided to lie low for a while,' Han said. This business of having to defend Bel Iblis was starting to feel uncomfortable.

'Could be,' Lando said. 'In that case, the question is why? What else could he be holding his ships and troops back for?'

Han chewed at the inside of his cheek. He saw where Lando was going with this, all right. 'You think he's made a deal with Fey'lya.'

'That's the obvious answer,' Lando agreed soberly. 'You heard how he talked about Mon Mothma, like he expected her to declare herself Emperor any day now. Fey'lya's influence?'

Han thought it over. It was still crazy, but not nearly as crazy as it had seemed at first blush. Though if Fey'lya thought he could stage a coup with six private Dreadnaughts, he was in for a rude surprise.

But on the other hand—'Wait a minute, Lando, this is crazy,' he said. 'If they're plotting against Mon Mothma, why bring us here?'

Lando hissed softly between his teeth. 'Well, that brings us to the worst-case scenario, Han old buddy. Namely, that your friend the Senator is a complete phony . . . and that what we've got here is a giant Imperial scam.'

Han blinked. '*Now* you've lost me.'

'Think about it,' Lando urged, lowering his voice as a group of uniformed men rounded a corner of one of the buildings and headed off in another direction. 'Garm Bel Iblis, supposedly killed, suddenly returned from the dead? And not only alive, but with his own personal army on top of it? An army that neither of us has ever heard of?'

'Yeah, but Bel Iblis wasn't exactly a recluse,' Han pointed out. 'There were a lot of holos and recordings of him when I was growing up. You'd have to go to a lot of effort to look and sound that much like him.'

'If you had those records handy to compare him with, sure,' Lando agreed. 'But all you've got is memories. It wouldn't take that much effort to rig a fairly close copy. And we know that this base has been sitting here for more than a year. Maybe abandoned by someone else; and it wouldn't take much effort to throw a fake army together. Not for the Empire.'

Han shook his head. 'You're skating on drive trails, Lando. The Empire's not going to go to this much effort just for us.'

'Maybe they didn't,' Lando said. 'Maybe it was for Fey'lya's benefit, and we just happened to stumble in on it.'

Han frowned. '*Fey'lya's* benefit?'

'Sure,' Lando said. 'Start with the Empire gimmicking Ackbar's bank account. That puts Ackbar under suspicion and ripe for someone to push him off his perch.

Enter Fey'lya, convinced that he's got the support of the legendary Garm Bel Iblis and a private army behind him. Fey'lya makes his bid for power, the New Republic hierarchy is thrown into a tangle; and while no-one's watching, the Empire moves in and takes back a sector or two. Quick, clean, and simple.'

Han snorted under his breath. 'That's what you call simple, huh?'

'We're dealing with a Grand Admiral, Han,' Lando reminded him. 'Anything is possible.'

'Yeah, well, possible doesn't mean likely,' Han countered. 'If they're running a con game, why would they bring *us* here?'

'Why not? Our presence doesn't hurt the plan any. Might even help it a little. They show us the setup, send us back, we blow the whistle on Fey'lya, and Mon Mothma pulls back ships to protect Coruscant from a coup attempt that never materializes. More chaos, and even more unprotected sectors for the Imperials to gobble up.'

Han shook his head. 'I think you're jumping at shadows.'

'Maybe,' Lando said darkly. 'And maybe you're putting too much trust in the ghost of a Corellian Senator.'

They had reached their quarters now, one of a double row of small square buildings each about five meters on a side. Han keyed in the lock combination Sena had given them, and they went inside.

The apartment was about as stark and simple as it could be while still remaining even halfway functional. It consisted of a single room with a compact cooking niche on one side and a door leading to what was probably a bathroom on the other. A brown fold-down table/console combo and two old-fashioned contour chairs upholstered in military gray occupied much of the space, with the cabinets of what looked like two fold-down beds positioned to take up the table's share of the floor space at night. 'Cozy,' Lando commented.

'Probably can be packed up and shipped offplanet on three minutes' notice, too,' Han said.

'I agree,' Lando nodded. 'This is exactly the sort of feel that lounge should have had, only it didn't.'

'Maybe they figured they ought to have at least one building around here that didn't look like it came out of the Clone Wars,' Han suggested.

'Maybe,' Lando said, squatting down beside one of the chairs and peering at the edge of the seat cushion. 'Probably pulled them out of that Dreadnaught up there.' Experimentally he dug his fingers under the gray material. 'Looks like they didn't even add any extra padding before they reupholstered them with this—'

He broke off, and abruptly his face went rigid. 'What is it?' Han demanded.

Slowly, Lando turned to look up at him. 'This chair,' he whispered. 'It's not gray underneath. It's blue-gold.'

'OK,' Han said, frowning. 'So?'

'You don't understand. The Fleet doesn't do the interiors of military ships in blue-gold. They've never done them in blue-gold. Not under the Empire, not under the New Republic, not under the Old Republic. Except one time.'

'Which was?' Han prompted.

Lando took a deep breath. 'The *Katana* fleet.'

Han stared at him, an icy feeling digging up under his breastbone. The *Katana* fleet ... 'That can't be right, Lando,' he said. 'Got to be a mistake.'

'No mistake, Han,' Lando shook his head. Digging his fingers in harder, he lifted the edge of the gray covering high enough to show the material beneath it. 'I once spent two whole months researching the Dark Force. This is it.'

Han gazed at the age-dulled blue-gold cloth, a sense of unreality creeping over him. The *Katana* fleet. The Dark Force. Lost for half a century ... and now suddenly found.

Maybe. 'We need something better in the way of proof,' he told Lando. 'This doesn't do it by itself.'

Lando nodded, still half in shock. 'That would explain why they kept us aboard the *Lady Luck* the whole way here,' he said. 'They'd never be able to hide the fact that their Dreadnaught was running with only two thousand crewers instead of the normal sixteen. The *Katana* fleet.'

'We need to get a look inside one of the ships,' Han persisted. 'That recognition code Irenez sent – I don't suppose you made a recording of it?'

Lando took a deep breath and seemed to snap out of it. 'We can probably reconstruct it,' he said. 'But if they've got any sense, their code for getting in won't be the same as their code for getting out. But I don't think we have to get aboard the ships themselves. All I need is a good, close look at that repeater display panel back in the head-quarters lounge.'

'OK,' Han nodded grimly. 'Let's go and get you that look.'

CHAPTER SIXTEEN

It took them only a few minutes to make their way back to the headquarters lounge. Han kept an eye on the pedestrian and vehicle traffic as they walked, hoping they were still early enough for the place to be empty. Getting a close look at that repeater display would be tricky enough without a whole bunch of people sitting around with nothing better to do than watch what was happening at the bar. 'What exactly are we looking for?' he asked as they came in sight of the building.

'There should be some specialized input slots on the back for the full-rig slave circuitry readouts,' Lando told him. 'And there'll be production serial numbers, too.'

Han nodded. So they were going to need to get the thing off the wall. Great. 'How come you know so much about the fleet?'

'Like I said, I did a lot of studying.' Lando snorted under his breath. 'If you must know, I got stuck with a fake map to it as part of a deal back when I was selling used ships. I figured if I could learn enough about it to look like an expert I might be able to unload the map on someone else and get my money back.'

'Did you?'

'You really want to know?'

'I guess not. Get ready; it's show time.'

They were in luck. Aside from the bartender and a couple of deactivated serving droids behind the bar, the place was deserted. 'Welcome back, gentlemen,' the bartender greeted them. 'What can I get you?'

'Something to take back to our quarters,' Han told him, giving the shelves behind the bar a quick once-over. They had a good selection here – there were probably a hundred bottles of various shapes and sizes. But there was also a door off to the side that probably led back to a small storeroom. That'd be their best bet. 'I don't suppose you'd have any Vistulo brandale on hand.'

'I think we do,' the bartender said, peering back at his selection. 'Yes – there it is.'

'What's the vintage?' Han asked.

'Ah—' The bartender brought the bottle over. 'It's a '49.'

Han made a face. 'Don't have any '46, do you? Maybe stashed in the back room somewhere?'

'I don't think so, but I'll check,' the bartender said agreeably, heading toward the door.

'I'll come with you,' Han offered, ducking under the bar and joining him. 'If you don't have any '46, maybe there'll be something else that'll do as well.'

For a second the bartender looked like he was going to object. But he'd seen the two of them having a friendly drink earlier with Bel Iblis himself; and anyway, Han was already halfway to the storeroom door. 'I guess that'd be OK,' he said.

'Great,' Han said, opening the door and ushering the bartender through.

He didn't know how long it would take Lando to get the repeater display off the wall, check it out, and then put it back up. On the theory it was better to play it safe, he managed to drag out the search for a '46 Vistulo for a full five minutes. Eventually, with cheerful good grace, he settled for a '48 Kibshae instead. The bartender led the way out of the room; mentally crossing his fingers, Han followed.

Lando was standing at the same place at the bar where he'd been when Han had left him, his hands on the bar, his face tight. And for good reason. Standing a few paces behind him, her hand on the butt of her blaster, was Irenez.

'Well, hello, Irenez,' Han said, trying his best innocent look on her. 'Funny meeting you here.'

The innocent look was wasted. 'Not all that funny,' Irenez said tartly. 'Sena asssigned me to keep an eye on you. You get what you came for?'

Han looked at Lando, saw the fractional nod. 'I think so, yeah,' he said.

'Glad to hear it. Let's go – outside.'

Han handed the bottle of Kibshae to the bartender. 'Keep it,' he said. 'Looks like the party's been canceled.'

There was an old five-passenger landspeeder waiting outside when they emerged from the lounge. 'Inside,' Irenez said, motioning to the vehicle's aft doorway.

Han and Lando obeyed. There, sitting with uncharacteristic stiffness in one of the passenger seats, Sena Leikvold Midanyl was waiting. 'Gentlemen,' she said gravely as they entered. 'Sit down, please.'

Han chose one of the seats, swiveled it to face her. 'Time for dinner already?'

'Irenez, take the controls,' Sena said, ignoring him. 'Drive us around the camp – I don't care where.'

Silently, Irenez made her way to the front of the vehicle; and with a slight lurch they were off. 'You didn't stay in your room very long,' Sena said to Han.

'I don't remember the Senator saying anything about being confined to quarters,' Han countered.

'He didn't,' Sena agreed. 'On the other hand, a properly brought up guest should know better than to wander unescorted around sensitive areas.'

'I apologize,' Han said, trying to keep a sarcastic edge out of his voice. 'I didn't realize your liquor supply was classified.' He glanced out the window. 'If you're trying to take us back to our quarters, you're going the wrong way.'

Sena studied his face a moment. 'I came to ask you a favor.'

It was about the last thing Han would have expected her to say, and it took him a second to find his voice again. 'What sort of favor?'

'I want you to talk to Mon Mothma for me. To ask her and the Council to invite Senator Bel Iblis to join the New Republic.'

Han shrugged. Was *that* why they'd brought him and Lando all the way over here? 'You don't need a special invitation to join up. All you have to do is contact someone on the Council and offer your services.'

A muscle in Sena's cheek twitched. 'I'm afraid that in the Senator's case it's not going to be quite that easy,' she said. 'It's not so much a matter of joining the New Republic as of *re*joining it.'

Han threw a frown at Lando. 'Oh?' he said carefully.

Sena sighed, half turning to gaze out the side window. 'It happened a long time ago,' she said. 'Before the various resistance groups fighting the Empire were formally consolidated into the Rebel Alliance. You know anything about that period of history?'

'Just what's in the official record,' Han said. 'Mon Mothma and Bail Organa of Alderaan got three of the biggest groups together and convinced them to make an alliance. After that the whole thing snowballed.'

'Have you ever heard the name of that first agreement?'

'Sure. It was called the Corellian Treaty—' Han broke off. 'The *Corellian* Treaty?'

'Yes,' Sena nodded. 'It was Senator Bel Iblis, not Mon Mothma, who convinced those three resistance groups to agree to a meeting. And, furthermore, who guaranteed protection for them.'

For a long minute the only sound in the speeder was the hum of the repulsorlifts. 'What happened?' Lando asked at last.

'To put it bluntly, Mon Mothma began to take over,' Sena said. 'Senator Bel Iblis was far better at strategy and tactics than she was, better even than many of the Rebellion's generals and admirals in those early days. But she had the gift of inspiration, the knack of getting diverse groups and species to work together. Gradually, she became the most visible symbol of the Rebellion, with Organa and the Senator increasingly relegated to the background.'

'Must have been hard for someone like Bel Iblis to take,' Lando murmured.

'Yes, it was,' Sena said. 'But you have to understand that it wasn't just pride that drove him to withdraw his support. Bail Organa had been a strong moderating influence on Mon Mothma – he was one of the few people whom she respected and trusted enough to pay serious attention to. After he was killed in the Death Star's attack on Alderaan, there was really no-one of equal status who could stand up to her. She began to take more and more power to herself; and the Senator began to suspect that she was going to overthrow the Emperor only to set herself up in his place.'

'So he pulled you out of the Alliance and started his own private war against the Empire,' Lando said. 'Did you know any of this, Han?'

'Never heard a whisper,' Han shook his head.

'I'm not surprised,' Sena said. 'Would *you* have advertised a defection by someone of the Senator's stature? Especially in the middle of a war?'

'Probably not,' Han conceded. 'I suppose the only surprise is that more groups didn't back out like you did. Mon Mothma can be pretty overbearing when she wants to be.'

'There wasn't any doubt as to who was in charge during the war, either,' Lando added dryly. 'I once saw her make Admiral Ackbar and General Madine both back down on one of their pet projects when she decided she didn't like it.'

Han looked at Sena, a sudden thought striking him. 'Is that why you've cut back your raids against the Empire? So that you'd be ready to move against Mon Mothma if she turned the New Republic into a dictatorship?'

'That's it exactly,' Sena said. 'We moved here to Peregrine's Nest just under three years ago, suspended all operations except material raids, and started working up

tactical contingency plans. And settled in to wait for the
Senator's triumphal vindication.' Her cheek twitched
again. 'And we've been waiting ever since.'

Han looked out the window at the camp passing by
outside, a hollow sense of loss filling him. The legendary
Senator Bel Iblis . . . waiting for a return to power that
would never come. 'It's not going to happen,' he told Sena
quietly.

'I know that.' She hesitated. 'Down deep, so does the
Senator.'

'Except that he can't swallow his pride long enough to
go to Mon Mothma and ask to be let back in.' Han nodded. 'So he gets you to ask us to—'

'The Senator had nothing to do with this,' Sena cut
him off sharply. 'He doesn't even know I'm talking to
you. This is on my responsibility alone.'

Han drew back a little. 'Sure,' he said. 'OK.'

Sena shook her head. 'I'm sorry,' she apologized. 'I
didn't mean to snap at you.'

'It's OK,' Han said, feeling some sympathetic ache of
his own. She could have all the good intentions and logic
in the galaxy on her side, but this probably still looked
and felt to her like betrayal. A stray memory clicked: the
expression on Luke's face, just before the Battle of Yavin
with the first Death Star. When he'd thought Han was
going to run off and abandon them . . .

'Han,' Lando said quietly.

Han looked over at his friend, shaking off the memory.
Lando raised his eyebrows slightly in reminder . . . 'We'll
make you a deal, Sena,' Han said, turning back to her.
'We'll talk to Mon Mothma about the Senator. You talk
to us about the *Katana* fleet.'

Sena's face went rigid. 'The *Katana* fleet?'

'Where your six Dreadnaughts came from,' Lando said. 'Don't bother denying it – I got a good look at that repeater display you've got up over the bar in the head-quarters lounge.'

Sena took a deep breath. 'No. I can't tell you anything about that.'

'Why not?' Lando asked. 'We're all about to be allies again, remember?'

An unpleasant tingle ran up Han's back. 'Unless you've already promised the fleet to Fey'lya.'

'We've promised Fey'lya nothing,' Sena said flatly. 'Not that he hasn't asked for it.'

Han grimaced. 'So he *is* trying for a coup.'

'Not at all,' Sena shook her head. 'Fey'lya wouldn't know what to do with a military coup if you gift wrapped it and handed it to him on a drinks tray. You have to understand that Bothans think in terms of political and persuasive influence, not military power. The typical Bothan's goal is to go through life getting more and more people to listen to what he has to say. Fey'lya thinks that being the one to bring the Senator back into the New Republic will be a large step in that direction.'

'Especially if Ackbar isn't around to oppose him?' Han asked.

Sena nodded. 'Yes, that's unfortunately another typical Bothan move. A Bothan leader who stumbles is invariably jumped on by all those who want to take over his position. In the distant past the attacks were literal – knives and usually death. Now, it's been modified to more of a verbal assassination. Progress, I suppose.'

'Ackbar's not a Bothan,' Lando pointed out.

'The technique is easily adapted to other races.'

Han grunted. 'What a great group to have as allies. So do they just stab, or do they also help with the tripping?'

'You mean the bank transfer?' Sena shook her head. 'No, I doubt that was Fey'lya's doing. As a rule Bothans don't stick their necks out far enough to concoct plots on their own. They much prefer to take advantage of other people's.'

'More like scavengers than hunters,' Han said sourly. Probably explained why he'd always disliked Fey'lya and his crowd. 'So what do we do about him?'

Sena shrugged. 'All you really need to do is get Ackbar cleared. As soon as he's not vulnerable to attack any more, Fey'lya should back off.'

'Great,' Han growled. 'Problem is, with a Grand Admiral in charge of the Empire, we might not have that much time.'

'And if we don't, neither do you,' Lando added. 'Wounded dignity aside, Sena, the Senator had better start facing reality. You're a small, isolated group with a line on the *Katana* fleet, and there's an Empire out there hungry for new warships. The minute the Grand Admiral tumbles to what you've got, he'll have the whole Imperial Fleet on you before you can blink twice. Bring the *Katana* fleet over to the New Republic and you get to be heroes. Wait too long, and you'll lose everything.'

'I know that,' Sena said, her voice almost too low to hear. Han waited, mentally crossing his fingers . . . 'We don't actually know where the fleet is,' she said. 'Our Dreadnaughts came from a man who says he stumbled on them about fifteen years ago. He's thin, below-average height, with a sort of weasely look about him. He has short white hair and a heavily lined face, though I suspect much of that appearance is due more to some past disease or injury than actual age.'

'What's his name?' Han asked.

'I don't know. He's never told us that.' She hesitated again, then plunged ahead. 'He loves to gamble, though. All our meetings with him have been aboard the *Coral Vanda*, usually across gaming tables. The staff there seemed to know him quite well, though the way he was throwing money around, that may not mean anything. Croupiers always get to know the losers quickly.'

'The *Coral Vanda*?' Han asked.

'It's a subocean luxury casino on Pantolomin,' Lando told him. 'Does three- and seven-day runs through the big network of reefs lying off the northern continent. I've always wanted to go there, but never had the chance.'

'Well, you've got it now,' Han said. He looked at Sena. 'I suppose the next question is how we're going to get out of here.'

'That won't be a problem,' she said, her voice sounding strained. Already having second thoughts, probably. 'I can get the *Harrier* to take you back to New Cov. When do you want to leave?'

'Right now,' Han said. He saw Sena's expression – 'Look, no matter when we go, you're going to have some explaining to do to the Senator. We're in a race with the Empire here – even a few hours might make a difference.'

'I suppose you're right,' she said with a reluctant nod. 'Irenez, take us to their ship. I'll make the arrangements from there.'

———

It turned out there was no need to make arrangements from the *Lady Luck*. Standing outside the ship's ramp as they arrived, clearly waiting for them, was Senator Bel Iblis.

'Hello, Solo; Calrissian,' he smiled as Han and Lando stepped out of the speeder. 'You weren't at your quarters, and I thought you might be here. I see I guessed right.'

His eyes flicked over Han's shoulder as Sena emerged from the speeder. Looked again into Han's face . . . and abruptly the easy smile vanished. 'Sena? What's going on?'

'They know about the *Katana* fleet, Commander,' she said quietly, coming up beside Han. 'And . . . I told them about our contact.'

'I see,' Bel Iblis said evenly. 'And so you're leaving. To see if you can persuade him to turn the Dark Force over to the New Republic.'

'That's right, sir,' Han said, matching his tone. 'We need the ships – need them pretty badly. But not as much as we need good fighters. And good commanders.'

For a long moment Bel Iblis gazed at him. 'I won't go to Mon Mothma like a beggar pleading to be let in,' he said at last.

'You left for good reasons,' Han persisted. 'You can come back the same way.'

Again, Bel Iblis's eyes flicked to Sena. 'No,' he said. 'Too many people know what happened between us. I would look like an old fool. Or like a beggar.'

He looked past Han, his eyes sweeping slowly across the buildings of Peregrine's Nest. 'I don't have anything to bring, Solo,' he said, his voice tinged with something that sounded like regret. 'Once I'd dreamed of having a fleet that would rival the best in the New Republic. A fleet, and a string of decisive and pivotal victories over the Empire. With that, perhaps I could have returned with dignity and respect.' He shook his head. 'But what we have here barely qualifies as a strike force.'

'Maybe so, but six Dreadnaughts aren't anything to sneer at,' Lando put in. 'And neither is your combat record. Forget Mon Mothma for a minute – every military person in the New Republic would be delighted to have you in.'

Bel Iblis cocked an eyebrow. 'Perhaps. I suppose it's worth thinking about.'

'Especially with a Grand Admiral in charge of the Empire,' Han pointed out. 'If he catches you here alone, you'll have had it.'

Bel Iblis smiled tightly. 'That thought has occurred to me, Solo. Several times a day.' He straightened up. 'The *Harrier* is leaving in half an hour to take Breil'lya back to New Cov. I'll instruct them to take you and the *Lady Luck* along.'

Han and Lando exchanged glances. 'You think it'll be safe to go back to New Cov, sir?' Han asked. 'There might still be Imperials hanging around.'

'There won't be.' Bel Iblis was positive. 'I've studied the Imperials and their tactics a long time. Aside from not expecting us to show up again so soon, they really can't afford to hang around any one place for long. Besides, we have to go there – Breil'lya will need to pick up his ship.'

Han nodded, wondering what kind of report Breil'lya would be giving to his boss when he got back to Coruscant. 'All right. Well . . . I guess we'd better get the ship prepped.'

'Yes.' Bel Iblis hesitated, then held out his hand. 'It was good to see you, Solo. I hope we'll meet again.'

'I'm sure we will, sir,' Han assured him, grasping the outstretched hand.

The Senator nodded to Lando. 'Calrissian,' he said. Releasing Han's hand, he turned and walked away across the landing field.

Han watched him go, trying to figure out whether he admired the Senator more than he pitied him or vice versa. It was a useless exercise. 'Our luggage is still back at our quarters,' he told Sena.

'I'll have it sent over while you get the ship prepped.' She looked at Han, her eyes suddenly blazing with a smoldering fire. 'But I want you to remember one thing,' she said with deadly earnestness. 'You can go now, with our blessings. But if you betray the Senator – in any way – you will die. At my hand, personally, if necessary.'

Han held her gaze, considering what to say. To remind her, perhaps, that he'd been attacked by bounty hunters and interstellar criminals, shot at by Imperial stormtroopers, and tortured at the direction of Darth Vader himself. To suggest that after all that, a threat coming from someone like Sena was too laughable to even take seriously. 'I understand,' he said gravely. 'I won't let you down.'

From the dorsal hatchway connection behind them came the creak of a stressed seal; and through the *Lady Luck*'s canopy the patch of stars visible around the bulk of the Dreadnaught abruptly flashed into starlines. 'Here we go again,' Lando said, his voice sounding resigned. 'How do I keep letting you talk me into these things?'

'Because you're the respectable one,' Han told him,

running an eye over the *Lady Luck*'s instruments. There wasn't a lot there to see, with the engines and most of the systems running at standby. 'And because you know as well as I do that we have to do it. Sooner or later the Empire's going to find out that the *Katana* fleet's been found and start looking for it themselves. And if they get to it before we do, we're going to be in big trouble.' And here they were, stuck uselessly for another two days in hyperspace while the *Harrier* took them back to New Cov. Not because they wanted to go there, but because Bel Iblis wasn't willing to trust them with the location of his stupid Peregrine's Nest base—

'You're worried about Leia, aren't you?' Lando asked into the silence.

'I shouldn't have let her go,' Han muttered. 'Something's gone wrong. I just know it. That lying little alien's turned her over to the Empire, or the Grand Admiral's out-thought us again. I don't know, but *something*.'

'Leia can take care of herself, Han,' Lando said quietly. 'And even Grand Admirals sometimes make mistakes.'

Han shook his head. 'He made his mistake at Sluis Van, Lando. He won't make another one. Bet you the *Falcon* he won't.'

Lando clapped him on the shoulder. 'Come on, buddy, brooding about it won't help. We've got two days to kill. Let's go break out a sabacc deck.'

The Grand Admiral read the dispatch twice before turning his glowing eyes on Pellaeon. 'You vouch for the reliability of this report, Captain?'

'As much as I can vouch for any report that doesn't originate with an Imperial agent,' Pellaeon told him. 'On the other hand, this particular smuggler has fed us fifty-two reports over the last ten years, forty-eight of which proved to be accurate. I'd say he's worth believing.'

Thrawn looked back at the reader. 'Endor,' he murmured, half to himself. 'Why Endor?'

'I don't know, sir,' Pellaeon said. 'Perhaps they were looking for another place to hide.'

'Among the Ewoks?' Thrawn snorted derisively. 'That would be desperation indeed. But no matter. If the *Millennium Falcon* is there, then so is Leia Organa Solo. Alert Navigation and Engineering; we leave immediately for Endor.'

'Yes, sir,' Pellaeon nodded, keying in the orders. 'Shall I have Khabarakh brought up from Nystao?'

'Yes. Khabarakh.' Thrawn said the name thoughtfully. 'Note the interesting timing here, Captain. Khabarakh comes back to Honoghr after a month's absence, just as Solo and Organa Solo head off on secret errands to New Cov and Endor. Coincidence?'

Pellaeon frowned. 'I don't follow you, sir.'

Thrawn smiled thinly. 'What I think, Captain, is that we're seeing a new degree of subtlety among our enemies. They knew that the return of a survivor from the failed Kashyyyk operation would catch my attention. They therefore arranged his release to coincide with their own missions, in the hope I would be too preoccupied to notice them. Doubtless when we break Khabarakh, we'll learn a great many things from him that will cost us countless man-hours to finally prove wrong.' Thrawn snorted again. 'No, leave him where he is. You may inform the dynasts that I have decided to permit them the full seven days of public shame, after which they may perform the rites of discovery as they choose. No matter how useless his information, Khabarakh may still serve the Empire by dying painfully. As an object lesson to his race.'

'Yes, sir.' Pellaeon hesitated. 'May I point out, though, that such a drastic psychological fragmentation and reconditioning is well outside the Rebellion's usual operating procedure.'

'I agree,' Thrawn said grimly. 'Which implies all the more strongly that whatever Organa Solo is looking for on Endor, it's considerably more vital to the Rebellion's war effort than mere sanctuary.'

Pellaeon frowned, trying to think of what might be on Endor that anyone could possibly want. 'Some of the material left over from the Death Star project?' he hazarded.

'More valuable than that,' the Grand Admiral shook his head. 'Information, perhaps, that the Emperor might have had with him when he died. Information they may think they can still retrieve.'

And then Pellaeon got it. 'The location of the Mount Tantiss storehouse.'

Thrawn nodded. 'That's the only thing I can think of that would be worth this much effort on their part. At any rate, it's a risk we can't afford to take. Not now.'

'Agreed.' Pellaeon's board pinged: Navigation and Engineering signaling ready. 'Shall I break orbit?'

'At your convenience, Captain.'

Pellaeon nodded to the helm. 'Take us out. Course as set by Navigation.'

Through the viewports the planet below began to fall away; and as it did so there was the short trill of a priority message coming through. Pellaeon pulled it up, read the heading. 'Admiral? Report from the *Adamant*, in the Abregado system. They've captured one of Talon Karrde's freighters. Transcript of the preliminary interrogation is coming through now.' He frowned as he glanced down to the end. 'It's rather short, sir.'

'Thank you,' Thrawn said with quiet satisfaction as he pulled up the report to his own station.

He was still reading it when the *Chimaera* made the jump to lightspeed. Reading it very, very carefully.

CHAPTER SEVENTEEN

———————— ✵ ————————

Mara had never been to the Abregado-rae Spaceport before; but as she walked along its streets she decided it deserved every bit of the rock-bottom reputation it had worked so hard to achieve.

Not that it showed on the surface. On the contrary, the place was neat and almost painfully clean, though with that grating antiseptic quality that showed the cleanliness had been imposed from above by government decree instead of from below by the genuine wishes of the inhabitants. It seemed reasonably peaceful, too, as spaceports went, with lots of uniformed security men patrolling the streets around the landing pits.

But beneath the surface glitter the rot showed straight through. Showed in the slightly furtive manner of the locals; in the half-hearted swaggering of the uniformed security men; in the lingering stares of the plainclothes but just as obvious quiet security men. The whole spaceport – maybe the whole planet – was being held together with tie wire and blaster power packs.

A petty totalitarian regime, and a populace desperate to escape it. Just the sort of place where anyone would betray anyone else for the price of a ticket offplanet.

Which meant that if any of the locals had tumbled to the fact that there was a smuggling ship sitting here under Security's nose, Mara had about ten steps to go before the whole place came down on top of her.

Walking toward a faded door with the equally faded sign 'Landing Pit 21' over it, she hoped sardonically that it wasn't a trap. She would really hate to die in a place like this.

The door to the landing pit was unlocked. Taking a deep breath, acutely conscious of the two pairs of uniformed security men within sight of her, she went inside.

It was the *Etherway*, all right, looking just as shabby and decrepit as it had when Fynn Torve had had to abandon it in Landing Pit 63 of this same spaceport. Mara gave it a quick once-over, checked out all the nooks and crannies in the pit where an armed ambush squad could be skulking, and finally focused on the dark-haired young man lounging in a chair by the freighter's lowered ramp. Even in that casual slouch he couldn't shake the military air that hovered around him. 'Hello, there,' he called to her, lowering the data pad he'd been reading. 'Nice day for flying. You interested in hiring a ship?'

'No,' she said, walking toward him as she tried to watch all directions at once. 'I'm more in a buying mood, myself. What kind of ship is this flying hatbox, anyway?'

'It's a Harkners-Balix Nine-Oh-Three,' the other sniffed with a second-rate attempt at wounded pride. 'Flying hatbox, indeed.'

Not much of an actor, but he was clearly getting a kick out of all this cloak-and-blade stuff. Setting her teeth firmly together, Mara sent a silent curse down on Torve's head for setting up such a ridiculous identification procedure in the first place. 'Looks like a Nine-Seventeen to me,' she said dutifully. 'Or even a Nine-Twenty-Two.'

'No, it's a Nine-Oh-Three,' he insisted. 'Trust me – my uncle used to make landing gear pads for them. Come inside and I'll show you how to tell the difference.'

'Oh, that'll be great,' Mara muttered under her breath as she followed him up the ramp.

'Glad you finally got here,' the man commented over his shoulder as they reached the top of the ramp. 'I was starting to think you'd been caught.'

'That could still happen if you don't shut up,' Mara growled back. 'Keep your voice down, will you?'

'It's OK,' he assured her. 'I've got all your MSE droids clattering around on cleaning duty just inside the outer hull. That should block out any audio probes.'

Theoretically, she supposed, he was right. As a practical matter ... well, if the locals had the place under surveillance they were in trouble, anyway. 'You have any trouble getting the ship out of impoundment?' she asked him.

'Not really,' he said. 'The spaceport administrator said the whole thing was highly irregular, but he didn't give me any major grief about it.' He grinned. 'Though I suppose the size of the bribe I slipped him might have had something to do with that. My name's Wedge Antilles, by the way. I'm a friend of Captain Solo's.'

'Nice to meet you,' Mara said. 'Solo couldn't make it himself?'

Antilles shook his head. 'He had to leave Coruscant on some kind of special mission, so he asked me to get the ship sprung for you. I was scheduled for escort duty a couple systems over anyway, so it wasn't a problem.'

Mara ran a quick eye over him. From his build and general manner . . . 'B-wing pilot?' she hazarded.

'X-wing,' he corrected her. 'I've got to get back before my convoy finishes loading. Want me to give you an escort out of here?'

'Thanks, but no,' she said, resisting the urge to say something sarcastic. The first rule of smuggling was to stay as inconspicuous as possible, and flying out of a third-rate spaceport with a shiny New Republic X-wing starfighter in tow didn't exactly qualify as a low-profile stance. 'Tell Solo thanks.'

'Right. Oh, one other thing,' Antilles added as she started past him. 'Han also wanted me to ask you if your people might be interested in selling information on our friend with the eyes.'

Mara sent him a sharp look. 'Our friend with the eyes?'

Antilles shrugged. 'That's what he said. He said you'd understand.'

Mara felt her lip twist. 'I understand just fine. Tell him I'll pass on the message.'

'OK.' He hesitated. 'It sounded like it was pretty important—'

'I said I'll pass on the message.'

He shrugged again. 'OK – just doing my job. Have a good trip.' With a friendly nod, he headed back down the ramp. Still half expecting a trap, Mara got the hatchway sealed for flight and went up to the bridge.

It took a quarter hour to run the ship through its preflight sequence, almost exactly the amount of time it took the spaceport controllers to confirm her for takeoff. Easing in the repulsorlifts, she lifted clear of the landing pit and made for space.

She was nearly high enough to kick in the sublight drive when the back of her neck began to tingle.

'Uh-oh,' she muttered aloud, giving the displays a quick scan. Nothing was visible; but this close to a planetary mass, that meant less than nothing. Anything could be lurking just over the horizon, from a single flight of TIE fighters all the way up to an Imperial Star Destroyer.

But maybe they weren't quite ready yet . . .

She threw full power to the drive, feeling herself pressed back into the seat cushion for a few seconds as the acceleration compensators fought to catch up. An indignant howl came from the controller on the comm speaker; ignoring him, she keyed the computer, hoping that Torve had followed Karrde's standard procedure when he'd first put down on Abregado.

He had. The calculation for the jump out of here had already been computed and loaded, just waiting to be initiated. She got the computer started making the minor adjustments that would correct for a couple of months of general galactic drift, and looked back out the forward viewport.

There, emerging over the horizon directly ahead, was the massive bulk of a *Victory*-class Star Destroyer.

Bearing toward her.

For a long heartbeat Mara just sat there, her mind skimming through the possibilities, all the time knowing full well how futile the exercise was. The Star Destroyer's commander had planned his interception with exquisite skill: given their respective vectors and the *Etherway*'s proximity to the planet, there was absolutely no way she would be able to elude the larger ship's weapons and tractor beams long enough to make her escape to lightspeed. Briefly, she toyed with the hope that the Imperials might not be after her at all, that they were actually gunning for that Antilles character still on the surface. But that hope, too, evaporated quickly. A single X-wing pilot could hardly be important enough to tie up a *Victory*-class Star Destroyer for. And if he was, they would certainly not have been so incompetent as to spring the trap prematurely.

'Freighter *Etherway*,' a cold voice boomed over her comm speaker. 'This is the Star Destroyer *Adamant*. You are ordered to shut down your engines and prepare to be brought aboard.'

So that was that. They had indeed been looking for her. In a very few minutes now she would be their prisoner.

Unless . . .

Reaching over, she keyed her mike. 'Star Destroyer *Adamant*, this is the *Etherway*,' she said briskly. 'I congratulate you on your vigilance; I was afraid I was going to have to search the next five systems to find an Imperial ship.'

'You will shut down all deflector systems—' The voice faltered halfway through the standard speech as the fact belatedly penetrated that this was not the normal response of the normal Imperial prisoner.

'I'll want to speak to your captain the minute I'm aboard,' Mara said into the conversational gap. 'I'll need him to set up a meeting with Grand Admiral Thrawn and provide me transport to wherever he and the *Chimaera* are at the moment. And get a tractor beam ready – I don't want to have to land this monster in your hangar bay myself.'

The surprises were coming too fast for the poor man. 'Ah – freighter *Etherway*—' he tried again.

'On second thought, put the captain on now,' Mara cut him off. She had the initiative now, and was determined to keep it as long as possible. 'There's no-one around who can tap into this communication.'

There was a moment of silence. Mara continued on her intercept course, a trickle of doubt beginning to worm its way through her resolve. *It's the only way*, she told herself sternly.

'This is the captain,' a new voice came on the speaker. 'Who are you?'

'Someone with important information for Grand Admiral Thrawn,' Mara told him, shifting from brisk to just slightly haughty. 'For the moment, that's all you need to know.'

But the captain wasn't as easily bullied as his junior officers. 'Really,' he said dryly. 'According to our sources, you're a member of Talon Karrde's smuggling gang.'

'And you don't believe such a person could tell the Grand Admiral anything useful?' she countered, letting her tone frost over a bit.

'Oh, I'm sure you can,' the captain said. 'I simply don't see any reason why I should bother him with what will be, after all, a routine interrogation.'

Mara squeezed her left hand into a fist. At all costs she had to avoid the kind of complete mind-sifting the captain was obviously hinting at. 'I wouldn't advise that,' she told him, throwing every bit of the half-remembered dignity and power of the old Imperial court into her voice. 'The Grand Admiral would be extremely displeased with you. *Extremely* displeased.'

There was a short pause. Clearly, the captain was starting to recognize that he had more here than he'd bargained for. Just as clearly, he wasn't ready yet to back down. 'I have my orders,' he said flatly. 'I'll need more than vague hints before I can make you an exception to them.'

Mara braced herself. This was it. After all these years of hiding from the Empire, as well as from everyone else, this was finally it. 'Then send a message to the Grand Admiral,' she said. 'Tell him the recognition code is Hapspir, Barrini, Corbolan, Triaxis.'

There was a moment of silence, and Mara realized she'd finally gotten through to the other. 'And your name?' the captain asked, his voice suddenly respectful.

Beneath her, the *Etherway* jolted slightly as the *Adamant*'s tractor beam locked on. She was committed now. The only way out was to see it all through. 'Tell him,' she said, 'that he knew me as the Emperor's Hand.'

They brought her and the *Etherway* aboard, settled her with uncertain deference into one of the senior officers' quarters . . . and then headed away from Abregado like a mynock with its tail on fire.

She was left alone in the cabin for the rest of the day and into the night, seeing no-one, speaking with no-one. Meals were delivered by an SE4 servant droid; at all other times the door was kept locked. Whether the enforced privacy was on the captain's orders or whether it came from above was impossible to tell, but at least it gave her time to do such limited planning as she could.

There was similarly no way of knowing where they were going, but from the labored sound of the engines, she could guess they were pushing uncomfortably far past a *Victory* Star Destroyer's normal flank speed of

Point Four Five. Possibly even as high as Point Five, which would mean they were covering a hundred twenty-seven light-years per hour. For a while she kept her mind occupied by trying to guess which system they might be making for; but as the hours ticked by and the number of possibilities grew too unwieldy to keep track of, she abandoned the game.

Twenty-two hours after leaving Abregado, they arrived at the rendezvous. At the last place Mara would have expected. At the very last place in the galaxy she would have wanted to go. The place where her universe had died a sudden and violent death.

Endor.

'The Grand Admiral will see you now,' the stormtrooper squad leader said, stepping back from the opening door and motioning her ahead. Mara threw a glance at the silent Noghri bodyguard standing on the other side of the doorway and stepped through.

'Ah,' a well-remembered voice called quietly from the command center in the middle of the room. Grand Admiral Thrawn sat in the double display ring, his red eyes glowing at her above the glistening white uniform. 'Come in.'

Mara stayed where she was. 'Why did you bring me to Endor?' she demanded.

The glowing eyes narrowed. 'I beg your pardon?'

'You heard me,' she said. 'Endor. Where the Emperor died. Why did you choose this place for the rendezvous?'

The other seemed to consider that. 'Come closer, Mara Jade.'

The voice was rich with the overtones of command,

and Mara found herself walking toward him before she realized what she was doing. 'If it's supposed to be a joke, it's in poor taste,' she bit out. 'If it's supposed to be a test, then get it over with.'

'It is neither,' Thrawn said as she came to the edge of the outer display ring and stopped. 'The choice was forced upon us by other, unconnected business.' One blue-black eyebrow raised slightly. 'Or perhaps not *entirely* unconnected. That still remains to be seen. Tell me, can you really sense the Emperor's presence here?'

Mara took a deep breath, feeling the air shuddering through her lungs with an ache as real as it was intangible. Could Thrawn see how much this place hurt her? she wondered. How thick with memories and sensations the whole Endor system still remained? Or would he even care about any of that if he did?

He saw, all right. She could tell that much from the way he was looking at her. What he thought of it she didn't much care. 'I can feel the evidence of his death,' she told him. 'It's not pleasant. Let's get this over with so I can get out of here.'

His lip quirked, perhaps at her assumption that she would in fact be leaving the *Chimaera*. 'Very well. Let's begin with some proof of who you were.'

'I gave the *Adamant*'s captain a high-level recognition code,' she reminded him.

'Which is why you're here instead of in a detention cell,' Thrawn said. 'The code isn't proof in itself.'

'All right, then,' Mara said. 'We met once, during the public dedication of the new Assemblage wing of the Imperial Palace on Coruscant. At that ceremony the Emperor introduced me to you as Lianna, one of his favorite dancers. Later, during the more private ceremony that followed, he revealed to you my true identity.'

'And what was that private ceremony?'

'Your secret promotion to the rank of Grand Admiral.'

Thrawn pursed his lips, his eyes never leaving her face. 'You wore a white dress to both ceremonies,' he said. 'Aside from the sash, the dress had only one decoration. Do you recall what that decoration was?'

Mara had to think back. 'It was a small shouldersculp,' she said slowly. 'Left shoulder. A Xyquine design, as I remember.'

'It was indeed.' Thrawn reached to his control board, touched a switch; and abruptly, the room was filled with holos of shouldersculps on ornate pillars. 'The one you wore is somewhere in this room. Find it.'

Mara swallowed, turning slowly as she looked around. She'd had literally hundreds of fancy dresses for her cover role as a member of the Emperor's entourage. To remember one particular shouldersculp out of all that . . .

She shook her head, trying to clear away the unpleasant buzzing sensation that hovered deep in her mind. She'd had an excellent memory once, one which the Emperor's training had made even better. Focusing her thoughts, fighting upstream against the disquieting aura of this place, she concentrated . . . 'That's it,' she said, pointing to a delicate filigree of gold and blue.

Thrawn's expression didn't change, but he seemed to relax a little in his seat. 'Welcome back, Emperor's Hand.' He touched the switch a second time, and the art gallery vanished. 'You've been a long time in returning.'

The glowing eyes bored into her face, the question unspoken but obvious. 'What was here for me before?'

she countered. 'Who but a Grand Admiral would have accepted me as legitimate?'

'Was that the only reason?'

Mara hesitated, recognizing the trip wire. Thrawn had been in command of the Empire for over a year now, and yet she hadn't approached him until now. 'There were other reasons,' she said. 'None of which I wish to discuss at this time.'

His face hardened. 'As, I presume, you don't wish to discuss why you helped Skywalker escape from Talon Karrde?'

YOU WILL KILL LUKE SKYWALKER.

Mara jerked, unsure for that first frozen heartbeat whether the voice had been real or just in her mind. The strange buzzing intensified, and for a moment she could almost see the Emperor's wizened face glaring at her. The image grew clearer, the rest of the room beginning to swim before her eyes . . .

She took a deep breath, forcing calmness. She would not fall apart. Not here; not in front of the Grand Admiral. 'It wasn't my idea to let Skywalker escape,' she said.

'And you were unable to alter that decision?' Thrawn asked, the eyebrow lifting again. 'You, the Emperor's Hand?'

'We were on Myrkr,' Mara reminded him stiffly. 'Under the influence of a planetful of ysalamiri.' She glanced over his shoulder at the ysalamir hanging from the nutrient frame behind his chair. 'I doubt you've forgotten their effect on the Force.'

'Oh, I remember it quite well,' Thrawn nodded. 'It's their dampening of the Force, in fact, that proves Sky-walker had help in his escape. All I need to know from you is whether it was Karrde himself who gave the order, or others of his group acting independently.'

So that he would know where to focus his revenge. Mara looked into those glowing eyes, beginning to remember now why the Emperor had made this man a Grand Admiral. 'It doesn't matter who's responsible,' she said. 'I'm here to offer a deal that'll clear the debt.'

'I'm listening,' Thrawn said, his face neutral.

'I want you to stop your harassment of Karrde and his organization. To cancel the cash bounty on all of us, and clear us with all Imperial forces and worlds that you control.' She hesitated; but this was no time to go all bashful. 'I also want a monetary credit of three million to be deposited under Karrde's name toward the purchase of Imperial goods and services.'

'Indeed,' Thrawn said, his lip twitching in an amused smile. 'I'm afraid Skywalker isn't worth nearly that much to me. Or do you propose to deliver Coruscant, as well?'

'I'm not offering Skywalker or Coruscant,' Mara said. 'I'm offering the *Katana* fleet.'

The amused smile vanished. 'The *Katana* fleet?' Thrawn repeated quietly, his eyes glittering.

'Yes, the *Katana* fleet,' Mara said. 'The Dark Force, if you prefer the more dramatic title. I presume you've heard of it?'

'I have indeed. Where is it?'

The tone of command again; but this time Mara was ready for it. Not that it would have done him any good anyway. 'I don't know,' she told him. 'But Karrde does.'

For a long moment Thrawn gazed at her in silence. 'How?' he asked at last.

'He was on a smuggling mission that went sour,' she

told him. 'They escaped past some Imperial watchdogs, but didn't have time to do a proper jump calculation. They ran into the fleet, thought it was a trap, and jumped again, nearly destroying the ship in the process. Karrde was on nav duty; later, he figured out what they'd hit.'

'Interesting,' he murmured. 'When exactly was this?'

'That's all I'll give you until we have a deal,' Mara told him. She caught the expression on his face— 'And if you're thinking of running me through one of Intelligence's sifters, don't bother. I really *don't* know where the fleet is.'

Thrawn studied her. 'And you would have blocks set up around it even if you did,' he agreed. 'All right. Tell me where Karrde is, then.'

'So Intelligence can sift him instead?' Mara shook her head. 'No. Let me go back to him, and I'll get you the location. Then we'll trade. Assuming the deal is to your liking.'

A dark shadow had settled across Thrawn's face. 'Do not presume to dictate to me, Mara Jade,' he said quietly. 'Not even in private.'

A small shiver ran up Mara's back. Yes; she was remembering indeed why Thrawn had been made a Grand Admiral. 'I was the Emperor's Hand,' she reminded him, matching the steel in his tone as best she could. Even to her own ears it came out a poor second. 'I spoke for him . . . and even Grand Admirals were obliged to listen.'

Thrawn smiled sardonically. 'Really. Your memory serves you poorly, Emperor's Hand. When all is said and done, you were little more than a highly specialized courier.'

Mara glared at him. 'Perhaps it is *your* memory that needs refreshing, Grand Admiral Thrawn,' she retorted.

'I traveled throughout the Empire in his name, making policy decisions that changed lives at the highest levels of government—'

'You carried out his will,' Thrawn cut her off sharply. 'No more. Whether you heard his commands more clearly than the rest of his Hands is irrelevant. It was still his decisions that you implemented.'

'What do you mean, the rest of his Hands?' Mara sniffed. 'I was the only—'

She broke off. The look on Thrawn's face ... and abruptly, all her rising anger drained away. 'No,' she breathed. 'No. You're wrong.'

He shrugged. 'Believe what you wish. But don't attempt to blind others with exaggerated memories of your own importance.' Reaching to his control board, he tapped a key. 'Captain? What report from the boarding party?'

The reply wasn't audible; but Mara wasn't interested in what Thrawn's men were doing, anyway. He was wrong. He *had* to be wrong. Hadn't the Emperor himself given her the title of Emperor's Hand? Hadn't he himself brought her to Coruscant from her home and trained her, teaching her how to use her rare sensitivity to the Force to serve him?

He wouldn't have lied to her. He wouldn't have.

'No, there's no point to that,' Thrawn said. He looked up at Mara. 'You don't happen to have any idea why Leia Organa Solo might have come to Endor, do you?'

With an effort, Mara brought her thoughts back from the past. 'Organa Solo is here?'

'The *Millennium Falcon* is, at any rate,' he said grimly. 'Left in orbit, which unfortunately leaves us no way of knowing where she might be. If she's there at all.' He turned back to his board. 'Very well, Captain. Have the ship brought aboard. Perhaps a closer examination will tell us something.'

He got an acknowledgement and keyed off the circuit. 'Very well, Emperor's Hand,' he said, looking up at Mara again. 'We have an agreement. The Dark Force for the lifting of our death mark against Karrde. How long will it take you to return to Karrde's current base?'

Mara hesitated; but that information wouldn't do the Grand Admiral much good. 'On the *Etherway*, about three days. Two and a half if I push it.'

'I suggest you do so,' Thrawn said. 'Since you have exactly eight days to obtain the location and bring it back here to me.'

Mara stared at him. 'Eight days? But that—'

'Eight days. Or I find him and get the location my way.'

A dozen possible retorts rushed through Mara's mind. Another look at those glowing red eyes silenced all of them. 'I'll do what I can,' she managed. Turning, she headed back across the room.

'I'm sure you will,' he said after her. 'And afterward, we'll sit down and have a long talk together. About your years away from Imperial service ... and why you've been so long in returning.'

Pellaeon stared rigidly at his commander, heart thudding audibly in his chest. 'The *Katana* fleet?' he repeated carefully.

'So our young Emperor's Hand told me,' Thrawn said. His gaze was fixed solidly on one of the displays in front of him. 'She may be lying, of course.'

Pellaeon nodded mechanically, the possibilities sweeping

out like a spread cloak before him. 'The Dark Force,' he murmured the old nickname, listening to the words echo through his mind. 'You know, I once had hopes of finding the fleet myself.'

'Most everyone your age did,' Thrawn returned dryly. 'Is the homing device properly installed aboard her ship?'

'Yes, sir.' Pellaeon let his gaze drift around the room, his eyes focusing without real interest on the sculptures and flats that Thrawn had on display today. The Dark Force. Lost for nearly fifty-five years. Now within their grasp . . .

He frowned suddenly at the sculptures. Many of them looked familiar, somehow.

'They're the various pieces of art that graced the offices of Rendili StarDrive and the Fleet planning department at the time they were working on the basic design of the *Katana*,' Thrawn answered his unspoken question.

'I see,' Pellaeon said. He took a deep breath and, reluctantly, brought himself back to reality. 'You realize, sir, how improbable this claim of Jade's really is.'

'Certainly it's improbable.' Thrawn raised glowing eyes to Pellaeon. 'But it's also true.' He tapped a switch, and part of the art gallery vanished. 'Observe.'

Pellaeon turned to look. It was the same scene Thrawn had showed him a few days earlier: the three renegade Dreadnaughts providing cover fire off New Cov so that the *Lady Luck* and that unidentified freighter could escape—

He inhaled sharply, a sudden suspicion flooding into him. '*Those* ships?'

'Yes,' Thrawn said, his voice grimly satisfied. 'The differences between regular and slave-rigged Dreadnaughts are subtle, but visible enough when you know to look for them.'

Pellaeon frowned at the holo, trying hard to fit all of it together. 'Your permission, Admiral, but it doesn't make sense for Karrde to be supplying this renegade Corellian with ships.'

'I agree,' Thrawn nodded. 'Obviously, someone else from that ill-fated smuggling ship also realized what it was they'd stumbled across. We're going to find that someone.'

'Do we have any leads?'

'A few. According to Jade, they escaped from an Imperial force on the way out of a botched job. All such incidents should be on file somewhere; we'll correlate with what we know about Karrde's checkered past and see what turns up. Jade also said that the ship was badly damaged in the process of doing its second jump. If they had to go to a major spaceport for repairs, that should be on file, as well.'

'I'll put Intelligence on it immediately,' Pellaeon nodded.

'Good.' Thrawn's eyes unfocused for a moment. 'And I also want you to get in contact with Niles Ferrier.'

Pellaeon had to search his memory. 'That ship thief you sent out to look for the Corellian's home base?'

'That's the one,' Thrawn said. 'Tell him to forget the Corellian and concentrate instead on Solo and Calrissian.' He cocked an eyebrow. 'After all, if the Corellian is indeed planning to join the Rebellion, what better dowry could he bring than the *Katana* fleet?'

The comm pinged. 'Yes?' Thrawn asked.

'Sir, the target has made the jump to lightspeed,' a voice reported. 'We've got a strong signal from the beacon; we're doing a probability extrapolation now.'

'Very good, Lieutenant,' Thrawn said. 'Don't bother with any extrapolations just yet – she'll change course at least once more before settling down on her true heading.'

'Yes, sir.'

'Still, we don't want her getting too far ahead of us,' Thrawn told Pellaeon as he keyed off the comm. 'You'd best return to the bridge, Captain, and get the *Chimaera* moving after her.'

'Yes, sir.' Pellaeon hesitated. 'I thought we were going to give her time to get the *Katana*'s location for us.'

Thrawn's expression hardened. 'She's not part of the Empire any more, Captain,' he said. 'She may want us to believe that she's coming back – she may even believe it herself. But she isn't. No matter. She's leading us to Karrde, and that's the important thing. Between him and our Corellian renegade we have two leads to the *Katana* fleet. One way or the other, we'll find it.'

Pellaeon nodded, feeling the stirrings of excitement again despite his best efforts to remain unemotional about this. The *Katana* fleet. Two hundred Dreadnaughts, just sitting there waiting for the Empire to take possession . . .

'I have the feeling, Admiral,' he said, 'that our final offensive against the Rebellion may be ready to launch a bit ahead of schedule.'

Thrawn smiled. 'I believe, Captain, that you may be right.'

CHAPTER EIGHTEEN

⬦

They had been sitting around the table in the maitra-kh's house since early morning, studying maps and floor plans and diagrams, searching for a plan of action that would be more than simply a complicated way of surrendering. Finally, just before noon, Leia called a halt. 'I can't look at this any more,' she told Chewbacca, closing her eyes briefly and rubbing her thumbs against throbbing temples. 'Let's go outside for a while.'

Chewbacca growled an objection. 'Yes, of course there are risks,' she agreed wearily. 'But the whole village knows we're here, and no-one's told the authorities yet. Come on; it'll be OK.' Stepping to the door, she opened it and went out. Chewbacca grumbled under his breath, but followed after her.

The late morning sunshine was blazing brightly down, with only a scattering of high clouds to interfere. Leia glanced upward at the clear sky, shivering involuntarily at the sudden sensation of nakedness that flooded in on her. A clear sky, all the way up to space . . . but it was all right. A little before midnight the maitrakh had brought the news of the Star Destroyer's imminent departure, a departure which she and Chewbacca had been able to watch with the macrobinoculars from the Wookiee's kit. It had been their first break since Khabarakh's arrest: just as it had begun to look like she and Chewbacca would be pinned down here until it was too late, the Grand Admiral had abruptly left.

It was an unexpected gift . . . a gift which Leia couldn't help but view with suspicion. From the way the Grand Admiral had been talking in the *dukha*, she'd expected him to stay here until Khabarakh's humiliation period had ended, after which the shipboard interrogation would begin. Perhaps he'd changed his mind and had taken Khabarakh back early, with a backhand gesture of contempt for Noghri tradition. But the maitrakh had said that Khabarakh was still on public display in the center of Nystao.

Unless she was lying about that. Or was herself being lied to about it. But if the Grand Admiral suspected enough to lie to the maitrakh, why hadn't a legion of Imperial troops already swooped down on them?

But he was a Grand Admiral, with all the cunning and subtlety and tactical genius that the title implied. This whole thing could be a convoluted, carefully orchestrated trap . . . and if it was, chances were she would never even see it until it had been sprung around her.

Stop it! she ordered herself firmly. Letting herself get caught up in the mythos of infallibility that had been built up around the Grand Admirals would gain her nothing but mental paralysis. Even Grand Admirals could make mistakes, and there were any number of reasons why he might have had to leave Honoghr. Perhaps some part of the campaign against the New Republic had gone sour, requiring his attention elsewhere. Or perhaps he'd simply gone off on some short errand, intending to be back in a day or two.

Either way, it meant that the time to strike was now. If they could only find something to strike at.

Beside her, Chewbacca growled a suggestion. 'We can't do that,' Leia shook her head. 'It'd be no better than a full-blown attack on the spaceport. We have to keep damage to Nystao and its people to an absolute minimum.'

The Wookiee snarled impatiently.

'I don't *know* what else to do,' she snapped back. 'All I know is that death and massive destruction won't do anything but put us back where we were before we came here. It certainly won't convince the Noghri that they should leave the Empire and come over to our side.'

She looked out past the cluster of huts at the distant hills and the brown *kholm-grass* rippling in the breeze. Glinting in the sunlight, the squat box shapes of a dozen decon droids were hard at work, scooping up a quarter cubic meter of topsoil with each bite, running it through some exotic catalytic magic in their interiors, and dumping the cleansed product out the back. Slowly but steadily bringing the people of Honoghr back from the edge of the destruction they'd faced ... and a highly visible reminder, if anyone needed it, of the Empire's benevolence toward them.

'Lady Vader,' a gravelly voice mewed from just behind her.

Leia jumped. 'Good morning, maitrakh,' she said, turning and giving the Noghri a solemn nod. 'I trust you are well this morning?'

'I feel no sickness,' the other said shortly.

'Good,' Leia said, the word sounding rather lame. The

maitrakh hadn't been so impolite as to say anything out loud, but it was clear enough that she considered herself to be in a no-win situation here, with dishonor and perhaps even death waiting for her family as soon as the Grand Admiral discovered what Khabarakh had done. It was probably only a matter of time, Leia knew, before she came to the conclusion that turning the intruders over to the Empire herself would be the least disastrous course still open to her.

'Your plans,' the maitrakh said. 'How do they go?'

Leia glanced at Chewbacca. 'We're making progress,' she said. It was true enough, after a fashion: the elimination of every approach they'd come up with *did* technically qualify as progress. 'We still have a long way to go, though.'

'Yes,' the maitrakh said. She looked out past the buildings. 'Your droid has spent much time with the other machines.'

'There isn't as much here for him to do as I'd thought there would be,' Leia said. 'You and many of your people speak Basic better than I'd anticipated.'

'The Grand Admiral has taught us well.'

'As did my father, the Lord Darth Vader, before him,' Leia reminded her.

The maitrakh was silent a moment. 'Yes,' she conceded reluctantly.

Leia felt a chill run up her back. The first step in a betrayal would be to put emotional distance between the Noghri and their former lord.

'That area will be finished soon,' the maitrakh said, pointing to the laboring decon droids. 'If they finish within the next ten days, we will be able to plant there this season.'

'Will the extra land be enough to make you self-sufficient?' Leia asked.

'It will help. But not enough.'

Leia nodded, feeling a fresh surge of frustration. To her, the Empire's scheme was as blatant as it was cynical: with careful tuning of the whole decontamination process, they could keep the Noghri on the verge of independence indefinitely without ever letting them quite make it over that line. She knew it; the maitrakh herself suspected it. But as for proving it . . .

'Chewie, are you familiar at all with decon droids?' she asked suddenly. This thought had occurred to her once before, but she'd never gotten around to following up on it. 'Enough that you could figure out how long it would take the number of droids they have on Honoghr to decontaminate this much land?'

The Wookiee growled an affirmative, and launched into a run-down of the relevant numbers – clearly, the question had occurred to him, too. 'I don't need the complete analysis right now,' Leia interrupted the stream of estimates and extrapolations and rules of thumb. 'Have you got a bottom line?'

He did. Eight years.

'I see,' Leia murmured, the brief flicker of hope fading back into the overall gloom. 'That would have put it right about the height of the war, wouldn't it?'

'You still believe the Grand Admiral has deceived us?' the maitrakh accused.

'I *know* he's deceiving you,' Leia retorted. 'I just can't prove it.'

The maitrakh was silent for a minute. 'What then will you do?'

Leia took a deep breath, exhaled it quietly. 'We have to leave Honoghr. That means breaking into the spaceport at Nystao and stealing a ship.'

'There should be no difficulty in that for a daughter of the Lord Darth Vader.'

Leia grimaced, thinking of how the maitrakh had effortlessly sneaked up on them a minute ago. The guards at the spaceport would be younger and far better trained. These people must have been fantastic hunters before the Emperor turned them into his private killing machines. 'Stealing a ship won't be too hard,' she told the maitrakh, aware of just how far she was stretching the truth here. 'The difficulty arises from the fact that we have to take Khabarakh with us.'

The maitrakh stopped short. 'What is that you say?' she hissed.

'It's the only way,' Leia said. 'If Khabarakh is left to the Empire, they'll make him tell everything that's occurred here. And when that happens, he and you will both die. Perhaps your whole family with you. We can't allow that.'

'Then you face death yourselves,' the maitrakh said. 'The guards will not easily allow Khabarakh to be freed.'

'I know,' Leia said, acutely aware of the two small lives she carried within her. 'We'll have to take that risk.'

'There will be no honor in such a sacrifice,' the old Noghri all but snarled. 'The clan Kihm'bar will not carve it into history. Neither will the Noghri people long remember.'

'I'm not doing it for the praise of the Noghri people,' Leia sighed, suddenly weary of banging her head against alien misunderstandings. She'd been doing it in one form or another, it seemed, for the whole of her life. 'I'm doing it because I'm tired of people dying for my mistakes. I asked Khabarakh to bring me to Honoghr – what's happened is my responsibility. I can't just run off and leave you to the Grand Admiral's vengeance.'

'Our lord the Grand Admiral would not deal so harshly with us.'

Leia turned to look the maitrakh straight in the eye. 'The Empire once destroyed an entire world because of me,' she said quietly. 'I don't ever want that to happen again.'

She held the maitrakh's gaze a moment longer, then turned away, her mind twisted in a tangle of conflicting thoughts and emotions. Was she doing the right thing? She'd risked her life countless times before, but always for her comrades in the Rebellion and for a cause she believed in. To do the same for servants of the Empire – even servants who'd been duped into that role – was something else entirely. Chewbacca didn't like any of this; she could tell that much from his sense and the stiff way he stood at her side. But he would go along, driven by his own sense of honor and the life-debt he had sworn to Han.

She blinked back sudden tears, her hand going to the bulge of her belly. Han would understand. He would argue against such a risk, but down deep he would understand. Otherwise, he wouldn't have let her come here in the first place.

If she didn't return, he would almost certainly blame himself.

'The humiliation period has been extended for four more days,' the maitrakh murmured beside her. 'In two days' time the moons will give their least light. It would be best to wait until then.'

Leia frowned at her. The maitrakh met her gaze

steadily, her alien face unreadable. 'Are you offering me your help?' Leia asked.

'There is honor in you, Lady Vader,' the maitrakh said, her voice quiet. 'For the life and honor of my thirdson, I will go with you. Perhaps we will die together.'

Leia nodded, her heart aching. 'Perhaps we will.'

But she wouldn't. The maitrakh and Khabarakh might die, and probably Chewbacca beside them. But not her. The Lady Vader they would take alive, and save as a gift for their lord the Grand Admiral.

Who would smile, and speak politely, and take her children away from her.

She looked out at the fields, wishing Han were here. And wondered if he would ever know what had happened to her.

'Come,' the maitrakh said. 'Let us return to the house. There are many things about Nystao which you must yet learn.'

'I'm glad you finally called,' Winter's voice came over the *Lady Luck*'s speaker, distorted slightly by a not-quite-attuned scrambler package. 'I was starting to worry.'

'We're OK – we just had to run silent awhile,' Han assured her. 'You got trouble back there?'

'No more than when you left,' she said. 'The Imperials are still hitting our shipping out there, and no-one's figured out what to do about it. Fey'lya's trying to persuade the Council that he could do a better job of defense than Ackbar's people, but so far Mon Mothma hasn't taken him up on the offer. I get the feeling that some of the Council members are starting to have second thoughts about his motivations for all of this.'

'Good,' Han growled. 'Maybe they'll tell him to shut up and put Ackbar back in command.'

'Unfortunately, Fey'lya's still got too much support to ignore completely,' Winter said. 'Particularly among the military.'

'Yeah.' Han braced himself. 'I don't suppose you've heard from Leia.'

'Not yet,' Winter said; and Han could hear the underlying tension in her voice. She was worried, too. 'But I *did* hear from Luke. That's why I wanted to get in touch with you, in fact.'

'Is he in trouble?'

'I don't know – the message didn't say. He wants you to rendezvous with him on New Cov.'

'New Cov?' Han frowned down at the cloud-speckled planet turning beneath them. 'Why?'

'The message didn't say. Just that he'd meet you at the, quote, money-changing center, unquote.'

'The—?' Han shifted his frown to Lando. 'What's that supposed to mean?'

'He's talking about the Mishra tapcafe in Ilic where he and I met while you were following Breil'lya,' Lando said. 'Private joke – I'll fill you in later.'

'So that means there's no question Luke sent the message?' Winter asked.

'Wait a minute,' Han put in as Lando started to answer. 'Didn't you talk to him personally?'

'No, the message came in printed,' Winter said. 'Not on any scrambler, either.'

'He doesn't have a scrambler on his X-wing, does he?' Lando asked.

'No, but he could get a message coded at any New

Republic diplomatic post,' Han said slowly. 'Is this private joke something only you two would know about?'

'Us two, plus maybe a hundred bystanders,' Lando conceded. 'You think it's a trap?'

'Could be. OK, Winter, thanks. We'll be checking in more often from now on.'

'All right. Be careful.'

'You bet.'

He signed off and looked at Lando. 'It's your ship, pal. You want to go down and take a look, or give it a miss and go check out this swimming casino of yours?'

Lando hissed a breath between his teeth. 'I don't think we've got much choice,' he said. 'If the message *was* from Luke, it's probably important.'

'And if it wasn't?'

Lando favored him with a tight grin. 'Hey, we've run Imperial traps before. Come on, let's take her down.'

After the way they'd blasted out of Ilic a few days earlier, it was doubtful the local authorities would be especially overjoyed to see the return of the *Lady Luck* to their city. Fortunately, he'd put the past two days' worth of leisure time to good use; and as they set down inside the domed landing area, the spaceport computer dutifully logged the arrival of the pleasure yacht *Tamar's Folly*.

'It's just terrific to be back,' Han commented dryly as he and Lando started down the ramp. 'Probably ought to snoop around a little before we head down to the Mishra.'

Beside him, Lando stiffened. 'I don't think we're going to have to bother with the Mishra,' he said quietly.

Han threw a quick glance at him, dropping his hand casually to his blaster as he shifted his gaze to where Lando was looking. Standing five meters from the end of the *Lady Luck*'s ramp was a bulky man in an ornate tunic, chewing on the end of a cigarra, and smiling with sly innocence up at them.

'Friend of yours?' Han murmured.

'I wouldn't go *that* far,' Lando murmured back. 'Name's Niles Ferrier. Ship thief and occasional smuggler.'

'He was in on the Mishra thing, I take it?'

'One of the key players, actually.'

Han nodded, letting his eyes drift around the space-port. Among the dozens of people moving briskly about their business, he spotted three or four who seemed to be loitering nearby. 'Ship thief, huh?'

'Yes, but he's not going to bother with anything as small as the *Lady Luck*,' Lando assured him.

Han grunted. 'Watch him anyway.'

'You bet.'

They reached the foot of the ramp and, by unspoken but mutual consent, stopped there and waited. Ferrier's grin broadened a bit, and he sauntered forward to meet them. 'Hello there, Calrissian,' he said. 'We keep bumping into each other, don't we?'

'Hello, *Luke*,' Han spoke up before Lando could reply. 'You've changed.'

Ferrier's smile turned almost sheepish. 'Yeah – sorry about that. I didn't figure you'd come if I put my own name on the message.'

'Where's Luke?' Han demanded.

'Search me,' Ferrier shrugged. 'He burned out of here same time you did – that was the last I saw of him.'

Han studied his face, looking for a lie. He didn't see one. 'What do you want?'

'I want to cut a deal with the New Republic,' Ferrier

said, lowering his voice. 'A deal for some new warships. You interested?'

Han felt a tingle at the back of his neck. 'We might be,' he said, trying to sound casual. 'What kind of ships are we talking about?'

Ferrier gestured to the ramp. 'How about we talk in the ship?'

'How about we talk out here?' Lando retorted.

Ferrier seemed taken aback. 'Take it easy, Calrissian,' he said soothingly. 'What do you think I'm going to do, walk off with your ship in my pocket?'

'What kind of ships?' Han repeated.

Ferrier looked at him for a moment, then made a show of glancing around the area. 'Big ones,' he said, lowering his voice. 'Dreadnaught class.' He lowered his voice still further. 'The *Katana* fleet.'

With an effort, Han kept his sabacc face in place. 'The *Katana* fleet. Right.'

'I'm not kidding,' Ferrier insisted. 'The *Katana*'s been found . . . and I've got a line on the guy who found it.'

'Yeah?' Han said. Something in Ferrier's face—

He turned around quickly, half expecting to see someone trying to sneak up over the edge of the ramp into the *Lady Luck*. But aside from the usual mix of shadows from the spaceport lights, there was nothing there. 'Something?' Lando demanded.

'No,' Han said, turning back to Ferrier. If the thief really did have a line on Bel Iblis's supplier, it could save them a lot of time. But if he had nothing but rumors – and was maybe hoping to wangle something a little more solid . . . 'What makes you think this guy has anything?' he demanded.

Ferrier smiled slyly. 'Free information, Solo? Come on – you know better than that.'

'All right, then,' Lando said. 'What do you want from us, and what are you offering in trade?'

'I know the guy's name,' Ferrier said, his face turning serious again. 'But I don't know where he is. I thought we could pool our resources, see if we can get to him before the Empire does.'

Han felt his throat tighten. 'What makes you think the Empire's involved?'

Ferrier threw him a scornful look. 'With Grand Admiral Thrawn in charge over there? He's involved in everything.'

Han smiled lopsidedly. At last they had a name to go with the uniform. 'Thrawn, huh? Thanks, Ferrier.'

Ferrier's face went rigid as he suddenly realized what he'd just given away. 'No charge,' he said between stiff lips.

'We still haven't heard what we're getting out of the deal,' Lando reminded him.

'Do you know where he is?' Ferrier asked.

'We have a lead,' Lando said. 'What are you offering?'

Ferrier shifted a measuring gaze back and forth between them. 'I'll give you half the ships we take out,' he said at last. 'Plus an option for the New Republic to buy out the rest at a reasonable price.'

'What's a reasonable price?' Han asked.

'Depends on what kind of shape they're in,' Ferrier countered. 'I'm sure we'll be able to come to an agreement.'

'Mmm.' Han looked at Lando. 'What do you think?'

'Forget it,' Lando said, his voice hard. 'You want to give us the name, fine – if it checks out, we'll make sure you're well paid once we've got the ships. Otherwise, shove off.'

Ferrier drew back. 'Well, fine,' he said, sounding more

hurt than annoyed. 'You want to do it all by yourselves, be my guest. But if we get to the ships first, your precious little New Republic's going to pay a lot more to get them. A *lot* more.'

Spinning around, he stalked off. 'Come on, Han, let's get out of here,' Lando muttered, his eyes on Ferrier's retreating back.

'Yeah,' Han said, looking around for the loiterers he'd spotted earlier. They, too, were drifting away. It didn't look like trouble; but he kept his hand on his blaster anyway until they were inside the *Lady Luck* with the hatch sealed.

'I'll prep for lift,' Lando said as they headed back to the cockpit. 'You talk to Control, get us an exit slot.'

'OK,' Han said. 'You know, with a little more bargaining—'

'I don't trust him,' Lando cut him off, running his hand over the start-up switches. 'He was smiling too much. And he gave up too easily.'

It was a hard comment to argue against. And as Han had noted earlier, it *was* Lando's ship. Shrugging to himself, he keyed for spaceport control.

They were out in ten minutes, once again leaving an unhappy group of controllers behind them. 'I hope this is the last time we have to come here,' Han said, scowling across the cockpit at Lando. 'I get the feeling we've worn out our welcome.'

Lando threw him a sideways glance. 'Well, well. Since when did you start caring what other people thought about you?'

'Since I married a princess and started carrying a government ID,' Han growled back. 'Anyway, I thought you were supposed to be respectable, too.'

'It comes and goes. Ah-*ha*.' He smiled humorlessly at Han. 'It looks like while we were talking to Ferrier, some-one sneaked up and put something on our hull. Ten'll get you one it's a homing beacon.'

'What a surprise,' Han said, keying his display for its location. It was on the rear lower hull, back near the ramp where it would be out of most of the lift-off turbu-lence. 'What do you want to do with it?'

'The Terrijo system's more or less on the way to Panto-lomin,' Lando said, consulting his display. 'We'll swing through there and drop it off.'

'OK.' Han scowled at his display. 'Too bad we can't put it on another ship right here. That way he wouldn't even know what direction we're going.'

Lando shook his head. 'He'll know we've spotted it if we put down on New Cov now. Unless you want to take it off up here and try to toss it onto another passing ship.' He glanced at Han; paused for a longer look. 'We're not going to try it, Han,' he said firmly. 'Get that look out of your eye.'

'Oh, all right,' Han grumbled. 'That'd get him off our backs, though.'

'And might get you killed in the process,' Lando retorted. 'And then *I'd* have to go back and explain it to Leia. Forget it.'

Han gritted his teeth. Leia. 'Yeah,' he said with a sigh.

Lando looked at him again. 'Come on, buddy, relax. Ferrier hasn't got a hope of beating us. Trust me – we're going to win this one.'

Han nodded. He hadn't been thinking about Ferrier, actually. Or about the *Katana* fleet. 'I know,' he said.

———

The *Lady Luck* disappeared smoothly through one of the ducts in the transparisteel dome, and Ferrier shifted his cigarra to the other side of his mouth. 'You're sure they won't find the second beacon?' he asked.

Beside him, the oddly shaped shadow between a pile of shipping crates stirred. 'They will not,' it said in a voice like cold running water.

'You'd better be right,' Ferrier warned, a note of menace in his voice. 'I didn't stand there and take that garbage from them for nothing.' He glared at the shadow. 'As it was, you almost gave the game away,' he said accusingly. 'Solo looked straight back at you once.'

'There was no danger,' the wraith said flatly. 'Humans need movement to see. Not-moving shadows are of no concern.'

'Well, it worked this time,' Ferrier was willing to concede. 'You're still lucky it was Solo and not Calrissian who looked – he saw you once before, you know. Next time, keep your big feet quiet.'

The wraith said nothing. 'Oh, go on, get back to the ship,' Ferrier ordered. 'Tell Abric to get 'er ready to lift. We've got ourselves a fortune to make.'

He threw a last look upward. 'And maybe,' he added with grim satisfaction, 'a smart-mouthed gambler to take out.'

CHAPTER NINETEEN

The *Etherway* was clearly visible now, dropping like a misshapen rock out of the sky toward its assigned landing pit. Standing in the protective shadow of the exit tunnel, Karrde watched its approach, stroking the grip of his blaster gently with his fingertips and trying to ignore the uneasiness still tickling the back of his mind. Mara was over three days late in bringing the freighter back from Abregado – not a particularly significant delay under normal conditions, but this trip had hardly qualified as normal. But there had been no other ships on her tail as she entered orbit, and she'd transmitted all the proper 'all clear' code signals to him as she dropped into the approach pattern. And aside from the incompetence of the controllers, who'd taken an inordinate amount of time to decide which pit she was actually being assigned to, the landing itself had so far been completely routine.

Karrde smiled wryly as he watched the ship come down. There had been times in the past three days when he'd thought about Mara's hatred of Luke Skywalker, and had wondered if she had decided to drop out of his life as mysteriously as she'd dropped into it. But it seemed now that his original reading of her had been correct.

Mara Jade wasn't the sort of person who gave her loyalty easily, but once she'd made a decision she stuck with it. If she ever ran out on him, she wouldn't do so in a stolen ship. Not stolen from him, anyway.

The *Etherway* was on its final approach now, rotating on its repulsorlifts to orient its hatchway toward the exit tunnel. Obviously, Karrde's reading of Han Solo had been correct, too. Even if the other hadn't been quite gullible enough to send a Mon Cal Star Cruiser out to Myrkr, he'd at least kept his promise to get the *Etherway* out of impoundment. Apparently, all of Karrde's private worrying of the past three days had been for nothing.

But the uneasiness was still there.

With a hiss of back-release outgassing, the *Etherway* settled to the stress-scored paving of the landing pit. His eyes on the closed hatchway, Karrde pulled his comlink from his belt and thumbed for his backup spotter. 'Dankin? Anything suspicious in sight?'

'Not a thing,' the other's voice came back promptly. 'Looks very quiet over there.'

Karrde nodded. 'All right. Keep out of sight, but stay alert.'

He replaced the comlink in his belt. The *Etherway*'s landing ramp began to swing down, and he shifted his hand to a grip on his blaster. If this was a trap, now would be the likely time to spring it.

The hatchway opened, and Mara appeared. She glanced around the pit as she started down the ramp, spotting him immediately in his chosen shadow. 'Karrde?' she called.

'Welcome home, Mara,' he said, stepping out into the light. 'You're a bit late.'

'I wound up making a little detour,' she said grimly, coming toward him.

'That can happen,' he said, frowning. Her attention was still flitting around the pit, her face lined with a vague sort of tension. 'Trouble?' he asked quietly.

'I don't know,' she murmured. 'I feel—'

She never finished the sentence. At Karrde's belt his comlink suddenly squawked, screeched briefly with the electronic stress of blanket jamming, and then went silent. 'Come on,' Karrde snapped, drawing his blaster and spinning back toward the exit. At the far end of the tunnel he could see shapes moving; lifting his blaster, he fired toward them—

The violent thunderclap of a sonic boom shattered the air around him, slamming hard against his head and nearly toppling him to the ground. He glanced up, ears ringing, just as two slower-moving TIE fighters swooped past overhead, laying down a spitting pattern of laser fire at the mouth of the exit tunnel. The paving erupted into steaming blocks of half-molten ceramic under the assault, blocking any chance of quick escape in that direction. Karrde snapped off a reflexive if meaningless shot toward the TIE fighters; and he was just beginning to shift his aim back toward the figures in the tunnel when a dozen stormtroopers suddenly leaped into view at the upper rim of the landing pit, sliding down droplines to the ground. 'Down!' he snapped at Mara, his voice hardly audible to his paralyzed sense of hearing. He dived for the ground, hitting awkwardly on his left arm and bringing his blaster to bear on the nearest stormtrooper. He fired, missing by half a meter . . . and he was just noticing the curious fact that the Imperials weren't returning fire when the blaster was deftly plucked from his hand.

He rolled half over, looking up at Mara with stunned disbelief. 'What—'

She was standing over him, her face so pinched with emotion he could hardly recognize it, her lips moving with words he couldn't hear.

But he didn't really need any explanation. Strangely, he felt no anger at her; not for concealing her Imperial past from him all this time, nor for now returning to her origins. Only chagrin that he'd been fooled so easily and so thoroughly . . . and a strange regret that he had lost such a skilled associate.

The stormtroopers hauled him to his feet and moved him roughly toward a drop ship that was settling onto the paving beside the *Etherway*; and as he stumbled toward it, a stray thought occurred to him.

He was betrayed and captured and probably facing death . . . but at least he now had a partial answer to the mystery of why Mara wanted to kill Luke Skywalker.

Mara glared at the Grand Admiral, her hands curled into fists, her body trembling with rage. 'Eight days, Thrawn,' she snarled, her voice echoing oddly through the background noises of the *Chimaera*'s vast shuttle bay. 'You said eight days. You *promised* me eight days.'

Thrawn gazed back with a polite calmness that made her long to burn him down where he stood. 'I changed my mind,' he said coolly. 'It occurred to me that Karrde might not only refuse to divulge the *Katana* fleet's location, but might even abandon you here for suggesting that he make such a deal with us.'

'The gates of hell you did,' Mara snapped back. 'You planned to use me like this right from the start.'

'And it got us what we wanted,' the red-eyed freak said smoothly. 'That's all that matters.'

Deep within Mara, something snapped. Ignoring the armed stormtroopers standing just behind her, she threw herself at Thrawn, fingers hooking like a hunting bird's talons for his throat—

And came to an abrupt, bone-wrenching stop as Thrawn's Noghri bodyguard sidled in from two meters away, threw his arm across her neck and shoulder, and spun her around and halfway to the deck.

She grabbed at the iron-hard arm across her throat, simultaneously throwing her right elbow back toward his torso. But the blow missed; and even as she shifted to a two-handed grip on his arm, white spots began to flicker in her vision. His forearm was pressing solidly against her carotid artery, threatening her with unconsciousness.

There wasn't anything to be gained by blacking out. She relaxed her struggle, felt the pressure ease. Thrawn was still standing there, regarding her with amusement. 'That was very unprofessional of you, Emperor's Hand,' he chided.

Mara glared at him and lashed out again, this time with the Force. Thrawn frowned slightly, fingers moving across his neck as if trying to brush away an intangible cobweb. Mara leaned into her tenuous grip on his throat; and he brushed again at his neck before understanding came. 'All right, that's enough,' he said, his voice noticeably altered, his tone starting to get angry. 'Stop it, or Rukh will have to hurt you.'

Mara ignored the order, digging in as hard as she

could. Thrawn gazed unblinkingly back at her, his throat muscles moving as he fought against the grip. Mara clenched her teeth, waiting for the order or hand movement that would signal permission for the Noghri to choke her, or for the stormtroopers to burn her down.

But Thrawn remained silent and unmoving . . . and a minute later, gasping for breath, Mara had to concede defeat.

'I trust you've learned the limits of your small powers,' Thrawn said coldly, fingering his throat. But at least he didn't sound amused any more. 'A little trick the Emperor taught you?'

'He taught me a great many tricks,' Mara bit out, ignoring the throbbing in her temples. 'How to deal with traitors was one of them.'

Thrawn's glowing eyes glittered. 'Have a care, Jade,' he said softly. '*I* rule the Empire now. Not some long-dead Emperor; certainly not you. The only treason is defiance of my orders. I'm willing to let you come back to your rightful place in the Empire – as first officer, perhaps, of one of the *Katana* Dreadnaughts. But any further outbursts like this one and that offer will be summarily withdrawn.'

'And then you'll kill me, I suppose,' Mara growled.

'My Empire isn't in the habit of wasting valuable resources,' the other countered. 'You'd be given instead to Master C'baoth as a little bonus gift. And I suspect you would soon wish I'd had you executed.'

Mara stared at him, an involuntary shiver running up her back. 'Who is C'baoth?'

'Joruus C'baoth is a mad Jedi Master,' Thrawn told her darkly. 'He's consented to help our war effort, in exchange for Jedi to mold into whatever twisted image he chooses. Your friend Skywalker has already walked into his web; his sister, Organa Solo, we hope to deliver soon.' His face hardened. 'I would genuinely hate for you to have to join them.'

Mara took a deep breath. 'I understand,' she said, forcing out the words. 'You've made your point. It won't happen again.'

He eyed her a moment, then nodded. 'Apology accepted,' he said. 'Release her, Rukh. Now. Do I take it you wish to rejoin the Empire?'

The Noghri let go of her neck – reluctantly, Mara thought – and took a short step away. 'What about the rest of Karrde's people?' she asked.

'As we agreed, they're free to go about their business. I've already canceled all Imperial search and detention orders concerning them, and Captain Pellaeon is at this moment calling off the bounty hunters.'

'And Karrde himself?'

Thrawn studied her face. 'He'll remain aboard until he tells me where the *Katana* fleet is. If he does so with a minimum of wasted time and effort on our part, he'll receive the three million in compensation which you and I agreed on at Endor. If not . . . there may not be much left of him to pay compensation to.'

Mara felt her lip twitch. He wasn't bluffing, either. She'd seen what a full-bore Imperial interrogation could do. 'May I talk to him?' she asked.

'Why?'

'I might be able to persuade him to cooperate.'

Thrawn smiled slightly. 'Or could at least assure him that you did not, in fact, betray him?'

'He'll still be locked in your detention block,' Mara reminded him, forcing her voice to stay calm. 'There's no reason for him not to know the truth.'

Thrawn lifted his eyebrows. 'On the contrary,' he said. 'A sense of utter abandonment is one of the more useful psychological tools available to us. A few days with only thoughts of that sort to relieve the monotony may convince him to cooperate without harsher treatment.'

'Thrawn—' Mara broke off, strangling back the sudden flash of anger.

'That's better,' the Grand Admiral approved, his eyes steady on her face. 'Especially considering that the alternative is for me to turn him directly over to an interrogator droid. Is that what you want?'

'No, Admiral,' she said, feeling herself slump a little. 'I just . . . Karrde helped me when I had nowhere else to go.'

'I understand your feelings,' Thrawn said, his face hardening again. 'But they have no place here. Mixed loyalties are a luxury no officer of the Imperial Fleet can afford. Certainly not if she wishes someday to be given a command of her own.'

Mara drew herself up again to her full height. 'Yes, sir. It won't happen again.'

'I trust not.' Thrawn glanced past her shoulder and nodded. With a rustle of movement, her stormtrooper escort began to withdraw. 'The deck officer's station is just beneath the control tower,' he said, gesturing to the large transparisteel bubble nestled in among the racked TIE fighters three-quarters of the way up the hangar bay's back wall. 'He'll assign you a shuttle and pilot to take you back to the surface.'

It was clearly a dismissal. 'Yes, Admiral,' Mara said.

Stepping past him, she headed toward the door he'd indicated. For a moment she could feel his eyes on her, then heard the faint sound of his footsteps as he turned away toward the lift cluster beyond the starboard blast doors.

Yes; the Grand Admiral had made his point. But it wasn't exactly the one he'd intended to make. With that single casual act of betrayal, he had finally destroyed her last wistful hope that the new Empire might someday measure up to the one that Luke Skywalker had destroyed out from under her.

The Empire she'd once been proud to serve was gone. For ever.

It was a painful revelation, and a costly one. It could erase in one stroke everything she'd worked so hard to build up for herself over the last year.

It could also cost Karrde his life. And if it did, he would die believing that she had deliberately betrayed him to Thrawn.

The thought twisted in her stomach like a heated knife, mixing with her bitter anger toward Thrawn for lying to her and her shame at her own gullibility in trusting him in the first place. No matter how she looked at it, this mess was her fault.

It was up to her to fix it.

Beside the door to the deck officer's office was the huge archway that led from the hangar bay proper into the service and prep areas behind it. Mara threw a glance over her shoulder as she walked, and spotted Thrawn stepping into one of the turbolifts, his tame Noghri at his side. Her stormtrooper escort, too, had disappeared, its members probably returning to their private section aft for debriefing over the mission they'd just completed. There were twenty or thirty other people in the bay, but none of them seemed to be paying any particular attention to her.

It was probably the only chance she would ever get. With her ear cocked for the shout – or the blaster shot – that would mean she'd been noticed, she bypassed the deck officer's office and stepped past the retracted blast doors into the prep area.

There was a computer terminal just inside the archway, built against the wall where it would be accessible to both the forward prep area and the aft hangar bay. Its location made it an obvious target for unauthorized access, and as a consequence it would undoubtedly be protected by an elaborate entry code. Probably changed hourly, if she knew Thrawn; but what even a Grand Admiral might not know was that the Emperor had had a private back door installed into the main computer of every Star Destroyer. It had been his guarantee, first during his consolidation of power and then during the upheaval of Rebellion, that no commander could ever lock him out of his own ships. Not him, and not his top agents.

Mara keyed in the backdoor entry code, permitting herself a tight smile as she did so. Thrawn could consider her a glorified courier if he liked. But she knew better.

The code clicked, and she was in.

She called up a directory, trying to suppress the creepy awareness that she might already have brought the stormtroopers down on top of her. The backdoor code was hardwired into the system and impossible to eliminate, but if Thrawn suspected its existence, he might well have set a flag to trigger an alarm if it was ever used. And if he had, it would take far more than another show of humble loyalty to keep her out of trouble.

No stormtroopers had appeared by the time the directory came up. She keyed for the detention section and ran her eye down the listing, wishing fleetingly that she had an R2 astromech droid like Skywalker's to help cut through all of it. Even if Thrawn had missed the backdoor code, he would certainly have alerted the deck officer to expect her. If someone in the control tower noticed she was overdue and sent someone out to look for her . . .

There it was: an updated prisoner list. She keyed for it, pulling up a diagram of the entire detention block while she was at it. A duty roster was next, with attention paid to the shift changes, then back to the daily orders and a listing of the *Chimaera*'s projected course and destinations for the next six days. Thrawn had implied he would be waiting a few days before beginning a formal interrogation, letting boredom and tension and Karrde's own imagination wear down his resistance. Mara could only hope she could get back before that softening-up period was over.

A drop of sweat trickled down her spine as she cleared the display. And now came the really painful part. She'd run through the logic a dozen times while walking across the hangar bay deck, and each time had been forced to the same odious answer. Karrde would almost certainly have had a backup spotter watching the *Etherway*'s approach, who would have had a front-row view of the stormtroopers' trap. If Mara now returned free and clear from the *Chimaera*, she would never be able to convince Karrde's people that she hadn't betrayed him to the Imperials. She'd be lucky, in fact, if they didn't burn her down on sight.

She couldn't rescue Karrde alone. She couldn't expect any help from his organization. Which left only one person in the galaxy she might be able to enlist. Only one person who might possibly feel he owed Karrde something.

Clenching her teeth, she keyed for the current location of a Jedi Master named Joruus C'baoth.

It seemed to take the computer an inordinate amount of time to dig out the information, and the skin on Mara's back was starting to crawl by the time the machine finally spat it out. She caught the planet's name – Jomark – and keyed off, doing what she could to bury the fact that this interaction had ever taken place. Already she'd pushed her timing way too close to the wire; and if they caught her here on a computer she shouldn't have been able to access at all, she was likely to find herself in the cell next to Karrde's.

She barely made it. She'd just finished her cleanup and started back toward the archway when a young officer and three troopers came striding through from the hangar bay, their eyes and weapons clearly ready for trouble. One of the troopers spotted her, muttered something to the officer—

'Excuse me,' Mara called as all four turned to her. 'Can you tell me where I can find the deck officer?'

'I'm the deck officer,' the officer said, scowling at her as the group came to a halt in front of her. 'You Mara Jade?'

'Yes,' Mara said, putting on her best unconcerned/innocent expression. 'I was told your office was over here somewhere, but I couldn't find it.'

'It's on the other side of the wall,' the officer growled. Brushing past her, he stepped to the terminal she'd just left. 'Were you fiddling with this?' he asked, tapping a few keys.

'No,' Mara assured him. 'Why?'

'Never mind – it's still locked down,' the officer muttered under his breath. For a moment he looked around the area, as if searching for some other reason Mara might have wanted to be back here. But there was nothing; and almost reluctantly, he brought his attention back to her again. 'I've got orders to give you transport down to the planet.'

'I know,' she nodded. 'I'm ready.'

The shuttle lifted and turned and headed off into the sky. Standing by the *Etherway*'s ramp, the stink of burned paving still thick in the air, Mara watched the Imperial craft disappear over the top of the landing pit. 'Aves?' she called. 'Come on, Aves, you've got to be here somewhere.'

'Turn around and put your hands up,' the voice came from the shadows inside the ship's hatchway. 'All the way up. And don't forget I know about that little sleeve gun of yours.'

'The Imperials have it now,' Mara said as she turned her back to him and raised her hands. 'And I'm not here for a fight. I came for help.'

'You want help, go to your new friends upstairs,' Aves retorted. 'Or maybe they were always your friends, huh?'

He was goading her, Mara knew, pushing for a chance to vent his own anger and frustration in an argument or gun battle. 'I didn't betray him, Aves,' she said. 'I got picked up by the Imperials and blew them a smoke ring that I thought would buy us enough time to get out. It didn't.'

'I don't believe you,' Aves said flatly. There was a muffled clank of boot on metal as he came cautiously down the ramp.

'No, you believe me,' Mara shook her head. 'You wouldn't have come here if you didn't.'

She felt a breath of air on the back of her neck as he stepped close behind her. 'Don't move,' he ordered. Reaching carefully to her left arm, he pulled the sleeve down to reveal the empty holster. He checked her other sleeve, then ran a hand down each side of her body. 'All right, turn around,' he said, stepping back again.

She did so. He was standing a meter away from her, his face tight, his blaster pointed at her stomach. 'Turn the question around, Aves,' she suggested. 'If I betrayed Karrde to the Imperials, why would I come back here? Especially alone?'

'Maybe you needed to get something from the *Etherway*,' he countered harshly. 'Or maybe it's just a trick to try to round up the rest of us.'

Mara braced herself. 'If you really believe that,' she said quietly, 'you might as well go ahead and shoot. I can't get Karrde out of there without your help.'

For a long minute Aves stood there in silence. Mara watched his face, trying to ignore the white-knuckled hand holding the blaster. 'The others won't help you, you know,' he said. 'Half of them think you've been manipulating Karrde from the minute you joined up. Most of the rest figure you for the type who switches loyalties twice a year anyway.'

Mara grimaced. 'That was true once,' she admitted. 'Not any more.'

'You got any way to prove that?'

'Yeah – by getting Karrde out,' Mara retorted. 'Look, I haven't got time to talk. You going to help, or shoot?'

He hesitated for a handful of heartbeats. Then, almost reluctantly, he lowered the blaster until it was pointed at the ground. 'I'm probably scribing my own death mark,' he growled. 'What do you need?'

'For starters, a ship,' Mara said, silently letting out a breath she hadn't realized she'd been holding. 'Something smaller and faster than the *Etherway*. One of those three boosted Skipray blastboats we brought in from Vagran would do nicely. I'll also need one of those ysalamiri we've been carrying around on the *Wild Karrde*. Preferably on a nutrient frame that's portable.'

Aves frowned. 'What do you want with an ysalamir?'

'I'm going to talk to a Jedi,' she said briefly. 'I need a guarantee he'll listen.'

Aves studied her a moment, then shrugged. 'I suppose I really don't want to know. What else?'

Mara shook her head. 'That's it.'

His eyes narrowed. 'That's *it*?'

'That's it. How soon can you get them to me?'

Aves pursed his lips thoughtfully. 'Let's say an hour,' he said. 'That big swamp about fifty kilometers north of the city – you know it?'

Mara nodded. 'There's a soggy sort of island near the eastern edge.'

'Right. You bring the *Etherway* to the island and we'll do the switch there.' He glanced up at the freighter towering over him. 'If you think it's safe to move it.'

'It should be for now,' Mara said. 'Thrawn told me he'd lifted all the search and detention orders for the rest of the group. But you'd better disappear anyway after I go. He'll have the whole Fleet screaming down your necks again if and when I get Karrde out. Better run a fine-edge scan on the *Etherway* before you take it any-where, though – there has to be a homing beacon aboard for Thrawn to have gotten the jump on me the way he did.' She felt her lip twitch. 'And knowing Thrawn, he's probably got someone tailing me, too. I'll have to get rid of him before I leave the planet.'

'I can give you a hand with that,' Aves said grimly. 'We're disappearing anyway, right?'

'Right.' Mara paused, trying to think if there was any-thing else she needed to tell him. 'I guess that's it. Let's get going.'

'Right.' Aves hesitated. 'I still don't know whose side you're on, Mara. If you're on ours . . . good luck.'

She nodded, feeling a hard lump settle into her throat. 'Thanks.'

Two hours later she was strapped into the Skipray's cock-pit, a strange and unpleasant sense of *déjà vu* burning through her as she drove toward deep space. It had been in a ship just like this one that she'd screamed off into the sky over the Myrkr forest a few weeks ago, in hot pursuit of an escaped prisoner. Now, like a twisted repeat of his-tory, she once again found herself chasing after Luke Skywalker.

Only this time, she wasn't trying to kill or capture him. This time, she was going to plead for his help.

CHAPTER TWENTY

The last pair of villagers detached themselves from the group standing at the back wall and made their way toward the raised judgement seat. C'baoth stood there, watching them come; and then, as Luke had known he would, the Jedi Master stood up. 'Jedi Skywalker,' he said, gesturing Luke to the seat. 'The final case of the evening is yours.'

'Yes, Master C'baoth,' Luke said, bracing himself as he stepped over and gingerly sat down. It was, to his mind, a thoroughly uncomfortable chair: too warm, too large, and far too ornate. Even more than the rest of C'baoth's home, it had an alien smell to it, and a strangely disturbing aura that Luke could only assume was a lingering aftereffect of the hours the Jedi Master had spent in it judging his people.

Now it was Luke's turn to do so.

Taking a deep breath, trying to push back the fatigue that had become a permanent part of him, he nodded at the two villagers. 'I'm ready,' he said. 'Please begin.'

It was a relatively simple case, as such things went. The first villager's livestock had gotten through the second's fence and had stripped half a dozen of his fruit bushes before they'd been discovered and driven back. The animals' owner was willing to pay compensation for the ruined bushes, but the second was insisting that he also rebuild the fence. The first countered that a properly built fence wouldn't have failed in the first place and that, furthermore, his livestock had suffered injuries from the sharp edges as they went through. Luke sat quietly and let them talk, waiting until the arguments and counter-arguments finally ended.

'All right,' he said. 'In the matter of the fruit bushes themselves, my judgement is that you' – he nodded to the first villager – 'will pay for the replacement of those damaged beyond repair, plus an additional payment to compensate for the fruit eaten or destroyed by your livestock. The latter amount will be determined by the village council.'

Beside him C'baoth stirred, and Luke winced at the disapproval he could sense from the Jedi Master. For a second he floundered, wondering if he should back up and try a different solution. But changing his mind so abruptly didn't sound like a good thing to do. And anyway, he really didn't have any better ideas.

So what was he doing here?

He looked around the room, fighting against a sudden flush of nervousness. They were all looking at him: C'baoth, the two supplicants, the rest of the villagers who'd come tonight for Jedi judgement. All of them expecting him to make the right decision.

'As to the fence, I'll examine it tomorrow morning,' he continued. 'I want to see how badly it was damaged before I make my decision.'

The two men bowed and backed away. 'I therefore

declare this session to be closed,' C'baoth called. His voice echoed grandly, despite the relatively small size of the room. An interesting effect, and Luke found himself wondering if it was a trick of the room's acoustics or yet another Jedi technique that Master Yoda had never taught him. Though why he would ever need such a technique he couldn't imagine.

The last of the villagers filed out of the room. C'baoth cleared his throat; reflexively, Luke braced himself. 'I sometimes wonder, Jedi Skywalker,' the old man said gravely, 'whether or not you have really been listening to me these past few days.'

'I'm sorry, Master C'baoth,' Luke said, an all-too-familiar lump sticking in his throat. No matter how hard he tried, it seemed, he was never quite able to measure up to C'baoth's expectations.

'Sorry?' C'baoth's eyebrows rose sardonically. 'Sorry? Jedi Skywalker, you had it all right there in your hands. You should have cut off their prattle far sooner than you did – your time is too valuable to waste with petty recriminations. You should have made the decision yourself on the amount of compensation, but instead gave it over to that absurd excuse of a village council. And as to the fence—' He shook his head in mild disgust. 'There was absolutely no reason for you to postpone judgement on that. Everything you needed to know about the damage was right there in their minds. It should have been no trouble, even for you, to have pulled that from them.'

Luke swallowed. 'Yes, Master C'baoth,' he said. 'But reading another person's thoughts that way seems wrong—'

'When you are using that knowledge to help him?' C'baoth countered. 'How can that be wrong?'

Luke waved a hand helplessly. 'I'm trying to understand, Master C'baoth. But this is all so new to me.'

C'baoth's bushy eyebrows lifted. 'Is it, Jedi Skywalker? Is it really? You mean you've never violated someone's personal preference in order to help him? Or ignored some minor bureaucratic rule that stood between you and what needed to be done?'

Luke felt his cheeks flush, thinking back to Lando's use of that illegal slicer code to get his X-wing repaired at the Sluis Van shipyards. 'Yes, I've done that on occasion,' he admitted. 'But this is different, somehow. It feels . . . I don't know. Like I'm taking more responsibility for these people's lives than I should.'

'I understand your concerns,' C'baoth said, less severely this time. 'But that is indeed the crux of the matter. It is precisely the acceptance and wielding of responsibility that sets a Jedi apart from all others in the galaxy.' He sighed deeply. 'You must never forget, Luke, that in the final analysis these people are primitives. Only with our guidance can they ever hope to achieve any real maturity.'

'I wouldn't call them primitive, Master C'baoth,' Luke suggested hesitantly. 'They have modern technology, a reasonably efficient system of government—'

'The trappings of civilization without the substance,' C'baoth said with a contemptuous snort. 'Machines and societal constructs do not define a culture's maturity, Jedi Skywalker. Maturity is defined solely by the understanding and use of the Force.'

His eyes drifted away, as if peering into the past. 'There was such a society once, Luke,' he said softly. 'A vast and shining example of the heights all could aspire to. For a thousand generations we stood tall among the lesser beings of the galaxy, guardians of justice and order. The creators of true civilization. The Senate could debate and pass laws; but it was the Jedi who turned those laws into reality.'

His mouth twisted. 'And in return, the galaxy destroyed us.'

Luke frowned. 'I thought it was just the Emperor and a few Dark Jedi who exterminated the Jedi.'

C'baoth smiled bitterly. 'Do you truly believe that even the Emperor could have succeeded in such a task without the consent of the entire galaxy?' He shook his head. 'No, Luke. They hated us – all the lesser beings did. Hated us for our power, and our knowledge, and our wisdom. Hated us for our maturity.' His smile vanished. 'And that hatred still exists. Waiting only for the Jedi to reemerge to blaze up again.'

Luke shook his head slowly. It didn't really seem to fit with what little he knew about the destruction of the Jedi. But on the other hand, he hadn't lived through that era. C'baoth had. 'Hard to believe,' he murmured.

'Believe it, Jedi Skywalker,' C'baoth rumbled. His eyes caught Luke's, burning suddenly with a cold fire. 'That's why we must stand together, you and I. Why we must never let down our guard before a universe that would destroy us. Do you understand?'

'I think so,' Luke said, rubbing at the corner of his eye. His mind felt so sluggish in the fatigue dragging at him. And yet, even as he tried to think about C'baoth's words, images flowed unbidden from his memory. Images of Master Yoda, gruff but unafraid, with no trace of bitterness or anger toward anyone at the destruction of his

fellow Jedi. Images of Ben Kenobi in the Mos Eisley cantina, treated with a sort of aloof respect, but respect
nonetheless, after he'd been forced to cut down those two
troublemakers.

And clearest of all, images of his encounter at the New
Cov tapcafe. Of the Barabel, asking for the mediation of
a stranger, and accepting without question even those
parts of Luke's judgement that had gone against him. Of
the rest of the crowd, watching with hope and expectation and relief that a Jedi was there to keep things from
getting out of hand. 'I haven't experienced any such
hatred.'

C'baoth gazed at him from under bushy eyebrows.
'You will,' he said darkly. 'As will your sister. And her
children.'

Luke's chest tightened. 'I can protect them.'

'Can you teach them, as well?' C'baoth countered.
'Have you the wisdom and skill to bring them to full
knowledge of the ways of the Force?'

'I think so, yes.'

C'baoth snorted. 'If you think but do not know then
you gamble with their lives,' he bit out. 'You risk their
futures over a selfish whim.'

'It's not a whim,' Luke insisted. 'Together, Leia and I
can do it.'

'If you try, you will risk losing them to the dark side,'
C'baoth said flatly. He sighed, his eyes drifting away
from Luke as he looked around the room. 'We can't take
that chance, Luke,' he said quietly. 'There are so few of us
as it is. The endless war for power still rages – the galaxy
is in turmoil. We who remain must stand together against
those who would destroy everything.' He turned his eyes

suddenly back on Luke. 'No; we can't risk being divided and destroyed again. You must bring your sister and her children to me.'

'I can't do that,' Luke said. C'baoth's expression changed – 'Not now, at least,' Luke amended hastily. 'It wouldn't be safe for Leia to travel right now. The Imperials have been hunting her for months, and Jomark isn't all that far from the edge of their territory.'

'Do you doubt that I can protect her?'

'I . . . no, I don't *doubt* you,' Luke said, choosing his words carefully. 'It's just that—'

He paused. C'baoth had gone abruptly stiff, his eyes gazing outward at nothing. 'Master C'baoth?' he asked. 'Are you all right?'

There was no reply. Luke stepped to his side, reaching out with the Force and wondering uneasily if the other was ill. But as always the Jedi Master's mind was closed to him. 'Come, Master C'baoth,' he said, taking the other's arm. 'I'll help you to your chambers.'

C'baoth blinked twice, and with what seemed to be an effort, brought his gaze back to Luke's face. He took a shuddering breath; and suddenly he was back to normal again. 'You're tired, Luke,' he said. 'Leave me and return to your chambers for sleep.'

Luke *was* tired, he had to admit. 'Are you all right?'

'I'm fine,' C'baoth assured him, a strangely grim tone to his voice.

'Because if you need my help—'

'I said leave me!' C'baoth snapped. 'I am a Jedi Master. I need help from no-one.'

Luke found himself two paces back from C'baoth without any recollection of having taken the steps. 'I'm sorry, Master C'baoth,' he said. 'I didn't mean any disrespect.'

The other's face softened a bit. 'I know you didn't,' he said. He took another deep breath, exhaled it quietly. 'Bring your sister to me, Jedi Skywalker. I will protect her from the Empire; and will teach her such power as you can't imagine.'

Far in the back of Luke's mind, a small warning bell went off. Something about those words . . . or perhaps the way C'baoth had said them . . .

'Now return to your chambers,' C'baoth ordered. Once again his eyes seemed to be drifting away toward nothing. 'Sleep, and we will talk further in the morning.'

He stood before her, his face half hidden by the cowl of his robe, his yellow eyes piercingly bright as they gazed across the infinite distance between them. His lips moved, but his words were drowned out by the throaty hooting of alarms all around them, filling Mara with an urgency that was rapidly edging into panic. Between her and the Emperor two figures appeared: the dark, imposing image of Darth Vader, and the smaller black-clad figure of Luke Skywalker. They stood before the Emperor, facing each other, and ignited their lightsabers. The blades crossed, brilliant red-white against brilliant green-white, and they prepared for battle.

And then, without warning, the blades disengaged . . . and with twin roars of hatred audible even over the alarms, both turned and strode toward the Emperor.

Mara heard herself cry out as she struggled to rush to her master's aid. But the distance was too great, her body too sluggish. She screamed a challenge, trying to at least distract them. But neither Vader nor Skywalker seemed to hear her. They moved outward to flank the Emperor . . . and as they lifted their lightsabers high, she saw that the Emperor was gazing at her.

She looked back at him, wanting desperately to turn away from the coming disaster but unable to move. A thousand thoughts and emotions flooded in through that gaze, a glittering kaleidoscope of pain and fear and rage that spun far too fast for her to really absorb. The Emperor raised his hands, sending cascades of jagged blue-white lightning at his enemies. Both men staggered under the counterattack, and Mara watched with the sudden agonized hope that this time it might end differently. But no. Vader and Skywalker straightened; and with another roar of rage, they lifted their lightsabers high –

YOU WILL KILL LUKE SKYWALKER!

And with a jerk that threw her against her restraints, Mara snapped out of the dream.

For a minute she just sat there, gasping for breath and struggling against the fading vision of lightsabers poised to strike. The small cockpit of the Skipray pressed tightly around her, triggering a momentary surge of claustrophobia. The back and neck of her flight suit were wet with perspiration, clammy against her skin. From what seemed to be a great distance, a proximity alert was pinging.

The dream again. The same dream that had followed her around the galaxy for five years now. The same situation; the same horrifying ending; the same final, desperate plea.

But this time, things were going to be different. This time, she had the power to kill Luke Skywalker.

She looked out at the mottling of hyperspace spinning around the Skipray's canopy, some last bit of her mind coming fully awake. No, that was wrong. She wasn't going to kill Skywalker at all. She was—

She was going to ask him for help.

The sour taste of bile rose into her throat; with an effort, she forced it down. *No argument*, she told herself sternly. If she wanted to rescue Karrde, she was going to have to go through with it.

Skywalker owed Karrde this much. Later, after he'd repaid the debt, there would be time enough to kill him.

The proximity alert changed tone, indicating thirty seconds to go. Cupping the hyperdrive levers in her hand, Mara watched the indicator go to zero and gently pushed the levers back. Mottling became starlines became the black of space. Space, and the dark sphere of a planet directly ahead.

She had arrived at Jomark.

Mentally crossing her fingers, she tapped the comm, keying the code she'd programmed in during the trip. Luck was with her: here, at least, Thrawn's people were still using standard Imperial guidance transponders. The Skipray's displays flashed the location, an island forming the center of a ring-shaped lake just past the sunset line. She triggered the transponder once more to be sure, then keyed in the sublight drive and started down. Trying to ignore that last image of the Emperor's face . . .

The wailing of the ship's alarm jerked her awake. 'What?' she barked aloud to the empty cockpit, sleep-sticky eyes flicking across the displays for the source of the trouble. It wasn't hard to find: the Skipray had rolled half over onto its side, its control surfaces screaming with stress as the computer fought to keep her from spinning out of the sky. Inexplicably, she was already deep inside the lower atmosphere, well past the point where she should have switched over to repulsorlifts.

Clenching her teeth, she made the switchover and then gave the scan map a quick look. She'd only been out of it for a minute or two, but at the speed the Skipray was doing even a few seconds of inattention could be fatal. She dug her knuckles hard into her eyes, fighting against the fatigue pulling at her and feeling sweat breaking out again on her forehead. Flying while half asleep, her old instructor had often warned her, was the quickest if messiest way to end your life. And if she had gone down there would have been no-one to blame but herself.

Or would there?

She leveled the ship off, confirmed that there were no mountains in her path, and keyed in the autopilot. The ysalamir and portable nutrient framework that Aves had given her were back near the aft hatchway, secured to the engine access panel. Unstrapping from her seat, Mara made her way back toward it—

It was as if someone had snapped on a light switch. One second she felt as if she had just finished a four-day battle; half a step later, a meter or so from the ysalamir, the fatigue abruptly vanished.

She smiled grimly to herself. So her suspicion had been correct: Thrawn's mad Jedi Master didn't want any company. 'Nice try,' she called into the air. Unfastening the ysalamir frame from the access panel, she lugged it back to the cockpit and wedged it beside her seat.

The rim of mountains surrounding the lake was visible now on the electropulse scanner, and the infrared had picked up an inhabited structure on the far side. Probably where Skywalker and this mad Jedi Master were, she decided, a guess that was confirmed a moment later as the sensors picked up a small mass of spaceship-grade metal just outside the building. There were no weapons emplacements or defense shields anywhere that she could detect, either on the rim or on the island beneath her. Maybe C'baoth didn't think he needed anything so primitive as turbolasers to protect him.

Maybe he was right. Hunching herself over the control board, hair-trigger alert for any danger, Mara headed in.

She was nearly to the midpoint of the crater when the attack came, a sudden impact on the Skipray's underside that kicked the entire craft a few centimeters upward. The second impact came on the heels of the first, this one centered on the ventral fin and yawing the ship hard to starboard. The ship jolted a third time before Mara finally identified the weapon: not missiles or laser blasts, but small, fast-moving rocks, undetectable by most of the Skipray's sophisticated sensors.

The fourth impact knocked out the repulsorlifts, sending the Skipray falling out of the sky.

CHAPTER TWENTY-ONE

Mara swore under her breath, throwing the Skip-ray's control surfaces into glide mode and keying for a contour scan of the cliff face beneath the rim building. A landing up on the rim was out of the question now; putting down on the limited area up there without her repulsorlifts might be possible, but not with a Jedi Master fighting her the whole way. Alternatively, she could go for the dark island beneath her, which would give her more room to operate but leave her with the problem of getting back up to the rim. Ditto if she tried to find a big enough landing area somewhere else down the mountains.

Or she could admit defeat, fire up the main drive and pull for space, and go after Karrde alone.

Gritting her teeth, she studied the contour scan. The rock storm had stopped after the fourth hit – the Jedi Master, no doubt, waiting to see if she'd crash without further encouragement on his part. With a little luck, maybe she could convince him that she was done for without actually wrecking the ship in the process. If she could just find the proper formation in that cliff face . . .

There it was, perhaps a third of the way down: a roughly hemispherical concavity where erosion had eaten away a layer of softer rock from the harder material surrounding it. The ledge that had been left beneath the indentation was relatively flat, and the whole thing was large enough to hold the Skipray comfortably.

Now all she had to do was get the ship there. Mentally crossing her fingers, she flipped the ship nose up and eased in the main sublight drive.

The glare of the drive trail lit up the near side of the rim mountains, throwing them into a dancing mosaic of light and shadow. The Skipray jerked up and forward, stabilized a little as Mara brought the nose a bit farther back off vertical. It threatened to overbalance, eased back as she tapped the control surfaces, twitched almost too far in the other direction, then steadied. Balancing on the drive like this was an inherently unstable operation, and Mara could feel the sweat breaking out on her forehead as she fought to keep the suddenly unwieldy craft under control. If C'baoth suspected what she was trying, it wouldn't take much effort on his part to finish her off.

Setting her teeth together, splitting her attention between the approach scope, the airspeed indicator, and the throttle, she brought the ship in.

She nearly didn't make it. The Skipray was still ten meters short of the ledge when its drive trail hit the cliff face below it with enough heat to ignite the rock, and an instant later the ship was sheathed in brilliantly colored fire. Mara held her course, trying to ignore the warbling of the hull warning sirens as she strained to see through the flames between her and her target. There was no time to waste with second thoughts – if she hesitated even a few seconds, the drive could easily burn away too much of the ledge for her to safely put down. Five meters away now, and the temperature inside the cabin was beginning to rise. Then three, then one—

There was a horrible screech of metal on rock as the Skipray's ventral fin scraped against the edge of the ledge. Mara cut the drive and braced herself, and with a stomach-churning drop, the ship dropped a meter to land tail-first on the ledge. For a second it almost seemed it would remain balanced there. Then, with ponderous grace, it toppled slowly forward and slammed down hard onto its landing skids.

Wiping the sweat out of her eyes, Mara keyed for a status readout. The airstilting maneuver had been taught to her as an absolute last-ditch alternative to crashing. Now, she knew why.

But she'd been lucky. The landing skids and ventral fin were a mess, but the engines, hyperdrive, life-support, and hull integrity were still all right. Shutting the systems back to standby, she hoisted the ysalamir frame up onto her shoulders and headed aft.

The main portside hatchway was unusable, opening as it did out over empty space. There was, however, a secondary hatch set behind the dorsal laser cannon turret. Getting up the access ladder and through it with the ysalamir on her back was something of a trick, but after a couple of false starts she made it. The metal of the upper hull was uncomfortably hot to her touch as she climbed out onto it, but the cold winds coming off the lake below were a welcome relief after the superheated air inside. She propped the hatchway open to help cool the ship and looked upward.

And to her chagrin discovered that she'd miscalculated. Instead of being ten to fifteen meters beneath the top of the crater, as she'd estimated, she was in fact nearly fifty meters down. The vast scale of the crater, combined with the mad rush of the landing itself, had skewed her perception.

'Nothing like a little exercise after a long trip,' she muttered to herself, pulling the glow rod from her belt-pack and playing it across her line of ascent. The climb wasn't going to be fun, especially with the top-heavy weight of the ysalamir frame, but it looked possible. Attaching the glow rod to the shoulder of her jumpsuit, she picked out her first set of handholds and started up.

She'd made maybe two meters when, without warning, the rock in front of her suddenly blazed with light.

The shock of it sent her sliding back down the cliff face to a bumpy landing atop the Skipray; but she landed in a crouch with her blaster ready in her hand. Squinting against the twin lights glaring down on her, she snapped off a quick shot that took out the leftmost of them. The other promptly shut off; and then, even as she tried to blink away the purple blobs obscuring her vision, she heard a faint but unmistakable sound.

The warbling of an R2 droid.

'Hey!' she called softly. 'You – droid. Are you Skywalker's astromech unit? If you are, you know who I am. We met on Myrkr – remember?'

The droid remembered, all right. But from the indignant tone of the reply, it wasn't a memory the R2 was especially fond of. 'Yes, well, skip all that,' she told it tartly. 'Your master's in trouble. I came to warn him.'

Another electronic warble, this one fairly dripping with

sarcasm. 'It's true,' Mara insisted. Her dazzled vision was starting to recover now, and she could make out the dark shape of the X-wing hovering on its repulsorlifts about five meters away, its two starboard laser cannons pointed directly at her face. 'I need to talk to him right away,' Mara went on. 'Before that Jedi Master up there figures out I'm still alive and tries to rectify the situation.'

She'd expected more sarcasm, or even out-and-out approval for such a goal. But the droid didn't say anything. Perhaps it had witnessed the brief battle between the Skipray and C'baoth's flying boulders. 'Yes, that was him trying to kill me,' she confirmed. 'Nice and quiet, so that your master wouldn't notice anything and ask awkward questions.'

The droid beeped what sounded like a question of its own. 'I came here because I need Skywalker's help,' Mara said, taking a guess as to the content. 'Karrde's been captured by the Imperials, and I can't get him out by myself. Karrde, in case you've forgotten, was the one who helped your friends set up an ambush against those stormtroopers that got both of you off Myrkr. You owe him.'

The droid snorted. 'All right, then,' Mara snapped. 'Don't do it for Karrde, and don't do it for me. Take me up there because otherwise your precious master won't know until it's too late that his new teacher, C'baoth, is working for the Empire.'

The droid thought it over. Then, slowly, the X-wing rotated to point its lasers away from her and sidled over to the damaged Skipray. Mara holstered her blaster and got ready, wondering how she was going to squeeze into the cockpit with the ysalamir framework strapped to her shoulders.

She needn't have worried. Instead of maneuvering to give her access to the cockpit, the droid instead presented her with one of the landing skids.

'You must be joking,' Mara protested, eyeing the skid hovering at waist height in front of her and thinking about the long drop to the lake below. But it was clear that the droid was serious; and after a moment, she reluctantly climbed aboard. 'OK,' she said when she was as secure as she could arrange. 'Let's go. And watch out for flying rocks.'

The X-wing eased away and began moving upward. Mara braced herself, waiting for C'baoth to pick up the attack where he'd left off. But they reached the top without incident; and as the droid settled the X-wing safely to the ground, Mara saw the shadowy figure of a cloaked man standing silently beside the fence surrounding the house.

'You must be C'baoth,' Mara said to him as she slid off the landing skid and got a grip on her blaster. 'You always greet your visitors this way?'

For a moment the figure didn't speak. Mara took a step toward him, feeling an eerie sense of *déjà vu* as she tried to peer into the hood at the face not quite visible there. The Emperor had looked much the same way that night when he'd first chosen her from her home . . . 'I have no visitors except lackeys from Grand Admiral Thrawn,' the figure said at last. 'All others are, by definition, intruders.'

'What makes you think I'm not with the Empire?' Mara countered. 'In case it escaped your notice, I was following the Imperial beacon on that island down there when you knocked me out of the sky.'

In the dim starlight she had the impression that C'baoth

was smiling inside the hood. 'And what precisely does that prove?' he asked. 'Merely that others can play with the Grand Admiral's little toys.'

'And can others get hold of the Grand Admiral's ysalamiri, too?' she demanded, gesturing toward the frame on her back. 'Enough of this. The Grand Admiral—'

'The Grand Admiral is your enemy,' C'baoth snapped suddenly. 'Don't insult me with childish denials, Mara Jade. I saw it all in your mind as you approached. Did you really believe you could take my Jedi away from me?'

Mara swallowed, shivering from the cold night wind and the colder feeling within her. Thrawn had said that C'baoth was insane, and she could indeed hear the unstable edge of madness in his voice. But there was far more to the man than just that. There was a hard steel behind the voice, ruthless and calculating, with a sense of both supreme power and supreme confidence underlying it all.

It was like hearing the Emperor speak again.

'I need Skywalker's help,' she said, forcing her own voice to remain calm. 'All I need to do is borrow him for a little while.'

'And then you'll return him?' C'baoth said sardonically.

Mara clenched her teeth. 'I'll have his help, C'baoth. Whether you like it or not.'

There was no doubt this time that the Jedi Master had smiled. A thin, ghostly smile. 'Oh, no, Mara Jade,' he murmured. 'You are mistaken. Do you truly believe that simply because you stand in the middle of an empty space in the Force that I am powerless against you?'

'There's also this,' Mara said, pulling her blaster from its holster and aiming it at his chest.

C'baoth didn't move; but suddenly Mara could feel a surge of tension in the air around her. 'No-one points a weapon at me with impunity,' the Jedi Master said with quiet menace. 'You will pay dearly for this one day.'

'I'll take my chances,' Mara said, retreating a step to put her back against the X-wing's starboard S-foils. Above and to her left she could hear the R2 droid chirping thoughtfully to itself. 'You want to stand aside and let me pass? Or do we do this the hard way?'

C'baoth seemed to study her. 'I could destroy you, you know,' he said. The menace had vanished from his voice now, leaving something almost conversational in its place. 'Right there where you stand, before you even knew the attack was coming. But I won't. Not now. I've felt your presence over the years, Mara Jade; the rising and falling of your power after the Emperor's death took most of your strength away. And now I've seen you in my meditations. Someday you will come to me, of your own free will.'

'I'll take my chances on that one, too,' Mara said.

'You don't believe me,' C'baoth said with another of his ghostly smiles. 'But you shall. The future is fixed, my young would-be Jedi, as is your destiny. Someday you will kneel before me. I have foreseen it.'

'I wouldn't trust Jedi foreseeing all that much if I were you,' Mara retorted, risking a glance past him at the darkened building and wondering what C'baoth would do if she tried shouting Skywalker's name. 'The Emperor did a lot of that, too. It didn't help him much in the end.'

'Perhaps I am wiser than the Emperor was,' C'baoth said. His head turned slightly. 'I told you to go to your chambers,' he said in a louder voice.

'Yes, you did,' a familiar voice acknowledged; and from the shadows at the front of the house a new figure moved across the courtyard.

Skywalker.

'Then why are you here?' C'baoth asked.

'I felt a disturbance in the Force,' the younger man said as he passed through the gate and came more fully into the dim starlight. Above his black tunic his face was expressionless, his eyes fixed on Mara. 'As if a battle were taking place nearby. Hello, Mara.'

'Skywalker,' she managed between dry lips. With all that had happened to her since her arrival in the Jomark system, it was only now just dawning on her the enormity of the task she'd set for herself. She, who'd openly told Skywalker that she would someday kill him, was now going to have to convince him that she was more trustworthy than a Jedi Master. 'Look – Skywalker—'

'Aren't you aiming that at the wrong person?' he asked mildly. 'I thought I was the one you were gunning for.'

Mara had almost forgotten the blaster she had pointed at C'baoth. 'I didn't come here to kill you,' she said. Even to her own ears the words sounded thin and deceitful. 'Karrde's in trouble with the Empire. I need your help to get him out.'

'I see.' Skywalker looked at C'baoth. 'What happened here, Master C'baoth?'

'What does it matter?' the other countered. 'Despite her words just now, she did indeed come here to destroy you. Would you rather I had not stopped her?'

'Skywalker—' Mara began.

He stopped her with an upraised hand, his eyes still on

C'baoth. 'Did she attack you?' he asked. 'Or threaten you in any way?'

Mara looked at C'baoth . . . and felt the breath freeze in her lungs. The earlier confidence had vanished from the Jedi Master's face. In its place was something cold and deadly. Directed not at her, but at Skywalker.

And suddenly Mara understood. Skywalker wouldn't need convincing of C'baoth's treachery after all. Somehow, he already knew.

'What does it matter what her precise actions were?' C'baoth demanded, his voice colder even than his face. 'What matters is that she is a living example of the danger I have been warning you of since your arrival. The danger all Jedi face from a galaxy that hates and fears us.'

'No, Master C'baoth,' Skywalker said, his voice almost gentle. 'Surely you must understand that the means are no less important than the ends. A Jedi uses the Force for knowledge and defense, never for attack.'

C'baoth snorted. 'A platitude for the simpleminded. Or for those with insufficient wisdom to make their own decisions. I am beyond such things, Jedi Skywalker. As you will be someday. *If* you choose to remain.'

Skywalker shook his head. 'I'm sorry,' he said. 'I can't.' He turned away and walked toward Mara—

'Then you turn your back on the galaxy,' C'baoth said, his voice now earnest and sincere. 'Only with our guidance and strength can they ever hope to achieve real maturity. You know that as well as I do.'

Skywalker stopped. 'But you just said they hate us,' he pointed out. 'How can we teach people who don't want our guidance?'

'We can heal the galaxy, Luke,' C'baoth said quietly. 'Together, you and I can do it. Without us, there is no hope. None at all.'

'Maybe he can do it without you,' Mara put in loudly, trying to break up the verbal spell C'baoth was weaving. She'd seen the same sort of thing work for the Emperor, and Skywalker's eyelids were heavy enough as it was.

Too heavy, in fact. Like hers had been on the approach to Jomark . . .

Stepping away from the X-wing, she walked over to Skywalker. C'baoth made a small movement, as if he were going to stop her; she hefted her blaster, and he seemed to abandon the idea.

Even without looking at him, she could tell when the Force-empty zone around her ysalamir touched Skywalker. He inhaled sharply, shoulders straightening from a slump he probably hadn't even noticed they had, and nodded as if he finally understood a hitherto unexplained piece of a puzzle. 'Is this how you would heal the galaxy, Master C'baoth?' he asked. 'By coercion and deceit?'

Abruptly, C'baoth threw back his head and laughed. It was about the last reaction Mara would have expected from him, and the sheer surprise of it momentarily froze her muscles.

And in that split second, the Jedi Master struck.

It was only a small rock, as rocks went, but it came in out of nowhere to strike her gun hand with paralyzing force. The blaster went spinning off into the darkness as her hand flared with pain and then went numb. 'Watch out!' she snapped to Skywalker, dropping down into a crouch and scrabbling around for her weapon as a second stone whistled past her ear.

There was a *snap-hiss* from beside her, and suddenly the terrain was bathed in the green-white glow of Skywalker's lightsaber. 'Get behind the ship,' he ordered her. 'I'll hold him off.'

The memory of Myrkr flashed through Mara's mind; but even as she opened her mouth to remind him of how useless he was without the Force, he took a long step forward to put himself outside the ysalamir's influence. The lightsaber flashed sideways, and she heard the double *crunch* as its brilliant blade intercepted two more incoming rocks.

Still laughing, C'baoth raised his hand and sent a flash of blue lightning toward them.

Skywalker caught the bolt on his lightsaber, and for an instant the green of the blade was surrounded by a blue-white coronal discharge. A second bolt shot past him to vanish at the edge of the empty zone around Mara; a third again wrapped itself around the lightsaber blade.

Mara's fumbling hand brushed something metallic: her blaster. Scooping it up, she swung it toward C'baoth—

And with a brilliant flash of laser fire, the whole scene seemed to blow up in front of her.

She had forgotten about the droid sitting up there in the X-wing. Apparently, C'baoth had forgotten about it, too.

'Skywalker?' she called, blinking at the purple haze floating in front of her eyes and wrinkling her nose at the tingling smell of ozone. 'Where are you?'

'Over here by C'baoth,' Skywalker's voice said. 'He's still alive.'

'We can fix that,' Mara growled. Carefully picking her way across the steaming ruts the X-wing's laser cannon had gouged in the ground, she headed over.

C'baoth was lying on his back, unconscious but breathing evenly, with Skywalker kneeling over him. 'Not even singed,' she murmured. 'Impressive.'

'Artoo wasn't shooting to kill,' Skywalker said, his fingertips moving gently across the old man's face. 'It was probably the sonic shock that got him.'

'That, or getting knocked off his feet by the shock wave,' Mara agreed, lining her blaster up on the still figure. 'Get out of the way. I'll finish it.'

Skywalker looked up at her. 'We're not going to kill him,' he said. 'Not like this.'

'Would you rather wait until he's conscious again and can fight back?' she retorted.

'There's no need to kill him at all,' Skywalker insisted. 'We can be off Jomark long before he wakes up.'

'You don't leave an enemy at your back,' she told him stiffly. 'Not if you like living.'

'He doesn't have to be an enemy, Mara,' Skywalker said with that irritating earnestness of his. 'He's ill. Maybe he can be cured.'

Mara felt her lip twist. 'You didn't hear the way he was talking before you showed up,' she said. 'He's insane, all right; but that's not all he is any more. He's a lot stronger, and a whole lot more dangerous.' She hesitated. 'He sounded just like the Emperor and Vader used to.'

A muscle in Skywalker's cheek twitched. 'Vader was deep in the dark side, too,' he told her. 'He was able to break that hold and come back. Maybe C'baoth can do the same.'

'I wouldn't bet on it,' Mara said. But she holstered her blaster. They didn't have time to debate the issue; and as long as she needed Skywalker's help, he had effective veto on decisions like this. 'Just remember, it's your back that'll get the knife if you're wrong.'

'I know.' He looked down at C'baoth once more, then back up at her. 'You said Karrde was in trouble.'

'Yes,' Mara nodded, glad to change the subject. Sky-walker's mention of the Emperor and Vader had reminded her all too clearly of that recurring dream. 'The Grand Admiral's taken him. I need your help to get him out.'

She braced herself for the inevitable argument and bargaining; but to her surprise, he simply nodded and stood up. 'OK,' he said. 'Let's go.'

With one last mournful electronic wail Artoo signed off; and with the usual flicker of pseudomotion, the X-wing was gone. 'Well, he's not happy about it,' Luke said, shutting down the Skipray's transmitter. 'But I think I've persuaded him to go straight home.'

'You'd better be more than just thinking you've persuaded him,' Mara warned from the pilot's chair, her eyes on the nav computer display. 'Sneaking into an Imperial supply depot is going to be hard enough without a New Republic X-wing in tow.'

'Right,' Luke said, throwing a sideways look at her and wondering if getting into the Skipray with her had been one of the smarter things he'd done lately. Mara had put the ysalamir away in the rear of the ship, and he could feel her hatred of him simmering beneath her consciousness like a half-burned fire. It evoked unpleasant memories of the Emperor, the man who'd been Mara's teacher, and Luke briefly wondered if this could be some sort of overly elaborate trick to lure him to his death.

But her hatred seemed to be under control, and there was no deceit in her that he could detect.

But then, he hadn't seen C'baoth's deceit either, until it was almost too late.

Luke shifted in his chair, his face warming with embarrassment at how easily he'd been taken in by C'baoth's act. But it hadn't all been an act, he reminded himself. The Jedi Master's emotional instabilities were genuine – that much he was convinced of. And even if those instabilities didn't extend as far as the insanity that Mara had alluded to, they certainly extended far enough for C'baoth to qualify as ill.

And if what she'd said about C'baoth working with the Empire was also true . . .

Luke shivered. *I will teach her such power as you can't imagine*, C'baoth had said about Leia. The words had been different from those Vader had spoken to Luke on Endor, but the dark sense behind them had been identical. Whatever C'baoth had once been, there was no doubt in Luke's mind that he was now moving along the path of the dark side.

And yet, Luke had been able to help Vader win his way back from that same path. Was it conceit to think he could do the same for C'baoth?

He shook the thought away. However C'baoth's destiny might yet be entwined with his, such encounters were too far in the future to begin planning for them. For now, he needed to concentrate on the immediate task at hand, and to leave the future to the guidance of the Force. 'How did the Grand Admiral find Karrde?' he asked Mara.

Her lips compressed momentarily, and Luke caught a

flash of self-reproach. 'They put a homing beacon aboard my ship,' she said. 'I led them right to his hideout.'

Luke nodded, thinking back to the rescue of Leia and that harrowing escape from the first Death Star aboard the *Falcon*. 'They pulled that same trick on us, too,' he said. 'That's how they found the Yavin base.'

'Considering what it cost them, I don't think you've got any complaints coming,' Mara said sarcastically.

'I don't imagine the Emperor was pleased,' Luke murmured.

'No, he wasn't,' Mara said, her voice dark with memories of her own. 'Vader nearly died for that blunder.' Deliberately, she looked over at Luke's hands. 'That was when he lost his right hand, in fact.'

Luke flexed the fingers of his artificial right hand, feeling a ghostly echo of the searing pain that had lanced through it as Vader's lightsaber had sliced through skin and muscle and bone. A fragment of an old Tatooine aphorism flickered through his mind: something about the passing of evil from one generation to the next . . . 'What's the plan?' he asked.

Mara took a deep breath, and Luke could sense the emotional effort as she put the past aside. 'Karrde's being held aboard the Grand Admiral's flagship, the *Chimaera*,' she told him. 'According to their flight schedule, they're going to be taking on supplies in the Wistril system four days from now. If we push it, we should be able to get there a few hours ahead of them. We'll ditch the Skipray, take charge of one of the supply shuttles, and just go on up with the rest of the flight pattern.'

Luke thought it over. It sounded tricky, but not ridiculously so. 'What happens after we're aboard?'

'Standard Imperial procedure is to keep all the shuttle crews locked aboard their ships while the *Chimaera*'s crewers handle the unloading,' Mara said. 'Or at least that was standard procedure five years ago. Means we'll need some kind of diversion to get out of the shuttle.'

'Sounds risky,' Luke shook his head. 'We don't want to draw attention to ourselves.'

'You got any better ideas?'

Luke shrugged. 'Not yet,' he said. 'But we've got four days to think about it. We'll come up with something.'

CHAPTER TWENTY-TWO

M ara eased the repulsorlifts off; and with a faint
metallic clank the cargo shuttle touched down on
the main deck of the *Chimaera*'s aft hangar bay. 'Shuttle
37 down,' Luke announced into the comm. 'Awaiting
further orders.'

'Shuttle 37, acknowledged,' the voice of the controller
came over the speaker. 'Shut down all systems and prepare for unloading.'

'Got it.'

Luke reached over to shut off the comm, but Mara
stopped him. 'Control, this is my first cargo run,' she
said, her voice carrying just the right touch of idle curiosity. 'About how long until we'll be able to leave?'

'I suggest you make yourselves comfortable,' Control
said dryly. 'We unload all the shuttles before any of you
leave. Figure a couple of hours, at the least.'

'Oh,' Mara said, sounding taken aback. 'Well ...
thanks. Maybe I'll take a nap.'

She signed off. 'Good,' she said, unstrapping and
standing up. 'That ought to give us enough time to get to
the detention center and back.'

'Let's just hope they haven't transferred Karrde off the

ship,' Luke said, following her to the rear of the command deck and the spiral stairway leading down to the storage area below.

'They haven't,' Mara said, heading down the stairs. 'The only danger is that they might have started the full treatment already.'

Luke frowned down at her. 'The full treatment?'

'Their interrogation.' Mara reached the center of the storage room and looked appraisingly around. 'All right. Just about . . . there should do it.' She pointed to a section of the deck in front of her. 'Out of the way of prying eyes, and you shouldn't hit anything vital.'

'Right.' Luke ignited his lightsaber, and began carefully cutting a hole in the floor. He was most of the way through when there was a brilliant spark from the hole and the lights in the storage room abruptly went out. 'It's OK,' Luke told Mara as she muttered something vicious under her breath. 'The lightsaber gives off enough light to see by.'

'I'm more worried that the cable might have arced to the hangar deck,' she countered. 'They couldn't help but notice that.'

Luke paused, stretching out with Jedi senses. 'Nobody nearby seems to have seen anything,' he told Mara.

'We'll hope.' She gestured to the half-finished cut. 'Get on with it.'

He did so. A minute later, with the help of a magnetic winch, they had hauled the severed section of decking and hull into the storage room. A few centimeters beneath it, lit eerily by the green light from Luke's lightsaber, was the hangar bay deck. Mara got the winch's grapple attached to it; stretching out flat on his stomach, Luke extended the lightsaber down through the hole. There he paused, waiting until he could sense that the corridor beneath the hangar deck was clear.

'Don't forget to bevel it,' Mara reminded him as the lightsaber bit smoothly into the hardened metal. 'A gaping hole in the ceiling would be a little too obvious for even conscripts to miss.'

Luke nodded and finished the cut. Mara was ready, and even as he shut down the lightsaber she had the winch pulling the thick slab of metal up into the shuttle. She brought it perhaps a meter up and then shut down the motor. 'That's far enough,' she said. Blaster ready in her hand, she sat gingerly on the still-warm edge of the hole and dropped lightly down to the deck below. There was a second's pause as she looked around— 'All clear,' she hissed.

Luke sat down on the edge and looked over at the winch control. Reaching out with the Force, he triggered the switch and followed her down.

The deck below was farther than it had looked, but his Jedi-enhanced muscles handled the impact without trouble. Recovering his balance, he looked up just as the metal plug settled neatly back down into the hole. 'Looks pretty good,' Mara murmured. 'I don't think anyone will notice.'

'Not unless they look straight up,' Luke agreed. 'Which way to the detention center?'

'There,' Mara said, gesturing with her blaster to their left. 'We're not going to get there dressed like this, though. Come on.'

She led the way to the end of the passage, then down a crossway to another, wider corridor. Luke kept his senses alert, but only occasionally did he detect anyone. 'Awfully quiet down here.'

'It won't last,' Mara said. 'This is a service supply area, and most of the people who'd normally be working here are a level up helping unload the shuttles. But we need to get into some uniforms or flight suits or something before we go much farther.'

Luke thought back to the first time he'd tried masquerading as an Imperial. 'OK, but let's try to avoid stormtrooper armor,' he said. 'Those helmets are hard to see through.'

'I didn't think Jedi needed to use their eyes,' Mara countered sourly. 'Watch it – here we are. That's a section of crew quarters over there.'

Luke had already sensed the sudden jump in population level. 'I don't think we can sneak through that many people,' he warned.

'I wasn't planning to.' Mara pointed to another corridor leading off to their right. 'There should be a group of TIE pilot ready rooms down that way. Let's see if we can find an empty one that has a couple of spare flight suits lying around.'

But if the Empire was lax enough to leave its service supply areas unguarded, it wasn't so careless with its pilot ready rooms. There were six of them grouped around the turbolift cluster at the end of the corridor; and from the sounds of conversation faintly audible through the doors, it was clear that all six were occupied by at least two people. 'What now?' Luke whispered to Mara.

'What do you think?' she retorted, dropping her blaster back in its holster and flexing her fingers. 'Just tell me which room has the fewest people in it and then get out of the way. I'll do the rest.'

'Wait a minute,' Luke said, thinking hard. He didn't want to kill the men behind those doors in cold blood; but neither did he want to put himself into the dangerous situation he'd faced during the Imperial raid on Lando's Nkllon mining operation a few months earlier. There, he'd successfully used the Force to confuse the attacking TIE fighters, but at the cost of skating perilously close to the edge of the dark side. It wasn't an experience he wanted to repeat.

But if he could just gently touch the Imperials' minds, instead of grabbing and twisting them . . .

'We'll try this one,' he told Mara, nodding to a room in which he could sense only three men. 'But we're not going to charge in fighting. I think I can suppress their curiosity enough for me to walk in, take the flight suits, and leave.'

'What if you can't?' Mara demanded. 'We'll have lost whatever surprise we would have had.'

'It'll work,' Luke assured her. 'Get ready.'

'Skywalker—'

'Besides which, I doubt that even with surprise you can take out all three without any noise,' he added. 'Can you?'

She glared laser bolts, but gestured him to the door. Setting his mind firmly in line with the Force, he moved toward it. The heavy metal panel slid open at his approach, and he stepped in.

There were indeed three men lounging around the monitor table in the center of the room: two in the Imperial brown of ordinary crewers, the other in the black

uniform and flaring helmet of a Fleet trooper. All three
looked up as the door opened, and Luke caught their idle
interest in the newcomer. Reaching out through the
Force, he gently touched their minds, shunting the curiosity away. The two crewers seemed to size him up and
then ignore him; the trooper continued to watch, but
only as a change from watching his companions. Trying
to look as casual and unconcerned as he could, Luke
went over to the rack of flight suits against the wall and
selected three of them. The conversation around the
monitor table continued as he draped them over his arm
and walked back out of the room. The door slid shut
behind him—

'Well?' Mara hissed.

Luke nodded, exhaling quietly. 'Go ahead and get into
it,' he told her. 'I want to try and hold off their curiosity
for another couple of minutes. Until they've forgotten I
was ever in there.'

Mara nodded and started pulling the flight suit on
over her jumpsuit. 'Handy trick, I must say.'

'It worked this time, anyway,' Luke agreed. Carefully,
he eased back his touch on the Imperials' minds, waiting
tensely for the surge of emotion that would show the
whole scheme was unraveling. But there was nothing
except the lazy flow of idle conversation.

The trick had worked. This time, anyway.

Mara had a turbolift car standing by as he turned
away from the ready room. 'Come on, come on,' she
beckoned impatiently. She was already in her flight suit,
with the other two slung over her shoulder. 'You can
change on the way.'

'I hope no-one comes aboard while I'm doing it,' he

muttered as he slipped into the car. 'Be a little hard to explain.'

'No-one's coming aboard,' she said as the turbolift door closed behind him and the car started to move. 'I've keyed it for nonstop.' She eyed him. 'You still want to do it this way?'

'I don't think we've got any real choice,' he said, getting into the flight suit. It felt uncomfortably tight over his regular outfit. 'Han and I tried the frontal approach once, on the Death Star. It wasn't exactly an unqualified success.'

'Yes, but you didn't have access to the main computer then,' Mara pointed out. 'If I can fiddle the records and transfer orders, we ought to be able to get him out before anyone realizes they've been had.'

'But you'd still be leaving witnesses behind who knew he'd left,' Luke reminded her. 'If any of them decided to check on the order verbally, the whole thing would fall apart right there. And I don't think that suppression trick I used in the ready room will work on detention center guards – they're bound to be too alert.'

'All right,' Mara said, turning back to the turbolift control board. 'It doesn't sound like much fun to me. But if that's what you want, I'm game.'

The detention center was in the far aft section of the ship, a few decks beneath the command and systems control sections and directly above Engineering and the huge sublight drive thrust nozzles. The turbolift car shifted direction several times along the way, alternating between horizontal and vertical movement. It seemed to Luke to be altogether too complicated a route, and he found himself wondering even now if Mara might be pulling some kind of double-cross. But her sense didn't indicate any such treachery; and it occurred to him that she might have deliberately tangled their path to put the *Chimaera*'s internal security systems off the scent.

At last the car came to a halt, and the door slid open. They stepped out into a long corridor in which a handful of crewers in maintenance coveralls could be seen going about their business. 'Your access door's that way,' Mara murmured, nodding down the corridor. 'I'll give you three minutes to get set.'

Luke nodded and set off, striving to look like he belonged there. His footsteps echoed on the metal deck, bringing back memories of that near-disastrous visit to the first Death Star.

But he'd been a wide-eyed kid then, dazzled by visions of glory and heroism and too naive to understand the deadly dangers that went with such things. Now, he was older and more seasoned, and knew exactly what it was he was walking into.

And yet was walking into it anyway. Dimly, he wondered if that made him less reckless than he'd been the last time, or more so.

He reached the door and paused beside it, pretending to study a data pad that had been in one of the flight suit's pockets until the corridor was deserted. Then, taking one last deep breath of clear air, he opened the door and stepped inside.

Even holding his breath, the stench hit him like a slap in the face. Whatever advancements the Empire might have made in the past few years, their shipboard garbage pits still smelled as bad as ever.

He let the door slide shut behind him, and as it did so

he heard the faint sound of an internal relay closing. He'd cut things a little too close; Mara must already have activated the compression cycle. Breathing through his mouth, he waited . . . and a moment later, with a muffled clang of heavy hydraulics, the walls began moving slowly toward each other.

Luke swallowed, gripping his lightsaber tightly as he tried to keep on top of the tangle of garbage and discarded equipment that was now starting to buck and twist around his feet. Getting into the detention level this way had been his idea, and he'd had to talk long and hard before Mara had been convinced. But now that he was actually here, and the walls were closing in on him, it suddenly didn't seem like nearly such a good idea any more. If Mara couldn't adequately control the walls' movement – or if she was interrupted at her task—

Or if she gave in for just a few seconds to her hatred for him . . .

The walls came ever closer, grinding together everything in their path. Luke struggled to keep his footing, all too aware that if Mara was planning a betrayal he wouldn't know until it was too late to save himself. The compressor walls were too thick for him to cut a gap with his lightsaber, and already the shifting mass beneath his feet had taken him too far away from the door to escape that way. Listening to the creak of tortured metal and plastic, Luke watched as the gap between the walls closed to two meters . . . then one and a half . . . then one . . .

And came to a shuddering halt just under a meter apart.

Luke took a deep breath, almost not noticing the rancid smell. Mara hadn't betrayed him, and she'd handled her end of the scheme perfectly. Now it was his turn. Moving to the back end of the chamber, he gathered his feet beneath him and jumped.

The footing was unstable, and the garbage compactor walls impressively tall, and even with Jedi enhancement behind the jump he made it only about halfway to the top. But even as he reached the top of his arc he drew his knees up and swung his feet out; and with a wrenching jolt to his legs and lower back, he wedged himself solidly between the walls. Taking a moment to catch his breath and get his bearings, he started up.

It wasn't as bad as he'd feared it would be. He'd done a fair amount of climbing as a boy on Tatooine and had tackled rock chimneys at least half a dozen times, though never with any real enthusiasm. The smooth walls here in the compactor offered less traction than stone would have, but the evenness of the spacing and the absence of sharp rocks to dig into his back more than made up for it. Within a couple of minutes he had reached the top of the compactor's walls and the maintenance chute that would lead – he hoped – to the detention level. If Mara's reading of the schedule had been right, he had about five minutes before the guard shift changed up there. Setting his teeth together, he forced his way through the magnetic screen at the bottom of the chute and, in clean air again, started up.

He made it in just over five minutes, to discover that Mara's reading had indeed been right. Through the grating that covered the chute opening he could hear the sounds of conversation and movement coming from the direction of the control room, punctuated by the regular hiss of opening turbolift doors. The guard was changing;

and for the next couple of minutes both shifts would be in the control room. An ideal time, if he was quick, to slip a prisoner out from under their noses.

Hanging on to the grating by one hand, he got his lightsaber free and ignited it. Making sure not to let the tip of the blade show through into the corridor beyond, he sliced off a section of the grating and eased it into the shaft with him. He used a hook from his flight suit to hang the section to what was left of the grating, and climbed through the opening.

The corridor was deserted. Luke glanced at the nearest cell number to orient himself and set off toward the one Mara had named. The conversation in the control room seemed to be winding down, and soon now the new shift of guards would be moving out to take up their positions in the block corridors. Senses alert, Luke slipped down the cross corridor to the indicated cell and, mentally crossing his fingers, punched the lock release.

Talon Karrde looked up from the cot as the door slid open, that well-remembered sardonic half smile on his face. His eyes focused on the face above the flight suit, and abruptly the smile vanished. 'I don't believe it,' he murmured.

'Me, neither,' Luke told him, throwing a quick glance around the room. 'You fit to travel?'

'Fit and ready,' Karrde said, already up and moving toward the door. 'Fortunately, they're still in the softening-up phase. Lack of food and sleep – you're familiar with the routine.'

'I've heard of it.' Luke looked both ways down the corridor. Still no-one. 'Exit's this way. Come on.'

They made it to the grating without incident. 'You must be joking, of course,' Karrde said as Luke maneuvered his way into the hole and got his feet and back braced against the chute walls.

'The other way out has guards at the end of it,' Luke reminded him.

'Point,' Karrde conceded, reluctantly looking into the gap. 'I suppose it'd be too much to hope for a rope.'

'Sorry. The only place to tie it is this grate, and they'd spot that in no time.' Luke frowned at him. 'You're not afraid of heights, are you?'

'It's the falling from them that worries me,' Karrde said dryly. But he was already climbing into the opening, though his hands were white-knuckled where he gripped the grating.

'We're going to rock-chimney it down to the garbage masher,' Luke told him. 'You ever done that before?'

'No, but I'm a quick study,' Karrde said. Looking back over his shoulder at Luke, he eased into a similar position against the chute walls. 'I presume you want this hole covered up,' he added, pulling the grating section from its perch and fitting it back into the opening. 'Though it's not going to fool anyone who takes a close look at it.'

'With luck, we'll be back at the hangar bay before that happens,' Luke assured him. 'Come on, now. Slow and easy; let's go.'

They made it back to the garbage compactor without serious mishap. 'The side of the Empire the tourists never see,' Karrde commented dryly as Luke led him across the tangle of garbage. 'How do we get out?'

'The door's right there,' Luke said, pointing down

below the level of the mass they were walking on. 'Mara's supposed to open the walls again in a couple of minutes and let us down.'

'Ah,' Karrde said. 'Mara's here, is she?'

'She told me on the trip here how you were captured,' Luke said, trying to read Karrde's sense. If he was angry at Mara, he was hiding it well. 'She said she wasn't in on that trap.'

'Oh, I'm sure she wasn't,' Karrde said. 'If for no other reason than that my interrogators worked so hard to drop hints to the contrary.' He looked thoughtfully at Luke. 'What did she promise for your help in this?'

Luke shook his head. 'Nothing. She just reminded me that I owed you one for not turning me over to the Imperials back on Myrkr.'

A wry smile twitched Karrde's lip. 'Indeed. No mention, either, of why the Grand Admiral wanted me in the first place?'

Luke frowned at him. The other was watching him closely ... and now that he was paying attention, Luke could tell that Karrde was holding some secret back from him. 'I assumed it was in revenge for helping me escape. Is there more to it than that?'

Karrde's gaze drifted away from him. 'Let's just say that if we make it away from here the New Republic stands to gain a great deal—'

His last word was cut off by a muffled clang; and with a ponderous jolt the compactor walls began slowly moving apart again. Luke helped Karrde maintain his balance as they waited for the door to be clear, stretching his senses outward into the corridor beyond. There were a fair number of crewers passing by, but he could sense no suspicion or special alertness in any of them. 'Is Mara doing all this?' Karrde asked.

Luke nodded. 'She has an access code for the ship's computer.'

'Interesting,' Karrde murmured. 'I gathered from all this that she had some past connection with the Empire. Obviously, she was more highly placed than I realized.'

Luke nodded, thinking back to Mara's revelation to him back in the Myrkr forest. Mara Jade, the Emperor's Hand . . . 'Yes,' he told Karrde soberly. 'She was.'

The walls reached their limit and shut down. A moment later there was a click of a relay. Luke waited until the corridor immediately outside was deserted, then opened it and stepped out. A couple of maintenance techs working at an open panel a dozen meters down the corridor threw a look of idle curiosity at the newcomers; throwing an equally unconcerned glance back their way, Luke pulled the data pad from his pocket and pretended to make an entry. Karrde played off the cue, standing beside him and spouting a stream of helpful jargon as Luke filled out his imaginary report. Letting the door slide closed, Luke stuffed the data pad back into his pocket and led the way down the corridor.

Mara was waiting at the turbolift cluster with the spare flight suit draped over her arm. 'Car's on its way,' she murmured. For a second, as her eyes met Karrde's, her face seemed to tighten.

'He knows you didn't betray him,' Luke told her quietly.

'I didn't ask,' she growled. But Luke could sense some of her tension vanish. 'Here,' she added, thrusting the flight suit at Karrde. 'A little camouflage.'

'Thank you,' Karrde said. 'Where are we going?'

'We came in on a supply shuttle,' Mara said. 'We cut an exit hole in the lower hull, but we should have enough time to weld it airtight before they send us back to the surface.'

The turbolift car arrived as Karrde was adjusting the fasteners on his borrowed flight suit. Two men with a gleaming power core relay on a float table were there before them, taking up most of the room. 'Where to?' one of the techs asked with the absent politeness of a man with more important things on his mind.

'Pilot ready room 33-129-T,' Mara told him, using the same tone.

The tech entered the destination on the panel and the door slid shut; and Luke took his first really relaxed breath since Mara had put the Skipray down on Wistril five hours ago. Another ten or fifteen minutes and they'd be safely back in their shuttle.

Against all odds, they'd done it.

The midpoint report from the hangar bay came in, and Pellaeon paused in his monitoring of the bridge deflector control overhaul to take a quick look at it. Excellent; the unloading was running nearly eight minutes ahead of schedule. At this rate the *Chimaera* would be able to make its rendezvous with the *Stormhawk* in plenty of time for them to set up their ambush of the Rebel convoy assembling off Corfai. He marked the report as noted and sent it back into the files; and he had turned his attention back to the deflector overhaul when he heard a quiet footstep behind him.

'Good evening, Captain,' Thrawn nodded, coming up beside Pellaeon's chair and giving the bridge a leisurely scan.

'Admiral,' Pellaeon nodded back, swiveling to face him. 'I thought you'd retired for the night, sir.'

'I've been in my command room,' Thrawn said, looking past Pellaeon at the displays. 'I thought I'd make one last survey of ship's status before I went to my quarters. Is that the bridge deflector overhaul?'

'Yes, sir,' Pellaeon said, wondering which species' artwork had been favored with the Grand Admiral's scrutiny tonight. 'No problems so far. The cargo unloading down in Aft Bay Two is running ahead of schedule, too.'

'Good,' the Grand Admiral said. 'Anything further from the patrol at Endor?'

'Just an addendum to that one report, sir,' Pellaeon told him. 'Apparently, they've confirmed that the ship they caught coming into the system was in fact just a smuggler planning to sift again through the remains of the Imperial base there. They're continuing to back-check the crew.'

'Remind them to make a thorough job of it before they let the ship go,' Thrawn said grimly. 'Organa Solo won't have simply abandoned the *Millennium Falcon* in orbit there. Sooner or later she'll return for it . . . and when she does, I intend to have her.'

'Yes, sir,' Pellaeon nodded. The commander of the Endor patrol group, he was certain, didn't need any reminding of that. 'Speaking of the *Millennium Falcon*, have you decided yet whether or not to do any further scan work on it?'

Thrawn shook his head. 'I doubt that would gain us anything. The scanning team would be better employed assisting with maintenance on the *Chimaera*'s own systems. Have the *Millennium Falcon* transferred up to vehicle deep storage until we can find some use for it.'

'Yes, sir,' Pellaeon said, swiveling back and logging the order. 'Oh, and there was one other strange report that came in a few minutes ago. A routine patrol on the supply base perimeter came across a Skipray blastboat that had made a crash landing out there.'

'A crash landing?' Thrawn frowned.

'Yes, sir,' Pellaeon said, calling up the report. 'It's underside was in pretty bad shape, and the whole hull was scorched.'

The picture came up on Pellaeon's display, and Thrawn leaned over his shoulder for a closer look. 'Any bodies?'

'No, sir,' Pellaeon said. 'The only thing aboard – and this is the strange part – was an ysalamir.'

He felt Thrawn stiffen. 'Show me.'

Pellaeon keyed for the next picture, a close-up of the ysalamir on its biosupport frame. 'The frame isn't one of our designs,' he pointed out. 'No telling where it came from.'

'Oh, there's telling, all right,' Thrawn assured him. He straightened up and took a deep breath. 'Sound intruder alert, Captain. We have visitors aboard.'

Pellaeon stared up at him in astonishment, fumbling fingers locating and twisting the alert key. 'Visitors?' he asked as the alarms began their throaty wailing.

'Yes,' Thrawn said, his glowing red eyes glittering with a sudden fire. 'Order an immediate check of Karrde's cell. If he's still there, he's to be moved immediately and put under direct stormtrooper guard. I want another guard ring put around the supply shuttles and an immediate ID check begun of their crews. And then' – he paused – 'have the *Chimaera*'s main computer shut down.'

Pellaeon's fingers froze on his keyboard. 'Shut *down*—?'

'Carry out your orders, Captain,' Thrawn cut him off.

'Yes, sir,' Pellaeon said between suddenly stiff lips. In all his years of Imperial service he had never seen a warship's main computer deliberately shut down except in space dock. To do so was to blind and cripple the craft. With intruders aboard, perhaps fatally.

'It will hamper our efforts a bit, I agree,' Thrawn said, as if reading Pellaeon's fears. 'But it will hamper our enemies' far more. You see, the only way for them to have known the *Chimaera*'s course and destination was for Mara Jade to have tapped into the computer when we brought her and Karrde aboard.'

'That's impossible,' Pellaeon insisted, wincing as his computer-driven displays began to wink out. 'Any access codes she might have known were changed years ago.'

'Unless there are codes permanently hard-wired into the system,' Thrawn said. 'Set there by the Emperor for his use and that of his agents. Jade no doubt is counting on that access in her rescue attempt; therefore, we deprive her of it.'

A stormtrooper stepped up to them. 'Yes, Commander?' Thrawn said.

'Comlink message from detention,' the electronically filtered voice announced. 'The prisoner Talon Karrde is no longer in his cell.'

'Very well,' the Grand Admiral said darkly. 'Alert all units to begin a search of the area between detention and the aft hangar bays. Karrde is to be recaptured alive – not necessarily undamaged, but alive. As to his would-be rescuers, I want them also alive if possible. If not—' He paused. 'If not, I'll understand.'

CHAPTER TWENTY-THREE

The wail of the alarm sounded over the overhead speaker; and a few seconds later the turbolift car came to an abrupt halt. 'Blast,' one of the two gunners who had replaced the service techs in the car muttered, digging a small ID card from the slot behind his belt buckle. 'Don't they ever get tired of running drills up there on the bridge?'

'Talk like that might get you a face-to-face with a stormtrooper squad,' the second warned, throwing a sideways glance at Luke and the others. Stepping past the first gunner, he slid his ID card into a slot on the control board and tapped in a confirmation code. 'It was a lot worse before the Grand Admiral took over. Anyway, what do you want 'em to do, announce snap drills in advance?'

'The whole thing's burnin' useless, if you ask me,' the first growled, clearing his ID the same way. 'Who they expect's gonna come aboard, anyway? Some burnin' pirate gang or something?'

Luke glanced questioningly at Karrde, wondering what they should do. But Mara was already moving toward the two gunners, the ID from her borrowed flight suit in hand. She stepped between them, reached the ID toward the slot—

And whipped the edge of her hand hard into the side of the first gunner's neck.

The man's head snapped sideways and he toppled to the floor without a sound. The second gunner had just enough time to gurgle something unintelligible before Mara sent him to join his friend.

'Come on, let's get out of here,' she snapped, feeling along the line where the door fitted into the car's cylindrical wall. 'Locked solid. Come on, Skywalker, get busy here.'

Luke ignited his lightsaber. 'How much time have we got?' he asked as he carved a narrow exit through part of the door.

'Not much,' Mara said grimly. 'Turbolift cars have sensors that keep track of the number of people inside. It'll give us maybe another minute to do our ID checks before reporting us to the system computer. I need to get to a terminal before the flag transfers from there to the main computer and brings the stormtroopers down on top of us.'

Luke finished the cut and closed down the lightsaber as Mara and Karrde lifted the section down and out of the way. Beyond was the tunnel wall, not quite in line with the hole. 'Good,' Mara said, easing through the gap. 'We were starting to rotate when the system froze down. There's room here to get into the tunnel.'

The others followed. The turbolift tunnel was roughly rectangular in cross-section, with gleaming guide rails along the walls, ceiling, and floor. Luke could feel the tingle of electric fields as he passed close beside the rails, and he made a mental note not to touch them. 'Where are we going?' he whispered down the tunnel toward Mara.

'Right here,' she whispered back, stopping at a red-rimmed plate set in the wall between the guide rails. 'Access tunnel – should lead back to a service droid storage room and a computer terminal.'

The lightsaber made quick work of the access panel's safety interlock. Mara darted through the opening, blaster in hand, and disappeared down the dark tunnel beyond. Luke and Karrde followed past a double row of deactivated maintenance droids, each with a bewildering array of tools fanned out from their limbs as if for inspection. Beyond the droids the tunnel widened into a small room where, as predicted, a terminal sat nestled amid the tubes and cables. Mara was already hunched over it; but as Luke stepped into the room he caught the sudden shock in her sense. 'What's the matter?' he asked.

'They've shut down the main computer,' she said, a stunned expression on her face. 'Not just bypassed or put it on standby. Shut it down.'

'The Grand Admiral must have figured out you can get into it,' Karrde said, coming up behind Luke. 'We'd better get moving. Do you have any idea where we are?'

'I think we're somewhere above the aft hangar bays,' Mara said. 'Those service techs got off just forward of the central crew section, and we hadn't gone very far down yet.'

'Above the hangar bays,' Karrde repeated thoughtfully. 'Near the vehicle deep storage area, in other words?'

Mara frowned at him. 'Are you suggesting we grab a ship from up there?'

'Why not?' Karrde countered. 'They'll probably be expecting us to go directly to one of the hangar bays. They might not be watching for us to come in via vehicle lift from deep storage.'

'And if they are, it'll leave us trapped like clipped mynocks when the stormtroopers come to get us,' Mara retorted. 'Trying to shoot our way out of deep storage—'

'Hold it,' Luke cut her off, Jedi combat senses tingling a warning. 'Someone's coming.'

Mara muttered a curse and dropped down behind the computer terminal, blaster trained on the door. Karrde, still weaponless, faded back into the partial cover of the service tunnel and the maintenance droids lined up there. Luke flattened himself against the wall beside the door, lightsaber held ready but not ignited. He let the Force flow through him as he poised for action, listening to the dark, purposeful senses of the troopers coming up to the door and recognizing to his regret that no subtle mind touches would accomplish anything here. Gripping his lightsaber tightly, he waited . . .

Abruptly, with only a flicker of warning, the door slid open and two stormtroopers were in the room, blaster rifles at the ready. Luke raised his lightsaber, thumb on the activation switch—

And from the tunnel where Karrde had disappeared a floodlight suddenly winked on, accompanied by the sound of metal grinding against metal.

The stormtroopers took a long step into the room, angling to opposite sides of the door, their blaster rifles swinging reflexively toward the light and sound as two black-clad naval troopers crowded into the room behind them. The stormtroopers spotted Mara crouching beside the terminal, and the blaster rifles changed direction to track back toward her.

Mara was faster. Her blaster spat four times, two shots per stormtrooper, and both Imperials dropped to the floor, one with blaster still firing uselessly in death reflex. The naval troopers behind them dived for cover, firing wildly toward their attacker.

A single sweep of the lightsaber caught them both.

Luke closed down the weapon and ducked his head out the doorway for a quick look around. 'All clear,' he told Mara, coming back in.

'For now, anyway,' she countered, holstering her blaster and picking up two of the blaster rifles. 'Come on.'

Karrde was waiting for them at the access panel they'd come in by. 'Doesn't sound like the turbolifts have been reactivated yet,' he said. 'It should be safe to move through the tunnels a while longer. Any trouble with the search party?'

'No,' Mara said, handing him one of the blaster rifles. 'Effective diversion, by the way.'

'Thank you,' Karrde said. 'Maintenance droids are such useful things to have around. Deep storage?'

'Deep storage,' Mara agreed heavily. 'You just better be right about this.'

'My apologies in advance if I'm not. Let's go.'

Slowly, by comlink and intercom, the reports began to come in. They weren't encouraging.

'No sign of them anywhere in the detention level area,' a stormtrooper commander reported to Pellaeon with the distracted air of someone trying to hold one conversation while listening to another. 'One of the waste chute gratings in detention has been found cut open – that must be how they got Karrde out.'

'Never mind how they got him out,' Pellaeon growled. 'The recriminations can wait until later. The important thing right now is to find them.'

'The security teams are searching the area of that turbolift alert,' the other said, his tone implying that anything a stormtrooper commander said must by definition be important. 'So far there's been no contact.'

Thrawn turned from the two communications officers who had been relaying messages for him to and from the hangar bays. 'How was the waste chute grating cut open?' he asked.

'I have no information on that,' the commander said.

'Get it,' Thrawn said, his tone icy. 'Also inform your search parties that two maintenance techs have reported seeing a man in a TIE fighter flight suit in the vicinity of that waste collector. Warn your guards in the aft hangar bays, as well.'

'Yes, sir,' the commander said.

Pellaeon looked at Thrawn. 'I don't see how it matters right now how they got Karrde out, sir,' he said. 'Wouldn't our resources be better spent in finding them?'

'Are you suggesting that we send all our soldiers and stormtroopers converging on the hangar bays?' Thrawn asked mildly. 'That we thereby assume our quarry won't seek to cause damage elsewhere before attempting their escape?'

'No, sir,' Pellaeon said, feeling his face warming. 'I realize we need to protect the entire ship. It just seems to me to be a low-priority line of inquiry.'

'Indulge me, Captain,' Thrawn said quietly. 'It's only a hunch, but—'

'Admiral,' the stormtrooper commander interrupted. 'Report from search team 207, on deck 98 nexus 326-KK.' Pellaeon's fingers automatically started for his keyboard; came up short as he remembered that there was no computer mapping available to pinpoint the location for him. 'They've found team 102, all dead,' the commander continued. 'Two were killed by blaster fire; the other two . . .' He hesitated. 'There seems to be some confusion about the other two.'

'No confusion, Commander,' Thrawn put in, his voice suddenly deadly. 'Instruct them to look for near-microscopic cuts across the bodies with partial cauterization.'

Pellaeon stared at him. There was a cold fire in the Grand Admiral's eyes that hadn't been there before. 'Partial cauterization?' he repeated stupidly.

'And then inform them,' Thrawn continued, 'that one of the intruders is the Jedi Luke Skywalker.'

Pellaeon felt his mouth drop open. '*Skywalker?*' he gasped. 'That's impossible. He's on Jomark with C'baoth.'

'*Was*, Captain,' Thrawn corrected icily. 'He's here now.' He took a deep, controlled breath; and as he let it out, the momentary anger seemed to fade away. 'Obviously, our vaunted Jedi Master failed to keep him there, as he claimed he'd be able to. And I'd say that we now have our proof that Skywalker's escape from Myrkr wasn't a spur-of-the-moment decision.'

'You think Karrde and the Rebellion have been working together all along?' Pellaeon asked.

'We'll find out soon enough,' Thrawn told him, turning to look over his shoulder. 'Rukh?'

The silent gray figure moved to Thrawn's side. 'Yes, my lord?'

'Get a squad of noncombat personnel together,' Thrawn ordered. 'Have them collect all the ysalamiri from Engineering and Systems Control and move them down to the hangar bays. There aren't nearly enough to cover the whole area, so use your hunter's instincts on their placement. The more we can hamper Skywalker's Jedi tricks, the less trouble we'll have taking him.'

The Noghri nodded and headed for the bridge exit. 'We could also use the ysalamiri from the bridge—' Pellaeon began.

'Quiet a moment, Captain,' Thrawn cut him off, his glowing eyes gazing unseeing through the side viewport and the edge of the planet turning beneath them. 'I need to think. Yes. They'll try to travel in concealment whenever possible, I think. For now, that means the turbolift tunnels.' He gestured to the two communications officers still standing beside his chair. 'Order turbolift control to put the system back into normal service except for the 326-KK nexus between deck 98 and the aft hangar bays,' he instructed them. 'All cars in that area are to be moved to the nearest cluster point and remain locked there until further notice.'

One of the officers nodded and began relaying the order into his comlink. 'You trying to herd them toward the hangar bays?' Pellaeon hazarded.

'I'm trying to herd them in from a specific direction, yes,' Thrawn nodded. His forehead was creased with thought, his eyes still gazing at nothing in particular. 'The question is what they'll do once they realize that. Presumably try to break out of the nexus; but in which direction?'

'I doubt they'll be foolish enough to return to the supply ship,' Pellaeon suggested. 'My guess is that they'll bypass the aft hangar bays entirely and try for one of the assault shuttles in the forward bays.'

'Perhaps,' Thrawn agreed slowly. 'If Skywalker is directing the escape, I'd say that was likely. But if Karrde is giving the orders . . .' He fell silent, again deep in thought.

It was somewhere to start, anyway. 'Have extra guards placed around the assault shuttles,' Pellaeon ordered the stormtrooper commander. 'Better put some men inside the ships, too, in case the intruders make it that far.'

'No, they won't make for the shuttles if Karrde's in command,' Thrawn murmured. 'He's more apt to try something less obvious. Perhaps TIE fighters; or perhaps he'll return to the supply shuttles after all, assuming we won't expect that. Or else—'

Abruptly, his head snapped around to look at Pellaeon. 'The *Millennium Falcon*,' he demanded. 'Where is it?'

'Ah—' Again, Pellaeon's hand reached uselessly for his command board. 'I ordered it sent to deep storage, sir. I don't know whether or not the order's been carried out.'

Thrawn jabbed a finger at the stormtrooper commander. 'You – get someone on the hangar bay computer and find that ship. Then get a squad there.'

The Grand Admiral looked at Pellaeon . . . and for the first time since ordering the intruder alert, he smiled. 'We have them, Captain.'

Karrde pulled away the section of cable duct that Luke had cut and carefully looked through the opening. 'No-one seems to be around,' he murmured over his shoulder, his voice almost inaudible over the background rumble of machinery coming through from the room beyond. 'I think we've beaten them here.'

'If they're coming at all,' Luke said.

'They're coming,' Mara growled. 'Bet on it. If there was one thing Thrawn had over all the other Grand Admirals, it was a knack for predicting his enemies' strategy.'

'There are a half dozen ships out there,' Karrde continued. 'Unmarked Intelligence ships, from the look of them. Any would probably do.'

'Any idea where we are?' Luke asked, trying to see past him through the cable duct. There was a fair amount of empty space out there surrounding the ships, plus a gaping light-rimmed opening in the deck that was presumably the shaft of a heavy vehicle lift. Unlike the one he remembered from the Death Star's hangar bay, though, this shaft had a corresponding hole in the ceiling above it to allow ships to be moved farther up toward the Star Destroyer's core.

'We're near the bottom of the deep storage section, I think,' Karrde told him. 'A deck or two above the aft hangar bays. The chief difficulty will be if the lift itself is a deck down, blocking us from access to the bay and entry port.'

'Well, let's get in there and find out,' Mara said, fingering her blaster rifle restlessly. 'Waiting here won't gain us anything.'

'Agreed.' Karrde cocked his head to the side. 'I think I hear the lift coming now. They're slow, though, and there's enough cover by the ships. Skywalker?'

Luke ignited his lightsaber again and quickly cut them a hole large enough to get through. Karrde went first, followed by Luke, with Mara bringing up the rear. 'The hangar bay computer link is over there,' Mara said, pointing to a freestanding console to their right as they crouched beside a battered-looking light freighter. 'As soon as the lift passes I'll see if I can get us into it.'

'All right, but don't take too long at it,' Karrde warned. 'A faked transfer order won't gain us enough surprise to be worth any further delay.'

The top of a ship was becoming visible now as it was lifted from the hangar bays below. A ship that seemed remarkably familiar . . .

Luke felt his mouth drop open in surprise. 'That's – no. No, it can't be.'

'It is,' Mara said. 'I'd forgotten – the Grand Admiral mentioned they were taking it aboard when I talked to him at Endor.'

Luke stared, a cold lump forming in his throat as the *Millennium Falcon* rose steadily up through the opening. Leia and Chewbacca had been aboard that ship . . . 'Did he say anything about prisoners?'

'Not to me,' Mara said. 'I got the impression he'd found the ship deserted.'

Which meant that wherever Leia and Chewbacca had gone, they were now stranded there. But there was no time to worry about that now. 'We're taking it back,' he told the others, stuffing his lightsaber into his flight suit tunic. 'Cover me.'

'Skywalker—' Mara hissed; but Luke was already jogging toward the shaft. The lift plate itself came into view, revealing two men riding alongside the *Falcon*: a naval trooper and a tech with what looked like a combined data pad/control unit. They caught sight of Luke—

'Hey!' Luke called, waving as he hurried toward them. 'Hold on!'

The tech did something with his data pad and the lift stopped, and Luke could sense the sudden suspicion in the trooper's mind. 'Got new orders on that one,' he said as he trotted up to them. 'The Grand Admiral wants it moved back down. Something about using it as bait.'

The tech frowned down at his data pad. He was young, Luke saw, probably not out of his teens. 'There's nothing about new orders here,' he objected.

'I haven't heard anything about it, either,' the trooper growled, drawing his blaster and pointing it vaguely in Luke's direction as he threw a quick look around the storage room.

'It just came through a minute ago,' Luke said, nodding back toward the computer console. 'Stuff's not transferring very fast today, for some reason.'

'Makes a good story, anyway,' the trooper retorted. His blaster was now very definitely pointed at Luke. 'Let's see some ID, huh?'

Luke shrugged; and, reaching out through the Force, he yanked the blaster out of the trooper's hand.

The man didn't even pause to gape at the unexpected loss of his weapon. He threw himself forward, hands stretching toward Luke's neck—

The blaster, heading straight toward Luke, suddenly reversed direction. The trooper caught the butt end full in the stomach, coughed once in strangled agony, and fell unmoving to the deck.

'I'll take that,' Luke told the tech, waving Karrde and Mara to join him. The tech, his face a rather motley gray, handed the data pad to him without a word.

'Good job,' Karrde said as he came up beside Luke. 'Relax, we're not going to hurt you,' he added to the tech, squatting down and relieving the gasping trooper of his comlink. 'Not if you behave, anyway. Take your friend to that electrical closet over there and lock yourselves in.'

The tech glanced at him, looked again at Luke, and gave a quick nod. Hoisting the trooper under the armpits, he dragged him off. 'Make sure they get settled all right, and then join me in the ship,' Karrde told Luke. 'I'm going to get the preflight started. Are there any security codes I need to know about?'

'I don't think so.' Luke glanced around the room, spotted Mara already busy with the computer console. 'The *Falcon*'s hard enough to keep functional as it is.'

'All right. Remind Mara not to waste too much time fiddling with that computer.'

He ducked under the ship and disappeared up the ramp. Luke waited until the tech had locked himself and the trooper into the electrical closet as ordered, and then followed.

'It has a remarkably fast start-up sequence,' Karrde remarked as Luke joined him in the cockpit. 'Two minutes, maybe three, and we'll be ready to fly. You still have that controller?'

'Right here,' Luke said, handing it to him. 'I'll go get Mara.' He glanced out the cockpit window—

Just as a wide door across the room slid open, to reveal a full squad of stormtroopers.

'Uh-oh,' Karrde murmured as the eight white-armored Imperials marched purposefully toward the *Falcon*. 'Do they know we're here?'

Luke stretched out his senses, trying to gauge the

stormtroopers' mental state. 'I don't think so,' he murmured back. 'They seem to be thinking more like guards than soldiers.'

'Probably too noisy in here for them to hear the engines in start-up mode,' Karrde said, ducking down in his seat out of their direct view. 'Mara was right about the Grand Admiral; but we seem to be a step ahead of him.'

A sudden thought struck Luke, and he threw a look through the side of the canopy. Mara was crouching beside the computer console, temporarily hidden from the stormtroopers' view.

But she wouldn't remain concealed for long ... and knowing Mara, she wouldn't just sit and wait for the Imperials to notice her. If there were only some way he could warn her not to fire on them yet ...

Perhaps there was. *Mara*, he sent silently, trying to picture her in his mind. *Wait until I give the word before you attack.*

There was no reply; but he saw her throw a quick look at the *Falcon* in response and ease farther back into her limited cover. 'I'm going back to the hatchway,' he told Karrde. 'I'll try to catch them in a cross fire with Mara. Stay out of sight up here.'

'Right.'

Keeping down, Luke hurried back down the short cockpit corridor. Barely in time; even as he came to the hatchway he could feel the vibration of battle-armored boots on the entry ramp. Four of them were coming in, he could sense, with the other four fanning out beneath the ship to watch the approaches. Another second and they would see him – a second after that and someone would notice Mara – *Mara; now.*

There was a flash of blaster fire from Mara's position, coming quickly enough on the tail of his command that Luke got the distinct impression Mara had planned to attack at that time whether she'd had his permission or not. Igniting his lightsaber, Luke leaped around the corner onto the ramp, catching the stormtroopers just as they were starting to turn toward the threat behind them. His first sweep took off the barrel of the lead stormtrooper's blaster rifle; reaching out with the Force, he gave the man a hard shove, pushing him into his companions and sending the whole bunch of them tumbling helplessly down to the lift plate. Jumping off the ramp to the side, he deflected a shot from another stormtrooper and sliced the lightsaber blade across him; caught a half dozen more shots before Mara's blaster fire took the next one out. A quick look showed that she'd already dealt with the other two.

A surge in the Force spun him around, to find that the group he'd sent rolling to the bottom of the ramp had untangled themselves. With a shout he charged them, lightsaber swinging in large circles as he waited for Mara to take advantage of his distraction to fire on them. But she didn't, and with the blaster bolts beginning to flash in at him there weren't many alternatives left. The lightsaber slashed four times and it was over.

Breathing hard, he closed down the lightsaber . . . and with a shock discovered why Mara hadn't been firing there at the end. The lift carrying the *Falcon* was dropping steadily down toward the deck below, well past the point where the stormtroopers would be out of Mara's line of fire. 'Mara!' he called, looking up.

'Yeah, what?' she shouted back, coming into view at

the rim of the lift, already five meters above him. 'What's Karrde doing?'

'I guess we're leaving,' Luke said. 'Jump – I'll catch you.'

An expression of annoyance flickered across Mara's face; but the *Falcon* was receding fast and she obeyed without hesitation. Reaching out with the Force, Luke caught her in an invisible grip, slowing her descent and landing her on the *Falcon*'s ramp. She hit the ramp running, and was inside in three steps.

She was seated beside Karrde in the cockpit by the time Luke got the hatchway sealed and made it up there himself. 'Better strap in,' she called over her shoulder.

Luke sat down behind her, suppressing the urge to order her out of the copilot's seat. He knew the *Falcon* far better than either she or Karrde did, but both of them probably had had more experience flying this general class of ship.

And from the looks of things, there was some tricky flying coming up. Through the cockpit canopy Luke could see that they were coming down, not into a hangar bay as he'd hoped, but into a wide vehicle corridor equipped with what looked like some kind of repulsorlift pads set across the deck. 'What happened with the computer?' he asked Mara.

'I couldn't get in,' Mara said. 'Though it wouldn't have mattered if I had. That stormtrooper squad had plenty of time to call for help. Unless you thought to jam their comlinks,' she added, looking at Karrde.

'Come now, Mara,' Karrde chided. 'Of course I jammed their comlinks. Unfortunately, since they probably had orders to report once they were in position, we still won't have more than a few minutes. If that much.'

'Is that our way out?' Luke frowned, looking along the corridor. 'I thought we'd be taking the lift straight down to the hangar bays.'

'This lift doesn't seem to go all the way down,' Karrde said. 'Offset from the hangar bay shaft, apparently. That lighted hole in the corridor deck ahead is probably it.'

'What then?' Luke asked.

'We'll see if this control can operate that lift,' Karrde said, holding up the data pad he'd taken from the tech. 'I doubt it, though. If only for security they'll probably have—'

'Look!' Mara snapped, pointing down the corridor. Far ahead down the corridor was another lift plate, moving down toward the lighted opening Karrde had pointed out a moment earlier. If that was indeed the exit to the hangar bays – and if the lift plate stopped there, blocking their way—

Karrde had apparently had the same thought. Abruptly, Luke was slammed hard into his seat as the *Falcon* leaped forward, clearing the edge of their lift plate and shooting down the corridor like a scalded tauntaun. For a moment it yawed wildly back and forth, swinging perilously near the corridor walls as the ship's repulsorlifts strobed with those built into the deck. Clenching his teeth, Luke watched as the lift plate ahead steadily closed the gap, the same bitter taste of near-helplessness in his mouth that he remembered from the Rancor pit beneath Jabba the Hutt's throne room. The Force was with him here, as it had been there, but at the moment he couldn't think of a way to harness that power. The *Falcon* shot toward the descending plate – he braced himself for the seemingly inevitable collision—

And abruptly, with a short screech of metal against metal, they were through the gap. The *Falcon* rolled over once as it dropped through to the huge room below, cleared the vertical lift plate guides—

And there, straight ahead as Karrde righted them again, was the wide hangar entry port. And beyond it, the black of deep space.

A half dozen blaster bolts sizzled at them as they shot across the hangar bay above the various ships parked there. But the shooting was reflexive, without any proper setup or aiming, and for the most part the shots went wild. A near miss flashed past the cockpit canopy; and then they were out, jolting through the atmosphere barrier and diving down out of the entry port toward the planet below.

And as they did so, Luke caught a glimpse across the entry port of TIE fighters from the forward hangar bays scrambling to intercept.

'Come on, Mara,' he said, slipping off his restraints. 'You know how to handle a quad laser battery?'

'No, I need her here,' Karrde said. He had the *Falcon* skimming the underside of the Star Destroyer now, heading for the ship's portside edge. 'You go ahead. And take the dorsal gun bay – I think I can arrange for them to concentrate their attack from that direction.'

Luke had no idea how he was going to accomplish that, but there was no time to discuss it. Already the *Falcon* was starting to jolt with laser hits, and from experience he knew there was only so much the ship's deflector shields could handle. Leaving the cockpit, he hurried to the gun well ladder, leaping halfway up, then climbing the rest of the way. He strapped in, fired up the quads . . . and as he looked around he discovered what Karrde had had in mind. The *Falcon* had curved up past the portside edge of the *Chimaera*, swung aft along the upper surface, and was now driving hard for deep space on a vector directly above the exhaust from the Star Destroyer's massive sublight drive nozzles. Skimming rather too close to it, in Luke's opinion; but it was for sure that no TIE fighters would be coming at them from underneath for a while.

The intercom pinged in his ear. 'Skywalker?' Karrde's voice came. 'They're almost here. You ready?'

'I'm ready,' Luke assured him. Fingers resting lightly on the firing controls, he focused his mind and let the Force flow into him.

The battle was furious but short, in some ways reminding Luke of the *Falcon*'s escape from the Death Star so long ago. Back then, Leia had recognized that they'd gotten away too easily; and as the TIE fighters swarmed and fired and exploded around him, Luke wondered uneasily whether or not the Imperials might have something equally devious in mind this time, too.

And then the sky flared with starlines and went mottled, and they were free.

Luke took a deep breath as he cut power to the quads. 'Good flying,' he said into the intercom.

'Thank you,' Karrde's dry voice came back. 'We seem to be more or less clear, though we took some damage around the starboard power converter pack. Mara's gone to check it out.'

'We can manage without it,' Luke said. 'Han's got the whole ship so cross-wired that it'll fly with half the systems out. Where are we headed?'

'Coruscant,' Karrde said. 'To drop you off, and also to follow through on the promise I made to you earlier.'

Luke had to search his memory. 'You mean that bit about the New Republic standing to gain from your rescue?'

'That's the one,' Karrde assured him. 'As I recall Solo's sales pitch to me back on Myrkr, your people are in need of transport ships. Correct?'

'Badly in need of them,' Luke agreed. 'You have some stashed away?'

'Not exactly stashed away, but it won't be too hard to put my hands on them. What do you think the New Republic would say to approximately two hundred pre-Clone Wars vintage Dreadnaught-class heavy cruisers?'

Luke felt his mouth fall open. Growing up on Tatooine had been a sheltered experience, but it hadn't been *that* sheltered. 'You don't mean . . . the Dark Force?'

'Come on down and we'll discuss it,' Karrde said. 'Oh, and I wouldn't mention it to Mara just yet.'

'I'll be right there.' Turning off the intercom, Luke hung the headset back on its hook and climbed onto the ladder . . . and for once, he didn't even notice the discontinuity as the gravity field changed direction partway down the ladder.

The *Millennium Falcon* shot away from the *Chimaera*, outmaneuvering and outgunning its pursuing TIE fighters and driving hard for deep space. Pellaeon sat at his station, hands curled into fists, watching the drama in helpless silence. Helpless, because with the main computer still only partially operational, the *Chimaera's* sophisticated weapons and tractor beam systems were useless against a ship that small, that fast, and that distant. Silent, because the disaster was far beyond the scope of any of his repertoire of curses.

The ship flickered and was gone . . . and Pellaeon prepared himself for the worst.

The worst didn't come. 'Recall the TIE fighters to their stations, Captain,' Thrawn said, his voice showing no sign of strain or anger. 'Secure from intruder alert, and have Systems Control continue bringing the main computer back on line. Oh, and the supply unloading can be resumed.'

'Yes, sir,' Pellaeon said, throwing a surreptitious frown at his superior. Had Thrawn somehow missed the significance of what had just happened out there?

The glowing red eyes glinted as Thrawn looked at him. 'We've lost a round, Captain,' he said. 'No more.'

'It seems to me, Admiral, that we've lost far more than that,' Pellaeon growled. 'There's no chance that Karrde won't give the *Katana* fleet to the Rebellion now.'

'Ah; but he won't simply *give* it to them,' Thrawn corrected, almost lazily. 'Karrde's pattern has never been to give anything away for free. He'll attempt to bargain, or else will set conditions the Rebellion will find unsatisfactory. The negotiations will take time, particularly given the suspicious political atmosphere we've taken such pains to create on Coruscant. And a little time is all we need.'

Pellaeon shook his head. 'You're assuming that ship thief Ferrier will be able to find the Corellian group's ship supplier before Karrde and the Rebellion work out their differences.'

'There's no assumption involved,' Thrawn said softly.

'Ferrier is even now on Solo's trail and has extrapolated his destination for us ... and thanks to Intelligence's excellent work on Karrde's background, I know exactly who the man is we'll be meeting at the end of that trail.'

He gazed out the viewport at the returning TIE fighters. 'Instruct Navigation to prepare a course for the Pantolomin system, Captain,' he said, his voice thoughtful. 'Departure to be as soon as the supply shuttles have been unloaded.'

'Yes, sir,' Pellaeon said, nodding the order on to the navigator and doing a quick calculation in his head. Time for the *Millennium Falcon* to reach Coruscant; time for the *Chimaera* to reach Pantolomin ...

'Yes,' Thrawn said into his thoughts. 'Now it's a race.'

CHAPTER TWENTY-FOUR

The sun had set over the brown hills of Honoghr, leaving a lingering hint of red and violet in the clouds above the horizon. Leia watched the fading color from just inside the *dukha* door, feeling the all-too-familiar sense of nervous dread that always came when she was about to go into danger and battle. A few more minutes and she, Chewbacca, and Threepio would be setting out for Nystao, to free Khabarakh and escape. Or to die trying.

She sighed and walked back into the *dukha*, wondering dimly where she'd gone wrong on this whole thing. It had seemed so reasonable to come to Honoghr – so *right*, somehow, to make such a bold gesture of good faith to the Noghri. Even before leaving Kashyyyk she'd been convinced that the offer hadn't been entirely her own idea, but instead the subtle guidance of the Force.

And perhaps it had been. But not necessarily from the side of the Force she'd assumed.

A cool breeze whispered in through the doorway, and Leia shivered. *The Force is strong in my family.* Luke had said those words to her on the eve of the Battle of Endor. She hadn't believed it at first, not until long afterward when his patient training had begun to bring out a hint of those abilities in her. But her father had had that same training and those same abilities ... and yet had ultimately fallen to the dark side.

One of the twins kicked. She paused, reaching out to gently touch the two tiny beings within her; and as she did so, fragments of memory flooded in on her. Her mother's face, taut and sad, lifting her from the darkness of the trunk where she'd lain hidden from prying eyes. Unfamiliar faces leaning over her, while her mother spoke to them in a tone that had frightened her and set her crying. Crying again when her mother died, holding tightly to the man she'd learned to call Father.

Pain and misery and fear ... and all of it because of her true father, the man who had renounced the name Anakin Skywalker to call himself Darth Vader.

There was a faint shuffling sound from the doorway. 'What is it, Threepio?' Leia asked, turning to face the droid.

'Your Highness, Chewbacca has informed me that you will be leaving here soon,' Threepio said, his prim voice a little anxious. 'May I assume that I will be accompanying you?'

'Yes, of course,' Leia told him. 'Whatever happens in Nystao, I don't think you'll want to be here for the aftermath.'

'I quite agree.' The droid hesitated, and Leia could see in his stance that his anxiety hadn't been totally relieved. 'There is, however, something that I really think you should know,' he continued. 'One of the decon droids has been acting very strangely.'

'Really?' Leia said. 'What exactly does this strangeness consist of?'

'He seems far too interested in everything,' Threepio said. 'He has asked a great number of questions, not only about you and Chewbacca, but also about me. I've also seen him moving about the village after he was supposed to be shut down for the night.'

'Probably just an improper memory wipe the last time around,' Leia said, not really in the mood for a full-blown discussion of droid personality quirks. 'I could name one or two other droids who have more curiosity than their original programming intended.'

'Your Highness!' Threepio protested, sounding wounded. 'Artoo is a different case altogether.'

'I wasn't referring only to Artoo.' Leia held up a hand to forestall further discussion. 'But I understand your concerns. I tell you what: you keep an eye on this droid for me. All right?'

'Of course, Your Highness,' Threepio said. He gave a little bow and shuffled his way back out into the gathering dusk.

Leia sighed and looked around her. Her restless wandering around the *dukha* had brought her to the genealogy wall chart, and for a long minute she gazed at it. There was a deep sense of history present in the carved wood; a sense of history, and a quiet but deep family pride. She let her eyes trace the connections between the names, wondering what the Noghri themselves thought and felt as they studied it. Did they see their triumphs and failures both, or merely their triumphs? Both, she decided. The Noghri struck her as a people who didn't deliberately blind themselves to reality.

'Do you see in the wood the end of our family, Lady Vader?'

Leia jumped. 'I sometimes wish you people weren't so good at that,' she growled as she regained her balance.

'Forgive me,' the maitrakh said, perhaps a bit dryly. 'I did not mean to startle you.' She gestured at the chart. 'Do you see our end there, Lady Vader?'

Leia shook her head. 'I have no vision of any future, maitrakh. Not yours; not even mine. I was just thinking about children. Trying to imagine what it's like to try to raise them. Wondering how much of their character a family can mold, and how much is innate in the children themselves.' She hesitated. 'Wondering if the evil in a family's history can be erased, or whether it always passes itself on to each new generation.'

The maitrakh tilted her head slightly, the huge eyes studying Leia's face. 'You speak as one newly facing the challenge of child-service.'

'Yes,' Leia admitted, her hand caressing her belly. 'I don't know if Khabarakh told you, but I'm carrying my first two children.'

'And you fear for them.'

Leia felt a muscle in her cheek twitch. 'With good reason. The Empire wants to take them from me.'

The maitrakh hissed softly. 'Why?'

'I'm not sure. But the purpose can only be an evil one.'

The maitrakh dropped her gaze. 'I'm sorry, Lady Vader. I would help you if I could.'

Leia reached over to touch the Noghri's shoulder. 'I know.'

The maitrakh looked up at the genealogy chart. 'I sent all four of my sons into danger, Lady Vader. To the Emperor's battles. It never becomes easier to watch them go forth to war and death.'

Leia thought of all her allies and companions who had died in the long war. 'I've sent friends to their deaths,' she said quietly. 'That was hard enough. I can't imagine sending my children.'

'Three of them died,' the maitrakh continued, almost as if talking to herself. 'Far from home, with none but their companions to mourn them. The fourth became a cripple, and returned home to live his shortened life in the silent despair of dishonor before death released him.'

Leia grimaced. And now, as the cost for helping her, Khabarakh was facing both dishonor and death—

The line of thought paused. 'Wait a minute. You said all four of your sons went to war? And that all four have since died?'

The maitrakh nodded. 'That is correct.'

'But then what about Khabarakh? Isn't he also your son?'

'He is my thirdson,' the maitrakh said, a strange expression on her face. 'A son of the son of my firstson.'

Leia looked at her, a sudden horrible realization flashing through her. If Khabarakh was not her son but instead her great-grandson; and if the maitrakh had personally witnessed the space battle that had brought destruction on Honoghr ... 'Maitrakh, how long has your world been like this?' she breathed. 'How many years?'

The Noghri stared at her, clearly sensing the sudden change in mood. 'Lady Vader, what have I said—?'

'*How many years?*'

The maitrakh twitched away from her. 'Forty-eight Noghri years,' she said. 'In years of the Emperor, forty-four.'

Leia put her hand against the smooth wood of the

genealogy chart, her knees suddenly feeling weak with shock. Forty-four years. Not the five or eight or even ten that she'd assumed. Forty-four. 'It didn't happen during the Rebellion,' she heard herself say. 'It happened during the Clone Wars.'

And suddenly the shock gave way to a wall of blazing-white anger. 'Forty-four years,' she snarled. 'They've held you like this for *forty-four years*?'

She spun to face the door. 'Chewie!' she called, for the moment not caring who might hear her. 'Chewie, get in here!'

A hand gripped her shoulder, and she turned back around to find the maitrakh gazing at her, an unreadable expression on her alien face. 'Lady Vader, you will tell me what is the matter.'

'Forty-four years, maitrakh, is what's the matter,' Leia told her. The fiery heat of her anger was fading, leaving behind an icy resolve. 'They've held you in slavery for almost half a century. Lying through their teeth to you, cheating you, murdering your sons.' She jabbed a finger down toward the ground beneath their feet. '*That* is not forty-four years' worth of decontamination work. And if they aren't just cleaning the dirt—'

There was a heavy footstep at the door and Chewbacca charged in, bowcaster at the ready. He saw Leia, roared a question as his weapon swung to cover the maitrakh.

'I'm not in danger, Chewie,' Leia told him. 'Just very angry. I need you to get me some more samples from the contaminated area. Not soil this time: some of the *kholm*-grass.'

She could see the surprise in the Wookiee's face. But he merely growled an acknowledgement and left. 'Why do you wish to examine the *kholm*-grass?' the maitrakh asked.

'You said yourself it smelled different than before the rains came,' Leia reminded her. 'I think there may be a connection here we've missed.'

'What connection could there be?'

Leia shook her head. 'I don't want to say anything more right now, maitrakh. Not until I'm sure.'

'Do you still wish to go to Nystao?'

'More than ever,' Leia said grimly. 'But not to hit and run. If Chewie's samples show what I think they will, I'm going to go straight to the dynasts.'

'What if they refuse to listen?'

Leia took a deep breath. 'They can't refuse,' she said. 'You've already lost three generations of your sons. You can't afford to lose any more.'

For a minute the Noghri gazed at her in silence. 'You speak truth,' she said. She hissed softly between her needle teeth, and with her usual fluid grace moved toward the door. 'I will return within the hour,' she said over her shoulder. 'Will you be ready to leave then?'

'Yes,' Leia nodded. 'Where are you going?'

The maitrakh paused at the door, her dark eyes locking onto Leia's. 'You speak truth, Lady Vader: they must listen. I will be back.'

The maitrakh returned twenty minutes later, five minutes ahead of Chewbacca. The Wookiee had collected a double handful of the *kholm*-grass from widely scattered sites and retrieved the analysis unit from its hiding place in the decon droid shed. Leia got the unit started on a pair of the ugly brown plants and they set off for Nystao.

But not alone. To Leia's surprise, a young Noghri female was already seated at the driver's seat of the open-topped landspeeder the maitrakh had obtained for them; and as they drove through the village at a brisk walking pace a dozen more Noghri joined them, striding along on both sides of the landspeeder like an honor guard. The maitrakh herself walked next to the vehicle, her face unreadable in the dim reflected light from the instrument panel. Sitting in the back seat next to the analysis unit, Chewbacca fingered his bowcaster and rumbled distrustingly deep in his throat. Behind him, wedged into the luggage compartment at the rear of the vehicle, Threepio was uncharacteristically quiet.

They passed through the village into the surrounding cropland, running without lights, the small group of Noghri around them virtually invisible in the cloud-shrouded starlight. The party reached another village, barely distinguishable from the cropland now that its own lights were darkened for the night, and passed through without incident. More cropland; another village; more cropland. Occasionally Leia caught glimpses of the lights of Nystao far ahead, and she wondered uneasily whether confronting the dynasts directly was really the wisest course of action at this point. They ruled with the assistance or at least the tacit consent of the Empire, and to accuse them of collaboration with a lie would not sit well with such a proud and honor-driven people.

And then, in the northeast sky, the larger of Honoghr's three moons broke through a thick cloud bank . . . and with a shock Leia saw that she and her original escort were no longer alone. All around them was an immense sea of shadowy figures, flowing like a silent tide along the landspeeder's path.

Behind her, Chewbacca growled surprise of his own. With his hunter's senses he had already been aware that the size of their party was increasing with each village they passed through. But even he hadn't grasped the full extent of the recruitment, and wasn't at all certain he liked it.

But Leia found some of the tightness in her chest easing as she settled back against the landspeeder's cushions. Whatever happened in Nystao now, the sheer size of the assemblage would make it impossible for the dynasts to simply arrest her and cover up the fact that she'd ever been there.

The maitrakh had guaranteed her a chance to speak. The rest would be up to her.

They reached the edge of Nystao just before sunrise ... to find another crowd of Noghri waiting for them.

'Word has arrived ahead of us,' the maitrakh told Leia as the landspeeder and its escort moved toward them. 'They have come to see the daughter of the Lord Vader and to hear her message.'

Leia looked at the crowd. 'And what is the message you've told them to expect?'

'That the debt of honor to the Empire has been paid in full,' the maitrakh said. 'That you have come to offer a new life for the Noghri people.'

Her dark eyes bored into Leia's face in unspoken question. Leia looked in turn over her shoulder at Chewbacca, and raised her eyebrows. The Wookiee rumbled an affirmative and tilted the analysis unit up to show her the display.

Sometime during their midnight journey the unit had
finally finished its work . . . and as she read the analysis,
Leia felt a fresh stirring of her earlier anger toward the
Empire at what they'd done to these people. 'Yes,' she
told the maitrakh. 'I can indeed prove that the debt has
been paid.'

Nearer now to the waiting crowd, she could see in the
dusky light that most of the Noghri were females. The
relative handful of males she could spot were either
the very light gray skin tone of children and young adolescents or the much darker gray of the elderly. But
directly in line with the landspeeder's path were a group
of about ten males with the steely-gray color of young
adults. 'I see the dynasts have heard the word, too,' she
said.

'That is our official escort,' the maitrakh said. 'They
will accompany us to the Grand *Dukha*, where the
dynasts await you.'

The official escort – or guards, or soldiers; Leia wasn't
quite sure how to think of them – remained silent as they
walked in arrowhead formation in front of the landspeeder. The rest of the crowd was alive with whispered
conversation, most of it between the city dwellers and the
villagers. What they were saying Leia didn't know; but
wherever her eyes turned the Noghri fell silent and gazed
back in obvious fascination.

The city was smaller than Leia had expected, particularly given the limited land area the Noghri had available
to them. After only a few minutes, they arrived at the
Grand *Dukha*.

From its name Leia had expected it to be simply a
larger version of the *dukha* back in the village. It was

certainly larger; but despite the similarity in design, there
was a far different sense to this version. Its walls and roof
were made of a silver-blue metal instead of wood, with
no carvings of any sort on their surfaces. The supporting
pillars were black – metal or worked stone, Leia couldn't
tell which. A wide set of black-and-red-marbled steps led
up to a gray flagstone entrance terrace outside the double
doors. The whole thing seemed cold and remote, very different from the mental picture of the Noghri ethos that
she'd built up over the past few days. Fleetingly, she wondered if the Grand *Dukha* had been built not by the
Noghri, but by the Empire.

At the top of the steps stood a row of thirteen middle-
aged Noghri males, each wearing an elaborately tooled
garment that looked like a cross between a vest and a
shawl. Behind them, his arms and legs chained to a pair
of upright posts in the middle of the terrace, was
Khabarakh.

Leia gazed past the row of dynasts at him, a ripple of
sympathetic ache running through her. The maitrakh
had described the mechanics of a Noghri public humiliation to her; but it was only as she looked at him that she
began to grasp the full depth of the shame involved in the
ritual. Khabarakh's face was haggard and pale, and he
sagged with fatigue against the chains holding his wrists
and upper arms. But his head was upright, his dark eyes
alert and watching.

The crowd parted to both sides as the landspeeder
reached the *dukha* area, forming a passage for the vehicle
to move through. The official escort went up the stairs,
forming a line between the crowd and the row of dynasts.
'Remember, we're not here to fight,' Leia murmured to

Chewbacca; and summoning every bit of regal demeanor she could muster, she stepped out of the landspeeder and walked up the stairs.

The last rustle of conversation in the crowd behind her vanished as she reached the top. 'I greet you, dynasts of the Noghri people,' she said in a loud voice. 'I am Leia Organa Solo, daughter of your Lord Darth Vader. He who came to you in your distress, and brought you aid.' She held out the back of her hand toward the Noghri in the center of the line.

He gazed at her for a moment without moving. Then, with obvious reluctance, he stepped forward and gingerly sniffed at her hand. He repeated the test twice before straightening up again. 'The Lord Vader is dead,' he said. 'Our new lord the Grand Admiral has ordered us to bring you to him, Leia Organa Solo. You will come with us to await the preparation of transport.'

From the bottom of the steps Chewbacca growled warningly. Leia quieted him with a gesture and shook her head. 'I have not come here to surrender to your Grand Admiral,' she told the dynast.

'You will do so nonetheless,' he said. He signaled, and two of the guards left their line and moved toward Leia.

She stood her ground, again signaling Chewbacca to do the same. 'Do you serve the Empire, then, or the people of Honoghr?'

'All Noghri of honor serve both,' the dynast said.

'Indeed?' Leia said. 'Does serving Honoghr now mean sending generation after generation of young men to die in the Empire's wars?'

'You are an alien,' the dynast said contemptuously. 'You know nothing about the honor of the Noghri.' He nodded to the guards now standing at Leia's sides. 'Take her into the *dukha*.'

'Are you then so afraid of the words of a lone alien woman?' Leia asked as the Noghri took her arms in a firm grip. 'Or is it that you fear your own power will be diminished by my coming?'

'You will speak no words of discord and poison!' the dynast snarled.

Chewbacca rumbled again, and Leia could sense him preparing to leap up the stairs to her aid. 'My words are not of discord,' she said, raising her voice loud enough for the whole crowd to hear. 'My words are of treachery.'

There was a sudden stirring from the crowd. 'You will be silent,' the dynast insisted. 'Or I will have you silenced.'

'I would hear her speak,' the maitrakh called from below.

'You will be silent as well!' the dynast barked as the crowd murmured approval of the maitrakh's demand. 'You have no place or speech here, maitrakh of the clan Kihm'bar. I have not called a convocate of the Noghri people.'

'Yet the convocate is here,' the maitrakh countered. 'The Lady Vader has come. We would hear her words.'

'Then you will hear them in prison.' The dynast gestured, and two more of the official guard left their line, heading purposefully toward the steps.

It was, Leia judged, the right moment. Glancing down at her belt, she reached out through the Force with all the power and control she could manage—

And her lightsaber leaped from her belt, breaking free from its quick-release and jumping up in front of her. Her eyes and mind found the switch, and with a *snap-hiss* the brilliant green-white blade flashed into existence, carving out a vertical line between her and the line of dynasts.

There was a sound like a hissing gasp from the crowd. The two Noghri who had been moving toward the maitrakh froze in midstride . . . and as the gasp vanished into utter silence, Leia knew that she'd finally gotten their complete attention. 'I am not merely the daughter of the Lord Vader,' she said, putting an edge of controlled anger into her voice. 'I am the *Mal'ary'ush*: heir to his authority and his power. I have come through many dangers to reveal the treachery that has been done to the Noghri people.'

She withdrew as much of her concentration as she could risk from the floating lightsaber to look slowly down the line of dynasts. 'Will you hear me? Or will you instead choose death?'

For a long minute the silence remained unbroken. Leia listened to the thudding of her heart and the deep hum of the lightsaber, wondering how long she could hold the weapon steady in midair before losing control of it. And then, from halfway down the line to her left, one of the dynasts took a step forward. 'I would hear the words of the *Mal'ary'ush*,' he said.

The first dynast spat. 'Do not add your own discord, Ir'khaim,' he warned. 'You see here only a chance to save the honor of the clan Kihm'bar.'

'Perhaps I see a chance to save the honor of the Noghri people, Vor'corkh,' Ir'khaim retorted. 'I would hear the *Mal'ary'ush* speak. Do I stand alone?'

Silently, another dynast stepped forward to join him. Then another did so; and another, and another, until nine of the thirteen stood with Ir'khaim. Vor'corkh hissed between his teeth, but stepped back to his place in line. 'The dynasts of Honoghr have chosen,' he growled. 'You may speak.'

The two guards released her arms. Leia counted out two more seconds before reaching a hand up to take the lightsaber and close it down. 'I will tell the story twice,' she said, turning to the crowd as she returned the weapon to her belt. 'Once as the Empire has told you; once as it truly is. You may then decide for yourselves whether or not the Noghri debt has been paid.

'You all know the history of how your world was devastated by the battle in space. How many of the Noghri were killed by the volcanoes and earthquakes and killer seas that followed, until a remnant arrived here to this place. How the Lord Darth Vader came to you, and offered you aid. How after the falling of the strange-smelling rains all plants except the *kholm*-grass withered and died. How the Empire told you the ground had been poisoned with chemicals from the destroyed ship, and offered machines to clean the soil for you. And you know all too well the price they demanded for those machines.'

'Yet the ground is indeed poisoned,' one of the dynasts told her. 'I and many others have tried through the years to grow food in places where the machines have not been. But the seed was wasted, for nothing would grow.'

'Yes,' Leia nodded. 'But it was not the soil that was poisoned. Or rather, not the soil directly.'

She signaled to Chewbacca. Reaching back into the landspeeder, he picked up the analyzer unit and one of the *kholm*-grass plants and brought them up the steps to her. 'I will now tell you the story that is true,' Leia said as the Wookiee went back down the steps. 'After the Lord Vader left in his ship, other ships came. They flew far and wide over your world. To any who asked they probably said they were surveying the land, perhaps searching for other survivors or other habitable places. But that was all a lie. Their true purpose was to seed your world with a new type of plant.' She held up the *kholm*-grass. 'This plant.'

'Your truth is dreams,' the dynast Vor'corkh spat. '*Kholm*-grass has grown on Honoghr since the beginning of knowledge.'

'I didn't say this was *kholm*-grass,' Leia countered. 'It looks like the *kholm*-grass you remember, and even smells very much like it. But not exactly. It is, in fact, a subtle creation of the Empire . . . sent by the Emperor to poison your world.'

The silence of the crowd broke into a buzz of stunned conversation. Leia gave them time, letting her gaze drift around the area as she waited. There must be close to a thousand Noghri pressed around the Grand *Dukha*, she estimated, and more were still coming into the area. The word about her must still be spreading, she decided, and glanced around to see where they were coming from.

And as she looked off to her left a slight glint of metal caught her eye. Well back from the Grand *Dukha*, half hidden in the long early-morning shadows beside another building, was the boxy shape of a decon droid.

Leia stared at it, a shiver of sudden horror running through her. A decon droid with unusual curiosity – Threepio had mentioned that, but she'd been too preoccupied at the time to pay any attention to his concerns. But for a decon droid to be in Nystao, fifty kilometers or more from its designated work area, was far more than just overdeveloped curiosity. It had to be—

She squatted down, mentally berating herself for her carelessness. Of course the Grand Admiral wouldn't have just flitted away on the spur of the moment. Not without leaving someone or something to keep an eye on things. 'Chewie – over there to your right,' she hissed. 'Looks like a decon droid, but I think it's an espionage droid.'

The Wookiee growled something vicious and started pushing his way through the crowd. But even as the Noghri made way for him, Leia knew he would never make it. Espionage droids weren't brilliant, but they were smart enough to know not to hang around after their cover had been blown. Long before Chewbacca could get over there it would be off and running. If it had a transmitter – and if there were any Imperial ships within range—

'People of Honoghr!' she shouted over the conversation. 'I will prove to you right now the truth of what I say. One of the Emperor's decon droids is there.' She pointed to it. 'Bring it to me.'

The crowd turned to look, and Leia could sense their uncertainty. But before anyone could move, the droid abruptly vanished around the corner of the building it had been skulking beside. A second later Leia caught a glimpse of it between two other buildings, scuttling away for all it was worth.

It was, tactically, the worst decision the droid could have made. Running away was as good as admitting guilt, particularly in front of a people who had grown up with the things and knew exactly what the normal behavioral range of a decon droid was. The crowd roared, and from the rear perhaps fifty of the older adolescents took off after it.

And as they did so, one of the guards on the terrace beside Leia cupped his hand around his mouth and sent a piercing half-scream into the air.

Leia jerked away, ears ringing with the sound. The guard screamed again, and this time there was an answer from somewhere in the near distance. The guard switched to a warble that sounded like a complicated medley of birdcalls; a short reply, and both fell silent. 'He calls others to the hunt,' the maitrakh told Leia.

Leia nodded, squeezing her hands into fists as she watched the pursuers disappear around a corner after the droid. If the droid had a transmitter it would right now be frantically dumping its data . . .

And then, suddenly, the pursuers were back in sight, accompanied by a half dozen adult Noghri males. Held aloft like the prize from a hunt, struggling uselessly in their grip, was the droid.

Leia took a deep breath. 'Bring it here to me,' she said as the party approached. They did so, six of the adolescents lugging it up the stairs and laying it on its back on the terrace. Leia ignited her lightsaber, her eyes searching the droid as she did so for signs of a concealed antenna port. She couldn't see one, but that by itself didn't prove anything. Steeling herself for the worst, she sliced a vertical cut through the droid's outer shell. Two more crosswise cuts, and its internal workings were laid out for all to see.

Chewbacca was already kneeling beside the droid as Leia shut down her lightsaber, his huge fingers probing delicately among the maze of tubes and cables and fibers. Near the top of the cavity was a small gray box. He threw a significant look at Leia and pulled it free from its connections.

Leia swallowed as he laid it on the ground beside him. She recognized it, all right, from long and sometimes bitter experience: the motivator/recorder unit from an Imperial probe droid. But the antenna connector jack was empty. Luck, or the Force, was still with them.

Chewbacca was poking around the lower part of the cavity now. Leia watched as he pulled several cylinders out of the tangle, examined their markings, and returned them to their places. The crowd was starting to murmur again when, with a satisfied murmur of his own, he pulled out a large cylinder and slender needle from near the intake hopper.

Gingerly, Leia took the cylinder from him. It shouldn't be dangerous to her, but there was no point in taking chances. 'I call on the dynasts to bear witness that this cylinder was indeed taken from the inside of this machine,' she called to the crowd.

'Is this your proof?' Ir'khaim asked, eyeing the cylinder doubtfully.

'It is,' Leia nodded. 'I have said that these plants are not the *kholm*-grass you remember from before the disaster. But I have not yet said what is different about them.' Picking up one of the plants, she held it up for them to see. 'The Emperor's scientists took your *kholm*-grass and changed it,' she told the crowd. 'They created differences that would breed true between generations. The altered smell you have noticed is caused by a chemical which the stem, roots, and leaves secrete. A chemical which has one purpose only: to inhibit the growth of all other plant life. The machines that the Grand Admiral claims are cleaning the ground are in fact doing nothing but destroying this special *kholm*-grass which the Empire planted.'

'Your truth is again dreams,' Vor'corkh scoffed. 'The droid machines require nearly two tens of days to cleanse a single *pirkha* of land. My daughters could destroy the *kholm*-grass there in one.'

Leia smiled grimly. 'Perhaps the machines don't require as much time as it appears. Let's find out.' Holding the *kholm*-grass out in front of her, she eased a drop of pale liquid from the tip of the needle and touched it to the stem.

It was as dramatic a demonstration as she could have hoped for. The drop soaked through the dull brown surface of the plant, and for a handful of seconds nothing seemed to happen. There was a faint sizzling sound; and then, without warning, the plant suddenly began to turn black and wither. There was a hissing gasp from the crowd as the patch of catalytic destruction spread along the stem toward the leaves and roots. Leia held it up a moment longer, then dropped it on the terrace. There it lay, writhing like a dry branch thrown into a fire, until there was nothing left but a short and unrecognizable filament of wrinkled black. Leia touched it tentatively with the toe of her boot, and it disintegrated into a fine powder.

She had expected another outburst of surprise or outrage from the crowd. Their dead silence was in its own way more unnerving than any noise would have been. The Noghri understood the implications of the demonstration, all right.

And as she looked around at their faces, she knew that she'd won.

She put the cylinder down on the terrace beside the destroyed plant and turned to face the dynasts. 'I have shown you my proof,' she said. 'You must now decide whether the Noghri debt has been paid.'

She looked at Vor'corkh; and moved by an impulse she couldn't explain, she unhooked her lightsaber from her belt and put it in his hand. Stepping past him, she went over to Khabarakh. 'I'm sorry,' she said softly. 'I didn't expect for you to have to go through anything like this because of me.'

Khabarakh opened his mouth in a needle-toothed Noghri smile. 'The Empire has long taught us that it is a warrior's pride and duty to face pain for his overlord. Should I do less for the *Mal'ary'ush* of the Lord Vader?'

Leia shook her head. 'I'm not your overlord, Khabarakh, and I never will be. The Noghri are a free people. I came only to try to restore that freedom to you.'

'And to bring us on your side against the Empire,' Vor'corkh said caustically from behind her.

Leia turned. 'That would be my wish,' she agreed. 'But I do not ask it.'

Vor'corkh studied her a moment. Then, reluctantly, he handed her lightsaber back to her. 'The dynasts of Honoghr cannot and will not make so important a decision in a single day,' he said. 'There is much to consider, and a full convocate of the Noghri people must be called.'

'Then call it,' Khabarakh urged. 'The *Mal'ary'ush* of the Lord Vader is here.'

'And can the *Mal'ary'ush* protect us from the might of the Empire, should we choose to defy it?' Vor'corkh countered.

'But—'

'No, Khabarakh, he's right,' Leia said. 'The Empire would rather kill you all than let you defect or even become neutral.'

'Have the Noghri forgotten how to fight?' Khabarakh scoffed.

'And has Khabarakh clan Kihm'bar forgotten what happened to Honoghr forty-eight years ago?' Vor'corkh snapped. 'If we defy the Empire now, we would have no option but to leave our world and hide.'

'And doing that would guarantee the instant slaughter of the commando teams that are out serving the Empire,' Leia pointed out to Khabarakh. 'Would you have them die without even knowing the reason? There is no honor in that.'

'You speak wisdom, Lady Vader,' Vor'corkh said, and for the first time Leia thought she could detect a trace of grudging respect in his eyes. 'True warriors understand the value of patience. You will leave us now?'

'Yes,' Leia nodded. 'My presence here is still a danger to you. I would ask one favor: that you would allow Khabarakh to return me to my ship.'

Vor'corkh looked at Khabarakh. 'Khabarakh's family conspired to free him,' he said. 'They succeeded, and he escaped into space. Three commando teams who were here on leave have followed in pursuit. The entire clan Kihm'bar will be in disgrace until they yield up the names of those responsible.'

Leia nodded. It was as good a story as any. 'Just be sure to warn the commandos you send to be careful when they make contact with the other teams. If even a hint of this gets back to the Empire, they'll destroy you.'

'Do not presume to tell warriors their job,' Vor'corkh retorted. He hesitated. 'Can you obtain more of this for us?' he asked, gesturing back at the cylinder.

'Yes,' Leia said. 'We'll need to go to Endor first and

pick up my ship. Khabarakh can accompany me back to Coruscant then and I'll get him a supply.'

The dynast hesitated. 'There is no way to bring it sooner?'

A fragment of conversation floated up from Leia's memory: the maitrakh, mentioning that the window for planting this season's crops was almost closed. 'There might be,' she said. 'Khabarakh, how much time would we save if we skipped Endor and went directly to Coruscant?'

'Approximately four days, Lady Vader,' he said.

Leia nodded. Han would kill her for leaving his beloved *Falcon* sitting in orbit at Endor like that, but there was no way around it. 'All right,' she nodded. 'That's what we'll do, then. Don't forget to be careful where you use it, though – you can't risk incoming Imperial ships spotting new cropland.'

'Do not presume, either, to tell farmers their job,' Vor'corkh said; but this time there was a touch of dry humor in his voice. 'We will eagerly await its arrival.'

'Then we'd better leave at once,' Leia said. She looked past him to the maitrakh, and nodded her head in thanks. Finally – finally – everything was starting to go their way. Despite her earlier doubts, the Force was clearly with her.

Turning back to Khabarakh, she ignited her lightsaber and cut him loose from his chains. 'Come on, Khabarakh,' she said. 'Time to go.'

CHAPTER TWENTY-FIVE

The *Coral Vanda* billed itself as the most impressive casino in the galaxy . . . and as he looked around the huge and ornate Tralla Room, Han could understand why he'd never heard of anyone challenging that claim.

The room had at least a dozen sabacc tables scattered around its three half-levels, plus a whole range of lugjack bars, tregald booths, holo-chess tables, and even a few of the traditional horseshoe-shaped warp-tops favored by hard-core crinbid fanatics. A bar bisecting the room stocked most anything a customer would want to drink, either to celebrate a win or forget a loss, and there was a serving window built into the back wall for people who didn't want to stop playing even to eat.

And when you got tired of looking at your cards or into your glass, there was the view through the full-wall transparent outer hull. Rippling blue-green water, hundreds of brilliantly colored fish and small sea mammals; and around all of it the intricate winding loops and fans of the famous Pantolomin coral reefs.

The Tralla Room was, in short, as fine a casino as Han had ever seen in his life . . . and the *Coral Vanda* had seven other rooms just like it.

Sitting at the bar beside him, Lando downed the last of his drink and pushed the glass away from him. 'So what now?' he asked.

'He's here, Lando,' Han told him, tearing his gaze from the reef outside and looking one more time around the casino. 'Somewhere.'

'I think he's skipped this trip,' Lando disagreed. 'Probably ran out of money. Remember what Sena said – the guy spends it like poisoned water.'

'Yeah, but if he was out of money he'd be trying to sell them another ship,' Han pointed out. He drained his own glass and got up from his seat. 'Come on – one more room to go.'

'And then we do it all over again,' Lando growled. 'And again, and again. It's a waste of time.'

'You got any other ideas?'

'Matter of fact, I do,' Lando said as they swung wide to get around a large Herglic balanced precariously across two of the seats and headed down the bar toward the exit. 'Instead of just wandering around like we have for the past six hours, we should plant ourselves at a sabacc table somewhere and start dropping some serious money. Word'll get around that there are a couple of pikers ripe for plucking; and if this guy loses money as fast as Sena says, he'll be plenty interested in trying to make some of it back.'

Han looked at his friend in mild surprise. He'd had the same idea a couple of hours ago, but hadn't figured on Lando going for it. 'You think your professional gambler's pride can take that kind of beating?'

Lando looked him straight in the eye. 'If it'll get me out of here and back to my mining operation, my pride can take anything.'

Han grimaced. He sometimes forgot that he'd kind of dragged Lando into all of this. 'Yeah,' he said. 'Sorry. Ok, tell you what. We'll give the Saffkin Room one last look. If he's not there, we'll come back here and—'

He broke off. There on the bar, in front of an empty seat, was a tray with a still-smoldering cigarra sitting in it. A cigarra with an unusual but very familiar aroma to it . . .

'Uh-oh,' Lando said quietly at his shoulder.

'I don't believe it,' Han said, dropping his hand to his blaster as he threw a quick look around the crowded room.

'Believe it, buddy,' Lando said. He touched the cushion of the vacant seat. 'It's still warm. He must be – there he is.'

It was Niles Ferrier, all right, standing beneath the ornate shimmerglass exit archway, another of his ever-present cigarras gripped between his teeth. He grinned at them, made a sort of mock salute, and disappeared out the door.

'Well, that's just great,' Lando said. 'Now what?'

'He wants us to follow him,' Han said, throwing a quick glance around them. He didn't see anyone he recognized, but that didn't mean anything. Ferrier's people were probably all around them. 'Let's go see what he's up to.'

'It could be a trap,' Lando warned.

'Or he could be ready to deal,' Han countered. 'Keep your blaster ready.'

'No kidding.'

They were halfway to the archway when they heard it: a short, deep-toned thud like a distant crack of thunder.

It was followed by another, louder one, and then a third. The conversational din of the casino faltered as others paused to listen; and as they did so, the *Coral Vanda* seemed to tremble a little.

Han looked at Lando. 'You thinking what I'm thinking?' he muttered.

'Turbolaser bursts hitting the water,' Lando murmured grimly. 'Ferrier's dealing, all right. Only not with us.'

Han nodded, feeling a hard knot settle into his stomach. Ferrier had gone ahead and made a deal with the Empire . . . and if the Imperials got their hands on the *Katana* fleet, the balance of power in the ongoing war would suddenly be skewed back in their favor.

And under the command of a Grand Admiral . . .

'We've got to find that ship dealer, and fast,' he said, hurrying toward the exit. 'Maybe we can get him out in an escape pod or something before we're boarded.'

'Hopefully, before the rest of the passengers start panicking,' Lando added. 'Let's go.'

They'd made it to the archway when their time ran out. There was a sudden thunderclap, not distant this time but seemingly right on top of them, and for a second the coral reef outside the transparent hull lit up with an angry green light. The *Coral Vanda* lurched like a wounded animal, and Han grabbed at the edge of the archway for balance—

Something caught his arm and pulled hard, yanking him out of the archway to his right. He grabbed reflexively for his blaster, but before he could draw it strong furry arms wrapped around his chest and face, pinning his gun hand to his side and blotting out all view of the sudden panic in the corridor. He tried to shout, but the arm was blocking his mouth as well as his eyes. Struggling uselessly, swearing under what breath he could get, he was hauled backwards down the corridor. Two more thunderclaps came, the second nearly throwing both him and his attacker off their feet. A change of direction sideways – his elbow banged against the side of a doorway—

A hard shove and he was free again, gasping for breath. He was in a small drinks storage room, with crates of bottles lining three of the walls almost to the ceiling. Several had already been knocked to the floor by the *Coral Vanda*'s lurching, and out of one of them a dark red liquid was oozing.

Lounging beside the door, grinning again, was Ferrier. 'Hello, Solo,' he said. 'Nice of you to drop in.'

'It was too kind an invitation to turn down,' Han said sourly, looking around. His blaster was hovering in front of a stack of crates two meters away, right in the middle of a thick and strangely solid shadow.

'You remember my wraith, of course,' Ferrier said blandly, gesturing at the shadow. 'He's the one who sneaked up onto the *Lady Luck*'s ramp to plant our backup homing beacon. The one *inside* the ship.'

So that was how Ferrier had managed to get here so fast. Another thunderclap shook the *Coral Vanda*, and another crate tottered too far and crashed to the floor. Han jumped back out of the way and took a closer look at the shadow. This time he was able to pick out the eyes and a glint of white fangs. He'd always thought wraiths were just space legend. Apparently not. 'It's not too late to make a deal,' he told Ferrier.

The other gave him a look of surprise. 'This *is* your deal, Solo,' he said. 'Why else do you think you're in here instead of out where shooting's about to start? We're just going to keep you here, nice and safe, until things settle down again.' He cocked an eyebrow. 'Calrissian, now – he's another story.'

Han frowned at him. 'What do you mean?'

'I mean that I'm tired of him getting in my way,' Ferrier said softly. 'So when the *Coral Vanda* finally gives up and surfaces, I'm going to make sure he's right up there in front, trying valiantly to protect poor Captain Hoffner from the evil stormtroopers. With any luck . . .' He spread his hands and smiled.

'Hoffner's the guy's name, huh?' Han said, fighting his anger down. Getting mad wasn't going to help Lando any. 'Suppose he's not on board? The Imperials won't be happy about that.'

'Oh, he's aboard,' Ferrier assured him. 'Getting a little stir-crazy, though. He's been sort of locked in our suite since about an hour after we sailed.'

'You sure you got the right guy?'

Ferrier shrugged. 'If not, the Grand Admiral has only himself to blame. He's the one who supplied me with the name.'

Another blast rocked the ship. 'Well, nice talking to you, Solo, but I've got a deal to close,' Ferrier said, regaining his balance and hitting the door release. 'See you around.'

'We'll pay you twice what the Empire's offering,' Han said, trying one last time.

Ferrier didn't even bother to answer. Smiling one last time, he slipped out the door and closed it behind him.

Han looked at the shadow that was the wraith. 'How about you?' he asked. 'You want to be rich?'

The wraith showed its teeth, but made no other reply. There was another thunderclap, and they were jerked hard to the side. The *Coral Vanda* was a well-built ship, but Han knew it couldn't stand up to this kind of pounding for long. Sooner or later, it would have to give up and surface . . . and then the stormtroopers would come.

He had just that long to find a way out of here.

The *Chimaera*'s turbolaser batteries fired again, and on the bridge holo display a short red line dug briefly into the sea near the tapered black cylinder that marked the *Coral Vanda*'s position. For an instant the red line was sheathed in the pale green of seawater suddenly flashed into superheated steam; and then the pale green spread outward in all directions, and the *Coral Vanda* rocked visibly as the shock wave passed it. 'They're stubborn, I'll give them that,' Pellaeon commented.

'They have a great many wealthy patrons aboard,' Thrawn reminded him. 'Many of whom would rather drown than give up their money under threat of force.'

Pellaeon glanced at his readouts. 'It won't be long until they're at that choice. Main propulsion's been knocked out, and they're developing microfractures in their hull seams. Computer projects that if they don't surface in ten minutes, they won't be able to.'

'They're a shipful of gamblers, Captain,' Thrawn said. 'They'll gamble on the strength of their ship while they seek an alternative.'

Pellaeon frowned at the holo display. 'What alternative could they possibly have?'

'Observe.' Thrawn touched his board, and a small white circle appeared on the holo in front of the *Coral*

Vanda, extending backward like the path of a crazed worm. 'There appears to be a path here beneath this section of the reef that would allow them to evade us, at least temporarily. I believe that's where they're heading.'

'They'll never make it,' Pellaeon decided. 'Not the way they're bouncing around down there. Best to be sure, though. A shot right at the entrance to that maze should do it.'

'Yes,' Thrawn said, his voice meditative. 'A pity, though, to have to damage any of these reefs. They're genuine works of art. Unique, perhaps, in that they were created by living yet nonsentient beings. I should have liked to have studied them more closely.'

He turned to Pellaeon again, gave a short nod. 'You may fire when ready.'

There was another clap of thunder as the Imperial ship overhead flash-boiled the water near them . . . and as the *Coral Vanda* lurched to the side Han made his move.

Letting the ship's motion throw him sideways, he half staggered, half fell across the storeroom to slam into one of the stacks of crates, turning at the last instant so that his back was to them. His hands, flung up over his head as if for balance, found the bottom corners of the topmost crate; and as the force of his impact shook the stack, he brought the box tipping over on top of him. He let it roll a quarter rotation toward his head, then shifted his grip and shoved it as hard as he could toward the wraith.

The alien caught it square on the upper torso, lost his balance, and crashed backward to the floor.

Han was on him in a second, kicking his blaster out of the wraith's hand and jumping after it. He caught up with the weapon, spun back up. The wraith had gotten clear of the box and was scrambling to get back to his feet on a floor now slippery with spilled Menkooro whiskey. 'Hold it!' Han snapped, gesturing with the blaster.

He might as well have been talking to a hole in the air. The wraith continued on to his feet—

And with the only other option being to shoot him dead, Han lowered his aim and fired into the pool of whiskey. There was a gentle *whoosh*; and abruptly, the center of the room burst into blue-tinged flame.

The alien leaped backward out of the fire, screaming something in his own language which Han was just as glad he couldn't understand. The wraith's momentum slammed him up against a stack of crates, nearly bringing the whole pile down. Han fired twice into the crate above the alien, starting twin waterfalls of alcohol cascading down around his shoulders and head. The alien screamed again, got his balance back—

And with one final shot, Han set the waterfalls on fire.

The wraith's scream turned into a high-pitched wail as it twisted away from the blaze, its head and shoulders sheathed in flame. More in anger than pain, though, Han knew – alcohol fires weren't all that hot. Given time, the wraith would slap out the fire, and then very likely break Han's neck.

He wasn't given that time. Midway through the wail the storeroom's automatic fire system finally sputtered into action, the sensors directing streams of fire foam straight into the wraith's face.

Han didn't wait to see the outcome. Ducking past the temporarily blinded alien, he slipped out the door.

The corridor, which had been crowded with panicking

people when he'd first been grabbed, was now deserted, the passengers on their way to the escape pods or the imagined safety of their staterooms. Firing a shot into the storeroom lock to seal it, Han hurried forward toward the ship's main hatchway. And hoped he'd get to Lando in time.

From far below him, almost lost among the shouts and screams of frightened passengers, Lando could hear the muffled hum of activated pumps. Sooner than he'd expected, the *Coral Vanda* was surrendering.

He swore under his breath, throwing another quick look over his shoulder. Where in blazes had Han gotten to, anyway? Probably hunting for Ferrier, wanting to see what the slippery ship thief was up to. Trust Han to run off and play a hunch when there was work to be done.

A dozen of the *Coral Vanda*'s crewers were busy taking up defensive positions inside the ship's main hatchway as he arrived. 'I need to talk to the captain or another officer right away,' he called to them.

'Get back to your room,' one of the men snapped without looking at him. 'We're about to be boarded.'

'I know,' Lando said. 'And I know what the Imperials want.'

That one rated him a quick look. 'Yeah? What?'

'One of your passengers,' Lando told him. 'He has something the Empire—'

'What's his name?'

'I don't know. I've got a description, though.'

'Wonderful,' the crewer grunted, checking the power level on his blaster. 'Tell you what you do – you head aft and start going door to door. Let us know if you find him.'

Lando gritted his teeth. 'I'm serious.'

'So am I,' the other retorted. 'Go on, get out of here.'

'But—'

'I said move it.' He pointed his blaster at Lando. 'If your passenger's got any sense he's probably already ejected in an escape pod, anyway.'

Lando backed away down the corridor, the whole thing belatedly falling together in his mind. No, the ship supplier wouldn't be in any escape pod. He probably wouldn't even be in his stateroom. Ferrier was here; and knowing Ferrier, he wouldn't have deliberately shown himself like that unless he'd already won the race.

The deck rocked slightly beneath his feet: the *Coral Vanda* had reached the surface. Turning, Lando hurried aft again. There was a passenger-access computer terminal a couple of corridors back. If he could get a passenger list from it and find Ferrier's room, he might be able to get to them before the Imperials took control of the ship. Breaking into a quick jog, he turned into a cross corridor—

They were striding purposefully toward him: four large men with blasters at the ready, with a thin, white-haired man almost hidden in the center of the group. The lead man spotted Lando, snapped his blaster up, and fired.

The first shot was a clean miss. The second sizzled into the wall as Lando ducked back behind the corner.

'So much for finding Ferrier's room,' Lando muttered. Another handful of shots spit past his barricade; and then, surprisingly, the firing stopped. Blaster in hand, hugging the corridor wall, Lando eased back to the corner and threw a quick look around it.

They were gone.

'Great,' he muttered, taking a longer look. They were gone, all right, probably into one of the crew-only areas that ran down the central core of the ship. Chasing after someone through an unfamiliar area was usually not a good idea, but there weren't a whole lot of other options available. Grimacing to himself, he started around the corner—

And yelped as a blaster bolt from his right scorched past his sleeve. He dived forward into the cross corridor, catching a glimpse as he fell of three more men coming toward him down the main corridor. He hit the thick carpet hard enough to see stars, rolled onto his side and yanked his legs out of the line of fire, fully aware that if any of the original group was watching from cover, he was dead. A barrage of blaster shots from the newcomers bit into the wall, with the kind of clustering that meant it was being used as cover fire while they advanced on him. Breathing hard – that crash dive had knocked the wind out of him – Lando got to his feet and started toward an arched doorway halfway down the cross corridor. It wouldn't give him much cover, but it was the best he had.

He had just made it to the doorway when there was a sudden curse from the direction of his attackers, a handful of shots from what sounded like a different model blaster—

And then, silence.

Lando frowned, wondering what they were pulling now. He could hear footsteps running toward him; flattening himself into the doorway as best he could, he leveled his blaster at the intersection.

The footsteps came to the intersection and paused. 'Lando?'

Lando lowered his blaster with a silent sigh of relief. 'Over here, Han,' he called. 'Come on – Ferrier's people have our man.'

Han rounded the corner and sprinted toward him. 'That's not all, buddy,' he panted. 'Ferrier's gunning for you, too.'

Lando grimaced. He hadn't missed by much, either. 'Never mind me,' he said. 'I think they must have gone down the ship's core. We've got to catch up with them before they reach the main hatchway.'

'We can try,' Han said grimly, looking around. 'Over there – looks like a crewer access door.'

It was. And it was locked.

'Ferrier's people got in,' Lando grunted, stooping down to examine the half-open release panel. 'Yeah. Here – it's been hot-wired. Let's see . . .'

He probed carefully into the mechanism with the tip of his little finger; and with a satisfying *click*, the panel unlocked and slid open. 'There we go,' he said. He got to his feet again—

And jumped back from the opening as a stuttering of blaster fire flashed through.

'Yeah, there we go all right,' Han said. He was against the wall on the other side of the opening, blaster ready but with no chance of getting a shot in through the rear guard's fire. 'How many people has Ferrier got on this ship, anyway?'

'A lot,' Lando growled. The door, apparently deciding that no-one was going through after all, slid shut again. 'I guess we do this the hard way. Let's get back to the main hatchway and try to catch them there.'

Han grabbed his shoulder. 'Too late,' he said. 'Listen.'

Lando frowned, straining his ears. Over the quiet hum of ship's noises, he could make out the rapid-fire spitting of stormtrooper laser rifles in the distance. 'They're aboard,' he murmured.

'Yeah,' Han nodded. The deck vibrated briefly beneath their feet, and abruptly the laser fire slackened off. 'Subsonic grenade,' he identified it. 'That's it. Come on.'

'Come on where?' Lando asked as Han set off down the cross corridor.

'Aft to the escape pod racks,' the other said. 'We're getting out of here.'

Lando felt his mouth drop open. But he looked at his friend, and his objections died unsaid. Han's face was set into tight lines, his eyes smoldering with anger and frustration. He knew what this meant, all right. Probably better than Lando did.

The escape pod bobbed on the surface of the sea, surrounded by a hundred other pods and floating bits of reef. Through the tiny porthole Han watched as, in the distance, the last of the Imperial assault shuttles lifted from the *Coral Vanda* and headed back to space. 'That's it, then?' Lando ventured from the seat behind him.

'That's it,' Han said, hearing the bitterness in his voice. 'They'll probably start picking up the pods soon.'

'We did all we could, Han,' Lando pointed out quietly. 'And it could have been worse. They could have blown the *Coral Vanda* out of the water – it might have been days before anyone came to get us then.'

Which would have given the Empire that much more of a head start. 'Oh, yeah, great,' Han said sourly. 'We're really on top of things.'

'What else could we have done?' Lando persisted. 'Scuttled the ship to keep them from getting him – never mind that we'd have killed several hundred people in the process? Or maybe just gotten ourselves killed fighting three assault shuttles' worth of stormtroopers? At least this way Coruscant has a chance to get ready before ships from the Dark Force start showing up in battle.'

Lando was trying – you had to give him that. But Han wasn't ready to be cheered up yet. 'How do you get ready to get hit by two hundred Dreadnaughts?' he growled. 'We're stretched to the limit as it is.'

'Come on, Han,' Lando said, his voice starting to sound a little irritated. 'Even if the ships are in mint condition and ready to fly, they're still going to need two thousand crewers apiece to man them. It'll be years before the Imperials can scrape that many recruits together and teach them how to fly the things.'

'Except that the Empire already had a call out for new ships,' Han reminded him. 'Means they already have a bunch of recruits ready to go.'

'I doubt they have four hundred thousand of them,' Lando countered. 'Come on, try looking on the bright side for once.'

'There's not much bright side here to look at.' Han shook his head.

'Sure there is,' Lando insisted. 'Thanks to your quick action, the New Republic still has a fighting chance.'

Han frowned at him. 'What do you mean?'

'You saved my life, remember? Shot those goons of Ferrier's off my back.'

'Yeah, I remember. What does that have to do with the New Republic's chances?'

'Han!' Lando said, looking scandalized. 'You know perfectly well how fast the New Republic would fall apart without me around.'

Han tried real hard, but he couldn't quite strangle off a smile on that one. He compromised, letting it come out twisted. 'All right, I give up,' he sighed. 'If I stop grousing, will you shut up?'

'Deal,' Lando nodded.

Han turned back to the porthole, the smile fading away. Lando could talk all he wanted; but the loss of the *Katana* fleet would be a first-magnitude disaster, and they both knew it. Somehow, they had to stop the Empire from getting to those ships.

Somehow.

CHAPTER TWENTY-SIX

───────── ⬩ ─────────

Mon Mothma shook her head in wonderment. 'The *Katana* fleet,' she breathed. 'After all these years. It's incredible.'

'Some might even put it more strongly than that,' Fey'lya added coolly, his fur rippling as he gazed hard at Karrde's impassive face. He'd been doing a lot of that throughout the hastily called meeting, Leia had noticed: gazing hard at Karrde, at Luke, at Leia herself. Even Mon Mothma hadn't been left out. 'Some might, in fact, have severe doubts that what you're telling us is true at all.'

Beside Karrde, Luke shifted in his seat, and Leia could sense his efforts to control his annoyance with the Bothan. But Karrde merely cocked an eyebrow. 'Are you suggesting that I'm lying to you?'

'What, a smuggler lie?' Fey'lya countered. 'What a thought.'

'He's not lying,' Han insisted, an edge to his voice. 'The fleet's been found. I saw some of the ships.'

'Perhaps,' Fey'lya said, dropping his eyes to the polished surface of the table. Of all those at the meeting, Han had so far been the only one to escape Fey'lya's posturing and his glare. For some reason, the Bothan seemed reluctant to even look at him. 'Perhaps not. There are more Dreadnaught cruisers in the galaxy than just the *Katana* fleet.'

'I don't believe this,' Luke spoke up at last, looking back and forth between Fey'lya and Mon Mothma. 'The *Katana* fleet's been found, the Empire's going after it, and we're sitting here arguing about it?'

'Perhaps the problem is that *you* believe too much, or too easily,' Fey'lya retorted, turning his gaze on Luke. 'Solo tells us the Empire is holding someone who can lead them to these alleged ships. And yet Karrde has said only he knows their location.'

'And as I've mentioned at least once today,' Karrde said tartly, 'the assumption that no-one else knew what we'd found was just that: an assumption. Captain Hoffner was a very astute man in his way, and I have no trouble believing that he might have pulled a copy of the coordinates for himself before I erased them.'

'I'm glad you have such faith in your former associate,' Fey'lya said. 'For myself, I find it easier to believe that it is Captain Solo who is wrong.' His fur rippled. 'Or has been deliberately deceived.'

Beside her, Leia felt Han's mood darken. 'You want to explain that, Councilor?' he demanded.

'I think you were lied to,' Fey'lya said bluntly, his eyes still not meeting Han's. 'I think this contact of yours – who I notice you've been remarkably reluctant to identify – told you a story and dressed it up with false evidence. That piece of machinery you say Calrissian examined could have come from anywhere. And you yourself admitted that you were never actually aboard any of the ships.'

'What about that Imperial raid on the *Coral Vanda*?'

Han demanded. '*They* thought there was someone there worth grabbing.'

Fey'lya smiled thinly. 'Or else they wanted us to believe that they did. Which they very well might ... if your unnamed contact is in fact working for them.'

Leia looked at Han. There was something there, beneath the surface. Some swirl of emotion she couldn't identify. 'Han?' she asked quietly.

'No,' he said, his eyes still on Fey'lya. 'He's not working for the Imperials.'

'So you say,' Fey'lya sniffed. 'You offer little proof of that.'

'All right, then,' Karrde put in. 'Let's assume for the moment that all of this is in fact a giant soap bubble. What would the Grand Admiral stand to gain from it?'

Fey'lya's fur shifted in a gesture Leia decided was probably annoyance. Between her and Karrde they'd pretty well burst the Bothan's theory that Thrawn was not, in fact, an Imperial Grand Admiral; and Fey'lya wasn't taking even that minor defeat well. 'I should think that was obvious,' he told Karrde stiffly. 'How many systems would we have to leave undefended, do you suppose, in order to reassign enough trained personnel to reactivate and transport two hundred Dreadnaughts? No, the Empire has a great deal to gain by hasty action on our part.'

'They also have a great deal to gain by our total lack of action,' Karrde said, his voice icy cold. 'I worked with Hoffner for over two years; and I can tell you right now that it won't take the Imperials a great deal of time to obtain the fleet's location from him. If you don't move quickly, you stand to lose everything.'

'If there's anything out there to lose,' Fey'lya said.

Leia put a warning hand on Han's arm. 'That should be easy enough to check,' she jumped in before Karrde could respond. 'We can send a ship and tech crew out to take a look. If the fleet is there and seems operational, we can start a full-scale salvage effort.'

From the look on Karrde's face she could tell that he thought even that was moving too slowly. But he nodded. 'I suppose that's reasonable enough,' he said.

Leia looked at Mon Mothma. 'Mon Mothma?'

'I agree,' the other said. 'Councilor Fey'lya, you'll speak to Admiral Drayson at once about assigning an Escort Frigate and two X-wing squadrons to this mission. Preferably a ship already here at Coruscant; we don't want anyone outside the system to get even a hint of what we're doing.'

Fey'lya inclined his head slightly. 'As you wish. Will tomorrow morning be sufficiently early?'

'Yes.' Mon Mothma looked at Karrde. 'We'll need the fleet's coordinates.'

'Of course,' Karrde agreed. 'I'll supply them tomorrow morning.'

Fey'lya snorted. 'Let me remind you, Captain Karrde—'

'Unless, of course, Councilor,' Karrde continued smoothly, 'you'd prefer I leave Coruscant tonight and offer the location to the highest bidder.'

Fey'lya glared at him, his fur flattening. But there was nothing he could do about it, and he knew it. 'In the morning, then,' he growled.

'Good,' Karrde nodded. 'If that's all, then, I believe I'll return to my quarters and rest awhile before dinner.'

He looked across at Leia . . . and suddenly, there was something different in his face or his sense. She nodded fractionally, and his gaze slid unconcernedly away from her as he stood up. 'Mon Mothma; Councilor Fey'lya,' he said, nodding to each in turn. 'It's been interesting.'

'We'll see you in the morning,' Fey'lya said darkly.

A faintly sardonic smile touched Karrde's lips. 'Of course.'

'Then I declare this meeting adjourned,' Mon Mothma said, making it official.

'Let's go,' Leia murmured to Han as the others began collecting their data cards together.

'What's going on?' he murmured back.

'I think Karrde wants to talk,' she told him. 'Come on – I don't want to get bogged down here talking to Mon Mothma.'

'Yeah, well, you go on,' Han said, his voice oddly preoccupied.

She frowned at him. 'You sure?'

'Yeah,' he said. His eyes flicked over her shoulder, and she glanced around in time to see Fey'lya stride from the room. 'Go on. I'll catch up with you.'

'All right,' she said, frowning at him.

'It's OK,' he assured her, reaching down to squeeze her hand. 'I just need to talk to Fey'lya for a minute.'

'What about?'

'Personal stuff.' He tried one of those lopsided smiles she usually found so endearing. It didn't look nearly so innocent this time as it normally did. 'Hey – it's OK,' he repeated. 'I'm just going to talk to him. Trust me.'

'I've heard *that* before,' Leia sighed. But Luke had already left the room, and Karrde was on his way out . . . and Mon Mothma had that look about her that signified that she was about to come over and ask Leia for a favor. 'Just try to be diplomatic, all right?'

His eyes flicked over her shoulder again. 'Sure,' he said. 'Trust me.'

Fey'lya was heading down the Grand Corridor toward the Assemblage chamber when Han caught sight of him, walking with that peculiar gait of someone who's in a terrific hurry but doesn't want anyone else to know it. 'Hey!' Han called. 'Councilor Fey'lya!'

The only response was a brief flush of pale red across the nearest of the line of ch'hala trees. Glowering at the back of Fey'lya's head, Han lengthened his stride, and within a dozen quick paces had caught up with the other. 'I'd like a word with you, Councilor,' he said.

Fey'lya didn't look at him. 'We have nothing to discuss,' he said.

'Oh, I think we do,' Han said, falling into step beside him. 'Like maybe trying to find a way out of the jam you're in here.'

'I thought your female was the diplomat of the family,' Fey'lya sniffed, throwing a sideways look at Han's shirtfront.

'We take turns,' Han told him, trying real hard not to dislike the other. 'See, what got you into trouble here was trying to play politics by Bothan rules. That bank thing made Ackbar look bad, so like any good Bothan, you jumped on him. Trouble is, no-one else jumped with you, so you were left there all alone with your neck stuck way out and your political reputation on the line. You don't know how to back out gracefully, and you figure the only way to salvage your prestige is to make sure Ackbar goes down.'

'Indeed?' Fey'lya said acidly. 'Did it ever occur to you that I might have stuck my neck out, as you put it, because I truly believed Ackbar was guilty of treason?'

'Not really, no,' Han told him. 'But a lot of other people think that, and that's what's got your reputation on the line. They can't imagine anyone making such a fuss without some proof.'

'What makes you think I haven't any proof?'

'For starters, the fact that you haven't shown it,' Han said bluntly. 'Then there's the fact that you sent Breil'lya scrambling out to New Cov to try and make some sort of high-prestige deal with Senator Bel Iblis. That *is* what Breil'lya was doing out there, isn't it?'

'I don't know what you're talking about,' Fey'lya muttered.

'Right. And that's the third thing: the fact that five minutes ago you were ready to throw Bel Iblis to the cravers if it would buy you enough time to bring in the *Katana* fleet.'

Abruptly, Fey'lya stopped. 'Let me speak frankly with you, Captain Solo,' he said, still not looking directly at Han's face. 'Whether you understand my motivations or not, I certainly understand yours. You hope to bring the *Katana* fleet to Coruscant yourself; and with that leverage to force my downfall and Ackbar's reinstatement.'

'No,' Han said tiredly, shaking his head. 'That's the whole point, Councilor. Leia and the others don't play by Bothan rules. They make decisions based on evidence, not prestige. If Ackbar is guilty, he gets punished; if he's innocent, he gets released. It's that simple.'

Fey'lya smiled bitterly. 'Take my advice, Captain Solo, and stick with smuggling and fighting and other things you understand. The private rules of politics are far beyond you.'

'You're making a mistake, Councilor,' Han said, trying one last time. 'You can back out now without losing anything – you really can. But if you keep going, you risk bringing the whole New Republic down with you.'

Fey'lya drew himself up to his full height. 'I do not intend to fall, Captain Solo. My supporters among the New Republic military will see to that. Ackbar will fall, and I will rise in his place. Excuse me, now; I must speak with Admiral Drayson.'

He turned and stalked off. Han watched him go, the sour taste of defeat in his mouth. Couldn't Fey'lya see what he was doing? That he was risking everything on a single long-shot bet?

Maybe he couldn't. Maybe it took an experienced gambler to see how the odds were stacked here.

Or a politician who wasn't so set in his own system that he couldn't change.

Fey'lya reached the end of the Grand Corridor and headed to the left toward the Admiralty center. Shaking his head, Han turned and headed back toward Karrde's guest quarters. First the *Coral Vanda*, and now this. He hoped it wasn't the start of a trend.

Mara stood at the window of her room, staring out at the Manarai Mountains in the distance, feeling the oppressive weight of black memories gathering around her mind. The Imperial Palace. After five years, she was back in the Imperial Palace. Scene of important governmental meetings, glittering social functions, dark and private intrigues. The place where her life had effectively begun.

The place where she'd been when it had ended.

Her fingernails grated across the carved swirls of the window frame as well-remembered faces rose before her: Grand Admiral Thrawn, Lord Vader, Grand Moff Tarkin, advisers and politicians and sycophants by the hundreds. But above them all was the image of the Emperor. She could see him in her mind's eye as clearly as if he were staring in at her through the window, his wrinkled face frowning, his yellow-tinged eyes bright with anger and disapproval.

YOU WILL KILL LUKE SKYWALKER.

'I'm trying,' she whispered to the words echoing through her mind. But even as she said it she wondered if it were really true. She'd helped save Skywalker's life on Myrkr; had come begging for his help on Jomark; and had now uncomplainingly come to Coruscant with him.

She wasn't in any danger. Neither was Karrde. There was no way she could think of why Skywalker would be useful to either her or any of Karrde's people.

She had, in short, no excuses left.

From the next room over came the faint sound of a door opening and closing: Karrde, returned from his meeting. Turning from the window, glad of an excuse to drop this line of thought, she headed toward the door connecting their rooms.

Karrde got there first. 'Mara?' he said, opening the door and poking his head through. 'Come in here, please.'

He was standing by the room's computer terminal

when she arrived. One look at his face was all she needed. 'What's gone wrong?' she asked.

'I'm not entirely sure,' he said, pulling a data card from the terminal's copy slot. 'That Bothan on the Council put up a surprising amount of resistance to our offer. He basically forced Mon Mothma to hold off on any serious retrieval mission until the location's been checked out. He's getting a ship set up now for a morning flight.'

Mara frowned. 'A double-cross?'

'Possibly, but I can't see any point to it.' Karrde shook his head. 'Thrawn already has Hoffner. He'll get to the fleet soon enough. No, I think it more likely Fey'lya's playing internal politics here, perhaps connected to his campaign against Admiral Ackbar. But I'd rather not take any chances.'

'I've heard stories about internal Bothan politics,' Mara agreed grimly. 'What do you want me to do?'

'I want you to leave tonight for the Trogan system,' he said, handing her the data card. 'Best guess is that's where Aves will have holed up. Make contact and tell him I want everything we have that can both fly and fight to rendezvous with me at the *Katana* fleet as soon as possible.'

Mara took the card gingerly, her fingers tingling at the touch of the cool plastic. There it was, in her hands: the *Katana* fleet. A lifetime's worth of wealth or power . . . 'I may have trouble persuading Aves to trust me,' she warned.

'I don't think so,' Karrde said. 'The Imperials will have reinstated the hunt for our group by now – that alone should convince him I've escaped. There's also a special recognition code on that data card that he'll know, a code

the Grand Admiral couldn't possibly have extracted from
me this quickly.'

'Let's hope he doesn't have a higher opinion of Imperial interrogation methods than you do,' Mara said, sliding
the data card into her tunic. 'Anything else?'

'No – yes,' Karrde corrected himself. 'Tell Ghent I'd
like him to come to Coruscant instead of going to the
Katana fleet. I'll meet him here after all this is over.'

'Ghent?' Mara frowned. 'Why?'

'I want to see what a really expert slicer can do with
that suspicious lump in Ackbar's bank account. Skywalker mentioned a theory that the break-in and deposit
happened at the same time, but he said that so far
no-one's been able to prove it. I'm betting Ghent can
do so.'

'I thought this involvement in New Republic politics
was supposed to be a one-shot deal,' Mara objected.

'It is,' Karrde nodded. 'I don't want to leave an ambi-
tious Bothan at my back when we leave.'

'Point,' she had to concede. 'All right. You have a ship
for me to use?'

There was a tap at the door. 'I will in a minute,' Karrde
said, crossing to the door and pulling it open.

It was Skywalker's sister. 'You wanted to see me?' she
asked.

'Yes,' Karrde nodded in greeting. 'I believe you know
my associate, Mara Jade?'

'We met briefly when you arrived on Coruscant,'
Organa Solo nodded. For a moment her eyes met Mara's,
and Mara wondered uneasily how much Skywalker had
told her.

'I need Mara to go on an errand for me,' Karrde said,

glancing both directions down the corridor before closing the door. 'She'll need a fast, long-range ship.'

'I can get her one,' Organa Solo said. 'Will a reconnaissance Y-wing do, Mara?'

'That'll be fine,' Mara said shortly.

'I'll call the spaceport and make arrangements.' She looked back at Karrde. 'Anything else?'

'Yes,' Karrde said. 'I want to know if you can throw together a tech team and get it into space tonight.'

'Councilor Fey'lya's already sending a team,' she reminded him.

'I know that. I want yours to get there first.'

She studied him a moment. 'How big a team do you want?'

'Nothing too elaborate,' Karrde told her. 'A small transport or freighter, perhaps a starfighter squadron if you can find one that doesn't mind risking official wrath. The point is not to have Fey'lya's presumably handpicked crew the only ones there.'

Mara opened her mouth; closed it again without speaking. If Karrde wanted Organa Solo to know that his own people would also be coming, he would tell her himself. Karrde glanced at her, back at Organa Solo. 'Can you do it?'

'I think so,' she said. 'Fey'lya has built up a lot of support in the military, but there are enough people who would rather have Admiral Ackbar back in charge.'

'Here are the coordinates,' Karrde said, handing her a data card. 'The sooner you can get the team moving, the better.'

'It'll be gone in two hours,' Organa Solo promised.

'Good,' Karrde nodded, his face hardening. 'There's

just one more thing, then. I want you to understand that there are exactly two reasons why I'm doing this. First, as gratitude to your brother for risking his life to help Mara rescue me; and second, to get the Imperials off my back by eliminating their chief reason to hunt me down. That's all. As far as your war and your internal politics are concerned, my organization intends to remain completely neutral. Is that clear?'

Organa Solo nodded. 'Very clear,' she said.

'Good. You'd better get moving, then. It's a long way to the fleet, and you'll want as much head start on Fey'lya as you can get.'

'Agreed.' Organa Solo looked at Mara. 'Come on, Mara. Let's get you your ship.'

The comm beside Wedge Antilles' bunk buzzed its annoying call-up signal. Groaning under his breath, he groped in the darkness and slapped in the general direction of the switch. 'Come on, give me a break, huh?' he pleaded. 'I'm still running on Ando time.'

'It's Luke, Wedge,' a familiar voice said. 'Sorry to drag you out of bed, but I need a favor. You feel like maybe getting your people into some trouble?'

'When *aren't* we in trouble?' Wedge countered, coming fully awake. 'What's the deal?'

'Get your pilots together and meet me at the spaceport in an hour,' Luke told him. 'Docking Pad 15. We've got an old transport; we should be able to fit all your X-wings aboard.'

'It's a long trip, then?'

'A few days,' Luke said. 'I can't tell you any more than that right now.'

'You're the boss,' Wedge said. 'We'll be there in one hour.'

'See you then. And thanks.'

Wedge keyed off and rolled out of bed, feeling a stirring of old excitement. He'd seen a lot of action in the decade he'd been with the Rebellion and New Republic; a lot of flying, a lot of fighting. But somehow, the missions he remembered as being the most interesting always seemed to be the ones where Luke Skywalker was also involved. He wasn't sure why; maybe Jedi just had a knack for that.

He hoped so. Between politics on Coruscant and cleaning up after Imperial raids across the New Republic, things were getting more and more frustrating around here. A change would do him good.

Keying on the light, he pulled a fresh tunic out of his wardrobe and started getting dressed.

There was no problem getting the midnight transport off Coruscant; Leia's authorization guaranteed that. But a freighter with a cargo consisting of a dozen X-wings was unusual enough to spark comment and speculation ... and it was inevitable that the speculation would eventually reach the ears of one of Fey'lya's supporters.

By morning, he knew everything.

'This goes well beyond internal political infighting,' he snarled at Leia, his fur rippling back and forth like short stalks of grain caught in a succession of dust devils. 'It was blatantly illegal. If not treasonous.'

'I'm not sure I'd go quite *that* far,' Mon Mothma said. But she looked troubled. 'Why did you do it, Leia?'

'She did it because I asked her to,' Karrde put in calmly.

'And since the *Katana* fleet is technically not yet under New Republic jurisdiction, I don't see how any activity related to it can be considered illegal.'

'We'll explain proper legal procedure to you later, smuggler,' Fey'lya said acidly. 'Right now, we have a serious breach of security to deal with. Mon Mothma, I request an executive order be made out for Solo's and Skywalker's arrest.'

Even Mon Mothma seemed taken aback by that one. 'An arrest order?'

'They know where the *Katana* fleet is,' Fey'lya bit out. 'None of their group has been cleared for that information. They must be sequestered until the fleet has been entirely brought into New Republic possession.'

'I hardly think that will be necessary,' Leia said, throwing a look at Karrde. 'Han and Luke have both handled classified information in the past—'

'This is not the past,' Fey'lya interrupted her. 'This is the present; and they have not been cleared.' His fur flattened. 'Under the circumstances, I think I had best take personal charge of this mission.'

Leia threw a look at Karrde, saw her own thought reflected in his face. If Fey'lya was able to personally bring back the *Katana* fleet – 'You're certainly welcome to come along, Councilor,' Karrde told the Bothan. 'Councilor Organa Solo and I will appreciate your company.'

It took a second for that to register. 'What are you talking about?' Fey'lya demanded. 'No-one's authorized either of you to come along.'

'*I'm* authorizing it, Councilor,' Karrde said coldly. 'The *Katana* fleet is still mine, and will remain so until the New Republic takes possession of it. Until then, I make the rules.'

Fey'lya's fur flattened again, and for a moment Leia thought the Bothan was going to launch himself physically at Karrde's throat. 'We will not forget this, smuggler,' he hissed instead. 'Your time will come.'

Karrde smiled sardonically. 'Perhaps. Shall we go?'

CHAPTER TWENTY-SEVEN

The proximity alert warbled, and Luke straightened up in his seat. After five days, they'd made it. 'Here we go,' he said. 'You ready?'

'You know me,' Han said from the pilot's seat beside him. 'I'm always ready.'

Luke threw a sideways glance at his friend. To all outward appearances, Han seemed perfectly normal, or at least as close to it as he ever got. But beneath the casual flippancy Luke had noticed something else over the past few days: a darker, almost brooding sense that had been with him since they left Coruscant. It was there now; and as he studied Han's face, Luke could see the tension lines there. 'You all right?' he asked quietly.

'Oh, sure. Fine.' The lines tightened a little further. 'But just once I'd like them to find someone else to go off on these little jaunts across the galaxy. You know Leia and I didn't even get a day together? We didn't see each other for a whole month; and we didn't even get a day.'

Luke sighed. 'I know,' he said. 'Sometimes I feel like I've been running full speed since we blasted out of Tatooine with the droids and Ben Kenobi way back when.'

Han shook his head. 'I hadn't seen her for a month,' he repeated. 'She looks twice as pregnant as she did when she left. I don't even know what happened to her and Chewie out there – all she had time to tell me was that those Noghri things are on our side now. Whatever *that* means. I can't get anything out of Chewie, either. Says it's her story, and that she should tell it herself. I'm about ready to strangle him.'

Luke shrugged. 'You have to face it, Han. We're just too good at what we do.'

Han snorted. But some of the tension left his face. 'Yeah. Right.'

'More to the point, I guess, we're on the list of people Leia knows she can trust,' Luke continued more seriously. 'Until we find that information tap the Empire's got into the Imperial Palace, that list is going to stay pretty short.'

'Yeah.' Han grimaced. 'Someone told me the Imperials call it Delta Source. You got any ideas who or what it might be?'

Luke shook his head. 'Not really. Got to be close in to the Assemblage, though. Maybe even to the Council. One thing's for sure – we'd better get busy and find it.'

'Yeah.' Han stirred and reached for the hyperdrive levers. 'Get ready . . .'

He pulled the levers; and a moment later they were again in the blackness of deep space. 'Here we are,' Han announced.

'Right.' Luke looked around, an involuntary shiver running up his back. 'Dead center in the middle of nowhere.'

'Should be a familiar feeling for you,' Han suggested, keying for a sensor scan.

'Thanks,' Luke said, 'but getting stuck between systems with a dead hyperdrive isn't something I want to get familiar with.'

'I didn't mean that,' Han said innocently as he keyed the comm. 'I was talking about Tatooine. Wedge?'

'Right here,' the other's voice came over the speaker.

'Looks like we've got a target at oh-four-seven mark one-six-six,' Han told him. 'You ready to fly?'

'Ready and eager.'

'OK.' Han took a last look out the viewport and keyed the cargo hatch release. 'Go.'

Luke craned his neck to look in the direction Han had indicated. At first all he could see was the normal scattering of stars, achingly bright against the total blackness around them. And then he saw them: the softer glow of a ship's running lights. His eyes traced the empty space between them, his brain forcing a pattern to the lights; and suddenly the image coalesced. 'It's a Dreadnaught, all right.'

'There's another one just past it,' Han said. 'And three more to port and a little below.'

Luke nodded as he located them, a strange tingle running through him. The *Katana* fleet. Only now did he realize just how little he'd really believed in the fleet's existence. 'Which one do we check out?' he asked.

'Might as well take the closest,' Han said.

'No,' Luke said slowly, trying to focus on the vague impression tingling through him. 'No. Let's try . . . that one over there.' He pointed to a set of running lights a few kilometers farther away.

'Any particular reason?'

'I don't really know,' Luke had to admit.

He could feel Han's eyes on him. Then the other shrugged. 'OK,' he said. 'Sure. We'll take that one. Wedge, you getting all this?'

'Copy, transport,' Wedge's voice confirmed. 'We're shifting into escort formation around you. So far it looks clean.'

'Good,' Han said. 'Stay sharp anyway.' He keyed the transport's intercom into the circuit and glanced at his chrono. 'Lando? Where are you?'

'Just inside the cargo hatch,' the other answered. 'We've got the sled loaded and ready to go.'

'OK,' Han said. 'We're heading in.'

They were approaching their target Dreadnaught now, close enough that Luke could see the faint outline of reflected starlight that marked the edge of the hull. Roughly cylindrical in shape, with a half dozen weapons blisters arranged around its midsection and a bow that he'd heard once described as a giant clam with an over-bite, the ship looked almost quaintly archaic. But it was a false impression. The Dreadnaught Heavy Cruiser had been the backbone of the Old Republic's fleet; and while it might not look as sleek as the Imperial Star Destroyer that had replaced it, its massive turbolaser batteries still packed an awesome punch. 'How do we get aboard?' he asked Han.

'There's the main docking bay,' Han said, pointing to a dim rectangle of lights. 'We'll take the ship inside.'

Luke looked at the rectangle doubtfully. 'If it's big enough.'

His fears proved groundless. The entrance to the docking bay was larger than it had appeared, and the bay itself even more so. With casual skill Han brought the transport in, swiveled it around to face the opening, and put it down on the deck. 'OK,' he said, keying the systems to standby and unstrapping. 'Let's get this over with.'

Lando, Chewbacca, and the four-man tech team were waiting at the cargo hatchway when Han and Luke arrived, the techs looking somewhat ill at ease with the unaccustomed blasters belted awkwardly to their sides. 'Checked the air yet, Anselm?' Han asked.

'It looks fine,' the head of the tech team reported, offering Han a data pad for inspection. 'Better than it should be after all these years. Must still be some droids on housekeeping duty.'

Han glanced at the analysis, handed back the data pad, and nodded to Chewbacca. 'OK, Chewie, open the hatch. Tomrus, you drive the sled. Watch out for blank spots in the gravity plates – we don't want you bouncing the sled off the ceiling.'

The air in the bay had a strangely musty odor about it; a combination of oil and dust, Luke decided, with a slight metallic tang. But it was fresh enough otherwise. 'Pretty impressive,' he commented as the group walked behind the repulsorlift sled toward the main hatchway. 'Especially after all this time.'

'Those full-rig computer systems were designed to last,' Lando said. 'So what's the plan, Han?'

'I guess we split up,' Han said. 'You and Chewie take Anselm, Tomrus, and the sled and go check out engineering. We'll head up to the bridge.'

For Luke, it was one of the eeriest trips of his life, precisely because it all looked so normal. The lights in the wide corridors were all working properly, as were the gravity plates and the rest of the environment system. Doors leading off the corridor slid open automatically whenever any of the group strayed close enough to trigger them, revealing glimpses of perfectly maintained machine shops, equipment rooms, and crew lounges. The faint mechanical noises of idling systems whispered behind the sound of their own footsteps, and occasionally they glimpsed an ancient droid still going about its business. To all appearances, the ship might just as well have been abandoned yesterday.

But it hadn't been. The ships had been floating here in the blackness for half a century . . . and their crews had not left, but had died here in agony and madness. Looking down empty cross corridors as they walked, Luke wondered what the maintenance droids had made of it all as they cleared away the bodies.

The bridge was a long walk from the docking bay. But eventually they made it. 'OK, we're here,' Han announced into his comlink as the blast doors between the bridge and the monitor anteroom behind it opened with only minor grating sounds. 'Doesn't seem to be any obvious damage. What have you got on the sublight engines?'

'Doesn't look good,' Lando reported. 'Tomrus says that six of the eight main power converters have been knocked out of alignment. He's still running a check, but my guess is this tub's not going anywhere without a complete overhaul.'

'Ask me if I'm surprised,' Han countered dryly. 'What about the hyperdrive? Any chance we can at least fly it somewhere in towing range of a shipyard?'

'Anselm is looking into that,' Lando said. 'Personally, I wouldn't trust it that far.'

'Yeah. Well, we're just here to look the thing over, not get it moving. We'll see what kind of control systems we've got left up here and that'll be it.'

Luke glanced up at the space over the blast doors. Paused for a second look at the elaborate name plaque fastened there. 'It's the *Katana*,' he murmured.

'What?' Han craned his neck for a look. 'Huh.' He looked oddly at Luke. 'Was that why you wanted this one?'

Luke shook his head. 'I guess so. It was just intuition through the Force.'

'Han, Luke,' Wedge's voice cut in suddenly. 'We've got incoming.'

Luke felt his heart jump. 'Where?'

'Vector two-ten mark twenty-one. Configuration . . . it's an Escort Frigate.'

Luke let out a quiet breath. 'Better give them a call,' he said. 'Let them know where we are.'

'Actually, they're calling us,' Wedge said. 'Hang on; I'll patch it through.'

'—tain Solo, this is Captain Virgilio of the Escort Frigate *Quenfis*,' a new voice came over Han's comlink. 'Do you read?'

'Solo here,' Han said. 'Calling from aboard the Old Republic ship *Katana*—'

'Captain Solo, I regret to inform you that you and your party are under arrest,' Virgilio cut him off. 'You will return to your own vessel at once and prepare to surrender.'

Virgilio's words, and the stunned silence that followed, echoed through the command observation deck above and behind the *Quenfis*'s bridge. Seated at the main board, Fey'lya threw a mocking smile at Leia, a slightly less insolent one at Karrde, then returned his attention to the distant X-wing drive trails. 'They don't seem to be taking you seriously, Captain,' he said toward the intercom. 'Perhaps launching your X-wing squadrons would convince them we're serious.'

'Yes, Councilor,' Virgilio said briskly, and Leia strained her ears in vain for any signs of resentment in that voice. Most of the warship captains she'd known would be highly annoyed at the prospect of taking line orders from a civilian, particularly a civilian with negligible military experience of his own. But then, Fey'lya would hardly have picked the *Quenfis* for this mission if Virgilio hadn't been one of his staunchest backers. Just one more indication, if she'd needed it, as to who was really in charge here. 'X-wings: launch.'

There were a series of dull thuds as the two squadrons of starfighters left the ship. 'Captain Solo, this is Captain Virgilio. Please respond.'

'Captain, this is Wing Commander Wedge Antilles of Rogue Squadron,' Wedge's voice cut in. 'May I ask your authorization to order our arrest?'

'Allow me, Captain,' Fey'lya said, touching the comm switch on the board behind him. 'This is Councilor Borsk Fey'lya, Commander Antilles,' he said. 'Though I doubt you're aware of it, Captain Solo is operating illegally.'

'I'm sorry, Councilor,' Wedge said, 'but I don't understand how that can be. Our orders came from Councilor Leia Organa Solo.'

'And these new orders come directly from Mon Mothma,' Fey'lya told him. 'Therefore, your authorization is—'

'Can you prove that?'

Fey'lya seemed taken aback. 'I have the order sitting here in front of me, Commander,' he said. 'You're welcome to examine it once you're aboard.'

'Commander, for the moment the origin of the arrest order is irrelevant,' Virgilio put in, annoyance starting to creep into his voice. 'As a superior officer, *I* order you to surrender and bring your squadron aboard my ship.'

There was a long silence. Leia threw a look at Karrde, seated a quarter of the way around the observation deck from her. But his attention was turned outward through the transparisteel bubble, his face impassive. Perhaps he was remembering the last time he'd been to this spot. 'What if I refuse?' Wedge asked at last.

'Forget it, Wedge,' Han's voice cut in. 'It's not worth risking a court martial over. Go on, we don't need you any more. Nice hearing from you, Fey'lya.' There was the faint click of a disconnecting comlink—

'Solo!' Fey'lya barked, leaning over the comm as if that would do any good. 'Solo!' He turned and glared at Leia. 'Get over here,' he ordered her, jabbing a finger at the comm. 'I want him back.'

Leia shook her head. 'Sorry, Councilor. Han won't listen to anyone when he's like this.'

Fey'lya's fur flattened. 'I'll ask you one more time, Councilor. If you refuse—'

He never had a chance to finish the threat. Something flickered at the edge of Leia's peripheral vision; and even as she turned to look, the *Quenfis*'s alarms went off. 'What—?' Fey'lya yelped, jerking in his seat and looking frantically around him.

'It's an Imperial Star Destroyer,' Karrde told him over the blaring of the alarms. 'And it appears to be coming this way.'

'We got company, Rogue Leader,' one of Wedge's X-wing pilots snapped as the sound of the *Quenfis*'s alarms came hooting over the comm. 'Star Destroyer; bearing one-seven-eight mark eighty-six.'

'Got it,' Wedge said, turning his ship away from its confrontation with the *Quenfis*'s approaching starfighters and bringing it around in a tight one-eighty. It was a Star Destroyer, all right: almost straight across from the *Quenfis*, with the *Katana* dead center between them. 'Luke?' he called.

'We see it,' Luke's voice came back tightly. 'We're heading for the docking bay now.'

'Right – hold it,' Wedge interrupted himself. Against the dark bulk of the Star Destroyer's lower hull a large group of drive trails had suddenly appeared. 'They're launching,' he told the other. 'Twelve marks – drop ships, probably, from the look of the drive trails.'

'So we hurry,' Han's voice came on. 'Thanks for the warning; now get back to the *Quenfis*.'

The comlink clicked and went dead. 'Like blazes we will,' Wedge muttered under his breath. 'Rogue Squadron: let's go.'

Captain Virgilio was trying to say something on the open channel. Switching to his squadron's private frequency, Wedge kicked the X-wing's drive to full power and set off toward the *Katana*.

In the near distance, just beyond the drive trails of the *Quenfis*'s X-wings, Rogue Squadron turned and blazed off in the direction of the Star Destroyer. 'They're going to attack,' Fey'lya breathed. 'They must be insane.'

'They're not attacking – they're running cover,' Leia told him, staring at the scenario unfolding outside the bubble and trying to estimate interception points. It was going to be far too close. 'We need to get over there and back them up,' she said. 'Captain Virgilio—'

'Captain Virgilio, you'll recall your X-wings at once,' Fey'lya cut her off. 'Navigation will prepare to make the jump to lightspeed.'

'Councilor?' Virgilio asked, his voice sounding stunned. 'Are you suggesting we abandon them?'

'Our duty, Captain, is to get out of here alive and sound the alarm,' Fey'lya countered sharply. 'If Rogue Squadron insists on defying orders, there's nothing we can do for them.'

Leia was on her feet. 'Captain—'

Fey'lya was quicker, slapping off the intercom before she could speak. 'I'm in charge here, Councilor,' he said as she started toward him. 'Authorized by Mon Mothma herself.'

'To blazes with your authority,' Leia snapped. For a handful of heartbeats she had the almost overwhelming urge to snatch her lightsaber from her belt and send it slicing through that bland face . . .

With an effort, she choked the urge down. Violent hatred was the path of the dark side. 'Mon Mothma didn't anticipate anything like this happening,' she said, fighting to keep her voice as calm as she could. 'Fey'lya, that's my husband and my brother out there. If we don't help them, they'll die.'

'And if we *do* help them, they'll most likely still die,' Fey'lya said coolly. 'And your unborn children along with them.'

An icy knife jabbed at Leia's heart. 'That's not fair,' she whispered.

'Reality is not required to be fair,' Fey'lya said. 'And the reality in this case is that I will not waste men and ships on a lost cause.'

'It's not lost!' Leia insisted, her voice breaking with desperation as she threw a look out the bubble. No; it couldn't end like this. Not after all she and Han had survived together. She took another step toward Fey'lya—

'The *Quenfis* will withdraw,' the Bothan said quietly; and suddenly, from some hiding place within the cream-colored fur, a blaster appeared in his hand. 'And neither you nor anyone else is going to change that.'

'Report from sensors, Captain,' the officer at the *Judicator*'s scan station called up to the command walkway. 'All the other Dreadnaughts in the region read negative for life-forms.'

'So they're concentrating on just the one,' Captain Brandei nodded. 'That's where we'll hit, then. The Rebels will be in far less of a hurry to open fire on a ship that has their own people aboard. Still just the one starfighter squadron moving to intercept?'

'Yes, sir. The Escort Frigate and other two squadrons haven't yet responded. They must have been caught off guard.'

'Perhaps.' Brandei permitted himself a slight smile. So it always went with rebels. They fought like crazed animals when they had nothing to lose; but give them a taste of victory and a chance to enjoy the spoils of war and suddenly they weren't nearly so eager to risk their lives any more. One of many reasons why the Empire would ultimately defeat them. 'Order the drop ships into defense formation,' he instructed the communications officer. 'And have Starfighter Command launch two squadrons of TIE fighters to intercept those X-wings.'

He smiled again. 'And send a message to the *Chimaera*. Inform the Grand Admiral that we have engaged the enemy.'

For a long minute Han gazed out the bridge observation bubble at the approaching Imperial ships, doing a quick estimate of times and distances and ignoring the fidgeting tech men waiting nervously at the bridge doorway. 'Shouldn't we be going?' Luke prompted from beside him.

Han came to a decision. 'We're not leaving,' he said, thumbing on his comlink. 'We'd get the transport out of the docking bay just in time to run into those drop ships and TIE fighters. Lando?'

'Right here,' Lando's voice came tensely back. 'What's happening out there?'

'Imperials on the way,' Han told him, moving over to the bridge fire-control panel and gesturing the techs to join him. 'Rogue Squadron's moving to intercept, but it sounds like Fey'lya's crowd is going to run for it.'

Lando swore under his breath. 'We can't just sit here and let Wedge tackle them alone.'

'We're not going to,' Han assured him grimly. 'Get busy back there and see what shape the power coupling to the turbolaser batteries is in. We'll check the fire control up here. And make it fast – once they break formation we won't be able to hit them.'

'Right.'

Han stuck the comlink back in his belt. 'How's it look, Shen?'

'Looks pretty solid,' the tech's muffled voice came from underneath the control board. 'Kline?'

'Connections look good here, too,' the other tech reported from a board across the room. 'If we can get the computer to enable the system . . . there we go.' He looked at Han. 'You're all set.'

Han sat down at the weapons panel, running his eyes over the unfamiliar arrangement of the controls and wondering if all this effort was more than just spitting in vacuum. Even these full-rigged, computer-centralized, slave-circuit-equipped Dreadnaughts still required over two thousand people to fly them.

But the Imperials wouldn't be expecting a derelict ship to fire. He hoped. 'Here we go,' he muttered to himself as he keyed for visual targeting. The drop ships were still flying in tight formation, using their overlapping shields to protect them from any lucky shots from the approaching X-wings. The faster TIE fighters had caught up with them now, sweeping around the group on all sides and starting to pass them.

'You've got just one shot at this,' Luke murmured.

'Thanks,' Han growled. 'I really needed to hear that.' He took a deep breath, held it, and gently squeezed the fire control triggers.

The *Katana* lurched, and as the multiple blazes of tur-bolaser light flashed outward he felt the double *thud* of a disintegrating capacitor bank through the deck. Luke had been right – the ship's first shot had been its last. But it had been worth it. The laser bolts hit the drop ship for-mation dead center; and suddenly the whole Imperial force seemed to come apart in a blaze of multiple explo-sions. For a few seconds everything was hidden behind secondary explosions and clouds of debris. Then, through the destruction, a handful of ships shot out. A few more joined them, this group moving with the distinctive limp of damaged property.

'Looks like you took out five of the drop ships,' Kline reported, peering through a set of macrobinoculars pressed tightly against his face. 'A few of the TIE fight-ers, too.'

'They're going into evasive maneuvers,' Luke added.

'OK,' Han said, getting up from the chair and pulling out his comlink. 'That's it for that game. Lando?'

'Whatever you just did, it made a real mess back here,' the other's voice came back. 'Took out the fire-control power coupling and at least one of the generators. What now?'

'We get ready for a boarding party,' Han told him. 'Meet us in the portside main corridor just forward of the docking bay. We'll see what kind of defense we can set up.'

'Right.'

Han shut down the comlink. 'Let's go,' he said.

'This had better be some defense,' Luke commented as they left the bridge and headed back down the portside corridor. 'Especially when we're talking maybe forty-to-one odds.'

Han shook his head. 'Never tell me the odds,' he admonished the other, glancing at his chrono. It could be any time now. 'Besides, you never know when the odds are going to change.'

'We can't just abandon them,' Leia said again, dimly aware that she was talking to Fey'lya as if he were a child. 'That's my husband and brother out there, and a dozen good X-wing pilots. We can't just leave them to the Imperials.'

'One mustn't place personal considerations above one's duty to the New Republic, Councilor,' Fey'lya said. His fur rippled, perhaps with appreciation of his own insight. But the blaster in his hand remained steady. 'Surely you understand that.'

'It's not just personal considerations,' Leia insisted, fighting hard to keep from losing her temper again. 'It's—'

'One moment,' Fey'lya interrupted her, touching the intercom switch. 'Captain? How soon to lightspeed?'

'Another minute,' Virgilio's voice came back. 'Perhaps two.'

'As quickly as you can, Captain,' Fey'lya said. He shut the intercom off again and looked back at Leia. 'You were saying, Councilor?'

Leia consciously unclenched her teeth. If Fey'lya's aim would only shift – even a little – she might be able to risk jumping him. But as matters stood, she was helpless. Her rudimentary abilities with the Force weren't nearly strong enough for her to grab or deflect the blaster, and he was nearly a meter out of reach of her lightsaber. 'Han and Luke are vitally important to the New Republic,' she said. 'If they die or are captured—'

'The *Katana*'s firing,' Karrde commented calmly, getting to his feet as if for a better view.

Leia glanced out the bubble as the distant Imperial ships were engulfed briefly in flame. 'They know a great deal about the workings of the New Republic, Fey'lya. Do you want the Empire to get that knowledge?'

'I'm afraid you're missing the Councilor's point, Leia,' Karrde said, walking over to where she sat. He passed in front of her, dropping a data pad casually onto the tracking console beside her as he did so. 'You're concerned about your family, of course,' he continued, walking on a couple of paces before turning to face Fey'lya. 'Councilor Fey'lya has a different set of priorities.'

'I'm sure he does,' Leia said, her mouth suddenly dry as she looked sideways at the data pad Karrde had set down. On its screen was a short message.

Turn on the intercom and comm.

She looked up again. Fey'lya's blaster was still pointed at her, but the Bothan's violet eyes were turned toward Karrde. Setting her teeth, Leia focused on the board behind him and reached out with the Force . . . and without even a click the intercom was on. Another effort and the comm was, too. 'I don't understand,' she said to Karrde. 'What other priorities could Councilor Fey'lya have?'

'It's simple enough,' Karrde said. 'Councilor Fey'lya is motivated solely by his own political survival. He's running away from the fight because he's put his most ardent supporters aboard this ship and he can't afford to lose any of them.'

Leia blinked. 'He's what? But I thought—'

'That this was the normal crew of the *Quenfis*?' Karrde

shook his head. 'Not at all. The captain and senior officers are all that remain, and they were mostly on his side in the first place. That's why Fey'lya wanted a few hours before leaving Coruscant: so that he could shift duty assignments around and make sure everyone aboard was fully loyal to him.' He smiled thinly. 'Not that any of them realized that, of course. They were given the impression that it was a special security arrangement.'

Leia nodded, feeling cold all over. So it wasn't just the captain. The entire ship was on Fey'lya's side.

Which meant it was over, and she had lost. Even if she was somehow able to take out Fey'lya himself, she had lost.

'So you can imagine,' Karrde went on offhandedly, 'how reluctant Fey'lya is to risk losing any of them over anything so outmoded as loyalty to one's comrades. Especially after having worked so hard to convince them of how much he cared for the average fighting man.'

Leia threw Karrde a sharp look, suddenly seeing where he was going with this. 'Is that true, Councilor?' she asked Fey'lya, putting disbelief in her voice. 'All this talk about being on the side of the military was nothing more than a play for political power?'

'Don't be foolish, Councilor,' Fey'lya said, fur rippling with contempt. 'What other use are soldiers to a politician?'

'Is that why you don't care if the men of Rogue Squadron die?' Karrde asked. 'Because they prefer to stay out of politics?'

'No-one cares if their enemies die,' Fey'lya said coldly. 'And all those who are not on my side are my enemies.'

He gestured with his blaster. 'I trust, Captain Karrde, that I need not say more.'

Karrde raised his eyes from Fey'lya to the view outside. 'No, Councilor,' he said. 'I believe you've said enough.'

Leia followed his gaze. Between the *Quenfis* and the *Katana*, in twos and threes, Fey'lya's X-wing squadrons were heading to Wedge's support. Deserting the politician who had just defined the limits of his consideration for their welfare. 'Yes,' she murmured. 'You've said enough.'

Fey'lya frowned at her; but even as he started to speak the door to the bridge slid open. Captain Virgilio stood there, flanked by two soldiers. 'Councilor Fey'lya,' he said stiffly. 'I respectfully request you return to your quarters. These men will accompany you.'

Fey'lya's fur flattened. 'I don't understand, Captain.'

'We're closing off this room, sir,' Virgilio said, his voice respectful but with an edge. Stepping over to the Bothan's seat, he leaned toward the intercom. 'This is the captain,' he called. 'All hands to battle stations.'

The alarm promptly went off . . . and in Fey'lya's eyes Leia could see the sudden shock of understanding. 'Captain—'

'You see, Councilor, some of us don't consider loyalty to be all that outmoded,' Virgilio cut him off, turning to Leia. 'Councilor Organa Solo, I'd like you to join me on the bridge at your convenience. We've called for a Star Cruiser to back us up, but it'll take awhile to get here.'

'We'll just have to hold them until then,' Leia said, standing up. She looked at Karrde. 'Thank you,' she said quietly.

'Not for you or your war,' Karrde warned her. 'Mara

and my people could be arriving at any time. I'd just as soon they not be facing a Star Destroyer alone.'

'They won't,' Virgilio said. 'Councilor?'

'It's a lost cause,' Fey'lya said, trying one last time as he surrendered his blaster to one of the soldiers.

'That's all right,' Virgilio said, smiling tightly. 'The whole Rebellion was considered nothing more than a lost cause. Excuse me, Councilor; I have a battle to run.'

The *Chimaera* was touring the region Pellaeon had privately dubbed the Depot when the report from the *Judicator* came in. 'Interesting,' Thrawn commented. 'They've responded faster than I'd expected.'

'Karrde must have decided to be generous,' Pellaeon said, skimming the follow-up report. Five drop ships and three TIE fighters destroyed; one of the Dreadnaughts apparently under Rebellion control and joining battle. It looked like a major scrap was shaping up out there. 'I recommend we send another Star Destroyer to assist, Admiral,' he said. 'The Rebellion may have larger ships on the way.'

'We'll go ourselves, Captain,' Thrawn said. 'Navigation: set us a course back to the *Katana* fleet.'

The navigation officer didn't move. He sat at his station, his back to them, unnaturally stiff. 'Navigation?' Thrawn repeated.

'Admiral, message coming through from the sentry line,' the comm officer reported suddenly. 'Unidentified *Lancer*-class Frigate has entered the system and is approaching. They insist on speaking with you, personally and immediately.'

Thrawn's glowing eyes narrowed as he tapped the

comm switch . . . and suddenly Pellaeon realized who it must be aboard that ship. 'This is Thrawn,' the Grand Admiral said. 'Master C'baoth, I presume?'

'You presume correctly,' C'baoth's voice boomed from the speaker. 'I would speak with you, Grand Admiral. Now.'

'We're on our way to assist the *Judicator*,' Thrawn said, his eyes flicking to the still-motionless nav officer. 'As you perhaps already know. When we return—'

'*Now*, Grand Admiral.'

Moving quietly in the brittle silence, Pellaeon keyed for a course projection on C'baoth's ship. 'It'll take at least fifteen minutes to bring him aboard,' he murmured.

Thrawn hissed softly between his teeth; and Pellaeon knew what he was thinking. In the fluid situation of a spontaneous battle, a fifteen-minute delay could easily be the difference between victory and defeat. 'Captain, order the *Peremptory* to assist the *Judicator*,' the Grand Admiral said at last. 'We'll remain here to consult our ally.'

'Thank you, Grand Admiral,' C'baoth said; and abruptly, the nav officer gasped and slumped in his chair. 'I appreciate your generosity.'

Thrawn reached to his board, and with a vicious flick of his wrist cut off the comm. He looked down into the crew pit and motioned to two bridge guards. 'Sick bay,' he told them, indicating the now-shivering nav officer.

'Where do you suppose C'baoth found that *Lancer*?' Pellaeon murmured as the guards helped the nav officer out of his seat and carried him aft.

'He most likely hijacked it,' Thrawn said, his voice tight. 'He's been sending messages for us over distances of several light-years, and he certainly knows how to take control of people. Apparently, he's learned how to meld the two abilities.'

Pellaeon looked down into the crew pit, a shiver running up his back. 'I'm not sure I like that, sir.'

'I don't much like it myself, Captain,' Thrawn agreed, turning his head to look out the viewport. 'It may be time,' he added thoughtfully, 'to reconsider our arrangement with Master C'baoth. To reconsider it very carefully.'

The *Katana*'s turbolasers flashed, disintegrating the center of the Imperials' drop ship formation, and one of Wedge's X-wing pilots gave a war whoop. 'Will you look at that?'

'Cut the chatter, Rogue Seven,' Wedge admonished, trying to see through the cloud of flaming debris. The Imperials had gotten a bloody nose, but that was about all. 'They've got lots more TIE fighters in reserve.'

'Wedge?'

Wedge switched channels. 'I'm here, Luke.'

'We've decided not to leave the ship,' Luke said. 'We'd run right into the Imperials, and you know how well transports fight. You might as well get your group out of here and go whistle up some help.'

The surviving drop ships, Wedge saw, were reconfiguring into an evasion pattern with the TIE fighters moving ahead to clear a path for them. 'You'll never be able to hold out,' he told Luke flatly. 'There could be three hundred troops aboard those drop ships.'

'We'll have a better chance against them than you will against a Star Destroyer,' Luke retorted. 'Come on, get going.'

Wedge clenched his teeth. Luke was right, and they both knew it. But to abandon his friends here—

'Rogue Leader, this is Gold Leader,' a new voice abruptly came on the comm. 'Requesting permission to join the party.'

Frowning, Wedge threw a glance out the back of his canopy. They were there, all right: the *Quenfis*'s two X-wing squadrons, coming up behind his group for all they were worth. 'Permission granted,' he said. 'I didn't think Councilor Fey'lya was going to let you come out and play.'

'Fey'lya doesn't have any say in it any more,' the other said grimly. 'Tell you about it later. Captain's turned things over to Organa Solo.'

'First good news I've heard today,' Wedge grunted. 'All right, here's the scheme. You detail four of your group to hit those drop ships; the rest of us will concentrate on the TIE fighters. With luck, we can clear them out before the next wave gets here. I don't suppose we've got any backup of our own coming?'

'Captain says there's a Star Cruiser on the way,' Gold Leader said. 'Don't know when it'll get here, though.'

Probably not soon enough, Wedge told himself silently. 'OK,' he said aloud. 'Let's do it.'

A new set of drive trails had appeared near the Star Destroyer's docking bay: the second wave of TIE fighters had launched. That was going to be trouble down the line; but for the moment, the X-wings had this batch of Imperials outnumbered. And the Imperials knew it. They were spreading out, trying to draw their attackers apart where they couldn't cover each other. Wedge did a quick evaluation of the situation – 'All X-wings: we'll do a one-on-one,' he said. 'Choose your target and go.'

Closer now, he could see that two of the Imperial star-fighters were the faster and more advanced TIE interceptors. Picking one of them for himself, he broke formation and headed after it.

Whatever erosion the Empire had experienced in the way of ships and trained personnel over the past five years, it was quickly clear that their starfighter training program hadn't suffered a lot. Wedge's target TIE interceptor slipped adroitly away from his initial attack, doing a sideways skid that simultaneously braked him out of the X-wing's way and swiveled his lasers around to track along its flight vector. Wedge threw the X-wing into a drop loop, wincing as the other's shot came close enough to trigger the starboard engines' heat sensors, and turned sharply to starboard. He braced himself for a second shot, but it didn't come. Bringing the X-wing out of its combination loop/turn, he looked around for his opponent.

'Watch your back, Rogue Leader!' the voice of Rogue Three snapped in his ear; and Wedge again threw the X-wing into a drop loop just as another laser blast sizzled past his canopy. Not only had the Imperial not been fooled by Wedge's corkscrew maneuver, he'd even managed to follow him through it. 'He's still with you,' Rogue Three confirmed. 'Go evasive – I can be there in a minute.'

'Don't bother,' Wedge told him. Through the spinning sky outside his canopy he'd caught a glimpse of another Imperial moving past him to portside. Hauling hard on his controls, he broke out of his loop and drove directly toward it. The TIE fighter jerked slightly as its pilot suddenly became aware of the threat bearing down on him and tried to veer out of the way.

Which was exactly what Wedge had counted on. Ducking beneath the TIE fighter, he threw the X-wing into an upward rolling turn, swinging perilously close to the Imperial's canopy and bringing his nose around to point back the way he'd come.

The TIE interceptor, which had instinctively swerved off Wedge's tail to keep from ramming one of his own ships, was caught flat-footed. A single point-blank blast from the X-wing's lasers blew it out of the sky.

'Nice flying, Rogue Leader,' Gold Leader commented. 'My turn.'

Wedge understood. Throwing power to his drive, he shot away from the TIE fighter he'd used for cover, getting clear just as Gold Leader's lasers caught it. 'How we doing?' Wedge asked as his canopy lit up briefly with the reflected light of the explosion.

'We're done,' Gold Leader said.

'We are?' Wedge frowned, bringing his X-wing around in a wide circle. Sure enough, the only things visible nearby were X-wings. Apart from expanding clouds of glowing debris, of course. 'What about the drop ships?' he asked.

'I don't know,' the other admitted. 'Gold Three, Gold Four; report.'

'We got six of them, Gold Leader,' a new voice said. 'I don't know what happened to the seventh.'

Wedge swore under his breath, switching comm channels as he glanced back towards the Star Destroyer. The new group of TIE fighters was coming up fast. No time for him to do anything for the *Katana* except maybe warn them. 'Luke? You've got company coming.'

'We know,' Luke's tight voice came back. 'They're already here.'

They came out of the drop ship with lasers blazing, laying down a heavy cover fire as they moved toward the two sets of blast doors that led forward from the docking bay. Luke couldn't see them from where he was, any more than he could see Han's group waiting silently for them behind the edge of the portside blast doors. But he could hear the Imperials' blaster fire, and he could sense their approach.

And there was something about that sense that set the back of his neck tingling. Something not quite right about them . . .

His comlink beeped. 'Luke?' Lando's voice came softly. 'They're coming. You ready?'

Luke closed down his lightsaber and gave his handiwork one last check. A large section of the corridor's ceiling was now hanging perilously by a few strands of metal, ready to come crashing down at the slightest provocation. Beyond it, two sections of the wall were similarly booby-trapped. 'All set,' he told Lando.

'OK. Here goes . . .'

And suddenly, the pitch of a different class of weapons joined the cacophony as the defenders opened up on the Imperials. For a few seconds the two groups of weapons vied with each other. Then, with a screech of strained metal, the sounds were cut off.

The four techs were the first around the corner to where Luke waited, their faces showing the mixture of fear and nervousness and exhilaration of men who've just survived their first firefight. Lando was next, with Han and Chewbacca bringing up the rear. 'Ready?' Han asked Luke.

'Yes.' Luke indicated the rigged sections of ceiling and wall. 'It's not going to hold them for long, though.'

'Doesn't have to,' Han grunted. 'As long as it takes a few of them out it's worth it. Let's go.'

'Hold it,' Luke said, stretching out with the Force. Those strangely disturbing minds ... 'They're splitting up,' he told Han. 'About half are still at the portside blast doors; the other half are going to the starboard Operations section.'

'Trying to flank us,' Han nodded. 'Lando, how well is that area sealed off?'

'Not very,' Lando admitted. 'The blast doors from the docking bay itself should hold for a while, but there's a whole maze of storage rooms and maintenance shops off of Operations that they can probably get back to the main starboard corridor from. There were too many doors for us to close it all off.'

From the blast doors they'd just left came the dull thud of a shaped charge. 'So this group keeps us busy thinking they're all here, while the other one tries to get behind us,' Han decided. 'Well, we didn't want to hold the whole corridor, anyway. Chewie, you and Lando take the others and fall back toward the bridge. Take out as many of them as you can on the way. Luke and I'll go across to starboard and see if we can slow that batch down a little.'

Chewbacca growled an acknowledgment and headed off, the four tech men already on their way. 'Good luck,' Lando said, and followed.

Han looked at Luke. 'Still in just the two groups?'

'Yes,' Luke said, straining to locate the enemy. The strange feeling was still there . . .

'OK. Let's go.'

They set off, Han leading the way down a narrow cross corridor lined with the kind of closely spaced doors that indicated crew quarters. 'Where are we going?' Luke asked as they hurried along.

'Number two starboard weapons blister,' Han said. 'Should be something nasty there we can use to flood the main corridor with – turbolaser coolant or something.'

'Unless they have life-support gear,' Luke pointed out.

'They don't,' Han said. 'At least, they weren't wearing any when they charged us. They had standard trooper air filters, but if we fill the whole corridor with coolant those won't do them much good. You never know,' he added reflectively. 'The coolant might be flammable, too.'

'Too bad the *Katana* fleet wasn't made up of Star Galleons,' Luke said, reaching out again toward the enemy. As near as he could tell, they were in the maze of rooms Lando had mentioned, working their way around toward the main starboard corridor. 'We really could have used those anti-intruder defenses they come equipped with.'

'If this was a Star Galleon, the Empire wouldn't be so anxious to take it away from us in one piece,' Han retorted. 'They'd just blow it out of the sky and be done with it.'

Luke grimaced. 'Right.'

They reached the main starboard corridor; and they were halfway across it when Han suddenly stopped short. 'What in blazes—?'

Luke turned to look. Ten meters down the corridor,

sitting in a patch of darkness beneath burned-out light panels, was a large metal box resting at a tilt on a half-seen tangle of cables and struts. Twin blaster cannon protruded from beneath a narrow viewpoint; the corridor walls immediately around it were warped and blackened, with a half dozen good-sized holes visible. 'What is it?' he asked.

'Looks like a scaled-down version of a scout walker,' Han said. 'Let's go take a look.'

'Wonder what it's doing here,' Luke said as they walked toward it. The floor beneath their feet was noticeably warped, too. Whoever had been in there firing had done a thorough job of it.

'Probably someone brought it out of storage during the hive virus thing that killed everyone,' Han suggested. 'Either trying to protect the bridge or else just gone crazy themselves.'

Luke nodded, shivering at the thought. 'It must have been a real trick to get it in here in the first place.'

'Well, we're sure not going to get it out,' Han said, peering down at the tangle of debris where the walker's right leg had been. He cocked an eyebrow at Luke. 'Unless . . . ?'

Luke swallowed. Master Yoda had lifted his X-wing out of a Dagobah swamp once . . . but Master Yoda had been far stronger in the Force than Luke was. 'Let's find out,' he said. Taking a deep breath, clearing his mind, he raised his hand and reached out with the Force.

The walker didn't even quiver. Luke tried again; and again. But it was no use. Either the machine was wedged too tightly against walls and ceiling to move, or Luke simply didn't have the strength to lift it.

'Well, never mind,' Han said, glancing back down the corridor. 'It would have been nice to have it mobile – we could have put it in that big monitor room behind the bridge and picked off anyone who came close. But we can use it here, too. Let's see if we can get in.'

Holstering his blaster, he climbed up the single remaining leg. 'They're getting closer,' Luke warned him, looking uneasily back down the corridor. 'Another couple of minutes and they'll be in sight.'

'Better get around behind me,' Han said. He was at the walker's side door now, and with a grunt he pulled it open—

'What?' Luke asked sharply as Han's sense abruptly changed.

'You don't want to know,' Han told him grimly. Visibly bracing himself, he ducked down and climbed inside. 'Still has power,' he called, his voice echoing slightly. 'Let's see . . .'

Above Luke, the blaster cannon traversed a few degrees. 'Still has maneuverability,' Han added with satisfaction. 'Great.'

Luke had made it to the top of the leg now, easing carefully past sharp edges. Whoever the walker had been fighting against had put up a good fight. The back of his mind tingled – 'They're coming,' he hissed to Han, slipping off the leg and landing silently on the deck. Dropping into a crouch, he peered back through the gap between the angled leg and the main part of the walker, hoping the darkness would be adequate to conceal him.

He'd gotten out of sight just in time. The Imperials were moving swiftly toward them down the corridor, spread out in a properly cautious military formation. The two point men paused as they caught sight of the broken walker, probably trying to decide whether to risk a straight advance or to give up the element of surprise by laying down cover fire. Whoever was in charge opted for a compromise; the point men glided forward while the rest of the party dropped prone or hugged the corridor walls.

Han let them get right up to the base of the walker. Then, swiveling the blaster cannon over their heads, he opened up on the main group.

The answering fire came instantly; but it was no contest at all. Han systematically raked the walls and the floor, driving back the handful who'd been fortunate enough to have a nearby doorway to duck into and annihilating those who hadn't. The two point men reacted instantly, one of them firing upward toward the viewport, the other scrambling up the leg toward the side door.

He reached the top to find Luke waiting for him. His companion down below got three shots off – all deflected – before the lightsaber found him, too.

Abruptly, the blaster cannon stopped firing. Luke glanced down the corridor, reaching out with the Force. 'There are still three of them left,' he warned as Han opened the walker's door and squeezed out.

'Leave 'em,' Han said, climbing carefully down the back of the damaged leg and consulting his chrono. 'We need to get back to Lando and Chewie.' He threw Luke a mirthless grin. 'Besides, the actuator crystals just burned up. Let's get going before they figure that out.'

———

The first wave of TIE fighters had been destroyed, as had all but one of the drop ships. The Rebel Escort Frigate and its X-wings were now engaged with Squadrons One and Three, and appeared to be holding their own quite well.

And Captain Brandei was no longer smiling.

'Squadron Four launching now,' Starfighter Control announced. 'Squadrons Five and Six are awaiting your orders.'

'Order them to stand by,' Brandei instructed. Not that he had much choice in the matter. Five and Six were recon and bomber squadrons – useful enough in their particular areas of expertise, but not in straight battle against Rebel X-wings. 'Anything further on the *Peremptory*?'

'No, sir. The last report from the *Chimaera* – before our shields went up – had their ETA as approximately 1519.'

Only about seven minutes away. But battles had been lost in less time than that; and from the look of things, this could very well become one of them.

Which left Brandei only one real option. Much as he disliked the idea of moving into range of that Dreadnaught's turbolasers, he was going to have to take the *Judicator* into combat. 'All ahead,' he ordered the helm. 'Shields at full strength; turbolaser batteries stand ready. And inform the leader of the boarding party that I want that Dreadnaught in Imperial hands *now*.'

'Yes, sir.' There was a dull roar through the deck as the sublight drive came up to power—

And, without warning, the roar was joined by the hooting of the ship's alarms. 'Bandits coming out of light-speed astern,' the sensor officer snapped. 'Eighteen craft – freighter class and smaller. They're attacking.'

Brandei swore viciously as he punched for the appropriate display. They weren't Rebel vessels, not this group, and he wondered who in the Empire they could be. But no matter. 'Come around to two-seven-one,' he ordered the helm. 'Bring aft turbolasers to bear on the bandits. And launch Squadron Six.'

Whoever they were, he would soon teach them not to meddle in Imperial business. As to their identity . . . well, Intelligence would be able to ascertain that later from the wreckage.

'Watch it, Mara,' Aves's voice warned over the comm. 'They're trying to come about. And we've got TIE fighters on the way.'

'Right,' Mara said, permitting herself a sardonic smile. For all the good that would do. The bulk of the Star Destroyer's starfighters were already engaged with the New Republic forces, which meant that all Karrde's people were likely to get would be recon ships and bombers. Nothing they couldn't handle. 'Dankin, Torve – swing down to intercept.'

The two pilots acknowledged, and she returned her attention to the inconspicuous spot beneath the Star Destroyer's central sublight drive nozzle where her Z-95's lasers were currently blasting away. Beneath the shielding at that point was a critical part of the lower-aft sensor package. If she could take it out, she and the others would have free run of the relatively undefended underside of the huge ship.

With a sudden puff of vaporized metal and plastic, the lasers punched through. 'Got it,' she told Aves. 'Lower-aft central sector is now blind.'

'Good job,' Aves said. 'Everyone: move in.'

Mara pulled the Z-95 away, glad to be leaving the heat and radiation of the drive emissions. The *Wild Karrde* and other freighters could handle the job of tearing into the Star Destroyer's outer hull now; her small starfighter would be better utilized in keeping the TIE fighters away from them.

But first, she had enough time to check in. 'Jade calling Karrde,' she said into the comm. 'You there?'

'Right here, Mara, thank you,' came a familiar voice; and Mara felt a little of her tension drain away. *Right here, thank you*, meant everything was fine aboard the New Republic ship.

Or as fine as could be expected while facing an Imperial Star Destroyer. 'What's the situation?' she asked.

'We've taken some damage, but we seem to be holding our own,' he said. 'There's a small tech team aboard the *Katana* and they have the turbolasers operational, which may account for the Star Destroyer's reluctance to move any closer. No doubt they'll overcome their shyness eventually.'

'They've overcome it now,' Mara said. 'The ship was under power when we arrived. And we're not going to be able to distract them for long.'

'Mara, this is Leia Organa Solo,' a new voice came on the comm. 'We've got a Star Cruiser on its way.'

'The Imperials will have backup coming, too,' Mara said flatly. 'Let's not be heroic to the point of stupidity, OK? Get your people off the *Katana* and get out of here.'

'We can't,' Organa Solo said. 'The Imperials have boarded. Our people are cut off from the docking bay.'

Mara looked across at the dark bulk of the Dread-naught, lit only by its own running lights and the flickers of reflected light from the battle raging near and around it. 'Then you'd better write them off,' she said. 'The Imperials aren't likely to be far away – their backup will get here long before yours does.'

And as if cued by her words, there was a flicker of pseudomotion off to her left; and abruptly three Dread-naughts in triangular formation appeared. 'Mara!' Aves snapped.

'I see them,' Mara said as a second triad flickered in behind and above the first. 'That's it, Karrde. Get out of there—'

'Attention, New Republic forces,' a new voice boomed over the channel. 'This is Senator Garm Bel Iblis aboard the warship *Peregrine*. May I offer our assistance?'

Leia stared at the comm speaker, a strange combination of surprise and disbelief flooding in on her. She glanced up at Karrde, caught his eye. He shrugged slightly, shook his head. 'I'd heard he was dead,' he murmured.

Leia swallowed. So had she . . . but it *was* Bel Iblis's voice, all right. Or else an excellent copy. 'Garm, this is Leia Organa Solo,' she said.

'Leia!' Bel Iblis said. 'It's been a long time, hasn't it? I didn't expect you to be out here personally. Though perhaps I should have. Was all this your idea?'

Leia frowned out the viewport. 'I don't understand what you mean by *all this*. What are you doing here, anyway?'

'Captain Solo sent my assistant the coordinates and asked us to come along as backup,' Bel Iblis said, a note of caution creeping into his voice. 'I assumed it was at your request.'

Leia smiled tightly. She should have guessed. 'Han's memory sort of slips sometimes,' she said. 'Though to be honest, we haven't had much time since we got back to compare notes.'

'I see,' Bel Iblis said slowly. 'So it wasn't actually an official request from the New Republic?'

'It wasn't, but it is now,' Leia assured him. 'On behalf of the New Republic, I hereby ask for your assistance.' She looked over at Virgilio. 'Log that, please, Captain.'

'Yes, Councilor,' Virgilio acknowledged. 'And speaking for myself, Senator Bel Iblis, I'm delighted to have you along.'

'Thank you, Captain,' Bel Iblis said, and in her mind's eye Leia could see the other's famous smile. 'Let's do some damage, shall we? *Peregrine* out.'

The six Dreadnaughts had moved into encirclement formation around the Star Destroyer now, smothering it with a flood of ion cannon fire and ignoring the increasingly sporadic turbolaser blasts raking them in return.

'Mara's right, though,' Karrde said, stepping close to Leia. 'As soon as we can get the tech team off that ship, we'd better get them and run.'

Leia shook her head. 'We can't just leave the *Katana* fleet to the Empire.'

Karrde snorted. 'I take it you haven't had a chance to count how many Dreadnaughts are left out there.'

Leia frowned. 'No. Why?'

'I did a scan,' Karrde said grimly. 'Earlier, when you were arguing with Fey'lya. Out of the original two hundred *Katana* ships . . . there are fifteen left.'

Leia stared at him. 'Fifteen?' she breathed.

Karrde nodded. 'I'm afraid I underestimated the Grand Admiral, Councilor,' he said, an edge of bitterness seeping in beneath the studied urbanity of his voice. 'I knew that once he had the location of the fleet he would start moving the ships away from here. But I didn't expect him to get the location from Hoffner this quickly.'

Leia shivered. She'd undergone an Imperial interrogation herself once. Years later, the memory was still vivid. 'I wonder if there's anything left of him.'

'Save your sympathy,' Karrde advised. 'In retrospect, it seems unlikely that Thrawn needed to bother with anything so uncivilized as coercion. For Hoffner to have talked so freely implies the Grand Admiral simply applied a large infusion of cash.'

Leia gazed out at the battle, the dark feeling of failure settling over her. They'd lost. After all their efforts, they'd lost.

She took a deep breath, running through the Jedi relaxation exercises. Yes, they'd lost. But it was just a battle, not the war. The Empire might have taken the Dark Force, but recruiting and training crewers to man all those Dreadnaughts would take years. A lot could happen in that time. 'You're right,' she told Karrde. 'We'd do best to cut our losses. Captain Virgilio, as soon as those TIE fighters have been neutralized I want a landing party sent to the *Katana* to assist our tech team there.'

There was no reply. 'Captain?'

Virgilio was staring out the bridge viewport, his face carved from stone. 'Too late, Councilor,' he said quietly.

Leia turned to look. There, moving toward the besieged

Imperial ship, a second Star Destroyer had suddenly emerged from hyperspace.

The Imperials' backup had arrived.

'Pull out!' Aves shouted, his voice starting to sound ragged. 'All ships, pull out! Second Star Destroyer in system.'

The last word was half drowned out by the clang of the Z-95's proximity warning as something got entirely too close. Mara threw the little ship into a sideways skid, just in time to get out of a TIE fighter's line of fire. 'Pull out where?' she demanded, turning her skid into a barely controlled spin that had the effect of killing her forward velocity. Her attacker, perhaps made overconfident by the appearance of the backup force, roared by too fast for more than a wild shot in her direction. Coolly, Mara blew him out of the sky. 'In case you've forgotten, some of us don't have enough computing power aboard to calculate a safe hyperspace jump.'

'I'll feed you the numbers,' Aves said. 'Karrde—'

'I agree,' Karrde's voice came from the Escort Frigate. 'Get out of here.'

Mara clenched her teeth, glancing up at the second Star Destroyer. She hated to turn tail and run, but she knew they were right. Bel Iblis had shifted three of his ships to meet the new threat, but even equipped with ion cannon, three Dreadnaughts couldn't hold down a Star Destroyer for long. If they didn't disengage soon, they might not get another chance—

Abruptly, her danger sense tingled. Again she threw the Z-95 into a skid; but this time she was too late. The ship lurched hard, and from behind her came the hissing scream of superheated metal vaporizing into space. 'I'm hit!' she snapped, one hand automatically slapping cut-off switches as the other grabbed for her flight suit's helmet seals and fastened them in place. Just in time; a second hiss, cut off almost before it began, announced the failure of cabin integrity. 'Power lost, air lost. Ejecting now.'

She reached for the eject loop ... and paused. By chance – or perhaps last-second instinct – her crippled fighter was aimed almost directly at the first Star Destroyer's hangar entry port. If she could coax a little more power out of the auxiliary maneuvering system ...

It took more than a little coaxing, but when she finally gripped the eject loop again she had the satisfaction of knowing that even in death the Z-95 would take a minor bit of revenge on the Empire's war machine. Not much, but a little.

She pulled down on the loop, and an instant later was slammed hard into her seat as explosive bolts blew the canopy clear and catapulted her out of the ship. She got a quick glimpse of the Star Destroyer's portside edge, an even quicker glimpse of the TIE fighter whipping past –

And suddenly there was an agonized squeal from the ejection seat's electronics, and the violent crackle of arcing circuits ... and with a horrible jolt Mara realized that she had made what might very well be the last mistake of her life. Intent on aiming her crippled Z-95 at the Star Destroyer's hangar bay, she had drifted too close to the giant ship and ejected directly into the path of the Dreadnaughts' ion beam bombardment.

And in that single crackle of tortured electronics she had lost everything. Her comm, her lights, her limited maneuvering jets, her life support regulator, her emergency beacons.

Everything.

For a second her thoughts flickered to Skywalker. He'd been lost in deep space, too, awhile back. But she'd had a reason to find him. No-one had a similar reason to find her.

A flaming TIE fighter roared past her and exploded. A large piece of shrapnel glanced off the ceramic armor that wrapped partially around her shoulders, slamming her head hard against the side of the headrest.

And as she fell into the blackness, she saw the Emperor's face before her. And knew that she hád again failed him.

They were approaching the monitor anteroom just behind the *Katana*'s bridge when Luke abruptly jerked. 'What?' Han snapped, looking quickly around down the corridor behind them.

'It's Mara,' the other said, his face tight. 'She's in trouble.'

'Hit?' Han asked.

'Hit and . . . and lost,' Luke said, forehead straining in concentration. 'She must have run into one of the ion beams.'

The kid was looking like he'd just lost his best friend, instead of someone who wanted to kill him. Han thought about pointing that out, decided at the last second they had more immediate things to worry about. Probably just one of those crazy Jedi things that never made sense anyway. 'Well, we can't help her now,' he said, starting forward again. 'Come on.'

Both the starboard and port main corridors fed into

the monitor anteroom, from which a single set of blast doors led the rest of the way forward into the bridge proper. Lando and Chewbacca were at opposite sides of the port corridor entranceway as Han and Luke arrived, huddling back from a barrage of laser fire and occasionally risking a quick shot back. 'What've you got, Lando?' Han asked as he and Luke joined them.

'Nothing good, buddy,' Lando grunted back. 'There are at least ten of them left. Shen and Tomrus were both hit – Shen will probably die if we don't get him to a medic droid in the next hour or so. Anselm and Kline are taking care of them inside the bridge.

'We did a little better, but we've still got a couple of them coming up behind us,' Han told him, doing a quick assessment of the rows of monitor consoles in the anteroom. They would provide reasonable cover, but given the layout, the defenders wouldn't be able to retreat farther without opening themselves to enemy fire. 'I don't think four of us can hold this place,' he decided. 'We'd better pull back to the bridge.'

'From which there's nowhere else to go,' Lando pointed out. 'I trust you considered that part?'

Beside him, Han felt Luke brace himself. 'All right,' Luke said. 'Into the bridge, all of you. I'll handle this.'

Lando threw him a look. 'You'll *what*?'

'I'll handle it,' Luke repeated. With a sharp *snap-hiss* he ignited his lightsaber. 'Get going – I know what I'm doing.'

'Come on,' Han seconded. He didn't know what Luke had in mind, but something about the kid's face suggested it wouldn't be a good idea to argue. 'We can backstop him from inside.'

A minute later they were set: Han and Lando just inside the bridge blast doors, Chewbacca a few meters farther in under cover of an engineering console, Luke standing alone in the archway with lightsaber humming. It took another minute for the Imperials to realize that they had the corridors to themselves; but once they did they moved swiftly. Cover fire began ricocheting around the monitor consoles, and as it did so the Imperials began diving one by one through the two corridor archways into the anteroom, taking cover behind the long consoles and adding their contribution to the laser fire storm.

Trying not to wince back from the attack, Han kept up his own fire, knowing full well that he wasn't doing much more than making noise. Luke's lightsaber flashed like something alive and hungry, deflecting the bolts that came too close. So far the kid didn't seem to have been hit . . . but Han knew that it couldn't last. As soon as the Imperials stopped laying down random cover fire and started concentrating on their aim, there would be too many shots for even a Jedi to stay clear of. Gritting his teeth, wishing he knew what Luke had in mind, he kept shooting.

'Ready!' Luke shouted over the screaming of the bolts . . . and even as Han wondered what he was supposed to be ready for, the kid took a step back and threw his lightsaber to the side. It spiraled across the anteroom, spun into the wall—

And with a crack like thunder, sliced the anteroom open to space.

Luke leaped backwards, barely making it into the bridge before the blast doors slammed shut against the explosive decompression. Alarms whistled for a moment until Chewbacca shut them off, and for another minute Han could hear the thudding of laser fire as the doomed Imperials fired uselessly at the blast doors.

And then the firing trailed off into silence . . . and it was all over.

Luke was already at the main viewport, gazing out at the battle taking place outside. 'Take it easy, Luke,' Han advised, holstering his blaster and coming up behind him. 'We're out of the fight.'

'We can't be,' Luke insisted, his artificial right hand opening and closing restlessly. Maybe remembering Myrkr, and that long trek with Mara across the forest. 'We've got to do something to help. The Imperials will kill everyone if we don't.'

'We can't fire, and we can't maneuver,' Han growled, fighting back his own feeling of helplessness. Leia was on that Escort Frigate out there . . . 'What's left?'

Luke waved a hand helplessly. 'I don't know,' he conceded. 'You're supposed to be the clever one. *You* think of something.'

'Yeah,' Han muttered, looking around the bridge. 'Sure. I'm supposed to just wave my hands and—'

He stopped short . . . and felt a slow, lopsided smile spread across his face. 'Chewie, Lando – get over there to those sensor displays,' he ordered, looking down at the console in front of him. Not the right one. 'Luke, help me find – never mind; here it is.'

'Here what is?' Lando asked, stepping in front of the display Han had indicated.

'Think about it a minute,' Han said, glancing over the controls. Good; everything still seemed to be engaged.

He just hoped it all still worked. 'Where are we, any-way?' he added, stepping over to the helm console and activating it.

'We're in the middle of nowhere,' Lando said with strained patience. 'And fiddling with that helm isn't going to get us anywhere.'

'You're right,' Han agreed, smiling tightly. 'It's not going to get *us* anywhere.'

Lando stared at him . . . and slowly, a smile of his own appeared. 'Right,' he said slyly. 'Right. This is the *Katana* fleet. And we're aboard the *Katana*.'

'You got it,' Han told him. Taking a deep breath, mentally crossing his fingers, he eased power to the drive.

The *Katana* didn't move, of course. But the whole reason the entire *Katana* fleet had disappeared together in the first place—

'Got one,' Lando called out, hunching over his sensor display. 'Bearing forty-three mark twenty.'

'Just one?' Han asked.

'Just one,' Lando confirmed. 'Count your blessings – after this much time we're lucky to have even one ship whose engines still work.'

'Let's hope they stay working,' Han grunted. 'Give me an intercept course for that second Star Destroyer.'

'Uh . . .' Lando frowned. 'Come around fifteen degrees portside and down a hair.'

'Right.' Carefully, Han made the necessary course change. It was a strange feeling to be flying another ship by slave-rig remote control. 'How's that?' he asked Lando.

'Looks good,' Lando confirmed. 'Give it a little more power.'

'The fire control monitors aren't working,' Luke

warned, stepping to Han's side. 'I don't know if you're going to be able to fire accurately without them.'

'I'm not even going to try,' Han told him grimly. 'Lando?'

'Shift a little more to portside,' Lando directed. 'A little more . . . that's it.' He looked up at Han. 'You're lined up perfectly.'

'Here goes,' Han said; and threw the throttle control wide open.

There was no way the Star Destroyer could have missed seeing the Dreadnaught bearing down on it, of course. But with its electronic and control systems still being scrambled by Bel Iblis's ion attack, there was also no way for it to move out of the way in time.

Even from the *Katana*'s distance, the impact and explosion were pretty spectacular. Han watched the expanding fireball fade slowly, and then turned to Luke. 'OK,' he said. '*Now* we're out of the fight.'

Through the *Judicator*'s side viewport Captain Brandei watched in stunned disbelief as the *Peremptory* died its fiery death. No – it couldn't be. It simply couldn't. Not an Imperial Star Destroyer. Not the mightiest ship in the Empire's fleet.

The *crack* of a shot against the bridge deflector screen snapped him out of it. 'Report,' he snapped.

'One of the enemy Dreadnaughts seems to have been damaged in the *Peremptory*'s explosion,' the sensor officer reported. 'The other two are on their way back here.'

To reinforce the three still blasting away with their ion cannon. Brandei gave the tactical display a quick check; but it was a meaningless exercise. He knew full well what their only course was. 'Recall all remaining fighters,' he ordered. 'We'll make the jump to lightspeed as soon as they're aboard.'

'Yes, sir.'

And as the bridge crew moved to comply, Brandei permitted himself a tight smile. Yes, they'd lost this one. But it was just a battle, not the war. They'd be back soon enough . . . and when they did, it would be with the Dark Force and Grand Admiral Thrawn to command it.

So he would leave the Rebels to enjoy their victory here. It might well be their last.

CHAPTER TWENTY-NINE

The repair party from the *Quenfis* got the anteroom hull breach patched in what was probably record time. The ship Luke had requested was waiting for him in the docking bay, and he was out in space again barely an hour after the destruction of the second Star Destroyer and the retreat of the first.

Locating a single inert ejection seat among all the debris of battle had been a nearly hopeless task for Karrde's people. For a Jedi, it was no trick at all.

Mara was unconscious when they found her, both from a dangerously depleted air supply and from what was probably a mild concussion. Aves got her aboard the *Wild Karrde* and set off at near-reckless speed toward the medical facilities of the Star Cruiser which had finally arrived. Luke saw them safely aboard, then headed back toward the *Katana* and the transport he and the rest of his team would be returning to Coruscant by.

Wondering why it had been so important for him to rescue Mara in the first place.

He didn't know. There were lots of rationalizations he could come up with, from simple gratitude for her assistance in the battle all the way up to the saving of lives being a natural part of a Jedi's duty. But none of them was more than simply a rationalization. All he knew for certain was that he had had to do it.

Maybe it was the guidance of the Force. Maybe it was just one last gasp of youthful idealism and naïveté.

From the board in front of him, the comm pinged. 'Luke?'

'Yes, Han, what is it?'

'Get back here to the *Katana*. Right away.'

Luke looked out his canopy at the dark ship ahead, a shiver running through him. Han's voice had been that of someone walking through a graveyard . . . 'What is it?'

'Trouble,' the other said. 'I know what the Empire's up to now. And it's not good.'

Luke swallowed. 'I'll be right there.'

'So,' Thrawn said, his glowing eyes blazing with cold fire as he looked up from the *Judicator*'s report. 'Thanks to your insistence on delaying me, we've lost the *Peremptory*. I trust you're satisfied.'

C'baoth met the gaze evenly. 'Don't blame the incompetence of your would-be conquerors on me,' he said, his voice as icy as Thrawn's. 'Or perhaps it wasn't incompetence, but the skill of the Rebellion. Perhaps it would be you lying dead now if the *Chimaera* had gone instead.'

Thrawn's face darkened. Pellaeon eased a half step closer to the Grand Admiral, moving a little farther into the protective sphere of the ysalamir beside the command chair, and braced himself for the explosion.

But Thrawn had better control than that. 'Why are you here?' he asked instead.

C'baoth smiled and turned deliberately away. 'You've made many promises to me since you first arrived on Wayland, Grand Admiral Thrawn,' he said, pausing to peer at one of the hologram sculptures scattered around the room. 'I'm here to make sure those promises are kept.'

'And how do you intend to do that?'

'By making certain that I'm too important to be, shall we say, conveniently forgotten,' C'baoth said. 'I'm hereby informing you, therefore, that I will be returning to Wayland . . . and will be assuming command of your Mount Tantiss project.'

Pellaeon felt his throat tighten. 'The Mount Tantiss project?' Thrawn asked evenly.

'Yes,' C'baoth said, smiling again as his eyes flicked to Pellaeon. 'Oh, I know about it, Captain. Despite your petty efforts to conceal the truth from me.'

'We wished to spare you unnecessary discomfort,' Thrawn assured him. 'Unpleasant memories, for example, that the project might bring to mind.'

C'baoth studied him. 'Perhaps you did,' he conceded with only a touch of sarcasm. 'If that was truly your motive, I thank you. But the time for such things has passed. I have grown in power and ability since I left Wayland, Grand Admiral Thrawn. I no longer need you to care for my sensitivities.'

He drew himself up to his full height; and when he spoke again, his voice boomed and echoed throughout the room. 'I am C'baoth; Jedi Master. The Force which binds the galaxy together is my servant.'

Slowly, Thrawn rose to his feet. 'And you are my servant,' he said.

C'baoth shook his head. 'Not any more, Grand Admiral Thrawn. The circle has closed. The Jedi will rule again.'

'Take care, C'baoth,' Thrawn warned. 'Posture all you wish. But never forget that even you are not indispensable to the Empire.'

C'baoth's bushy eyebrows lifted ... and the smile which creased his face sent an icy shiver through Pellaeon's chest. It was the same smile he remembered from Wayland.

The smile that had first convinced him that C'baoth was indeed insane.

'On the contrary,' the Jedi Master said softly. 'As of now, I am all that is *not* indispensable to the Empire.'

He lifted his gaze to the stars displayed on the room's walls. 'Come,' he said. 'Let us discuss the new arrangement of our Empire.'

Luke looked down at the bodies of the Imperial troops who had died in his sudden decompression of the *Katana*'s bridge anteroom. Understanding at last why they'd felt strange to his mind. 'I don't suppose there's any chance of a mistake,' he heard himself say.

Beside him, Han shrugged. 'Leia's got them doing a genetic check. But I don't think so.'

Luke nodded, staring down at the faces laid out before him. Or rather, at the single face that was shared by all of the bodies.

Clones.

'So that's it,' he said quietly. 'Somewhere, the Empire's found a set of Spaarti cloning cylinders. And has gotten them working.'

'Which means it's not going to take them years to find

and train crews for their new Dreadnaughts,' Han said, his voice grim. 'Maybe only a few months. Maybe not even that long.'

Luke took a deep breath. 'I've got a really bad feeling about this, Han.'

'Yeah. Join the club.'

To Be Concluded . . .